I0938551

HABITS

That Haunt Me

*The Horse
and
The Rose*

Patricia Sorg

HABITS
that Haunt Me

Patricia Sorg

ISBN 978-1-953278-27-2 Hard Back
ISBN 978-1-953278-28-9 Soft Back
ISBN 978-1-953278-29-6 E-Book

Published by

 INDIGNOR HOUSE™

Chesapeake, Virginia
www.IndignorHouse.com

"To walk the spiritual path is
to continually step out into
the unknown."

~Wallace Huey

THE HORSE AND THE ROSE

PROLOGUE

It was the first time since the three had died that they were once again together inside the old mansion. What unforgettable memories their spirits held … lovely memories of intense and long-lived lives mixed within sudden and unexpected deaths. The small table was perfectly set for tea. Porcelain cups decorated with the aroma of freshly cut roses created an environment of love and companionship. Juan Ignacio had brought the flowers just for Sara. He worked to arrange the stems with difficulty as the vase was small, and his hands trembled from age.

"If we were to count," Juan Ignacio asked, "how many years would it add up to now?"

"If we added up all our time here together?" Sara replied with a grin. "Hundreds, Juancho, why?" The tender gaze of his blue eyes gave her reason to pause as she remembered his subtle gentleness. Juancho's eyes still held the loving splendor that Sara had loved so much. She frowned as she studied his once tall stature that now resembled more of a slouch. Juancho struggled to stand, and Sara reached out and grabbed his arm.

"These legs …" — the old man sighed — "… always give me problems."

"Sit down," Sara said softly.

He sat with difficulty, and Sara watched as he worked with his bony and aging fingers, that to this day, demonstrated he never had to work hard a day in his life. She hugged Juancho and kissed the top of his head … a man who was once young and full of energy … a man who was, at one time, her greatest love.

"You're beautiful, Sara, as always," he whispered.

"Was that a tremor?" Rogelio, the old farmhand, darted into the room and stared up at the swinging iron chandelier.

"Perhaps a slight one," Sara replied, nodding. "Nothing to worry about. Remember that everything belongs to the other world now. Just like us … we're from that other world." Sara walked over to the tall windows and placed her hands on her hips. She frowned and shook her head. "We should open these curtains so we can admire the outside." Sara yanked back the drapes and stared out at the dimming horizon.

Rogelio stood near the fireplace and rubbed his hands together. He still held that peasant appearance that was a leftover from his childhood. Short of stature and donning a shabby, straw hat, Rogelio's happy smile framed his crisp, yellow teeth. Tanned and cracked skin from years of working under the hot sun now added to the deep furrow that crisscrossed his forehead, and he walked with a slowed and stooped gait.

"There …" Sara said, enjoying the view. "Now, we can see the boarding school and the belfry."

"The sunset is beautiful," Juancho said. "Look at those silhouettes of the volcanoes against that magenta and orange sky." He took in a deep breath as he held onto the windowsill for support.

"Tea?" Sara offered while still taking a peek.

"That's why we're here," Rogelio replied.

Sara's hands shook as she held the teapot. The porcelain clinked when the hot brew flowed into the delicate cups. "Remember how we jumped like goats when we were kids?" She giggled. "We were always so happy … so innocent and so amazed at life."

"Happy times." Juancho smiled and nodded.

"Are we telling the story now?" Rogelio kept rubbing his hands together. "Yes or no?"

"Of course," Sara replied. "It's still fresh in our minds. Shall we recite it together?"

"And where do we begin?" Rogelio asked. "At the convent? The city? The boarding school?"

"We'll just tell it as she would have told it," Sara whispered, before taking a sip of her tea.

CHAPTER I

The decision between having another drink or dropping an Alka-Seltzer into a glass of water was an easy one. Not much was left in the bottle, and a migraine was looming just beyond Brisa's reach. The door swung open and she sat her glass onto the table. However, her reach fell short.

"Sorry." Sonia frowned at the now shattered glass. "The door was open."

"I'll get a broom." Brisa's head pounded. "I only had a few drinks this morning." Her eyes focused on the withered roses Sonia was carrying. "Did I miss something?"

"The funeral?" Sonia nodded. "Manager of PROE S.A. where we work … remember?"

"I'm dressed in black." Brisa waved at her skirt.

"You're always dressed in black."

"Shit!" Brisa whispered. "I'm an idiot. Didn't the deceased ever explain that I was a push-over? Easy to manipulate and other stuff that doesn't describe me in the best of light?"

"What's going on with you?" Sonia opened the fridge. "Have you eaten today? Other than vodka … wine … beer … is this your life now?"

Brisa grabbed a glass from the counter and filled it from the tap. She dropped an Alka-Seltzer tablet and watched as the bubbles fizzed.

Sonia looked at the woman and frowned. "You didn't go to the funeral. You didn't go to the burial. And *he* was the only person who actually trusted you. Do you do this shit on purpose? Or are you deliberately trying to destroy what's left of your small world?"

"He's dead … who cares? Everyone dies … eventually." Brisa shrugged and snapped her fingers. "We'll all disappear like a puff of smoke one day."

"Lately, you're like a different person." Sonia leaned against the kitchen table and picked up a damp towel. She played with it before tossing it onto the counter. "Brisa, I'm thankful for how you've helped me. When I really needed you, you were there. But lately, you've been acting … off."

Brisa shrugged. Her friend was probably right, and she couldn't explain what was running through her mind. It was as if her recent separation from her husband, Mariano, had deposited her near a dead end. A place where her thoughts sought vengeance and something else loomed. Something that eluded her. "Did anyone miss me?"

"Angela was asking about you. I called several times. You never called me back." They both looked at the withered roses that Sonia had brought. "These are the flowers *you* asked me to buy. I thought they were for the funeral." Sonia sighed.

"What did Angela want?" Brisa shrugged. "To say goodbye to me? Fire me?"

"Things don't look good." Sonia shook her head. "She did say she needed to see you … in private."

"When?"

"Tomorrow. At nine."

Brisa sat and scratched her head. "Damn."

"You need a bath …" – Sonia took in a deep breath – "… and sleep." She walked across the room and placed her hands on her hips. "Dyed your hair? Looks darker. Can still see your roots."

"So, I colored it," Brisa snapped. "Blondes are not respected in the workplace. Brunettes are given more authority."

"Hair coloring has nothing to do with it. Your priorities are all upside down." Sonia growled. "I've always envied you, Brisa. You're pretty … you have … I don't know, how many post-graduate degrees? Everything comes so easy for you."

"Easy? What do you know about easy?" Brisa walked into the bathroom.

Sonia walked over to the baby crib and ran her fingers along the top. She frowned. "I'm sorry about the …"

Brisa grabbed a half-emptied bottle of vodka and hurried back to the kitchen table. She filled a glass that was sitting next to the still-fizzling water. "You've always been a *busybody*, Sonia. Always fussing about me and Mariano. Whether he liked this one or that one, and what does so and so think …" Brisa gulped the liquor, and a tear rolled down her cheek. "Annulment! *He* annulled *our* marriage … remember?"

"Because of the —"

"Stop it!" Brisa slammed the glass onto the table. She pointed to the door and yelled out as another tear fell. "Get out! Get out of my life! Don't come back and don't come anywhere near me."

Sonia grabbed the wilted roses and aimed for the hallway. "Nobody's going to come anywhere near you, Brisa. Nobody! And that's the problem. You push everyone away. You only see a glass as half empty … of alcohol." She pointed to the empty glass on the table. "You see everything wrong. You're an architect and the opportunities are out there. You just can't see through those damn bloodshot eyes of yours." She flipped Brisa the finger and threw the flowers into the trashcan. As she walked down the hallway, Sonia yelled, "At nine in the morning, with Angela."

Brisa's head was still pounding. Desperation ran through her veins hotter than the alcohol she was drinking. Since her separation from Mariano, Brisa believed that her personal life was over, and it seemed that her professional career was also finished. She had left her work behind to become a housewife and mother. Mariano, her ex-husband of only a few months, was now the one working her projects. The future resembled more an empty bottle of vodka than a bright sunrise.

Brisa picked up the disheveled roses. The aroma surrounded her and she smiled. After filling a vase with water, she carefully arranged the dented stems so they looked a little better. Running her fingers across the wilting petals, their fragility frightened her for they somehow resembled what surrounded her right now.

After walking into the bathroom, Brisa glanced into the mirror. *I need to dye my roots.* She pulled out a box of coloring from off the shelf. She sat on the toilet seat, and soon, the dark dye was burning deeply into her scalp. With each sip from her glass, and with each passing second, her migraine pounded harder … stronger. She showered and wrapped a towel around her head. Two more Alka-Seltzers were dropped into a fresh glass of water, and the red roses now looked beautiful as if suddenly renewed by an invisible force.

"What in the world?" She blinked several times. "Can I trust my eyes?" She leaned over and her head pounded harder. The fragrance sent a mixed sensation of freedom combined with imprisonment all through her. "Can't I trust anybody?"

Brisa nervously climbed the steps to the entrance of PROE S.A. With each step, her heart pounded and her hands shook for today could be the last time she ever walked through those doors. On the second floor, she aimed for the coffee maker. As she passed a large mirror, she stopped and stared at her reflection. A woman with darkened eyes, and wearing a frail and sickly complexion, stared back.

Sonia walked behind her, and her friend's reflection flashed a slight look of concern before fading into one of total disgust. Sonia did not stop to chat. Although a pretty girl, Sonia was a little overweight. Normally, she wore a beautiful smile but not today.

Brisa stepped into her office and thought about her small stash of personal items — two photos, three diplomas, and a name plate … Brisa Murillo - Architect/Civil Engineer. Brisa placed her little trinkets inside a small cardboard box and shrugged. She would carry them out to her car after the meeting. After she was fired. A set of plans for a project called Antaño Heights reflected back the morning light. She had spent many long hours working on the architectural designs and structural calculations. Disappointment rained down around her, and she wiped away a tear. Brisa picked up a frame that held one of her diplomas and a tear fell.

"I will no longer build things," she whispered, before pushing the thought from her mind. "Don't want to live in Antaño anyway."

Mariano, her ex, stopped at her door and tapped on the wall. When she turned around, he acted as if he hadn't seen her. Brisa stepped into the hallway and the man glanced over at her. Flipping him off, she smiled. He was not the person she wanted to run into this morning. Hesitating for only a moment at the entrance to Angela's office, she shot some breath spray onto her tongue before entering.

"Come in, Brisa!" Angela's overly cheery words echoed through the room.

Fearing what the woman was about to say, Brisa spoke first. "I'm sorry about engineer López. He was a wonderful person."

Angela nodded. "Sit down, Brisa. I need to discuss something important."

"Listen, Angela. I understand. I want you to know that I'm grateful for —"

"You worked on these plans, yes?" Angela ignored Brisa's words and pointed to several sets of plans from the Antaño Heights project that were laying on her desk.

"The architectural and structural ones, yes." Brisa nodded as her hands shook.

"We're giving *you* the project." Angela smiled and sat on the corner of her desk. "The one at the Herradura ranch. You'll manage it all."

"Excuse me?" Brisa's voice trembled. "You're serious?"

The secretary walked in and placed several documents on Angela's desk. Angela nodded at the young woman before glancing back at Brisa and adding, "López wanted *you* to work the project." She nodded again. "No one else."

"But … he isn't here anymore. He died, remember?"

"Mariano's begging for the work." Angela snickered. "However, the board also agrees that it should be yours."

"I don't —"

"Look … your ex is working hard to land *this* project and take it away from you. I know you've been busy on the divorce —"

"Annulment." Brisa said the word so fast that she surprised even herself.

"Annulment." Angela laughed. "You're perfect for this project. Antaño Heights was *your* design. *Your* idea. We need you out there. It'll be a lot of work. Demand your full attention. Are you up to it?"

"To be honest —"

"You've been sitting on the sidelines lately, which is understandable." Angela stood and walked over to the windows. "You were focused on making a home and raising a kid."

"That's over now." Brisa glanced at her hands and frowned. She placed them under her legs, praying that Angela wouldn't see them shaking. "I thought you were going to …"

"Going to what? Fire you?" Angela sat in her chair. "Thought about it. But … I felt it important to give you another opportunity to prove yourself. You need this project, Brisa. It's now or never. And we can't wait."

"Why the rush?"

"UNESCO is about to declare Antaño a world heritage site. Something about its historic colonial worth. This project must be completed before they can finalize their plans. You'll live in Antaño during the construction. Not here in the city."

"May I think it over?" The thought of living in such a small town did not excite Brisa.

"You have objections?" Angela stared at her. "You never cease to surprise me."

Brisa frowned. "I was born in Antaño. After drawing up these plans, I promised myself I'd never return."

"You were born there? In Antaño?" Angela laughed and shook her head. "Me, too. What a coincidence. I thought you were born in Mexico. That's where you were living when we hired you. And … didn't you complete your postgraduate there?"

Brisa didn't reply.

"Is there a problem?" Angela stared at her. "Want me to hand the project over to your ex?"

Brisa stood and glanced into the hallway. Employees walking past were talking to each other and enjoying their morning. Brisa stood by the door, and memories flooded her vision as she watched herself fill a cup with coffee from that little kitchen. It was only a few months ago, and it was when her body was completely out of control. Her hands refused to stop shaking. The coffee splashed and stained her new, white skirt. As her thoughts played out, Mariano stepped out of an office with a young female draped across his arm. Brisa took in a deep breath and sighed. The pressure of feeling smothered almost suffocated her. *Could she be … the one?*

"Brisa?" Angela said a little sterner. "We *will* need an answer soon."

"It's not that I'm ungrateful." Brisa was once again doubting herself. She walked over to the plans and ran her fingers across the dark lines and small lettering. "Yes, Angela. I accept and thank you for the opportunity."

"Perfect." Angela placed her hands onto the drawings.

The secretary poked her head around the corner and whispered, "The Honorable Mayor of Antaño, Mr. Pablo Mencos, is here to see you."

"Five minutes." Angela waved. She turned to Brisa and looked directly at the trembling hands. "You can do this. I trust in you. But … you'll have to stop drinking."

"How did you —"

"Everyone knows." She shook her head as she walked back over to the window. "The question is can you quit?"

Brisa nodded. "I have a little self-will left."

An attractive, tall man stood in the doorway. He reached out his hand, and Angela ran to accept it. "Come in, Pablo! Please … meet Brisa Murillo, our lead architect for the project."

The mayor extended his hand and smiled. "Pablo, please."

"Yes," Brisa replied, stepping forward. "We met once in Antaño when I was measuring the site."

"Sit, Pablo," Angela said, pushing the man toward a chair. "Any updates on the permits?"

"Two to go," he replied, nodding. "Local licenses are easy enough to get from the National Council. Are you aware of our plans for the demolition?" He looked directly at Brisa.

"Yes."

"What's left of the girls' boarding school must go," he said, raising his chin and smiling.

"The old mansion at the entrance …" Brisa stepped over to the plans and studied the large sheets of paper. "It's a beautiful colonial and I propose to save it for social events, weddings, and the like." She grinned at the mayor. "Would be perfect for an event hall or a clubhouse. I conducted a structural study, and the building is in great condition. Would add a colonial touch to the project."

"Just a bunch of old, mossy bricks," Angela stated. "It all must go. The tremors have already destroyed the upper floors. We're using the first floor for the temporary construction offices."

"I know, but —"

"It's just a very old house," Angela stated again. "Not at all colonial. Demolishing that old convent may be a bit more of an issue. Could be considered heritage. Then again, it's located inside our parcels, and hopefully we're taking care of that problem. Correct, Pablo?"

The mayor glanced over at Angela and nodded. "Does the architect know about the other obstacle?"

Brisa looked at the man and frowned. It felt odd having someone talk as if she weren't in the room.

"Yes," Angela replied. "Nothing our legal department can't handle." Angela glanced over at Brisa and sighed. "A relative with the last name of Herradura filed a lawsuit about the rights. Nothing to worry about. You'll supervise the demolition and leveling of the land. After that, you'll proceed with the construction as depicted in your plans. Explain to Pablo your ideas for the project."

Brisa nodded. "If no changes, the first six months will focus on the demolition of the abandoned town in the lower terrain … by the hollow. Just small houses that once belonged to the workers when the place was a farm. And a temporary supply road will need to be built."

"You don't have any issues with demolishing the old nunnery?" the mayor asked. "Are you religious?"

Brisa shook her head. "I would appreciate it if you would consider retaining the old mansion and a few of the older buildings to add a little aesthetic. As for the boarding school, I have no objections. I spoke to the demolition company and it would be easy to exclude the mansion and convent. I suggest you reconsider my proposal as a whole."

"We'll take a look at it," Angela said, without paying much attention to Brisa's proposal.

"I'm in favor of demolishing everything." Pablo stood and took in a deep breath. "I don't like old buildings. Full of mold and asbestos and nasty, little critters … ironic …" – he laughed – "… with all the tremors lately, you'd think not much would be left." He walked over to the door and paused. "I wish a strong one would hit. Get rid of those damn buildings once and for all." He walked back over to Brisa and patted her on the shoulder.

Brisa nodded. "I won't disappoint you."

"Since you'll be living in town …" – he winked – "… I'll see you often."

"Thank you, Mr. Mayor."

"Pablo," he replied. "Please, just Pablo."

"Brisa …" Angela stepped between the two and smiled. "Pablo is an active partner in our company. Indirectly, by way of another corporation, of course." Angela laughed. "Being the mayor creates a slight conflict of interest. However, we simply overlook that here … understand?"

Brisa stared at the woman.

"Once this development is finished," Angela added, "let's consider the possibility of making *you* a full partner. What do you think, Brisa? Would you like that?"

"I'll work to ensure that nothing hampers our plans." Brisa smiled. "Nothing and nobody."

"Great! Then, welcome to the Antaño Heights project." Angela reached out and grabbed Brisa's hand.

Brisa left the two standing together inside Angela's office. Angela was practically a stranger to her, and if she knew how fragile Brisa's emotional state was at the moment, the whole project could crash down around her. Brisa could not show anyone any signs of insecurity. Angela was an unusual paradox at that office, always had been, always would be. She held an MBA and an engineering license, and now, with the passing of engineer López, she was the managing director. The two were never close, and Brisa never believed the woman ever liked her much. Angela was a little older than Brisa by about six or eight years. With her green eyes and fair complexion, Angela's high cheekbones gave her a rather exotic appeal. From Brisa's perspective, Angela was an attractive and ambitious woman who walked and talked with a high level of expectations when it came to leadership and control. She appeared to be cultured, but every now and then, a provincial tinge appeared despite her efforts to hide it.

Brisa felt confused and excited, and her hangover still pounded from somewhere inside the dark recesses of her brain. She again glanced into the mirror at the end of the hallway and frowned. The woman looked aged, tired, rundown, and weak.

"Will you succeed, Brisa?" Brisa asked her reflection.

The reflection did not answer back.

She rode the elevator to the ground floor and entered one of the stores. After buying a small bottle of vodka, she carefully placed it inside her handbag. Across the street sat a bistro. The place was eclectic and housed an urban bar. She sat near a corner where she faced a man who refused to stop staring at her.

"A whiskey sour," Brisa said, before changing her words to, "I mean … plain orange juice."

The stranger was rather tall and rough looking. His brownish-gray eyes gazed into his coffee for only a moment before glancing back up. His intense stare penetrated deeply through her inner being without even a blink. Sporting disheveled hair, combed unevenly, and wearing a wrinkled shirt, he reminded her of a cowboy or a farmer or a rancher or … who knows what. He looked completely out of place in the up-scale bistro. And, for that matter, out of place in such a big city.

As she watched the stranger watch her, a strong hand jerked Brisa backward. She gasped as she tried to steady herself. She turned and stared directly into her ex-husband's eyes.

"You will *never* work that project!" Mariano stated firmly. He squinted and a large scowl covered his face.

A wave of triumph washed over Brisa and she smiled. Her ex-husband looked defeated and it sent waves of success all through her. She glared at him and smirked. To her surprise, the love that once filled her with wonderment and a sense of longing no longer seemed to torment her. She felt nothing for the man. No love and no hate … just nothing.

"A beer!" Mariano shouted out to the bartender before sitting down next to Brisa.

The enigmatic-looking man from the next table slapped his hand between Mariano and his beer. He winked at Brisa before frowning at Mariano.

"Leave," Brisa stated firmly.

"The miss is asking you to leave," the man said, glaring at Mariano.

Mariano looked up at him and squinted. He huffed a few times before standing. Brisa snickered because she understood that her ex would never push for a fight. Not in this way.

"You!" Mariano grumbled and pointed directly at Brisa before stomping out of the bistro and never once looking back.

The stranger glanced over at the bartender and asked for the bill. He leaned over and whispered to Brisa, "It seems you have enemies, miss. Name's Sebastián Salguero." He extended a hand.

"Brisa Murillo." She stared at the hand and smiled.

"Take care of yourself." The man tapped on his cowboy hat as if to say goodbye. He walked out and into the light without looking back.

She sighed. "What a shitty day …"

The bartender nodded.

"Tab, please."

"Your new friend already paid." The bartender chuckled.

CHAPTER II

"**B**risa! You've given away everything," Sonia shouted, stepping into the small and empty apartment. "By the way, Carlos Calderón, the architect, is coming with us." Sonia picked up the historical and tourism books about the small city of Antaño and laughed. "I see *you've* been doing your homework."

"It's a charming place for tourists but a boring place to live," Brisa replied.

"It'll be interesting … us working together. You as the builder and me as the seller." Sonia looked up at the ceiling as if daydreaming. "Sonia Paz, Marketing Manager. The name Antaño Heights has a nice ring to it, don't you think? A concept that should sell. A remote city dominated from the start by the Herradura family."

"Herradura?" Brisa repeated.

"Yes. The colonial city was founded by the famous Francisco de Herradura. His name is still relevant. I'd say it's a town that remained frozen in time. Even if they do call it a city now."

"It has interesting ruins." Brisa nodded.

"Ruins?" Sonia repeated. "You mean the pile of rubble they call a convent and their old-fashioned citizens with their spooky legends? The nice part … those old legends will help sell to the retirees. I'll use them during startup. Tourists love that shit."

"Hmm."

"Brisa, this could be a new beginning for you. Remember when you helped me to begin anew?"

"I don't need a new beginning." Brisa shook her head. "Besides, why should I start over in the place where I started from?"

"You're from Antaño?" she asked and her eyes widened. "I thought you were from Mexico. I saw photographs of your parents and of your life. Even your diplomas are from there. You even met Mariano in —"

"And your point?" Brisa locked the door behind them as they walked toward the street.

A man standing by the car opened the door when he saw them. He nodded and said, "Architect, Carlos Calderón. In Antaño they call me Carlitos, and it's where everything feels homier."

"Interesting." Brisa laughed. "Thanks, Carlitos."

"What about the car the company gave you?" Sonia asked Brisa.

"In the shop."

"You'll need a good car, Miss Architect," Carlitos added.

"Brisa," she corrected him. "If we're going to work together, we should call each other by our first names. I'll call you, Carlitos."

"The land for the project is broken and uneven," Carlitos said, "and the streets in the town are cobbled. They ruin cars. Especially in winter. Make sure you have new tires."

"I know." Brisa smiled at him from inside the rear-view mirror. "I have the proper car. It's in the shop. Thanks for driving us today."

The highway to Antaño was surrounded by lush, green valleys and tall, snow-topped volcanoes. As they approached the small city, Brisa admired the wild roses that were invading the fields with an enchanting scarlet hue.

"There are many greenhouses that cultivate the roses in these mountains," Carlitos explained. "They export them to Holland. However, these types are unique. They grow only as climbing roses here, and that makes them a special species."

"I understand that the building codes are stricter now that UNESCO placed their interest in Antaño," Brisa stated.

"Yes, and the city changed its name. The official name was always *Antaño de Herradura*, but today it is known as just *Antaño*.

"Antaño." Sonia laughed. "The name means *yesteryears*, or little remote town of the past. And, if we keep driving in a straight line, we'd reach the beach."

"Carlitos, you were born here?" Brisa asked.

"Yes. To live in Antaño is like going back in time. I feel it when I return from the capital. Is the demolition crew ready, Miss Architect?"

"Please, Carlitos. Call me, Brisa."

"Brisa," he corrected himself. "The Mexican demolition consultants began their work, and we have an engineer on site. I thought you recommended them. They're highly qualified professionals. Do you know who completed the calculations?"

"I did for the architectural and structural plans," Brisa replied, enjoying the view.

"You specialize in anti-seismic structures?" he asked.

Brisa nodded. "Are we okay with the building permits?"

"Missing a couple … red tape and all. Like you mentioned in your email, if we start with the lower demolition and level the ground first, we'll gain some time as we work to pull the missing permits. As for your office, you'll need to pick out a space."

Carlitos seemed knowledgeable about the project, and Brisa had a lot to digest. She tried to visualize her new incursion into Antaño Heights.

"I'm sorry about the other afternoon," Brisa whispered to Sonia.

"Forget it. I forgive you all the time. You're the same Brisa I've known for years."

Brisa sighed.

"This is a town where the earth shakes," Sonia said. "I understand that after a while a person tends to ignore it."

"One does become accustomed." Carlitos laughed. "If only one could tell when the earth will shake next. Brisa, you should know. It's your specialty."

"No way to predict," Brisa replied. "I just build."

"Did you train in Mexico?" he asked.

"Yes."

"At the office they told me," Sonia interjected, "that there was someone called Mother Rosa. That she was a nun at the old convent that's on the property. They say she's well-known around these parts. We could take advantage of her notoriety when marketing the project."

"A nun?" Brisa glanced over at Carlitos. "I haven't heard about her."

Carlitos looked into the rear-view mirror.

"There are ruins ... a convent and school," Brisa added. "Both are scheduled for demolition. I know nothing about a nun."

"Are you talking about *the* Mother Rosa?" Carlitos asked. "She's our blessed Mother."

"Blessed?"

"Yes, it's Vatican terminology and is used before someone is appointed as a saint. She's a legend from many years ago. Believers like me consider her the patroness. The saint of our home. As for tourists, it's only a matter of curiosity. They sell souvenirs of her in town."

Sonia and Brisa stared at each other and smiled.

Carlitos looked at the women through the rear-view mirror and frowned. "She's done several miracles for me," he said.

"Tell me about you," Brisa said.

"I'm the resident architect in Antaño," he replied. "I graduated from a small college not far from here and have researched many of the superstitions that still haunt the smaller towns and cities."

"Los Arcos!" Sonia yelled out. "We're here. Los Arcos ... the lodge that will be your home away from home for the next year or so. I'll stay here too when I'm in town."

Brisa tapped Sonia on the arm. "Don't do that!"

"Do what?" Sonia asked.

"Jump up and scream like that, you scared the crap out of me!"

Carlitos nodded.

The lodge was of a colonial style and surrounded by colorful flowers and red rose bushes that scaled the walls. Arched walkways gave the place a rather romantic appeal. A courtyard with tables and umbrellas allowed visitors to enjoy the warmth of the day while ignoring the burning rays from the noonday sun. Large pots scattered about with smaller trees provided the place with a more country stance.

Carlitos and Sonia pulled out the bags and suitcases and handed them to an attendant. "You go to work. I'll check us in," Sonia said.

"Carlitos and I do need to see the site," Brisa replied. "See you in a while, Sonia."

Carlitos drove Brisa up to the project site. Some of the land had already been cleared, but the old mansion was still there. She was impressed when she first saw the pictures. An old building that, to her surprise and disappointment, was now scheduled for demolition along with the other historic ruins.

"Shame to tear all this down," Carlitos said, as if reading Brisa's mind.

An elderly man circled through the main gate. He looked to be either a peasant or a laborer. He smiled and his twisted, yellow teeth filled his mouth. He lifted his hat slightly as if sharing a signal of greeting.

Brisa felt for the bottle in her bag and sighed. She watched for Carlitos to react to the stranger, but he didn't seem to care about the old man's drunkenness. It bothered Brisa, and a strange sensation ran up her back. She shivered. *How could Carlitos allow such a person to be on the payroll?* She didn't want to come right out and ask. No need to criticize so early in the project. But something felt off. She nodded to Carlitos and remained quiet.

The day passed and Brisa and Sonia were soon alone. They remained awake and talked into the wee hours of the morning. Although she would have preferred to be well rested for the first real day of work, Brisa couldn't refuse her friend a little personal one-on-one time. Now, Brisa stood in front of the old mansion and couldn't stop yawning.

"Our first adventure," Sonia said as the mini taxi inched its way down the dirt road. The mini taxis were small, wooden carriages pulled by a single horse. The easiest way to travel over Antaño's cobbled streets.

Carlitos smiled and yelled out, "Good morning, ladies. Did you enjoy your ride? Picturesque, are they not?"

"Yes, picturesque," Brisa repeated. "Very bouncy."

"Come in, come in." Carlitos waved his arms to guide them into the foyer. "This is the operation center. I'll show you to your office. Let me know of any changes you would like to make."

They entered the large vestibule, and Brisa glanced up at the beautiful and majestic forged-iron chandelier.

"It's our seismographer." Carlitos pointed up.

"I get it," Sonia said. "It moves during a tremor?"

Carlitos bounced on his heels.

The lobby connected to a set of grandiose stairs that led to a second floor that was decorated with an arched-paneled window that allowed for the early morning light. In a strange way, the light gave the place a mysterious, yet captivating feel. The building was in bad shape with worn steps that could use a good coat of paint. Years of neglect had left the walls pitted and cracked. Carlitos pointed to what must have been a dining room once but was now filled with office desks and computers. Near the front, Brisa noticed a huge living room with a beautiful rock fireplace. The place was empty except for a few pieces of furniture that were stacked neatly in a corner. As they walked, their footsteps echoed off the plastered walls.

"Here, near the fireplace, will be your office," Carlitos said. "We placed the workers in the smaller rooms. Over there sits the assistant architects. Back there in the old library is the blueprint room. And way in the back is demolition. More personnel will be assigned as the time for construction changes. Decide what you want to do. We can always lease a trailer if you'd prefer."

Brisa walked through the daunting rooms and sighed. The huge windows allowed for a full view of the distant volcanoes. Off to one side, the church ruins with its bell tower decorated the hillside. The place was amazing. Then again, Brisa felt a cold chill run up her arms. The house seemed creepy and a bit sinister. She thought about the number of souls that had once lived here and wondered what their lives might have been like. They were probably rich … of lineage, for sure.

"Cracks on the ceiling." Sonia pointed up.

"Doesn't look structural," Brisa replied.

"Any spooks, Carlitos?" Sonia mused.

"This area is surrounded by an electromagnetic field." He laughed and whispered, "People sometimes mix the phenomena with spirits. Maybe you know about this?"

Brisa shook her head. "Not my field of study. I know that when an environment is permeated by these fields, energies can be present that may alter reality. That's why people confuse the two. I do not believe we have ghosts."

A young girl, almost a child, offered the small group a cup of coffee. "Would you like some, ma'am?" The girl nodded to Brisa.

"Thanks, Selena." Carlitos took a cup. "Selena helps with the cleaning and such around here."

"Thank you, Selena," Brisa said. "Carlitos, you'll need to introduce me to the employees and colleagues. And we'll need a conference room for our corporate meetings. This room could definitely work for that. The fireplace is nice. My desk would look wonderful over there in the corner too." Brisa pointed across the room. "I could watch the progress from here. Not to mention the view is absolutely beautiful." Brisa walked over to the large windows and stared out.

"What's upstairs?" Sonia asked. "Why the yellow caution tape across the stairs?"

"Structure is old," Carlitos replied.

"I would love to see the upstairs," Brisa added, turning and heading for the stairs.

"Is it safe?" Sonia asked.

"Oh, quite safe," Carlitos replied.

"All the peeling and broken pieces," Sonia said as they climbed. "I see why nobody wants us on the upper floors."

"Just superficial," Brisa replied as she stepped closer to examine the cracks and missing plaster. "Definitely not structural. I'm sure it's just cosmetic. I could live here." Brisa entered what she considered was once a bedroom. Perhaps the master. She felt a strange connection to the place as if she'd been in this room before.

"You could sleep here?" Carlitos asked, raising his brows.

"Why not?" Brisa asked.

"There's a furniture store in town." Carlitos nodded at Brisa.

"I would only need a mattress. Look at this old-fashioned headboard." Brisa walked over and ran her hand down the intricately carved wood.

"I could have the electric brought up," Carlitos added. "Set up in no time."

Brisa walked over and stood by one of the windows. She studied the placement of the old school and church.

"What a shame that this view will not be here much longer," Carlitos said.

The bell tower rang out … ding … dong … ding …

"Is the tower empty?" Brisa asked.

"Abandoned years ago," Carlitos replied. "Just pigeons live in there now. You know how pigeons *love* old buildings."

"Sonia, you're awfully quiet," Brisa said, turning to her.

"You must be absolutely crazy!" Sonia flailed her arms. "You can't stay here. This is … I don't know, Dracula's castle?"

"Let's look at the rest of the rooms," Brisa added, ignoring her friend's outburst. A strange sound echoed down the hall and she paused. "What's that? Is someone up here?"

"Prohibited," Carlitos replied.

"It's as if someone's watching us," Sonia whispered loudly.

Brisa followed the hallway toward the back of the house, enjoying the sweet aroma of history. The other rooms were mostly dust and cobwebs, although, odd pieces of broken furniture were scattered throughout. In places, the walls still held an old, oil painting or discolored photograph from a time long since forgotten. A black-and-white of an older woman caught Brisa's eye, and she stepped up to get a better look. The woman's face had a sinister appeal about it — almost dreamlike and spiritual in some strange way.

"That's Lady Delfina Herradura," Carlitos said. "This house was the home of the Herradura family for more than a century. She was the last to actually live here. A bad reputation that one owned."

"That noise was probably from rats or mice," Sonia said, peering around doors and searching the rooms for little creatures. "Yes, probably rats making that awful noise."

"I will call for an exterminator," Carlitos said. "It may also be the shifting rocks. The house settles as the temperature changes. This place just needs a good cleaning and a little love."

"Brisa!" Sonia stepped up next to her friend and shook her arm. "I've got chills running up and down my back. How could you possibly sleep here … alone?"

"Empty places do not frighten me." Brisa laughed and shrugged off her friend. "Besides, I *love* old buildings. Goes with my profession."

"You might like them … but to want to live in one!" Sonia glanced around nervously. "Can we at least turn the picture of that old lady around or something? She's creepy. Her eyes frighten me. It's as if she's watching us. To stay here is not a good idea. I'm going downstairs."

"I'll be down in a few." She watched as Sonia ran cautiously down the hallway. Brisa giggled as she entered each room to memorize the layout.

"I could have this place ready for you in a couple of days," Carlitos whispered.

From the top of the stairs, Brisa admired the majestic fireplace that covered one wall in the great hall. "I love these types of fireplaces," Brisa yelled down at Sonia. "Baroque in style and one that really warms a place up. Not like today's fake ones. Ingenious engineering back then."

Sonia stared up at Brisa and shook her head. "I'll wait for you outside." She aimed for the front door. "I need fresh air."

Brisa followed her friend, and once outside, she took in a deep breath. She allowed her eyes to search the grounds while they talked to Carlitos and a few of the other young professionals. She would have preferred to wait and meet them in more of an official setting, but then again, any introduction was better than none. Brisa watched as the old man walked up a small hill and stood under a large tree. She excused herself and aimed for where the old man was standing. He reeked of alcohol and Brisa cringed.

"Plots of our saint Mother Rosa," the old man said. He glanced up at the bell tower and pointed over at the ruins of the convent.

How could they allow such a drunkard to work on the site? Brisa wondered if she might have to assess the staff a little more closely. It felt odd talking to the old man, and her nerves crawled as if wanting to escape. Carlitos walked up behind Brisa and coughed.

"This nun that's to be beatified … what's her name again?" Brisa asked Carlitos.

"Mother Rosa," Carlitos replied. "And that's what they say. I'm told that a tremor will soon open her coffin, and her body will still be intact … in perfect condition, and she'll be surrounded with nothing but red roses."

"Oh?"

"Yes, and it will mark the beginning of the return of her teachings. Lessons that have been forgotten throughout time. For us, she's just Saint Mother Rosa and we venerate her."

"Thanks for the history lesson." Brisa looked over at the elderly man who seemed disinterested in joining the conversation.

"Do not believe?" Carlitos asked.

"Not really." Brisa smiled.

"Do you believe in anything about God or the world beyond?" Carlitos asked.

"I do not believe in miracles." Brisa glanced back at the mansion that seemed to be beckoning her. "Hard to grasp religion sometimes. And the dead are simply dead. Sometimes, I don't even believe in those that are still alive."

Carlitos laughed. "Mother Rosa is sometimes seen walking around here. You'll meet people that'll gladly talk about our ghosts and how our dead frighten them. Quite common with our townsfolk. That's why I prefer living in the capital. No spirits." He laughed again. "I can introduce you to the workers down below now if you'd like."

"Later. I've scheduled an introductory meeting for after lunch."

"Before I forget," Carlitos said, stepping a little closer. "You need to know about a lady who visits the boarding school on a regular basis. She never asks for permission, and I've explained to her that she cannot just barge in here.

However, she never heeds my direction. Perhaps you can deal with her. Her name's Marta and she wears the uniform of the Ministry of Culture."

"Is that her?" Brisa pointed to a petite woman who was opening the door of the boarding school.

"That's her."

Brisa sighed and turned to talk to the old man, however, the drunk was gone.

CHAPTER III

Marta would not stop talking. Brisa pretended to be listening, but her attention was busy trying to convince the woman that the boarding school they were walking through was sitting on private property. She explained to Marta about her company's decision to demolish everything, however, the woman ignored her and instead began an official tour.

"This is the front lobby and main office …" Marta said, disregarding Brisa's comments. Her nervous laughter displayed a golden tooth that twinkled in the sunlight. She wore a tight-fitting, dark blue uniform, and her overall appearance seemed quite out of fashion. Especially her permanent-induced, wavy hair. "Would you like to see the library?" Marta possessed a certain childish demeanor and mischievous attitude. She fumbled with a bunch of keys that seemed to overwhelm her otherwise small stature.

"Yes, please."

"This may be the last visit before everything comes down, you know." Marta sighed a long, drawn-out sigh. Her smile seemed to renew when the large, wooden gate roared and slowly opened. "These are not colonial ruins, of course. Just an old building from the sixties that once housed a boarding school for wayward girls. The remains of that church and bell tower … now, those *are* Spanish colonial and was where the original nunnery was located."

Brisa glanced down the long and dark hallway that led to a common patio. Tall arches that once protected the gardens from direct sunlight were now cracking and covered in run-away vines.

"Soon, our city will be called the Antaño World Heritage Site," Marta whispered. "They do it for the money, yah know." She shook her head and sighed again. "Everything's about the money these days. They want the tourists to come. And that UNESCO place has us twisted around their little finger with the stuff about ruin preservation. Very few authentic edifications are left these days. Especially any that hold as much history and legends as ours." Marta sighed again. "City of Antaño de Herradura."

"I prefer just Antaño." The romanticism that saturated the name flooded Brisa with remorse.

"The name Herradura implies lineage." Marta continued to ramble. "It was a name that held class once. Today, hardly anyone uses it anymore. There may only be a hundred or so Herraduras left in the world. I searched for it on the internet once. I love the internet. Did you know that the Herraduras coat of arms has disappeared!" She nodded. "No trace of it anywhere."

"I did not know that," Brisa replied, still following the woman.

"Around here, there are only a few who carry that last name. Although, none to my liking if I must say, but of course, nobody is asking me." Marta kept talking as if she were a living dictionary of information.

"Marta, I'm sorry for interrupting, but I need to see your authorization that allows you to be here."

Marta ignored the statement and kept walking down the shadowy hallway that held a musty and damp odor with a slight flavor of history. The corridors were filled with niche arches that now housed only broken statues. Most were headless, probably from the frequent tremors. Marta did not reply to Brisa's statement but continued with her monologue.

"It shakes a lot here. Why demolish anything? If you wait just a bit longer, the tremors will take care of it for you." Marta laughed.

Voices echoed out from beyond the walls and Brisa paused. The voices seemed to be heading their way. The sounds would fade only to suddenly spring back. She strained to hear where they were coming from.

"Did you hear that?" Brisa asked.

"Hear what, Architect?" Marta replied, looking up and frowning.

"Nothing."

Marta stood still and listened. She hunched her shoulders and sighed. Then, she started walking again.

"You may call me Brisa."

Marta opened a door that led to a darker hallway that was lined with tall, boarded-up windows and many wooden doors. The domed ceiling was cracked on all sides, and scattered pieces of plaster now rested on the floor.

Marta paused by a set of large, double doors and pulled out her keys. "This was the school's library once." The lock clicked and Marta stepped inside. "When I first walked in here, books were laying around everywhere. I picked up most of them."

They entered an old office near the front that was filled with scattered piles of papers. Books and boxes were strewn about. Dust covered everything. Furniture, sheltered with aging sheets and long cobwebs, decorated the floor.

"I'm not the person that cleans." Marta shrugged. "Where's your office, Miss Architect? In the mansion?"

"Yes. It's a beautiful house."

"You like it?" Marta sighed. "It's a grim place."

"Perfect place to live," Brisa whispered.

"You're not thinking of staying in that old crypt are you?"

Brisa didn't reply. She picked up a book and flipped through the dusty pages.

Marta sat down at the only desk.

"What's behind that wall?"

"Nothing," Marta replied, checking her phone. "Just more corridors. I don't have a key for that area."

Brisa walked through the large room and read through a few titles that still rested on the shelves. When she returned, Marta was standing in the hallway tapping on her phone. Again, faint voices echoed through the room. Brisa walked over to a window and tried to glance out between the boards.

Could they be coming from a hidden corridor. Singing? No wait ... just children playing outside. The sounds of young voices drifted through the air. "Marta, do you hear anything?"

The woman looked up and frowned.

"I hear children."

"Little girls?" Marta asked, somewhat correcting Brisa. "Or ... more precisely, adolescent girls. Not everyone can hear them. You must have the gift."

Brisa walked into the hallway and glanced around. Not seeing anyone, she returned to the library office.

"They are simply echoes from the past," Marta said. "Do not be afraid."

"Echoes?" Brisa repeated.

"Yes, echoes ... voices from the yesteryears," Marta whispered. "Sounds that are trapped between the fabric of time. An acoustic manifestation. Energy that's caught inside an abandoned building. Sounds that bounce off the walls forever, never coming to rest."

"Nonsense!" Brisa glared at her. "It's true that sometimes under a dome we can experience unusual acoustic phenomena but only when people are present. Not from past voices."

"Honestly, Architect?" Marta dropped her phone into her bag and sighed. "In a place where dramatic events have happened, a residual energy always remains. Sometimes the vicious circle never stops." She pointed to a pattern carved into the ceiling. "I've seen shows about this type of phenomena on the internet ... I love the internet ... look it up on Google. It has a scientific name, you know."

"This is not science."

Marta glared at Brisa.

"A bunch of nonsense."

Marta frowned and shook her head. She huffed a few times and continued to sort through her keys.

"Must be kids playing outside." Brisa had no explanation for what she was hearing, however, it was likely that the sounds were from children. Then again, they were quite a ways from most of the local homes.

"You're an architect with many college courses behind you. You believe you know all there is to know about the dead." Marta picked out a key and stood. "Well, Architect, I'm a professional too, and I work for the Ministry of Culture. I'm a state employee!"

"I didn't mean to offend you. But in this small town there are many superstitions floating around." Brisa felt the urge to grab the keys and kick the woman out of the building. "Marta, you can no longer enter this site without permission. Company rules prohibit it."

"I'm leaving," Marta said. "However, I must sign some papers before I go." Marta pulled out her phone and tapped on the screen.

As the woman talked to someone, Brisa aimed for the main door. "I'll wait for you outside."

Marta stepped away with a slight wave, still talking on her phone.

Brisa lingered for only a moment before walking toward the large, wooden gate. The silence returned and the eerie hush felt overwhelming. A strong ringing from the bell tower echoed through the walls, and Brisa's heart pounded as she ran from the building. After a few minutes, Marta stepped out and approached a young man who apparently was waiting for her. As the two talked, Brisa stepped up to them.

"Why does that bell ring like that?" Brisa asked, interrupting their conversation.

"Those are birds." Marta pointed to the tower. "Blackbirds and pigeons make their nests up there. They fly into the bell and it rings."

Marta walked away with the young man, and Brisa stared up at the tower and frowned. The ringing sounded again and filled the air with a resonance that vibrated everything it touched. *That's no bird.* Brisa glanced at her watch. It was noon. She walked toward the mansion, and as the ringing stopped, she sighed. The quiet felt peaceful. Brisa glanced around. There were no birds, no insects, and no wind. She entered the mansion and the building was empty except for Sonia who was sitting at a small desk.

"Everyone's out for lunch." Sonia smiled. "Only Carlitos, you, and I are left."

The big, empty house felt mysterious and ominous. Then again, it also sent an invitation of intense awareness that somehow soothed her soul. Its enchantments were obvious. While the lady in the photograph was not very welcoming, the house was, for it emanated a magnetism that deeply attracted Brisa.

"Please, don't stay here," Sonia begged. "You'll be vulnerable. Stay at the lodge with me. Are you not frightened by ghosts?"

"I'm more afraid of the living." Brisa laughed. "What can the dead do to me? The living, however, can do a lot. There's something about this place that calls to me. I can't explain it."

Sonia rolled her eyes. "If that's what you want." She scratched her head. "Stay here until they come with the wrecking ball for all I care."

"I'm going to fight against the demolition," Brisa said. "Conserving this place is in the best interest of the project. Should be profitable and Antaño deserves it." She placed her hands on her hips.

"You're not thinking about going against Angela, are you?"

"Don't be silly. I'll stay at the lodge until they have this place ready, which should take about a week. Isn't that right, Carlitos?"

Carlitos nodded.

"Carlitos, who's that old man who walks around here? What's his position?"

"What old man?" Carlitos asked. "I'm not sure who you're talking about."

"Hmm, not important then," Brisa replied.

Carlitos dropped Sonia and Brisa off at the lodge for lunch. That afternoon, Brisa finally met the rest of the project staff. The younger interns were working on the street plans, and José Peña was acting as the demolition coordinator. He seemed quiet and somewhat of an introvert. The accounting section was situated in the mansion's dining room, and to Brisa's surprise, the kitchen remained a common area for everyone to use.

Only a few days had passed, and the mansion was ready to welcome Brisa home. Carlitos was sweeping the upper floor when Brisa carried up a few of her things. He had improvised the electrical elements from what was installed on the ground floor. Downstairs, workers hustled in and out, however, the upstairs remained quiet and peaceful. It was as if she were entering a whole new world — a world that was now the property of just Brisa. The mansion, at times, felt a little ominous. Then again, it was also enigmatic and regal.

The original paintings and photos were left on the walls. The only thing she removed and stored in a back closet was the black-and-white photo of Lady Delfina de Herradura. Her presence just felt sinister. Nights were mostly noisy from the creaking of the ancient wood that was constantly shaking. Several broken windows allowed in the wind, and it took about a week for Brisa to settle down and become accustomed to the various creaks and cracks. To her surprise and despite the warnings from Sonia, Brisa ran into no ghost.

Many times during the night, however, Brisa would hear footsteps as if someone were walking up or down the stairs. A couple of times, she even ran downstairs to see if someone was there. Each time, everything was fine and she was alone. Brisa kept reminding herself about the microseisms that some people experienced on a daily basis. Perhaps most of the squeaks and rumbles were from the smaller quakes. She was not typically the type to allow herself to be influenced by such foolishness. No one else had access to the upper floors, and she had the whole place to herself. As the days passed, her mind eased and the place felt a little more like a home.

Every Monday, Brisa was required to return to the capital for a meeting at the main office. She always brought an update regarding their progress. Today's session was fairly short and with nothing else to do, Brisa headed back to Antaño. It was just a little before lunch and the first time she had driven the long drive alone. For some reason that she didn't completely understand, she was happy to be back at her job. But mostly, she was happy to be returning to that big, old house.

The trip from the capital was fraught with detours and heavy traffic. After sitting in the hot car for what seemed like hours, Brisa was relieved to receive a call from Angela.

"Sorry we didn't have time to talk in person today ..." Angela said, "... about not knocking down a couple of the buildings? We can cover that at a later time. And ... I'm not convinced you should be living in that old house by yourself. I know you adore old buildings, but you should have discussed it with me first. I didn't want to ask you about it in front of everyone ... but how *are* you doing with the *other thing*?"

Brisa knew what the *other thing* was all about. It was about her marriage, or non-marriage, and the drinking. Brisa's face flushed and her heart raced. After a deep breath, she replied, "Don't worry about me. And I gotta go. Big detour coming up."

"Okay, goodbye."

The traffic was extremely heavy. As she waited, she dictated a few emails on her phone. After setting her phone down, Sonia's name popped up on the small screen.

"Hello, Sonia?"

"Get your car back yet?"

"Yep, what's up?"

"Why are you returning to Antaño today? It's a holiday. No work, remember? Don't want to be nosy, but …"

"You're being nosy," Brisa mused. *And foolish.* However, she bit her tongue. "I want to experience Antaño alone. Experience living within the soul of the small town. Call you later."

This time, Brisa turned off her phone. She lowered the window and waved at a pedestrian. "Hey, can I go this way?"

"They're paving up ahead," the stranger said. "You cannot get through."

"Is there another route to Antaño?" Brisa asked.

"Take the first right and follow the detour. It'll lead to the coast and on to Antaño. You'll pass a few mountain towns along the way."

Brisa nodded.

"Just follow the traffic," he said.

Brisa waited patiently until she reached the detour. She turned down the dirt road and cringed. The traffic was crazy, and her nerves were already frayed. Dust billowed out from the speeding cars, and she could hardly see a thing. The narrow road was wall-to-wall with buses and trucks running every which way. Her hands were sweating, and her breathing grew heavy. As her heart pounded faster, Brisa believed her nerves would snap.

For what seemed like hours, she endured the crazy dirt and traffic and sudden turns. She took a right and followed the car in front of her. A large dump truck flew past, and the dust and rocks pelted her windshield. Her last vision was of a light tan of swirls. Her steering wheel twirled and locked in place. Brisa screamed. The car refused to obey her commands. She pumped on the brakes, but the car seemed to be speeding up. Brisa screamed again as the car jerked to a sudden stop. It felt as if she had just ridden a rollercoaster, and the front was facing up and toward the heavens. She could feel her back being pushed into the seat. A wall of dust had her trapped inside a bubble of utter silence.

When she slowly opened her eyes and coughed, dust and grit had covered everything. Shaking off her hands only seemed to make matters worse. She still couldn't see a thing. Her mind whirled as she tried to understand where she was and what had just happened. A knock on her window startled her and she jumped. A dark figure loomed only briefly at her car window before the door was flung open and a hand reached inside. Brisa screamed and covered her face.

"Ma'am? Are you okay?" a male voice asked.

"What?"

"Cami!" the male voice shouted out. "Stay in the car!"

As the dust settled, Brisa tried to see where she was. It looked as if she had landed on a large sand dune. Another man stood down in the street and waved his arms toward the highway.

"Lady!" The stranger reached over and unfastened her safety belt. "You okay? Damn! Still no signal."

Brisa felt stunned and weak. Her mind refused to comprehend what had happened.

"Ma'am?" the man said again. "Are you hurt?"

"I don't believe so," Brisa said, swinging her feet out the door. She stood and slapped at the swirling dust and sand. "What happened?"

The man was covered with dirt. He spat and coughed as he talked. "No signal on this side of the mountain." He held up his phone.

She sat back on her seat and reached for her phone.

"There's no signal," he said again.

Brisa stood and stared at her car that now rested on a steep slope of sand. The main road was several feet below.

"You ran up the emergency ramp," he said. "That truck almost hit you." The man led Brisa to the back seat of his jeep. "Camelia," he said to a young girl sitting in the front, "the lady's coming with us."

"My name's Brisa," Brisa forced a smile.

The man handed Brisa her purse. "Had it not been for the ramp, you'd probably be dead about now. I'll take you to the medical center."

"I'm fine. Are we far from Antaño?"

"This is a detour, and the road's used mostly by locals. Too steep for tourists. Dangerous if you're not familiar with the area." The man spoke on his CB radio and ordered a tow truck. "This sand will kill a car's brakes." He removed his hat and dusted off his hair. He picked up a bottle of water and rinsed out his mouth. He spat and took another drink. Upon removing his sunglasses, the whites around his eyes gave him a raccoon appearance. He turned and smiled. His light gray eyes were impressive, and in a strange way, the stranger looked almost familiar. He leaned back and rolled down Brisa's window.

"Forgive me," he said. "Water?"

"Yes, thank you." Brisa gulped the cool liquid.

His gaze spread an eerie feeling of déjà vu all through her. She sat quietly and studied the man. Did she know him from somewhere? As each second ticked by, Brisa checked for a signal. She glanced out the window and knew they were close to Antaño.

"I know you," he said.

"You do look familiar."

"I met you in the capital." He smiled. "A man was bothering you. Are you escaping from another threat like the day at the café?" He laughed.

"No." Brisa smiled back. "Just disoriented."

"Where are you going in Antaño?"

"Los Arcos lodge."

"Cami and I stay there sometimes."

"Are you from around here?"

"Camelia Ranch," the girl replied. "It is called Camelia just like me. But I'm called Cami. We live in Palmas Rojas. We have horses."

"Really? Tell me more."

The girl looked to be between six and eight. Brisa wasn't sure for she never was very good around kids.

"In Antaño, they're spooks," the girl said.

Brisa frowned for the statement didn't seem to match their conversation.

"By day they hide, by night their souls walk the streets."

"Who walks the streets?" Brisa asked.

"Spanish conquistadors," the girl replied. "Nuns and priests. People who used to live here. They're spooks now."

"Sorry," the man said, interrupting the child. "She's into legends and old stories. I'm Sebastián Salguero and this is my daughter, Cami."

"Brisa Murillo."

"Like the breeze from the sea?" Cami asked.

"Why, yes." Brisa smiled.

"We have horses," Cami said. "Do you have a horse? My mare is Princesa. Do you like to ride?"

"I love to ride," Brisa replied.

"Brisa can ride my mare," Cami said to her father.

"We'll see, Cami."

"Brisa, if you drive down that road over there, you'll reach the ocean. If you keep going toward those peaks, you'll be in Mexico. Isn't that right, Papa?"

"Yes, Cami. Antaño is near the border."

"Tourists love Antaño. Brisa, see that rock over there. It's where the city starts. And it's now Mother Rosa's place. Right, Papa?"

"It's only a rock, Cami."

"She's going to be a saint soon, and when that happens, they'll open her coffin and she'll be sleeping in roses."

"Oh?" Brisa was amazed with the child's knowledge of the legend. "Why would anyone want to open her coffin?"

"An earthquake will open it," Cami explained.

"It's just a legend, Cami." Her father sighed. "I explained that already."

"People pray to her and leave her roses," Cami said. "Nanita asks her for miracles because she's beautiful."

"Beatified," he said, correcting her. "Cami, you talk too much."

It was an intriguing story. Perhaps it would be a good idea to include it in the launch of the project. Brisa decided she should probably pay more attention to the story about the nun, Mother Rosa. Locals seemed to honor her. Brisa somewhat envied the girl. She would have enjoyed believing in something or someone divine to defend her from her insecurities. Maybe she wouldn't feel so alone all the time if she had a little faith in her life. Unfortunately, the stories were probably just nonsenses — a small town's dream.

"Papa, show Brisa how the hill deceives us." Cami turned to Brisa and smiled. "You'll see the spook!"

He frowned.

"Stop the car!" the girl yelled.

The car slowed and they sat silently on the dirt road. A loud creak filled Brisa's ears as the man pulled on the emergency brake.

"Wait for it," Cami said. "Now, we say … Mother Rosa, come be with us!"

The car shook before slowly rolling up the hill. Brisa's eyes widened as she stared out the window. It was as if they had just entered a different dimension or something.

Cami laughed. "You see? They're spooks." She laughed again. "Papa says it's just electromag forces."

"Electromagnetic," her father stated. He laughed as he started the engine.

The wild, red flowers completely filled her view, and Brisa tried to count the rose bushes, but there were too many.

"It only happens here between the roses," Cami said.

They soon arrived at the lodge, and Brisa invited them in for a visit.

"Cami, ice cream?" her father asked.

Cami nodded.

"Beer?" Sebastián asked Brisa.

"No, but I'd love a soda."

The man placed the order while Cami played in the little park. Brisa found a shady seat under an umbrella. After handing Cami a cone, Sebastián took a seat next to Brisa. Something about Sebastián's eyes intrigued her. They seemed to change color with his mood. Right now, they looked more of a coffee color. He handed Brisa a soda and took a sip of his beer. His gaze caught Brisa off guard, although, it felt good to look at him.

His phone rang and he answered. He nodded and pointed to Brisa as he spoke. "They'll tow your car to a garage," he said. "What's your number and I'll text you their info." He handed her his phone.

Brisa typed her number into his phone. It felt odd having her name in a stranger's address book. "Don't know how to thank you."

"I like rescuing pretty, young women." He laughed. "You work near the bar in town?"

"Yes. My office is across the street … and you?"

"I'm no city guy. My lawyer is a few buildings down from the bistro. In my small town there are only fields, plantations, and cattle … no lawyers."

"Brisa?" A hand touched her shoulder.

Brisa turned and smiled. "Sonia? What are you doing here? Thought you were staying in the city?"

"Surprise? I was bored. What took you so long and where's your car?"

"Slight bump on the road. This is Sebastián. My car's broken again."

Sonia smiled a fake smile and nodded.

Sebastián stood. "Cami! We're leaving."

"Thanks again, Sebastián." Brisa stood and nodded.

"Papa, can we bring Brisa to the ranch? I want her to meet my horse."

"Maybe someday." Sebastián nodded directly at Brisa as he placed his hat back on his head.

Brisa stood next to Sonia and watched as the two walked away.

Sonia glanced at Brisa and said, "What a hunk!"

"He's okay."

"Wrinkled shirt," Sonia said. "Poor guy probably doesn't have anyone to iron it for him. Do you like to iron, Brisa?" She smiled.

Brisa shook her head and took a sip of her soda.

"Did you see how he looked at you?"

"No, I didn't."

"Talk about electromagnetic attraction." Sonia laughed.

"I believe I heard something about that just a little while ago."

"Everyone here talks about it. And you two, there's something. Something that's between electricity and magnetism. A reality-altering force." She laughed again. "What do you think about my scientific analogy? I've researched it and can tell you, *wow*, around here it's strong!"

"You're being silly, Sonia."

Sonia shook her head.

"What I just experienced left my knees shaking."

"Gotta be," she mused. "You ran into that mango ... literally."

"I need a glass of wine."

Sonia glared at Brisa and frowned.

"I'm heading home," Brisa said, ignoring Sonia's negative response. "Need some rest."

"I'll be here if you want company. Call me if you can't sleep in that *spooky* house."

Brisa waved down a mini taxi and enjoyed the time with the beautiful horse that was pulling the small carriage. She thought about the conversation with Cami. The carriage stopped and Brisa climbed out. The driver nodded and she shrugged. She almost ran inside and wanted nothing more than a warm fire to give her new place a homey feel.

After stacking the wood inside the fireplace, she lit the papers she had carefully placed underneath. The smoke billowed out and dimmed the light.

"How can this be?"

This type of Spanish fireplace was usually efficient and safe. She tapped out the fire and sighed. Brisa really wanted to enjoy one. As she glanced out toward the convent and fields, her chaotic day ran through her mind. When her phone rang, she answered.

"Tell me ... did you get your car back?" Sonia asked.

"Not yet," Brisa sighed loud enough for her to hear. "It's in the shop. I just left you and I need some rest, okay?"

"Want me to call that handsome guy and ask about your car?" Sonia snickered.

"Drop it already."

"He asked *me* for your number." Sonia laughed.

"He asked for my number?" Brisa squinted and frowned.

"Well ... not him exactly. The little girl asked for it. Said she wanted to show you some books and a collection of rosaries she had that were Mother Rosa's."

"I thought they left just before I did?"

"No, they returned and checked in. The girl grabbed me before they went to their room."

"Good night, Sonia."

Brisa entered the office and held up the liquor bottle she had brought with her. She stared at it. She really needed a drink — just one — to relax. The glorious bottle and her next step ran through her mind. But she couldn't do it. Couldn't sabotage herself or the project. She held the bottle close to her chest and studied the dead fireplace. It was massive, however, from the outside the chimney and the ash pit hid most of the actual size. The hearth was just too clean, as if it were never used. The hearth in the bedroom, meanwhile, was caked with built-up soot. *Maybe this one never worked?* Brisa stuck her hand into the damper and felt around. The old wall that led to the exhaust seemed different somehow. The bricks inside the fireplace were situated at unusual angles. Cogs that felt like rungs were stacked into the mortar that led upward. Brisa ducked down and inched her way inside. It was dark and she couldn't see much.

After a few moments, she crawled back out and dusted herself off. She glanced around for a good place to hide her bottle. A place where no one would find it but with easy access for her … in case of an emergency. A small, hidden shelf on the old mantel seemed to be the perfect spot.

"You will be well sheltered." Brisa smiled at the little bottle as if it were an old friend.

She placed the bottle on the shelf and pushed it back, so it would be hidden within the shadows. As she pushed, it tumbled backward and fell. The clanking of glass echoed as it disappeared into the darkness.

"That's why the chimney didn't work!"

She crawled back into the hearth and stood. Using her phone as a light, she lit the flue and snapped a few pictures. The throat that regulated the draft looked as if it were closed. Perhaps she could fix it. It was such a majestic fireplace, and therefore, very much worth the trouble. Brisa took a few more photos of the fascia. She could examine it a little later. Her phone rang and she jumped. An unknown number.

"Hello?"

"Brisa?" a soft voice asked. "It's Cami."

"Hello, Cami."

"I have a rosary that I used for my first communion and some clips about Mother Rosa. Remember the story of the sleeping nun? When you come to the ranch … well, I also have cards about horses and —"

"I'm sorry, Rocío …" a male voice said, "… but Cami was insisting …"

"Brisa," Brisa said, correcting the caller.

"She's very outgoing," he replied.

"It's fine. Cami can call as often as she wants." She rolled her eyes. Cami was a charismatic girl, but Brisa needed to finish out the day and settle in for the night.

"Camelia, let the lady rest," he said to the young girl. "Did they call about your car?"

"Not yet."

"Make sure the mechanic does not hand you a bill. I already paid. I'm letting you know so you're not charged twice."

"Oh? How can I pay you back?"

"Someday and … if not … then courtesy of Camelia Ranch!"

"But —"

He had hung up.

Brisa thought about the strange encounters she had with the man recently and shrugged, for it was time for some much-needed rest. Tomorrow, she would purchase a new bottle to replace the one that had just disappeared. She stared at the fireplace and frowned.

"Odd."

CHAPTER IV

Brisa laced up her work boots, strapped on her leather tool belt, and tapped on her helmet twice. It was time for her morning walk about. Workers driving heavy equipment were busy removing gravel from the hollow. About half of the small dwellings were already gone. As a crane swiveled and heavy trucks sped up the small hill, Brisa glanced at her watch. It was still just a little before six in the morning.

Mr. Rogelio stood under the large tree with a goat at his side. He smiled as she approached. "Good morning, ma'am." Rogelio nodded. "I come here because I enjoy watching them move the good ole' Mother Earth." He frowned. "However, if you'd prefer that I …"

"You're fine, Mr. Rogelio," Brisa replied. "Just be cautious of the heavy equipment."

He nodded. "That convent was built before the time of Mother Rosa. Did you know that?"

Brisa smiled. "Have you always worked here?"

"Yes, ma'am." He nodded again. "I was born on this land." He smiled and his missing teeth made her shiver. "My father worked the farm when I was little. We lived here until the good boss died. It was then that Lady Delfina sent us to live in the valley." As he talked, the crane pushed over a small structure. "It was where the field hands lived. The cranes just knocked one over."

"Lady Delfina?"

"Yes. Lady Delfina de Herradura. She took this place over when the good boss died. She was a very bad person."

Brisa thought about the sinister portrait of the old woman and how she had stashed it in an empty closet. Lady Delfina was the last occupant of the old mansion. She looked at the man but didn't say anything. Wouldn't be too wise to become too chummy.

"She was the step-grandmother of the children, Juancho and Lucía. We used to play together, and they treated me as a friend, as their peer. Sara played with us too. We chased each other inside the old tunnels."

The old man seemed sober today. Therefore, no need to say anything to the personnel department. "Tunnels? Where do they lead?"

"Everywhere and nowhere." He laughed. "Just passageways. This city was built on top of another that was destroyed during an earthquake."

"Does everyone know that you drink up here?" Brisa asked.

He nodded. "Look, ma'am. When one has a drinking problem, everyone knows. Everyone except the person with the problem." He glanced away.

Brisa smiled.

"Are the entrances to the catacombs going to disappear, ma'am?" he asked. "Will you dynamite them?"

"No, they're not in the way. They won't interfere with the new construction."

"Down there ..." – the man pointed to the old church – "Will there be more demolition?"

"Not a lot. I hope to save a good deal of it."

Brisa possessed polarized feelings on just about everything. She didn't know what she wanted or what she was looking for. Right now, the only thing for sure was the project. It was the one thing she could control. Brisa hurried toward the mansion and Mr. Rogelio followed.

"Many secrets remain underground," he said. "Sara will no longer have any place to walk."

"Sara? Who's Sara?"

"She lived here many, many years ago. Mother Rosa granted her a miracle once. I'm still waiting for mine. One should never lose faith."

Brisa sighed.

"To quit drinking, ma'am," he added. "That would be my miracle."

"Rogelio …" Brisa looked at him. "Who hired you?"

"When you want more stories about those that lived in that house," – he winked – "come see me." He nodded and walked away.

"Brisa!" Carlitos called out as he approached from a small field. "Engineer Peña needs you to look at some dates. We've started on the gravel removal below the river and the demolition of the little huts is on schedule."

"I'll be down there as soon as I can."

"Having second thoughts?" Carlitos asked.

"What?"

"About the ruins."

"Sentimental, are we?" Brisa mused. "I'll walk through the ruins and evaluate the area, then write up a protocol for the cracks. We'll need to fence the place off."

"Be careful, ma'am."

"With the ruins?"

"No, the rose bushes. Thorns are everywhere. Most of the roses grow around those ruins. Some say that Mother Rosa sleeps under them."

"Thank you, Carlitos," Brisa replied, walking away. "I'll be careful."

Brisa circled the ruins before glancing up at the belfry. The original bronze bell was still in place. Definitely baroque. The structure was huge with many tall and intricate arches but just barely. It was difficult to believe that the tremors hadn't already knocked them down.

Echoes of someone screaming pulled her from her thoughts. Before she could figure out who it was, her phone dinged.

```
Carlitos:    Accident on one of the cranes. We need you down
             here.
```

Brisa wanted to run straight there, but the accident was not accessible from where she stood. She had to take a detour. A few minutes later, she stood next to Carlitos and frowned. A backhoe had turned over, and a worker was trapped underneath. Workers had already called for an ambulance and were now struggling to dig out the trapped man. A religious-looking woman knelt down and held the man's head. Eventually, the paramedics arrived and soon the man was whisked away. Brisa glanced around for the religious-looking woman, but there was no trace of her.

"He'll be okay," Carlitos said.

"Who was that woman who was with him?"

"Woman?" Carlitos asked. "What woman?"

"Never mind," Brisa said, shaking her head.

As she walked back toward the ruins, her mind wandered. Those old buildings probably held some equally old and dark secrets. Would it be difficult for her to give the order to knock them down? Maybe the mayor would approve her preliminary plans to retain the mansion and ruins.

An unknown number flashed across her phone and she paused. *Sebastián?* It was a silly thought and she pushed it from her mind. The call was from José who was sorry about the mishap. He had completed the evaluation phase of the demolition and wanted to let her know.

"The topographers are ready as soon as we clear the gravel," José continued. "I think I'll order a retraining of the operators. To be on the safe side."

"Agreed." Brisa nodded. "Always good to review safety protocols. We can't afford another incident. On another note, you know that we're not touching the ruins, right?"

"Yes, Carlitos told me."

"Please ban anyone from going inside. I wish to save what remains and use them as an event hall or for other functions."

Pablo, the mayor, visited the project at least three times a week. His masculine demeanor, although he didn't take care of his figure or posture, was somewhat attractive. Then again, Brisa couldn't quite put her finger on what it was that she didn't like about him. He wasn't quite forty yet and was tall with curly, black hair and lively, dark eyes. His skin was tinted with a copper hue that made him look provincial. At times, she felt as if he were hiding behind his urban clothing. It sometimes seemed that he wore his clothes ensuring that the brand name was on the outside. An ostentatious, gold watch and chain contradicted his efforts to look sophisticated. A wide and tactless smile always decorated his face, especially when he was bragging. He was definitely a fan of the project, and a bigger fan of the total demolition of the old buildings. Since he asked about every little detail, he reminded Brisa of a kid with a new toy. Sometimes, he gave the impression that his work at City Hall didn't require his attention as much as the project.

Brisa waved at Pablo and Carlitos who were deep in conversation.

"That matter of the Herradura family heir is becoming more of a burden," Carlitos said to Pablo. "The guy wants custody. Claims that Juancho is his uncle."

"Custody of who?" Brisa asked.

"His uncle, Juancho Herradura," Carlitos repeated.

"I don't understand why Mr. Herradura would want custody," Brisa replied. "And what would that have to do with us? I wish someone would explain it to me."

"Long story," Pablo said.

"They're small but troublesome complications that come with the territory," Carlitos explained. "The old man's a paraplegic. I believe he also inherited some of the family's senility. His legal guardian had agreed to invest in our project. However, his guardian recently died and now a different family member is claiming legal possession to the land. He's challenging the signed agreements. Basically, this guy is interested in his uncle's money. Rich family members die and the heirs bleed out from the woodwork."

"It sounds like a delicate matter," Brisa said. "Reminds me of something, but not sure what. Do we have all the permits to take down the ruins?"

"Of course." Pablo laughed. "I am the city!" He winked at her.

Carlitos didn't reply.

"Look, Brisa, you proceed as planned," Pablo said. "I'm happy with the progress so far. Angela will handle the legal issues. We have lawyers on the payroll."

"If anyone knows how to handle these types of problems, it's you," Carlitos said, nodding to the mayor.

Carlitos aimed for the fields, and Pablo aimed for his car. Brisa waved goodbye before walking toward the boarding school. As the mayor drove down the dirt road, Marta ran across the yard with her cluster of keys.

"Marta!" Brisa yelled, running toward the woman and waving her arms. "You cannot enter the school! They're preparing for demolition, and no one is allowed inside!"

"I'm sorry, Architect," Marta said, frowning. "I have orders from the Ministry of Culture. Although the school may not be sitting on an archaeological site, it could still house old relics."

"Does the mayor know about this?"

"Of course." She sighed. "My office is in City Hall and only a few doors from his. However, I report directly to the ministry and not to the municipality."

"This is just an old school from the sixties and not from the colonial era." Brisa pointed to the old buildings. "What could possibly be of any interest between these walls?"

"This is a delicate matter," Marta replied. "You're an outsider and will just never understand. We must know what remains of the colonial ruins. The ministry may have claims to them, and if so, then the land would not belong to the Herraduras or your company."

"The mayor is not worried about this?"

"He's acting on his own self-interest."

"You'll need a hardhat." Brisa took her hat from her head and handed it to the woman. "Construction rules."

"Are you following me in?" she asked.

"I have more hats in my office, so I'll join you shortly." Brisa turned to leave and Marta followed her. "It's the only way you can enter. You can no longer be inside these ruins by yourself, and I'm sure the mayor has everything under control."

"That's what he thinks," Marta said, almost talking to herself. "There are two sides to every story, yah know. The one that's buried by the earthquakes and most convenient, and the others that will be uncovered by excavation. Once uncovered, they could be of great importance to this small city."

Brisa sighed as Marta followed her into the office. She grabbed another hardhat, and the two walked back toward the old school.

"Inside that girls' boarding school, many atrocities were committed," Marta said. "Much has been forgotten or swept under the rug. Not many care but others do. If we're not careful, time will erase everything."

Brisa considered the possibilities. Could young girls have been buried there? Young girls who suddenly turned up missing? "I think the demolition will do more damage than good, unless we can find a way to stop the mayor from moving forward with his plans."

Marta used her keys and unlocked the wooden gate and then opened the door. The two walked down the empty hall, and the echoes gave Brisa reason to pause. When they arrived at the old library, a large painting of a nun that almost covered one wall, made Brisa think.

"Is that her?" Brisa asked. "The Mother?"

Marta nodded.

The oils had darkened from time, which made the woman's features difficult to make out.

"It'll be given to the bishop. However, if it's a true relic … it actually belongs to the convent."

"The one that the blessed Mother Rosa founded?"

"It is so, even if it seems a little odd," Marta said, crossing her arms and nodding. "It's documented and they'll eventually come for it."

The silhouette of the religious woman with a soft and far-away gaze somewhat blended into the darker background. The canvas had almost completely surrendered to the constant bombardment of dust and mold.

"Needs to be restored." Brisa sighed and stepped closer. Using the light from her phone, she studied the portrait.

The mysterious woman wore a black habit with a reddish-brown tunic. Her veil and white scapulary were complimented by the common band that rolled around the tunic near her waist. Her right hand, with a rose tattoo, rested on a rosary, and her left hand caressed a brown notebook.

"The book of the teachings." Marta pointed. "She was a pilgrim who helped to build the convent. Most of her written doctrines are lost, and now, only oral traditions remain."

"Oh?" Brisa said.

"She was an advocate for abused girls suffering from sexual abuse. Girls long abandoned by their single mothers. She gave them shelter. Education. That was centuries ago. Lady Delfina Herradura changed the benevolent course of the convent when she walked in as protector. She was the major beneficiary of the congregation. She changed things and not for the good. Undid the incredible work accomplished by the Holy Mother. We're hoping that old documents or relics that once belonged to the Mother are hidden somewhere around here."

"Who would hide them?" Brisa asked.

"The nuns." Marta laughed. "Who else?"

Brisa thought about it and her interest sparked. "Mother Rosa was a saint who lived centuries ago, and Lady Delfina de Herradura is a more recent story by just a few decades … the seventies?"

"That's right." Marta nodded. "A friendly woman who was also very bad. Both good and bad people once lived here — divinity versus evil."

Brisa didn't know what to think. A long time ago, a holy woman walked these halls, and then a very evil woman took them over — Lady Delfina. What was the relevance? Was there a connection?

"Now then," Marta said, "regarding the atrocities that took place and remains in the consciousness of the Herraduras. Be they living or dead is none of my never mind. I just do my job."

"Yes, Marta, but there are rules we must follow. This land was legally purchased. Anything else is water under the bridge. I understand that this is important to you. However, this property now belongs to my company."

"I will still visit every day … until the demolition. Not even the mayor can stop me."

"What are you looking for? I see only trash, and no other representatives have stepped forward to verify your claims."

"There's a legal action in place challenging your project." Marta grinned. "Is there not?"

"I can't deny that." Brisa sighed again. "But legal matters are handled by our attorneys. I do not become involved in such things." Brisa frowned. "I must ask for the keys that you are carrying."

"No!" Marta took several steps back and glared at her. "I cannot give you *my* keys!" Marta pushed on the door, but Brisa blocked it with her foot. Marta grunted a few times before walking away.

Brisa left the door ajar and aimed for the mansion. Angela was sitting behind her desk when she entered the office.

"I have news for you, Brisa. The good first. We need only one signature from the mayor and then the last permit will be complete. Your work is moving forward according to schedule. Liquidity is on budget."

Brisa crossed her arms. "What's the bad?"

"The project is threatened … temporarily."

"Legal?"

"Nothing special." Angela smiled. "Just that the Herradura relative is trying to stake a claim."

"Why make such a fuss? I thought everything was in place?"

"The Herraduras are a high-profile family." She shook her head. "But they've lost most of their power over the last few years."

"I understand that these lands belonged to the Herraduras since the founding of Antaño in 1525."

"Look." Angela stood and took a couple of steps forward. "I'm fed up with all this legal stuff. Change of topic. Sonia says you've taken a liking to these old walls."

"I'm not clinging to them," Brisa replied. "I just like old buildings."

"According to Sonia, you have abandonment issues."

"Abandonment issues?" Brisa laughed. "Sonia is nosy and always trying to psychoanalyze me."

"Brisa …" Angela frowned.

"Sonia talks too much. I only look at numbers and calculate the profit. Saving the mansion and ruins for special events could be a moneymaker. That's where my interest ends. Most think of me as being sentimental. However, I honestly believe these old buildings could benefit the project."

Angela smiled. "Pablo's not swayed with the idea. He's prepared to knock it all down. Wants new construction."

Brisa frowned and looked away.

"He's a governing partner and a board member."

"I'll make them all change their minds."

"Your orders are simple," Angela said. "Just follow the approved plans."

Brisa walked over to the window and stared out at the rising hills. The sun was just about to crest a distant ridge. She turned to Angela. "Is it legal for Pablo to be a partner?"

"I explained it to you already," Angela said with her voice rising. "It's a corporate relationship. The only ones who know of his connections are in upper management."

"I'm tired," Brisa said, holding the front door open.

Angela walked out without another word. Brisa's mind whirled through the possibilities. Marta's stories left her feeling at odds with the place and the whole situation. After Angela's car rolled down the dirt road, Brisa walked the path toward the old school. The sun barely reached her now. She opened the door that she had left ajar and stepped inside.

"Why didn't Marta have this place cleaned out?"

Marta seemed concerned about what remained and all Brisa saw was rubbish — trash and broken glass scattered everywhere. She walked through the darkened halls and listened to the echoes of her steps. It wasn't difficult to imagine girls ambling across these floors and playing in the courtyards. Standing still, she could almost hear their voices.

"Residual sonic waves that are physically trapped?" Brisa said. "Now, I'm losing it."

She shook her head and stepped toward the library. The massive room gave her chills. Reaching down, she picked up several books, *Don Quixote*, a bible, and a novel from a distant but classical time. All were torn or mildewed. She turned on her phone light and strolled between the tall bookcases.

Running her fingers along a shelf, the dust that collected on her hand felt gritty. She brushed off the dirt and shook her head.

"Sad," Brisa whispered.

Stuffed into a corner of a bookshelf, an old notebook caught her attention. She read the title: Vida y Milagros de la Madre Rosa, Fundadora de la Congregación de las Servidoras de la Corona de Espinas — *Life and Miracles of Mother Rosa, Founder of the Congregation Servants of the Crown of Thorns.*

It didn't look to be centuries old … maybe only fifty years or so. And it seemed odd that Marta had not yet found it. Brisa stuffed the small notebook into her tool belt. She would surprise the woman with it tomorrow.

Near a back wall, a door stood open and beckoned to her. A closet, maybe? Brisa entered and flashed around her light. Many old desks were stacked next to one wall. *An old schoolroom?* Papers scattered across the floor had already invited the rats. As several critters ran from her light, she turned to leave. But her eyes followed the light along the floor instead, and a metal grate reflected back.

"Ventilation?"

It would only be sensible that fresh air was able to enter. Although, this wall should face the outside. There should be nothing on the other side but the old rose bushes. Brisa stepped up to the grate and rubbed her hand along the old wallpaper. A few pieces crumbled and fell to the floor. She hit the wall softly and listened for an echo. An odd sound floated through the air. *Another room? How can I find it? Does this school have a basement?* Many older buildings were often built on top of basements or older structures. If they had to fill in after demolition, her costs would increase. Not a good thing. Brisa snapped a few photos before leaving. She stepped into the hallway and glanced around. Another opened door at the far end looked enticing.

Brisa's curiosity was pulling her in. The old building housed many nooks and hallways and stairs that led both up and down. She stepped into what had once been a kitchen. Twisted frying pans still hung over a wood burning stove. It was huge and hogged the center of the room. Nothing else of interest was in here. It was becoming dark and about time for her to return to the mansion for the evening. Brisa walked up to the front office and stopped. She pushed the door open and entered. After pounding her foot on the floor, she waited for the squeaks and scratches to die down. She flashed her light through the room and little, yellow eyes stared back from inside the dark shadows.

Brisa laughed and browsed through the old notebooks that contained accounting information. The pages were dated from 1962. She took a few photos. The paper files had somewhat decayed, so she left most of them alone. A disquieting silence hung in the air. Every sound was multiplied by an echo. Even her flipping through the old pages bounced off the ancient walls. She ran her fingers down a line of charges and strange voices floated around her. Brisa froze. The voices sounded louder than before ... closer. She stepped into the hall and flashed her light into the darkness. Empty. She hurried back to the kitchen, and again, the room was empty.

She shrugged and walked back toward the mansion. Her stomach growled and her mind remained fixated on the old convent and its stories. She couldn't shake the enigma of the famous nun or the *evil* Lady Delfina de Herradura. *How could anyone mistreat young girls like that?*

"Good evening," a voice said from under the large tree.

Brisa turned and smiled. "Mr. Rogelio ... nice evening."

"I am sober, ma'am," Rogelio said. "Did you have a good afternoon?"

Brisa didn't respond. The man was not supposed to be out here, but she was not about to say anything. She turned to leave and the old school bell rang. Brisa glanced up at the old tower and smiled. The bell sounded every day at noon and at six. No one paid it any attention except for her and Rogelio. He noticed it. She entered the house, as she had named the mansion, and relaxed since the staff had already left for the day. She shivered and pulled her sweater tighter around her shoulders. A perfect night to read a book in front of a warm fire. She ate a light dinner and then changed into something a little more comfortable. She grabbed a novel and stepped up to her bed. As she reached for the covers, she froze. A single rose rested on top of one of the pillows.

"Who …?"

She glanced around and thought about Sebastián but immediately pushed that idea away. After placing the rose on the nightstand, she climbed in between the covers and opened the book. Reading the first few lines made her eyes feel heavy and she yawned. The rhythm of a light rain hitting the windows sounded soothing.

It was the footfalls upon the stairs that startled her. She jumped and flipped on the hallway light. Every night this week, Brisa had darted out of bed just to find the hallway empty. After climbing again between the sheets, she pulled the covers over her head and fell asleep.

The light of day woke her early, and the outside world appeared gray and solemn. Sitting up, she glanced around. The bedroom really looked gloomy on such a cloudy day. She tried to fall back to sleep, but again, heard the footsteps. *This old house makes all kinds of noises.* Small tremors visited the area every day. Giving up, she sighed and swung her legs off the bed. The bedroom door flew open.

"Selena?" she asked, believing it to be the cleaning girl.

"Morning, Brisa," a female voice replied.

"Sonia! How did you get in?" Did she not lock the door last night?

Sonia turned and glanced down the hallway. "What a spooky place!"

"I'll get dressed," Brisa said, standing.

"What's down there?" Sonia asked as she snooped through the empty rooms.

A nose echoed and Sonia ran back into Brisa's room. With her face pale and eyes wide, she yelled out, "A white shadow! I saw a white shadow. I thought shadows were supposed to be dark!" She was panting and shaking.

Brisa tried to calm her, but her friend's yelling upset her instead. "Let's go downstairs." Brisa pulled on Sonia's arm. "I'll make coffee."

A white light flashed briefly and lit the hallway. Brisa turned to get a better view, but it happened so fast that she had almost missed it. Another flash on the stairs, and she ran after the light. Whatever it was floated into the fireplace and vanished. Her knees shook, and when she glanced back at Sonia, Brisa shook her head and laughed.

"I swear," Sonia said, "that white *thing* was coming after me!"

"Okay." Brisa glanced back at the stairs.

"A woman!" Sonia stated. "It was a woman!"

"I believe you."

"No, you don't," Sonia frowned. "You shouldn't be in this house alone!"

"Take it easy."

The two entered the kitchen, and Brisa started the coffee. "Carlitos talked to Selena, and she agreed to sleep in the maid's room," Brisa said. "Maybe she was here last night, or she came early today."

"This weekend you're having breakfast with me at the lodge." Sonia huffed. "You should stay a few days in my room while I'm in the city. I have to get you outta here, even if it's for just one day."

"Coffee's ready." Brisa grabbed two cups.

"I wanted to surprise you. Tell you I was taking you away for a short vacation. But the one who was surprised was me ... I'm leaving this hell hole!" Sonia gulped down her coffee. "I'll see you tomorrow."

Brisa nodded and touched her friend's shoulder. "I believe you, Sonia. I believe that you saw a light. I saw a light too. There just has to be a logical explanation."

Sonia darted to her car without saying goodbye.

Brisa stepped outside and watched as her friend sped away. Rogelio was asleep near the back door. Had Sonia seen him? He reeked of alcohol. Brisa covered him with an old blanket before reentering the house. She filled her cup with coffee and walked through the mansion. Her curiosity was growing as she thought about how strange everything was becoming. Despite her vulnerability and daily struggles with wanting a drink, Brisa was surviving through her panic attacks and the mysterious nightly footsteps. Lately, nothing seemed to frighten her. Not even a momentary apparition.

She was, however, terrified of what people might think about her allowing that drunk to hang around. Even more than that was her ex-husband. A man who had stopped loving her. He had abandoned and betrayed her. Brisa was in constant panic about the indifference displayed by others, and therefore, things from the other side didn't frighten her. Only things from this side could hurt her, and someone already had. Could it be that Brisa did not believe in ghosts? For the first time, she opened herself up to the possibility that something otherworldly might be happening. Or was it that she was not trusting in what she was seeing? Brisa definitely did not believe in *herself.* Only one thing planted her feet on firm soil — numbers, estimates, and her designs — for they were tangible and real.

CHAPTER V

S unday arrived and she readied herself for breakfast at the lodge with Sonia. A loud noise in the street startled her, and she now regretted bringing her car. Sonia had not yet arrived from the capital, and with several minutes to spare, Brisa sat to watch the news in the lobby.

"Do you remember me?" a deep voice asked.

It was Sebastián. He looked a little more unkempt than usual and seemed a little taller than before.

"Spending the weekend in Antaño?" Brisa asked.

"May I?" He pulled up a chair. "What are you drinking?"

"Espresso."

"Me, too." He ordered two fresh cups. "Are you heading back to the capital?"

"No, staying here."

"Today's a holiday and many from the capital are here to enjoy the celebrations."

"Ah, that's the noise I hear. I thought it strange … seeing so many cars parked along the street."

"You alone?"

"Waiting for my friend. We're having breakfast together. You met her the other day."

Sonia walked up and Sebastián stood. "Don't wish to intrude," he said, looking directly at Brisa. "I just needed to tell you that I've blocked your car.

The lot was full. When you're leaving, just ask the attendant for my keys." He nodded. "See you later, ma'am." He tapped his hat and flashed a half-smile.

"Ma'am?" Sonia repeated, shaking her head. "What an insult. Ma'am! That's for old ladies." She laughed. "I guess you can forgive him a little 'cause he's handsome." Sonia shrugged. "So, tell me, what's going on between you two? Are you and the unruly-haired hunk an item?" She sat back and crossed her arms. "He was asking about you in the lobby of the PROE S.A. building."

"Asking about me?"

"He was asking to speak to a Miss Rocío Murillo. They told him no one by that name worked there. He pulled out a receipt from some place, probably to get your name right. Then he said, 'Sorry, I meant Brisa Murillo.' The receptionist didn't want to give out any information, and I was about to step into the middle of it, but my phone rang."

"Maybe he wants payment for the repairs."

"It was definitely him. He had the same not-well-ironed shirt. What's going on between you two?"

"Nothing," Brisa replied. "Not seen or heard from him since the accident … until today."

"Right …" Sonia whined. "Change of topic. Can we walk through the fair?"

"Not interested. Let's have breakfast so I can return home. I need some peace and quiet. Want to read a good book while wearing my pajamas."

"Come on, Brisa!" Sonia pleaded. "Lots of tourists and there's games —"

"Exactly. I want silence."

"You and that spooky house!"

"I figured out what that light was. It enters through the large windows. And one of them is cracked, which makes the morning sun bounce through the halls. Especially when a cloud passes, and the light —"

"You believe that?" Sonia asked.

"I do. I also say it's just a light." Brisa tried to reassure her friend. She didn't want Sonia making a scene in public.

"Think whatever you want." Sonia huffed. "I know what I saw, and it tried to talk to me!"

They ate breakfast, and every once in a while, they'd look at each other before looking away. They agreed to meet later that day, and Sonia left for the festivities. Sebastián's car with a horse trailer was definitely blocking Brisa's car.

"Didn't he leave his keys with you?" Brisa asked.

"Mr. Sebastián?" the attendant asked. "No. He must have forgotten. I'm sure he's nearby."

Brisa didn't want to wait. She searched for a mini taxi but all were busy. Instead, she walked up the hill toward the mansion. Many citizens were decorating their windows with colorful pots and paper flyers, and the cobbled streets were now covered with a carpet of sawdust. Some villagers were on horseback, and the locals and tourists were ready to party.

"Brisa!" Sebastián rode up on a beautiful, white stallion, looking as handsome as ever. "Was looking for you. Forgive me, I forgot to leave the keys. I took Cami to her mother's. We can go for your car now."

"Thanks. I've walked this far, I'm sure I can walk the rest. My car's fine where it is."

"I'll take you then."

"On your horse?"

He smiled.

Brisa hesitated as she studied the beautiful animal.

Sebastián slid down. "Put your foot on the stirrup, and I'll raise you up."

"In front or back?"

"Front."

"Been a long time since I last rode." She giggled.

"Still want to be alone?" he asked.

"Don't like crowds."

"Then I know the perfect place."

"Place?"

"Just lean back and enjoy the ride."

Sebastián said hello to others as they strolled through the streets. Brisa was surprised since he was not living in Antaño and so many still greeted him. He leaned forward and her back rested against his warm chest. It felt odd but soothing. When they reached an open field, he nudged the horse to gallop. Everything blurred and his heavy breathing somewhat comforted her. She felt his arms as they pushed against hers. When he rested his hands on the horn, his arms completely surrounded her. Now intertwined and not sure where they were headed, she prayed the trip would last forever.

The horse slowed and stopped by an old, iron gate where an ancient fence barely stood. Sebastián slid down before helping Brisa.

"What is this place?" she asked.

"I own this land," he said, tying the horse to a nearby post.

"There's nothing out here," she added.

"Follow me."

They walked to a small mound with a sloping grade. The field was covered with overgrown grass and brush, and they followed a narrow path that was lined with wild roses.

"Watch out for thorns," he said, taking the lead.

They stopped at a picket fence, and Sebastián pushed on the dilapidated, wooden gate. When a cool breeze blew up from the stairs that led below ground, she shivered.

"Catacombs?" Brisa asked.

He nodded. "Very old passageway."

They stepped inside using the lights from their phones. The corridor was narrow and not easy to maneuver. Sebastián had to hunch over. Brisa was short and could stand with an inch or two gap remaining above her head. The passageway eventually opened into a higher and prolonged hallway that was filled with many niches. Cracked statues filled some of the open sections. Sunlight penetrated through the skylights that were placed strategically along the top as if designed by modern engineers. The place was strangely inviting. Brisa felt surrounded and alone at the same time. She wasn't sure how to react, because she was walking through a catacomb with a person she hardly knew and was feeling excited and afraid at the same time.

"Impressive engineering." Brisa examined the walls as if interested in the construction. "Do these halls lead to monasteries and convents from the time of the conquistadors?"

Sebastián nodded. "The houses of the heralds of the time. Affluent families. See these niches? Tombs of the nobles. There are wells for communal ossuaries, and at one time, prisoners who never saw the light of day were kept here."

"I've heard of that. Medieval architects added water wells to protect them from earthquakes. People believed they were safer underground when the earth shook."

"You know of these stories?"

"I'm an architect ..."

He nodded.

Brisa could feel the tension growing between them. A sexual tension that attracted her. It felt as if they were trying to cover up their feelings for each other. The silence soon pushed the awkwardness and comfort meter into the danger zone.

"Is it true that the first monasteries and convents were connected with secret passageways?" Brisa asked. "I've heard of old stories about monks that used to communicate with the priests secretly through the walls."

"Old stories," he repeated.

As they walked, their steps echoed, reminding Brisa of the old school. The air was stale and made it hard to breathe. It was probably her nerves, but she couldn't stop talking.

"Antaño is full of secrets," Brisa said. "I met an old man, and he told me all types of stories."

"The old ones know about the secrets. When I was a kid, they told us many legends and myths. I could listen for hours."

"What is this?" Brisa pointed to a slab with a hole.

"A colonial-era refrigerator." He laughed. "Monasteries kept their food cold down here. There was a wooden door here once. Ingenious, actually."

Their bodies touched and he glanced down at her. *Could he be interested in me?* She didn't know what to think. They stepped into a larger and more open space.

"Take those stairs and you'll find an old kitchen," he said, pointing. "Sunlight enters from up there." He pointed again.

Brisa glanced up at the grids. The vents sent a fresh breeze across her face.

"Pantry and wood stove." He pointed around the room as he talked. "Feel the dry air?"

"Natural insulation?"

He nodded. "You are indeed an architect."

"And you?"

"Amateur archaeologist," he mused. "My *real* thing is cattle. I seem to get along better with animals than people."

His tone and closeness made her shiver. "Do you believe in the stories about that nun ... Mother Rosa?" she asked.

"No. But you have to respect the people who do." He touched her hair and allowed a few strands to fall through his fingers. "Air fresher now?"

"A little." Brisa's heart pounded. She was gasping more from her nerves than the staleness. "Let's sit for a moment."

"This space looks comfy." He pointed to a niche next to a stack of old firewood.

He took off his leather jacket and placed it on the stone slab. She sat and looked up at him. He knelt and their lips met. It was hard for Brisa to believe what was happening but it felt wonderful. She responded without thinking or objecting. She could feel the beating of her heart and wondered if he could hear it.

Her mind was spinning. She contradicted herself knowing she could not allow this but also yearning for the luxury of a romantic adventure. Would he also disappoint her? Brisa's fear turned into excitement as Sebastián leaned back and caressed her arms. He stopped to look into her eyes before leaning in again. His eyes turned from a stark coffee hue to a light amber. She never saw anything like it before. His hands glided across her blouse, and before she knew it, they were both naked. The cold was not bothersome, and they made love as the corridors filled with their wails that sounded strange and mysterious. She was afraid to stop, for she would have to face the fact that she had dropped her guard again. Although she feared her own self-reproach, she also found herself clinging to him.

They ended exhausted. He studied her in silence. Brisa had enjoyed his heavy breathing. He tenderly touched her face and kissed her lips.

"I need to get back," Brisa whispered.

They dressed in silence. Every so often, he'd glance over and smile. They walked to the exit, and before they stepped into the sunlight, he kissed her again.

"I have to find my car." Brisa gently pushed him away.

He nodded and took her hand. They left the catacombs and laughed as the horse studied them.

"Can we stop at my house?" she asked. "I need my jacket."

"Mine doesn't warm you?"

"I only live a short distance."

They rode gingerly along the street that led directly to the big house. He didn't seem in a hurry. Brisa leaned back and enjoyed his arms embracing her.

"Are we close?" he asked.

She nodded.

"I don't know much about you," he said. "Lunch at the lodge?"

Brisa nodded again.

Perhaps this was not a mistake after all. She wanted to tell him about herself and wanted to know everything about him. Now that she lived in Antaño, and he seemed to visit quite a bit, maybe it was a good idea after all.

"Here," Brisa said, pointing to the house. "Stop here."

"Here?"

"No, not here. At the house." Brisa pointed at the old mansion.

"The big one?"

"It's the only one out here."

She slid from the horse and ran inside. When she returned, Sebastián didn't say anything. They rode to the lodge amid a strange and painful silence. All the passion she had felt just a few moments before now mimicked a horrible tension.

Why isn't he speaking to me? "We're here," Brisa said, feeling a little nervous.

His attitude had changed, and so suddenly, that even his eye coloring was different. They now appeared darker, almost black. It was as if she had come out after grabbing her jacket to find a completely different man waiting for her.

"Goodbye, Brisa," he said.

Shame filled her and she nodded. "I don't have your number."

"It's better this way. I'm sorry. This was a mistake."

"What?"

His eyes darkened a little more. He turned the horse around. "Goodbye, Brisa." His voice was deep, and cold, and lifeless.

She stood there, alone and speechless. It felt as if a bucket of cold water had just splashed against her bleeding heart.

About a month after her encounter with Sebastián, Brisa, again, dyed her hair. Only this time, she used black coloring and not a dark brown. Without thinking, she also began to wear darker clothing. Now, her outward apparel matched her inner feelings.

"You are just divorced, Brisa," Sonia said. "You didn't become a widow. It looks like you're in mourning. Nobody has died."

"Somebody doesn't have to die for a person to feel sad." Sonia had caught her right in the middle of a sensitive moment, and it was not the time for jokes. "And there are many types of losses. And … an annulment … remember? A divorce would have at least acknowledged that we were once a couple."

"You're sad because of your … ex?"

"No, not really. I can mourn for other things, like … my mother, or father, or child …"

Sonia stared at her. "Brisa … the other day, you said you were from Antaño. I thought your parents lived in Mexico?"

"My adoptive parents were Mexican. When my dad died, my mother committed suicide. Marvelous story," Brisa said sarcastically.

"And your biological parents?" she asked.

"They annulled me from their life just as Mariano annulled our marriage. No trace, no record … the relationship never existed."

"I'm sorry."

"Don't feel sorry for me. I have this project, and I'm putting into practice everything I've learned. I feel fulfilled and satisfied. My work doesn't abandon me. No deceptions. I do it well, and I know what I'm getting in return. PROE

S.A. is my life now. I will not let anyone or anything get in the way of the success of this project. I'm in control."

"It would do you good to meet someone. A partner to have some fun with."

"Mind your own business," Brisa snapped.

"Are you still in love with Mariano?"

"Of course not! Stick to your own love affairs and leave mine alone."

Brisa stared out the window and sighed. Marta had returned to the school. The woman seemed to be visiting the site every day now, just as she had promised. For some strange reason, Marta never wanted to talk about her visits, and the mayor was refusing to discuss the convertion of the mansion and ruins into event venues. Brisa was worried.

She had lost interest in trying to convince everyone of her plans for preservation. Instead, she ran with the flow. A crane, parked and now locked, filled most of the yard. It was to be used for the demolition of the mansion, the convent, and the old church. Trucks, ladened with gravel, were the order of the day with their comings and goings from the rubble of the shanty town.

Brisa thought about the shipment of explosives that Angela had said was due from Mexico next week. Neither Pablo nor Angela had said any more about it. Their original agreement was to follow her proposal, which meant to demolish it all in a mechanical way, not blow the place to pieces.

Her phone beeped and when she saw Angela's name she shrugged. "Hello, Angela."

"I gave the new dates to the engineer," Angela said.

"Dates for what?"

"Explosives."

"José knows nothing about it. I thought we agreed that the demolition would be mechanical. I don't understand what you're doing."

"That's why I'm calling. Let me add Pablo to the line."

Brisa waited.

"Pablo, you there?" Angela asked.

"Yes," he replied. "We're sending the cargo as a precaution. To guarantee no delays. In case we need to hurry things along."

"There's no budget for explosives," Brisa replied.

"You're doing an excellent job," Angela said. "Everything's on schedule. It's only a precaution, as Pablo said. If you don't use them, you can return them, that's all. I'll keep you posted in regard to the revised budget."

"I have another call," Pablo stated and hung up.

Angela was not acting like herself. Her sudden decisions were not making any sense. Something was going on, and Brisa had to figure it out.

"Angela, you're acting nervous," Brisa said. "What is it?" The phone quieted and Brisa could hear Angela's breathing.

"Mr. Herradura has disappeared. Kidnapped or something. It could hold things up, and that's a bit worrying. God, I hate that family!"

Brisa sighed. "All the permits are approved, yes?"

"One is still pending. The one from the Council for the Conservation of Antaño."

"Any news from UNESCO? Any problems from that end?"

"Still in process. It's slow but the extra time gives us a chance to solve other … problems."

"I see." Brisa didn't see but she agreed anyway.

"I'm glad we ordered explosives. Have they arrived yet?"

"No, and I still don't —"

Angela had hung up. Brisa stared at her phone. Something strange was going on, and she needed to know what it was. A movement from outside grabbed her attention. She watched as Marta walked out of the boarding school to meet another person. At least both were wearing hardhats. Brisa darted out of the old mansion.

"Marta!" Brisa yelled as she ran up to her. "You cannot enter without someone else from the project."

"In that case," Marta said, crossing her arms, "you come with me and help. I must remove a piece of furniture. It's too heavy for just me, and I need to prepare the portrait of the Mother for pick up."

Brisa nodded.

"Wait for me out here," Marta said to her friend.

"You've run out of time," Brisa said as they walked inside. "All this will soon be nothing but rubble."

"Don't worry," Marta replied. "My work is done as of today."

"I'm very busy these days. Don't have time to walk these halls with you."

"I am also busy, if not more," Marta said and her voice sounded tense. "I do have responsibilities, and my organization relies on *me* for results."

What was Marta up to for they walked in silence unlike the other times when Marta talked nonstop.

"Where is this heavy furniture? I can find a couple workers to help you. And the portrait … didn't you say someone would be picking it up?"

Marta stopped and grinned. "Would you like to take a stroll with me to where the voices are louder? To say your final goodbyes."

Brisa shrugged. Was Marta here for furniture or for something else? "Voices?"

"Yes," Marta replied. "You can listen to the echoes of the past."

Brisa shrugged. "If you wish." She was more curious than anything else. However, if it was the only way she could get rid of the woman, then so be it.

"A stroll down memory lane!" Marta said as her grin widened. Marta stopped and her odd gaze sent chills up Brisa's spine. "You've been snooping around here?"

"There's nothing here to snoop at," Brisa replied. "It's only an old building with trash."

"Oh?" Marta laughed. "Then follow me." Marta's laughter echoed down the hall, which made her presence seem a little more sinister. "Look at these old pictures." Marta walked over to several black-and-white photos that were still in frames. "These students are trying to tell you something." She pointed at the young face. "They speak to you, don't they? They speak to me." Marta sighed. "And now you will bury their voices with this building."

The ringing bell vibrated through the walls, and Brisa glanced at her watch — noon.

"It's twelve," Marta stated.

Brisa sighed. "I told you … I do not believe in ghosts. I don't even believe in the living."

Marta stared at Brisa's chest and frowned. "That bell started ringing the day you returned, and you have a rose tattoo just above your breast. Why?"

"It's not a tattoo." Brisa tried to close up her blouse a little. "A birthmark. Nevus Flammeus is the scientific name."

"We need to be friends … you and me. Antaño is a small town, and we'll run into each other. Why don't we meet up and have some wine. We could talk … get to know each other better."

"Why?" Brisa asked.

Marta smiled and her golden tooth shined. The bell rang again. "Damn pigeons!"

"I've heard the voices," Brisa said, now following Marta. "What are they? And … what makes that bell ring, and don't say it's the birds."

Marta laughed. "Let's play a little listening game."

"A listening game?"

They walked past what was left of the old kitchen, and Marta stopped in front of a dumbwaiter that was probably once used to transport vegetables from an underground pantry. Brisa glanced back at the wood burning stove and the huge ovens with their domed roofs.

"I want you to experience the true magic of these walls." Marta smiled. "Stand here in this corner and wait for me."

Brisa nodded to play along.

"I'm going into the other room. Count to fifty and then whisper a secret. Say it softly so no one can hear. Something no one knows."

Brisa smiled and nodded again. She had studied acoustic phenomena and had stood inside a whisper gallery. But nothing compared to what she was hearing inside these old walls. She flashed her phone light up at the ceiling. The flat bricks didn't seem ideal for this type of game.

She started counting and when she reached fifty, she whispered, "For the love of Sebastián Salguero."

Brisa panicked. Her thoughts were way out of bounds. *How stupid of me! How could I mention his name?* Brisa felt her pride sink. Then, she giggled. She was too far away for Marta to have heard.

An eerie woman's voice seeped out from behind her. "You're in danger, Brisa, run."

The voice had escaped through the bricks as if there were a hidden speaker or open piping somewhere behind her. Brisa glanced around. What a cheap parlor trick Marta was playing. She took in a deep breath, and her throat felt dry and her hands shook.

Marta's footsteps echoed as she ran into the room. She grabbed Brisa by the arm and yanked her toward the hallway. Marta's eyes were wide and her face pale. "Let's get out of here!"

Marta ran toward an old, back gate and pulled out her keys. The woman seemed to have a key for every door or entry. They entered an area that looked much older, and the lingering aroma of wetness was overwhelming.

"This is part of the original convent," Marta said and her voice sounded strained.

Brisa looked closely at the cracked walls and sighed. "This structure is colonial, and these walls might date back over five hundred years."

"Only a small part," Marta replied. "This area was once the nun's sleeping quarters. It was never a part of the original school. Young girls aspiring to become nuns communicated secretly through these walls. I believe it was their only way to remain sane. They could use these walls as if they were a phone. It's Mother Rosa's voice that flows through these walls now."

"That's ridiculous." Brisa laughed as she hurried behind Marta. "You're enjoying this. You want to impress me with your little stunts. With all due respect to the nuns, I do not believe they communicated secretly through these bricks. It's true that there is such a thing as auditive experiences, but that requires very specific conditions. And those conditions are not present here. How did you do it? What was your trick? And how did you make that bell ring?"

"We talked just like the nuns used to," Marta replied. "You're in danger, Brisa. You said the family name Salguero."

Brisa rubbed her hands against her slacks. Her body shook and she felt weak.

"I heard you say that name and Mother Rosa's reply," Marta stated firmly. "You need to be careful. Do you know who he is? Does he know you're working this project?"

"I don't —" Brisa's anger was rising. "Mother Rosa's reply?"

"If he approaches you, it's only out of self-interest. He's a Herradura."

"Herradura?" Brisa repeated. "Sebastián Salguero?"

"Salguero-Herradura," Marta whispered. "He's the one that filed the lawsuit. Because of him, your project is paralyzed."

"What? The project isn't stopped."

"He's placing obstacles in the way," Marta stated. "Your job and soul depend on you not becoming involved with that man."

"What are you talking about?"

"Brisa! He's from the Herradura linage. He lives on the coast in Palmas Rojas. He's a powerful figure around these parts. I've even heard rumors that some want to make him the new mayor of Antaño."

"I don't know why you're telling me this." Now Brisa's voice cracked.

Marta stopped walking and turned. "If you say so. I still advise you to not mention that name again, especially while inside these ruins."

Brisa breathed in deeply.

"As I was saying," Marta continued. "This was not your run-of-the-mill boarding school. Many unwilling girls were transferred to the novitiate. Illegally, by order of Lady Delfina, of course."

Brisa's phone dinged. She glanced at it and frowned. A text from Carlitos had arrived.

```
Carlitos:   We have started the grading.
```

"I gotta go." Brisa looked around. "I'm not interested in these old stories. I don't really know Sebastián Salguero. We only recently met. Please excuse me if I offended you, but for me, those old tales are just silly legends from the past. Voices and mysteries of a yesterday that has nothing to do with me or my project." Brisa walked over to a glass door and tried to open it.

Marta pulled out her keys and unlocked it.

"Most typical of a small town," Brisa continued. "This building will be sealed off soon. Take out what you need today. I'll send over a worker to help you with the heavier furniture. Please, Marta, no more wasting my time."

Brisa felt like a complete idiot. Darting out the door, she almost tripped over a fallen branch. After walking up the small hill, she reached down and rubbed her knees. They were trembling. She glanced up at the sun and took in a deep breath, and the warmth felt wonderful and refreshing. While glancing back at the old school, she sighed. Marta was now standing motionless at the yellowed glass door staring at her.

CHAPTER VI

Every Monday, Brisa woke early in order to attend the weekly meeting at the capitol. Today, however, she was running a little late. When she arrived, a younger male lawyer had just finished his presentation. Brisa walked in offering her apologies.

"Come in, Brisa," Angela said, greeting her. "Your ex-husband's lawyer just finished his talk. Can you update us on the project and your projections for the next few weeks?"

Brisa nodded and proudly presented their progress and goals. She deliberately avoided the obstacles that were outside her control. During the questions and answers, an engineer expressed his concerns.

"I understand …" he stated as he leaned back, placing the end of his pen to his mouth, "… that legal problems are haunting phase two. I'm concerned they will cause a delay of starting phase three. Can you elaborate on it and maybe alleviate some of our fears?"

Brisa glanced over at the legal team and shrugged.

One of the counselors stood and said, "Mr. Sebastián Salguero-Herradura filed in family court requesting custody of his uncle, Juan Ignacio."

Brisa held back a cough when she heard Sebastián's name. She took in a deep breath and tried to hide her fears.

"Nothing directly against PROE S.A.," he continued. "His complaint does not stop our project. We are still proceeding as planned. Although …" he glanced around, "… there could be a change of guardianship that could affect our original agreement."

"Oh?" An engineer from across the room sat up straight and tapped his pen on the table.

"Yes," the lawyer replied. "We signed with the previous guardian. If Mr. Salguero is named the new guardian, the original agreement could be nullified."

"Why is Mr. Juan Ignacio in need of a legal guardian?" the same engineer asked.

The mayor stood and looked over at the man. "From what I understand, it's a family matter. Nothing that concerns us. Juan Ignacio Herradura is also known as Juancho. According to medical records, he's a paraplegic. The eldest brother took custody years ago when Lady Delfina died. The brother then died a few months ago, and a new guardian must be appointed. Therefore, Mr. Salguero has filed for legal custody. Perfectly normal."

Brisa's hands felt damp, and she wiped them on her skirt. She sat and shoved them under her legs. The shaking was just too obvious. Her heart raced and it almost hurt to breathe.

Angela stood and added, "We're looking into the matter just in case things become complicated." She smiled but her grin looked strained. "We are not too concerned. We have the signature and approval of the previous guardian, and we believe it will hold."

Brisa's mind twirled from the conflicting statements, and her mouth reacted before she could stop it. "Then, Mr. Salguero has no legal standing. Am I hearing you correctly?"

"Not in the project directly," one of the representatives replied, "but if he is appointed in family court, he could proceed to annul the original agreement. Then we're back in negotiations."

Another man stood and said, "Is there anyone here who knows this man personally and could perhaps reach an agreement with him?"

Angela rubbed her hands together. She glanced over at the mayor and nodded. "This gentleman is bad blood. I've tried to reason with him, and it's obvious he wants to control the rights to become the sole inheritor. I do not believe he's interested in his uncle's health, only the wealth that's involved."

"No possibility to renegotiate?" the man asked.

"Impossible," Angela said, shaking her head. "He's arrogant and demanding things *his* way."

The meeting ended with statements of concern over the project's potential success. Brisa watched as each individual gathered their things and shook hands before walking out. She prayed that no one would ever find out that she had an intimate encounter with Sebastián.

Brisa drove home thinking about how much Sebastián had excited her. She perceived him to be sensitive, gentle, and tender. Socially, however, he acted a little rough around the edges. Then again, he had treated her like crap. She was fascinated by the man, which was a given, and for a few brief moments, she even wondered if she were falling in love. The idea sent chills all through her. Brisa could never love someone who openly wished for her failure. It was obvious that they were on opposite sides of a battle that she was now determined to win. She would build Antaño Heights no matter what it took or who it affected.

Their passionate love scene flew through her mind. Her body had responded in ways that she never believed it could. From her perspective, he had felt the same way. Was she making a mistake … again? Confusing lust for love? Brisa remembered when he rode her to the mansion on his horse. All she wanted to do was grab a jacket. It was only now that everything became crystal clear. She was living in the residence of the Herraduras, and he had instantly decided that she was the enemy. She was wiping her forehead with a paper towel when her phone rang.

"Hello?"

"Brisa? It's Carlitos."

"Hey."

"I found the original plans for the old boarding school. You asked me to look for them, remember?"

"Yes."

"They were registered in town. But the ones for the convent are not there. I doubt if they ever existed. Maybe the mayor might know. I'm dropping off what I have at the mansion."

"Thanks, Carlitos. I'm on my way home now."

"You feeling all right? You sound a little agitated."

"I'm fine. Just tired. On second thought, can you drop them off tomorrow?"

Her eyes landed on the large mansion, and she could hardly breathe. She had to gasp for air. It was as if she were walking through a nightmare and was stuck somewhere within the deep recesses of her imagination. She parked her car and stumbled toward the large structure. She sat on the bench that was near the front door. With each deep breath, she felt a little better, but each gasp sent a searing pain down her back. The strong stench of stale liquor attacked her senses and she cringed.

Did I stop at a bar? Am I drunk?

Fear rippled up and down her spine. She tried to think, but a dense fog saturated her reality with massive amounts of doubt and guilt. Her eyes closed, and if she opened them now, she'd have to face the reality of a possible relapse. Afterall, she could not remember the drive home. The disgusting odor grew stronger. Brisa tried to stand but her head pounded.

I definitely relapsed.

Tears filled her eyes and her stomach rolled. Her ears rang and her mouth felt dry.

"Ma'am? Brisa?" Rogelio shook her arm and pulled her hair from her face.

"What happened?" she asked, slowly opening her eyes.

"You fainted, ma'am." He held her by the arm, and the strong stench of alcohol made her stomach churn.

"You're drunk?" She pushed him away. "Go sleep under your tree, old man!"

"Brisa," he said. "I'm not drunk. Only a small sip to steady my tremors. I am part of the ground, for I shake as she does now."

Relief flooded through her as she realized she had not relapsed. Her annoyance faded as she looked at the man who seemed trapped by his vice. Nobody better than Brisa could understand how addiction imprisoned a person. They were the same — him and her. Two alcoholics, tossed together, differentiated only by their social or cultural differences. After all, she did bring a bottle with her, which now resided … probably broken … behind the old fireplace.

"Rogelio." She blinked several times as her head tried to clear. "Thank you for helping me. I need to move. Would you walk with me?"

He nodded.

They headed for the street and neither spoke. When they reached a small church, Brisa read the sign that was an announcement for alcoholics. Someday, she would step through similar doors, and maybe this place was waiting just for her. Many times she would peek at the sign on her way to the lodge but never paid it much attention. In reality, the sign actually bothered her. Instead of hiding behind her insecurities, those two words — *Alcoholic Anonymous* — released her inner demons. To face one's fears meant accepting who a person had become. And Brisa didn't like who she had become. Maybe this small sign made the truth behind her addiction too real … too much in the present and not something unspoken from the past. The two stepped up to the door and Brisa smiled. Rogelio narrowed his eyes.

"Would you come with me?" he asked.

He suddenly reminded her of a little boy who was too afraid to be by himself. "You go," she said, giving him a little push. "I'll wait here."

It felt good to help him, but Brisa was actually the more grateful one. Although, he was the one with the problem and not her. It was obvious that he was feeling sorry for himself just as she had felt sorry for herself. He walked inside as if he knew most of the people. After a few moments, and with no additional thought, Brisa walked away. She had not relapsed after all, which meant that she did possess the strength to handle all that life had to throw at her.

The bottle that had fallen behind the chimney inched its way to the surface of her memory. *Can I rescue it?* Then again, why was she thinking about it? She had just left the old man at a recovery circle, and now she was worried as to the condition of her bottle? For some odd reason, Brisa needed to know that it was safe and in one piece. Not that she needed a drink, but to possess a sense of security by just knowing it was somewhere close.

The fireplace looked huge inside that living room. Outside, the true size was mostly concealed. She stared at the opening and clean hearth. Even though she was a petite woman, it was still amazing that she could easily fit inside. After removing the flashlight from her tool belt and clipping it to her belt loop, she knelt and paused. As she crawled on hands and knees into the small opening, she wondered if she had finally lost her mind. She stood and could tell that something was definitely wrong with the overall design.

"This was never built to house a fire! But why?"

No soot covered the aging bricks. She flashed the light up the flue. The damper was definitely closed. *Then, where was the bottle?* She pushed her hand between the bricks and felt around the smoke chamber. There should be a shelf, but she felt nothing. Something cold and slender brushed against her fingers and she paused. *Maybe it's what opens the damper?* She clasped tighter to the handle and wiggled it. However, nothing moved. She yanked harder on the slender rod, and it shimmied into place. A loud grating shrieked as the hinges moved. She flinched when the flap banged open just above her head. A large opening showing nothing but darkness and a huge empty space greeted her. A space that should not be there.

"A hidden passageway?"

She crawled out of the fireplace and walked outside, studying the design of the chimney. The bricks were pushed inward in certain places as if made for someone's hands and feet. The damper had definitely been altered, but why? From inside the chimney, it was obvious that the column was leaning at an incorrect angle. But from outside, everything looked … perfect. The defect was only noticeable if one stepped inside the chimney.

This is nuts!

Brisa crawled back into the hearth. She allowed her fingers to explore the upper bricks. These bricks felt more like stairs than just a vertical structure to allow smoke to escape. Shining her light above her head, no open sky greeted her. The chimney was not made for warmth but for travel. Several of the bricks that stuck out at odd angles enticed her to give it a try. She climbed with ease, and after a few short moments, she faced a black void that she had to traverse. Her life was nothing more than a black void. Sections of time segmented apart as if mimicking a chapter of a book. Why was her life so dark and empty?

"What in the world?"

Brisa climbed a little higher and inched herself into the darkness. She flashed her light and from where she stood, she could only see more bricks. She secured her light to her belt loop and climbed higher. When she reached another opening, she hoisted herself inside. Using the bricks as leverage, she scooted her head and chest into the narrow space. Her legs dangled, and the pressure on her stomach gave her reason to pause. She kicked against the bricks and slowly scooted herself into an opening just large enough to crawl through.

"Where does this go?"

Brisa felt around in the darkness and found nothing but emptiness ahead of her. She flipped on her light. She was now inside a smaller passageway that was only large enough to sit or crawl through. On hands and knees, she inched slowly forward until she came to another opening. Again, she used her light and found nothing but another dark void. She flashed it along the sides and gasped, for the bottom remained hidden. However, steps that led up or down were now right in front of her. Struggling to move, she squeezed her legs under her and sat up. She nudged herself forward and toward the opening. The stairs were narrow, just wide enough for one foot at a time. Balancing precariously on two bricks, she stood. Using the sides for support, she again flashed her light around. Nothing, except single bricks that followed the inside of the large chimney.

Brisa chose down. Leaning slightly, she used the opposite wall for support. Slowly, she made her way down the narrow staircase. After what felt like forever, she giggled. The lost bottle had shattered on one of the bricks. She continued down and when she finally stepped onto a solid floor, she sighed and took in a deeper breath. Around her, the darkness gloomed. Brisa was standing in an underground passageway that ran in two directions, and it didn't feel inviting. Between the walls was only about three feet, and the ceiling was just a few inches above her head. At least she could stand and walk.

Which way?

The hall leading to what she thought would be the old school seemed the most logical choice. With her light showing the path, she made her way through the darkness. After a while, a corridor with a tall, domed ceiling opened up before her. Metal grates several feet above her served as skylights and lit the upper bricks. The structure was of an ingenious design. Whoever built this place knew what they were doing. Turning her light off, the natural light of the day bounced down the walls and mysteriously lit the floor, which was made from an unknown, polished stone.

She continued to creep through the eerie passage. Notches along the way that once held statues were now bare. She ran her hand along the wall and felt nothing but cold smoothness. As she walked, no sounds touched her ears. Not even her footsteps echoed. The hallway was somehow sheltered from any noise. She entered a circular room that resembled a small chapel and held various entranceways that led off to unknown destinations. Fresh air caressed her cheeks, and she took in several long, deep breaths. *Where is the air coming from?* The slight breeze was cool, not warm and not cold. Very unlike what she had experienced while making love to Sebastián.

The round crypt, surrounded by several niches, held a few tall statues that were probably once ancient saints. They stared down at her as if judging her thoughts and fears. In the middle of the large room, a huge cross, that was sculpted from the cave's rock, rose up to the ceiling. She flashed her light upward and was rewarded with a colorful fresco of angels and clouds. She took a few pictures with her phone. Noticing the time, she sighed. It was late and her battery was about to die. She turned to leave when soft voices floated out from one of the hallways. She stood still and listened.

She made her way down a dark corridor. Near the end, a light shone out through a grid several feet above her. The bricks were not as smooth and shot out at various odd angles. It was as if the spirits had left her a ladder to help her explore. She slowly inched her way up and peeked through the thin, metal slats. She was now looking across the old floor of the school's library office and was peeking out over the baseboard near the main door. Two different pairs of women's shoes walked back and forth across the worn-out, red carpet. As she listened she nodded for she knew who was talking.

"I just don't trust that woman!" It was Marta's voice.

"The best thing would be for me to take her out of the way," a different woman's voice replied. "We're running out of time."

Who's Marta talking to?

"No, I will handle things myself," Marta said. "No need to involve another."

Brisa tried to see more through the grate, but the view was somewhat blocked by an old chair. Marta walked over to a partially boarded window, and her hand swayed as she walked. Brisa gasped for the woman was holding a pistol. She waved it around before shoving it into a large canvas bag that hung from her shoulder. Brisa tried to understand and her thoughts whirled as she put the pieces together. Marta pulled out her phone and tapped on the screen. Brisa's phone vibrated from inside her back pocket, and a loud ding echoed through the chamber. She jumped down and fumbled with her phone. She'd just received a text from Marta. Brisa lowered the volume to off and inched herself deeper into the folds of darkness. *Could Marta have heard the ding?* Brisa tapped on her phone and read the message.

```
Marta: Can I drop by and say hi? Are you home?
```

What hypocrisy! Brisa ran back the way she had come and stood, shaking inside the small chapel. She studied the message before replying.

```
Brisa: Of course. Some coffee perhaps?
```

Brisa darted down the hallway and back toward the mansion. She climbed up the single-brick staircase in the same manner as she had used them coming down. When she found the small opening, she crawled in backwards, which wasn't easy. Soon, her legs dangled in the air, and she had to inch herself out over the edge and down into the hearth. She crawled out of the chimney and brushed herself off before walking to the kitchen. After washing her hands, she stood quietly, watching out the window for any movement.

Within a few minutes, a knock echoed out from the old front door. Brisa waited in the kitchen and listened as Selena greeted the woman.

Acting as calm as possible, she walked casually into the foyer and smiled. "Why … hello, Marta. Would you like some coffee or tea?"

"No, thanks. I just wanted to stop by and invite you to have a little wine with me. Just as we talked about. We could get to know each other a little better. Outside of work and all."

What could Marta possibly want with her other than to lodge a bullet inside her skull? Was the woman pretending and just stringing her along?

"Of course," Brisa replied. Her hands shook and her voice cracked.

"Good," Marta said. "I'll plan it all out. Oh … I'll call when it's time for our next treasure hunt. Okay?"

Brisa sighed. "Good day, Marta."

Marta left without speaking another word. Brisa closed the door and stood back. Her heart pounded and her hands were still shaking. Marta could have called, so why come here in person? She sat on the sofa as Selena entered.

"Brisa, ma'am. Do you need anything?"

"No, thank you, Selena." Brisa thought for a moment before adding, "Do they sell liquor around here?"

Selena frowned. "Only in the bars. I would buy it for you but I'm too young …"

"I can go if you tell me where."

"My great-grandmother lives only a few blocks away, and they sell beer in a bar next to her. I can take you there."

"Yes, please."

They walked in silence along the cobbled streets where the sounds of hooves and carriages echoed across the houses. The homes were made from colorful stucco, and their charm always felt overwhelming. A few of the houses were decorated with flowering, climbing roses that stretched up to greet the rooftops. Many windows were adorned with painted boxes that were overflowing with fragrant flowers. Parked bikes rested peacefully against a few of the walls.

"Look, ma'am," Selena said. "By day, there are nuns and it's the religious who walk here. But at night, only the drunks stumble through our streets." Selena pointed to a group of men drinking heavily near a corner. "My great-grandmother says the teachings of Mother Rosa are needed now more than ever."

"And what teachings would that be?" Brisa asked.

"My great-grandmother used to help care for abused women. She taught them how to fend for themselves. Taught good things and how to be a better person. Look, ma'am." Selena pointed to a modest home about halfway down the block. "My aunt's house. Very humble. Don't be scared now."

They stepped up and the door was open. Stairs that led to a dark upper floor seemed somewhat uninviting. Next door was a bar, and the men inside were drinking something that made them quite happy and cheerful.

"Come, Brisa. I will introduce you to my aunt." Selena grabbed Brisa's hand and pulled her inside. "My aunt is taking appointments today. That is why the door is open."

"Appointments?" Brisa repeated. "Appointments for what?"

"She tells people about their future."

"You mean a mystic?" Brisa stepped back. "No, Selena. Just let me order my beer and leave."

Selena frowned.

Brisa stepped out of the house and into the bar. She ordered a beer to go, and Selena waited for her by the door. The man behind the counter handed Brisa a brown bottle before accepting her money. After stepping back into the afternoon sunlight, Brisa whispered so no one else could hear. "I don't have time for such foolishness."

Selena brushed her foot across the sidewalk.

Guilt flowed through Brisa. "Fine." With just a slight shrug, Brisa followed Selena into the old house of the mystic. They stepped up to the second floor, and the place looked empty. "She's not here," Brisa whispered. "We should go."

"Hail, Mary!" A woman stepped out from behind a partition and clasped her hands together. "Please, come in!"

"This is my mother," Selena said. "She helps around here sometimes. Mother, we came to see Aunt Conchita."

Selena's mother pointed to an elderly woman sitting alone in a rocking chair that creaked as the woman rocked. The room reeked of fresh flowers, and several candles flickered from inside the shadows. When the light glittered against the paintings of various saints, Brisa shivered. On a small table, a smoldering incense challenged the aroma from the flowers. The old woman stretched out her hand and pointed to a nearby chair. Her aging eyes looked almost transparent.

Brisa sat and smiled.

"Welcome," the old woman whispered. "I can feel your air of . . ." — Conchita took in a deeper breath and hesitated — "roses?" The woman reached out and stole the brown bottle away from Brisa. She sat it on the table next to her. As she swiped her fingers across Brisa's birthmark, she said, "This is a rose . . . it is *the* mark. Oh, how much your mother loved you. And how much more your children will love you!"

Brisa jerked back and the spell broke. Her heart pounded and sweat dripped down her face.

"Your mother is here now, my child." Conchita reached out and touched Brisa's chest again. "She's here visiting you from beyond the heavens. And she will remain with you throughout this journey. As you walk together across the petals of time, she will help you mark out the path of your destiny."

The elderly woman had just slit through the barrier that separated Brisa from her world of safety and flung her straight back into the painful void of her memories, as if the barrier never existed. How dare this old woman awaken the sleeping curse? Brisa stared at the woman as her anger grew. She stood so quickly that the small chair fell over, banging against the floor.

"I'm leaving, Selena!"

Brisa stared down at the woman who glared back with a mesmerizing and peaceful gaze. She reached for the beer, but the woman placed her hand on top of the bottle. The old woman closed her eyes and hummed.

"I never had a mother!" Brisa yelled as tears filled her eyes. "Besides, someone who commits suicide isn't exactly accepted into heaven. And regarding *my* children … I can't have any!" Brisa frowned over at Selena. "Your aunt is a cheap old witch and a charlatan!"

"I am not a witch, my daughter," the woman said with a softer voice. "I'm a nun of the Holy Order of our Lord, and our beloved saints talk through me."

Selena's eyes teared and she frowned.

Brisa's skin crawled and she felt as small as an obnoxious worm. She stood by the door and whispered, "Forgive me." She ran down the cobbled street, aiming for the mansion. It was important for her to find Rogelio, but he was not there. She had to talk to him. She sat on the bench outside her front door and cried.

"I don't have a mother!" Brisa screamed out. "And I can't have children. I have nobody!"

Brisa cried and screamed as the bad times suddenly rushed back to her. She glanced around and wished she had grabbed the beer the old woman had stolen from her. When her eyes finally dried, Brisa slowly climbed the stairs and fell onto her bed. She glanced outside and the night sky felt evil.

"Please, God," Brisa whispered, "do not let me wake up."

The following morning, she felt renewed somehow. Although her veil of guilt still lingered, she asked herself how she could have lashed out at that old nun like that. She grabbed her phone and ordered a basket of flowers and food. After they arrived, she knocked on Selena's bedroom door. "Can you come with me?"

Selena hesitated before nodding.

"I have something for your Aunt Conchita," Brisa said as she drove her car down the cobblestone street. "I must apologize for my bad behavior."

The daytime street looked vastly different from the night time one. Everything was brighter and much more colorful. When they arrived, Selena ran up the stairs. Brisa waited at the front door.

A different young girl greeted them this time. "Follow me, please."

Brisa stepped cautiously up the stairs and stood quietly next to Selena with her arms full of flowers and snacks.

"She's my cousin," Selena whispered and nodded over to the other young girl. "Aunt Conchita is sleeping now. She didn't have a good night."

"Can you give her this when she wakes?" Brisa handed the gifts to the cousin. "Tell her it's from Brisa, and I'll come back another time."

The girl nodded.

They returned home and Brisa felt energetic and a little more sure of herself. She searched for the liquor bottle she thought she had recently stashed, but it remained hidden. She checked the fridge and her bag and the fireplace. Nothing. Brisa breathed a huge sigh of relief. No liquor in the old house anywhere. She wanted to start a new life that was focused on her job and taking better care of herself. Maybe a good spirit was watching over her after all.

CHAPTER VII

"It's been three weeks ..." Angela said over the phone. "I'm tired and you're exhausted."

"I'm okay." Brisa sighed. "Time has flown, and with so much movement in the field, it sometimes feels like it's too much for me or Carlitos to handle. But we're making do."

"In the capital, everyone's stressed and running around like crazy. I'm happy with your performance." Angela laughed. "You're a key player now. You sound good. Any more panic attacks?"

"None recently." Brisa glanced out the window. "A few weeks ago, I went through a rough spot but I'm good now."

"It's that house!" Angela paused. "That environment's just not healthy." She paused again. "Take a few days. Lawyers are handling things here. You're in a good, quiet place. A few days off would renew your energy. Once construction starts, you won't be able to rest."

"You're having personal problems too. I hear ... with your child and family?" Brisa paused now. "Sonia told me in case you're wondering. Sonia's a two-way gossiper."

"What if we take off together? Visit the spa at the lodge and relax?"

"That sounds wonderful. When?" Brisa didn't want to go, however, she needed to please Angela and maybe shake off a little stress.

"Make us an appointment for Saturday."

"Will do."

Angela and Brisa spent the day at the spa as planned, although, they didn't talk much. Once in a while Angela would say a little something about her ex or family court. Other than that, she didn't provide any details and Brisa didn't ask. Brisa did invite Angela to stay with her … a little space to allow her nerves to unravel. Instead of accepting, Angela assigned Brisa to a short business trip to Palmas Rojas to negotiate a small parcel of land for a new road for the project. Brisa accepted, although, it was one of her free weekends.

She drove alone, and two hours into the trip, the damp sea air was making her hair curl. The car ride on the steep mountain highways no longer challenged her. She had become accustomed to slowing down, and now she handled the curves and slopes with ease. Her phone beeped several times. It was José.

"Morning, Brisa," José said through her car's speakers. "The farm is called El Tejar. Alberto will be waiting for us. Where are you?"

"At kilometer 210."

"Good, you're about half an hour behind me." The connection was not good.

The sign to Palmas Rojas flew past, and Brisa thought about Sebastián and his daughter, Cami. It would have been wonderful to visit his ranch and ride the horses. Who would have thought that a work visit would bring her down this path?

Her phone rang again. "Hello?"

"Brisa?"

"Angela? Are you not with José?"

"No. I need you to represent me." Angela sounded frazzled. "The courts have the dates for my custody hearing all mixed up, so I must meet with my lawyer. Just remember that this visit is to establish good relations with Alberto.

That land will be used to build a road to connect our property in Antaño. It'll make Mexican investors more interested in phase three."

"All right, Angela. No worries. Take care of your family."

The phone call ended.

Brisa turned onto Alberto's property, and José's car was already parked under a tree. The heat felt suffocating, and only a slight breeze was attempting to bring any relief. A farmhand escorted her to a large shed, and the table loaded with refreshments was a welcoming sight.

José stood as she walked up. "Hi, Brisa. Good ride?"

"Yes." Brisa nodded. "No issues."

"Good, good." José stood next to a man who was rather tall and quite thin. His graying temples gave him a moderately seductive but wiser look. "This is Alberto. Alberto, this is Ms. Murillo."

"Just Brisa," Brisa said, accepting the man's hand.

"She's our lead engineer and architect," José said a little too quickly.

"It's a pleasure to talk business with such a young and beautiful professional," Alberto replied. "Please, sit and enjoy our refreshments. You *are* still interested in the property?"

"Yes," Brisa replied, pouring herself a glass of lemonade.

"Have you seen it yet?"

"Brisa has not but I have," José replied. "I told her it's rocky, but since it's her job to build roads, she said it wouldn't be a problem … if the price is right."

"I'm sure we can reach a mutual agreement," Alberto said, smiling.

"Would you like a beer or gin and tonic?" a young boy offered.

Brisa would have given anything for a drink. However, she felt a little confident and therefore renewed, and not to mention, she still had to drive home. "What I have is fine," Brisa replied, holding up her glass of lemonade.

Alberto frowned. "I'm not really interested in selling the land. It's rocky and not of much use, other than my family's sentiment. I'm an old man, and this land has been in my family for centuries." He nodded and smiled again. "There's another farm just up the road. Has the perfect terrain for what you're looking for. Easy land to move and better access to the mountains that border Antaño. I know the owner. Nice man. Perhaps I could put in a good word for you."

"We're open to suggestions," José said, "although it would mean another trip."

"What is that over there?" Brisa pointed to a lagoon with a peculiar characteristic.

"A crater," Alberto replied. "A sleeping volcano. Over time, water collected in it and now we have a pond."

A truck rolled in and parked a few feet in front of the small lake. A man wearing a cowboy hat stepped out and waved at Alberto.

"Speak of the devil!" Alberto said, waving back. "He is the owner of the farm I was just telling you about. His name's Sebastián."

"Alberto!" Sebastián yelled out. "How're you?"

"Good, ol' boy." Alberto stood and shook Sebastián's hand. "Sit with us for a while?"

Chills ran up and down Brisa's spine as she searched for a hole to climb into. Instead of running away, she smiled.

"I saw this boy grow up," Alberto said. "Rode a horse since he was a mischievous child. This is Brisa and José. Engineers on that project in Antaño."

Sebastián smiled and nodded. It was obvious that he was in his natural habitat. "Do you have a beer for me?" Sebastián asked before sitting down.

Alberto motioned for the young boy to return.

"It's a pleasure," Sebastián said, removing his hat. "I've already met the architect. You don't drink, correct?"

Brisa didn't answer.

"Sensible. Should I call you Architect or Engineer?" Sebastián asked.

"Architect is fine," Brisa replied with a slight grin. Was Sebastián deliberately trying to embarrass her? They had made love, and he had left her standing alone and feeling like a piece of used meat, and now he was insulting her?

"You know each other? I hope no hard feelings on account of those legal problems. In this life, everything can be solved with goodwill," Alberto said.

Sebastián accepted a beer from the boy and took a long, slow drink.

"I'd like to know," Alberto said, staring at Sebastián. "If you're not interested in the inheritance of the Herraduras' land, then why object to the development? Sell them the access, and you'd have an easier ride to the town. They don't need that much. Make a few bucks in the process."

"I don't want to talk business," Sebastián replied. "It's Sunday, Alberto. One needs rest on a Sunday. It's the Lord's desire."

"You never rest!" Alberto laughed. "Besides, we need to take advantage of you before you become mayor of Antaño."

Brisa's heart stopped and she glared at Sebastián.

"Just a proposal," Sebastián said, holding up a hand. "They made a proposal and I'm considering it. I'm not sure if I'll take it or not."

"You never cease to amaze me!" Alberto banged on the table. "You're from Antaño. Although, I believe you feel as if you're more from Palmas Rojas. Son, you could do much for the place of your birth."

"Let's forget about business and politics on this beautiful Sunday afternoon," Sebastián said, taking another drink.

"I appreciate this small banquet, but I must be going." José stood. "I look forward to checking out the land with our architect." José stretched out his hand to Alberto.

"You leaving?" Brisa asked, standing.

"One of our warehouses was just broken into and a security guard was hurt. Didn't steal anything. Police are on their way. They've asked me to come over."

"I should go too, José."

"No, Brisa." José used his hand to signal her to sit. "I'll take care of it. It's one of our warehouses down below. The guard that was hurt is not in any danger. You're the best for this negotiation. Stay, I'll take care of it."

Brisa nodded.

José shook Sebastián's hand and walked away.

Alberto stood and yawned. "I too will retire to take my afternoon nap. I'm not of an age to be conducting business meetings." He nodded at Sebastián. "Take the Architect to see the lagoon and the good things at your ranch. It is a wonderful day."

Brisa stood and ran to José's car. She grabbed the window and held back the urge to climb inside. "They want me to go to Salguero's farm. Come with me, please!"

"I can't, Brisa. You go. You know what we need. Smooth things over with Salguero. Remember what Angela said about public relations? Do it for the project. Angela will appreciate it. Hey, if you can't beat them, join them. Isn't that what they always say?"

Brisa slowly walked back to Sebastián and watched as he took another long sip of his beer.

"Did your partner bail out on you?" he asked with a smirk.

Brisa didn't respond. She sat and took a long drink of her lemonade.

"Want to see the lagoon?" he asked, chuckling.

Brisa nodded and frowned. "You didn't tell me that you're Salguero-Herradura."

"And you didn't tell me you were the coordinator for the Antaño Heights project. Not to mention the one in charge of the demolition." He shook his head.

They walked in silence toward the lagoon, and a cool wind slapped gently across her face. She sat on a large rock to admire the view.

"Beautiful breeze, Brisa," he said.

Play on words? If yes, it wasn't funny. Brisa squinted and replied, "I don't know if this makes you happy or sad, but your uncle doesn't even know you're alive. He has no idea what's going on around him. Does he even recognize you?"

"I didn't abduct him," he said, wiping his forehead with a small cloth. "And … I don't have to explain anything to you. You don't know me. You don't know my family. I will tell you one thing … family is family. Respect is both felt and recognized. That man, *my uncle* who's in a *wheelchair*, has suffered much more than *anyone* should endure during a lifetime. He deserves to live out his days in a friendly environment. If the judge grants my petition, that is what he'll have." He sighed. "Love and peace."

Brisa tossed a rock into the water, and the ripples rolled out in a circle.

"He treated me the best when I was a boy. Taught me to love and respect archaeology."

"I know … you're an archaeologist," she whispered.

"Aficionado. It's a hobby."

"What did you study in college?" Brisa asked.

"Business administration, animal husbandry, agronomy. Nothing about archaeology. It was Uncle Juancho who got me started." His gaze lowered and he frowned. "It's *my* obligation and responsibility to care for him. Can we set the ironies aside and pick them up another day?"

"Obligation?"

"Obligation to myself and my deceased brother," Sebastián said. "It's complicated. Are you *really* living alone in that old house?"

"Yes." Brisa nodded. "It's the house of your ancestors."

"Ever since my step-grandmother died that house has been abandoned. I was never interested in entering it again."

"Why? Cause of the strange things that happen there?" Brisa asked, smiling.

"Ghosts and such are nothing more than foolish talk. Why do you insist on living there?"

"That house attracts me." She glanced away and tossed another rock into the water. "It's difficult to explain. I've seen photos of your step-grandmother."

"My father said she was an evil witch. I've seen photos of my uncle and mom … when they were kids. Even a few of Sara. Unless that old witch burned them, they should still be in that house somewhere."

"I've found pictures of a nun," Brisa said.

"That was probably Sara. A novice."

"Sara? You mean Juancho's Sara? What can you tell me about her."

"My Uncle Juancho was in love and would have done anything for her. That man knew how to treat a woman. He was not like me. I'm awkward and not very committed. Their love story was a sad one. And now, Sara's dead."

They both stared out at the water and tossed in a rock.

"What is it that we share?" Brisa asked, looking over at him.

"I don't know," he replied. "Sexual attraction, maybe? I don't want to be insensitive but there's nothing more. There can never be anything more."

His words felt more painful than a slap to the face.

"There can never be anything between us," he said again. Only this time, his words were a little stronger and louder.

"I believe the same," Brisa lied.

"Our relationship must remain professional. Unless we become enemies."

Sebastián stood and she followed him back to the table. Alberto had awakened from his nap and was waiting to see them.

"Brisa should really see the Camelia Ranch," Alberto said, staring at Sebastián.

"It would be my pleasure," Sebastián replied in a very unemotional tone.

"Yes, Architect," Alberto said. "Go! Perhaps this will be the start of a grand accord among the parties."

Sebastián and Brisa smiled but refused to look at each other.

"Shall we go, lady architect?" Sebastián asked, tapping on his hat. "I can drive."

"I prefer to follow in my car," Brisa replied not knowing how to escape the situation.

"I hope that your brakes do not fail," Sebastián mused.

"Thank you for everything, Alberto," she said, shaking his hand. "It's been a pleasure."

Camelia Ranch was only a few minutes away. The highway was decorated with beautiful flowers, and the air was mixed with the aroma of sugarcane and coffee. How different it was to see palm trees in contrast with the conifers. It was incredible that this area bordered the project's site and looked so different. Sebastián acted way too sure of himself, looking all manly and sweaty with his unruly hair that he kept crunched under his hat. His brownish-gray eyes were as vast and mysterious as the rolling hills of his self-proclaimed accomplishments.

The main house, rustic and simple, didn't resemble the home of a true-blooded Herradura. It didn't match what the people said about his lineage. It was large and pretty but without luxuries. Just a somber and rural home.

"Is this where your wife lives, Cami's mom?" she asked to break the ice.

"I don't have a wife." He laughed. "A little late to be asking that question. Don't you think?"

He opened the door and they entered. An older woman stepped out of the kitchen and nodded.

"Nanita, please show the Architect to where she can make herself at home."

"This way," she said with a friendly voice.

Brisa entered the spare bedroom and aimed for the bathroom. She had traveled in her work clothes — boots and all — and was not prepared to meet with a man whom she'd had a sexual encounter with. Her heart pounded and her hands shook. She breathed in deeply and tried to control her emotions.

A child's voice echoed out from the hallway. "Brisa, Brisa! You came to see my horse?" Cami ran in and hugged her. "I'm glad you like to ride. My mother hates them."

Cami was charismatic and it felt comfortable being around her, despite the fact that Brisa didn't like children. However, Cami was somehow special. The girl grabbed Brisa's hand.

"I want to show you our big rocks. It's where the river runs by our ranch. And my Mother Rosa stamps! And my collection of horse stickers."

"Brisa is an architect," Sebastián said. "She's here for work, not for play. I'm showing her our property." Sebastián stood in the hallway, shaking his head. "Don't you have homework that's due on Monday?"

Cami sighed and looked down at the floor.

Sebastián laughed. "Fine. When we're done, you can show her your things. Okay?"

"Mom scolds me when I talk of Mother Rosa," Cami whispered. "She doesn't like her. A worker told me that my mother was evil."

Brisa glance over at Sebastián but he had already left. "I will see you later, Cami."

Sebastián had disappeared. A ranch manager was the one who escorted Brisa to see the property … and what a marvelous piece of land. Huge stables that took her breath away, reminded her of her dreams as a young child. A place she always wanted to live. Camelia Ranch was vast and extended out in all directions. His farm bordered tall mountains on one side, the ocean on another, and the Herradura property near the back — the property where Brisa now worked. Although Sebastián was part of the Herradura family, their worlds were far apart. Much more vast than any ocean or mountain.

Brisa stood under a tree and sipped on some water. Cami and Nanita walked over.

"She wants to hang out with you," Nanita said. "She finished her homework."

Cami was a pretty girl … a big talker and surprisingly precocious. Something about her was special and difficult to describe. Brisa felt at home around Cami and it was obvious that Cami felt the same. Cami introduced her to her horse, her room, her toys, and … of course … her collection of stamps, as well as a rosary that supposedly once belonged to Mother Rosa. They were alone for quite some time while they waited for Cami's dad to return.

Sebastián did return, but much later that night. He looked tired, dirty, and sweaty. He'd been working and did not seem to care about Brisa having to fend for herself.

"A good deal of my cattle escaped into the neighbor's fields," he said as if Brisa were a part of his family. "A few were stuck in the fence. The veterinarian is doing what he can. I might be called out to shoot one or two."

"They still do that?" Brisa asked.

He frowned and then smiled. "I didn't forget you were here. I trust that you walked the property?" He grinned and ignored her question.

"Yes, your worker showed me around. I should be leaving. It's already dark."

"Why not stay?" he said. "No need to be driving at night."

"No, thank you. I've really got to go."

"Allow me to shower," he said. "I'll be quick."

Brisa sat on the front porch and stared out at the rising full moon. Her mind kept telling her that she had to leave. It *was* dark and the roads *were* dangerous at night.

Sebastián stepped onto the porch and stretched. "A short stroll?" he asked. "Under the full moon. It's really only dusk."

"Okay." Brisa heard herself say the word, although her mind was telling her to leave. They walked to a small cluster of palm trees and stared out over the hillside. "Cami showed me the horses."

"She took you to the main stables?"

"No, just the small one near the house."

"Then let me show you." He threated his arm through hers, and they walked down the hill. "We can see the sea from up here."

A splendid view with the moonlight reflecting across the water sent chills all through her. Where the mountain touched the shore, the sea splashed before rolling back out. Brisa's questions were many, but she preferred to remain quiet and enjoy her time with Sebastián. As they walked, several wooden structures came into view.

"The stables?" she asked.

"My second home," he said. "Every afternoon, I'm down here, brushing and feeding the horses. I even have a living room." They entered a small area with a couch and a chair. "No TV, no radio, no internet. Just peace and quiet."

"And that cabin?" She pointed to a tiny house that sat on top of a small hill.

He did not reply.

Brisa petted several horses who poked their heads out of the stalls. Even in early childhood, she possessed a passion for horses. "I really must be going," she said.

Sebastián turned and kissed her. Brisa responded, although a small part of her was screaming for her to stop.

She pulled back and looked at him. "Did you love her? Do you still love her?"

"Who?"

"Cami's mom."

"I never did." He sighed. "Irresponsible on my part."

"Was she your wife?"

"No, and she's not good for Cami. I could never love her. Let's change the subject."

"We don't know each other," she said. "You know nothing about me."

"I know more than you realize."

"May I snap a few pictures of that log cabin? Could we walk closer?"

"It's just an abandoned hunting lodge." Sebastián kissed her neck, her cheek, her …

She gently pushed him away. "I really need to go."

Her mind said to shove him away, but her heart said to step closer. They kissed passionately. He stopped for a moment to look deeply into her eyes. A tenderness that Brisa had never experienced before felt overwhelming. It was as if Sebastián were asking for permission to take their love to a deeper depth. Brisa softly pushed on his chest again.

"We'll regret this in the morning," she whispered.

"Are you feeling what I'm feeling?" he asked. "What is it that we have?"

Brisa unbuttoned her blouse, and he gazed at her rose-shaped mark. He gently ran his fingers across it, and to Brisa, it felt like a moment of love. As much as she wanted to, she didn't dare say the words. Sebastián gazed into her eyes, and his hands explored her body.

"Is this … love?" he asked.

He gently caressed her breasts as if finding a lost treasure … cautiously … ravishingly. His eyes were still asking the question, and Brisa wanted to reply that, *yes*, it was love. However, her fear of rejection was simply too powerful, too controlling.

"You tell me," she whispered as she gasped for air.

Her voice cracked as she placed her hands against his chest. Her fingers faded within his masculinity and she sighed deeply. His aroma excited her and she couldn't talk. Their lips met and she allowed their passion to flow. His hand slid down, and they soon committed fully to each other. Without words, they moaned through the caresses as their bodies moved to a rhythm she had never danced before. A sound of a hoof hitting the ground or snout sniffing the air only added to her pleasure … to a lasting memory. The moonlight glowed through an opened window, and the sweet fragrance of the saltwater mixing with the delicate scent from the sugarcane filled her with a deeper yearning. A yearning to love and be loved. Again, they touched and again their passion grew.

The moon finally dipped completely behind the mountains, and with the rebirth of a new evening, they stepped outside and breathed in the fresh air. An awkward silence crept across the fields and into their souls. They glanced out at the sea, and a loneliness from the vast recesses of her essence flowed through her.

She sighed and whispered, "Why can't we explore the cabin?"

"Nobody ever goes in there." His voice was sharp and stern.

"Forgive me," Brisa whispered, lowering her eyes. "I didn't mean to intrude."

Sebastián scratched his head and his eyes scanned along the heavens. He looked down at her and frowned. "When a woman means something to me in here …" — he touched his chest — "… there can be no secrets."

"Because I'm involved in the project. What if we agree on things one day?" Brisa had spoken the one word that was forbidden … *agree.*

Sebastián's stance turned rigid and he growled. Through clenched teeth, he spoke slowly. "I will never agree!"

Brisa took a step back.

"I don't expect you to understand. I'm sorry, but I'm not ready for this."

"For what?" she asked.

"A romantic relationship. I'm not good at it. I went through hell with Cami's mother." He looked back out at the water. "I just want to focus on my daughter and ranch. Are you ready for a relationship so soon after your separation?"

The question took her by surprise. "I hadn't really thought about it."

"Or," he said, "are you doing this to better your career? Seems convenient to have the engineer fall in love with the property owner. Don't you think? Remove the major obstacle?"

Brisa took another step back. The man she had just made love to was now slapping her in the face with his harsh words. Her heart and head pounded. She wanted to run and escape, protect herself within the walls of the mansion.

"You're an ass, Sebastián! What am I ... a glorified slut? Something to use and toss away when you're satisfied?"

"I'm sorry, Brisa. I shouldn't have lost control." He looked down at her and smiled. "Let's use a little common sense for a moment. Are *you* ready for a relationship? And a relationship with someone who is fighting you in court about the project that you're in charge of?"

Brisa thought for only a moment. She really wasn't ready for a full-time lover ... not yet. And the project? It could definitely establish her future. "No," she whispered. She took a step and turned. He was handsome and wonderful, however, he *was* still the enemy. "Since you brought it up." She chuckled. "You're the one who should be concerned over the legal issues, not me."

He shook his head and laughed. "The lawsuit is not the question here. My part is nothing more than a family obligation. When I tell you to quit this project, I only say it on your behalf. Not mine."

Brisa ignored his hurtful words and followed him toward the main house and her car.

"You and I are opponents." His voice sounded full of an odd type of sarcasm.

Brisa glanced down and frowned. His boots had kicked up a little dirt, and within the dust, her spirit was fading. She would miss seeing his cowboy boots and talking to Cami. Tonight, when they say their goodbyes, it would be final. Her chest pounded and her world twirled, for this moment was most definitely the ending of their short and wonderful relationship.

"Please, stay the night," Sebastián said. "A room's ready for you. It's late and you should not be on the road. Too dangerous."

"No, thank you, Sebastián." Her voice sounded flat and felt unreal. It was her mind talking now and not her heart. "I'd prefer it if we never see each other again. Whether by accident or on purpose. Stay away from me and … *this,*" — she waved her arms through the air — "will never happen again."

"I'd rather not see you either." He looked directly into her eyes. His face held no emotion. "Please tell your company to send someone else to negotiate the land deal."

She opened her car door and climbed in. She looked at him and frowned. "Please give my fondest goodbyes to Cami." As she drove down the dark and forbidden road of regret, her tears fell.

CHAPTER VIII

The busy worksite gave Brisa comfort. Angela had said the team was working diligently with Pablo on the legal issues. Carlitos was still hustling through the red tape trying to pull the remaining permit. Brisa, however, concentrated on last-minute changes, signing checks, and authorizing documents. With little time to think about Sebastián, her workdays seemed to fly by. Every now and then, a subtle reminder of *him* made her push a little harder.

Marta never mentioned her invite for wine and cheese again. She still visited the property at the same time every day, as did the mayor. However, they somehow were able to avoid each other. Although Brisa had confiscated the keys from the woman, Marta would simply walk into the office and retrieve them. Brisa always relented despite her reservations. She just didn't have the time or patience to deal with the woman's ancient ghost stories.

When a possible extension during the second phase popped up, Brisa laughed. Perhaps that was one of Marta's ghosts. The negotiations with Alberto to purchase land for a road to the coast had come to a complete halt. No movement and Brisa wondered if Sebastián had anything to do with it.

"Do you want another architect to help with the pre-planning?" Carlitos' eyes looked dark and sullen. "You seem a little over your head with work these days."

"So are you," Brisa snapped. "We have one week to go before the workload slows down. Anyway, we don't have the budget to hire anyone else."

"No word from Salguero on the land?"

"Not that I'm aware."

"Seems he's on the run for mayor these days. He's nowhere to be found. Not in Antaño or in Palmas Rojas. Maybe he went and got himself killed."

"Why would you say such a thing?"

"He has many enemies." Carlitos laughed.

His last statement gave her a moment of pause. She left the mansion and walked down to the boarding school. The outside air felt cool and the sun's rays warm. Now standing in the hallway, everything seemed a little colder, and a wave of uneasiness washed through her. The light filtering in through the dirty windows gave the place a ghostly atmosphere. She lit a cigarette and took a long drag as familiar-sounding voices echoed off the walls. She dropped her cigarette and stepped on it.

"The permit cannot be expedited …"

Was that the mayor?

"Even with that …" Marta's voice replied, "… we still have other issues to solve."

Brisa ducked into an empty room and peeked out the door.

"Let's get out of here," Marta said with a stern voice. "We can't be seen together."

Brisa wasn't exactly sure who the man she was talking to was, but it was obvious that Marta was nervous. And even with that … she had an extra set of keys, for she had not stopped by the office today.

That bitch!

Brisa pushed her back against the wall as the two walked down the hallway toward the kitchen. Her heart pounded. Looking at the woman from the back, she was definitely Marta. But who was the other one? Was that Pablo? No, the person didn't look tall enough. As soon as they turned a corner, Brisa darted out the front doors. Carlitos stood outside, staring up at the bell tower.

"Your demolition plans should work," he said as Brisa approached. "The second dumping site is now open, so the debris can be easily removed."

"Guarantees protection of our workers," Brisa replied.

"You talk with a certain melancholy." Carlitos laughed. "Everything okay?"

"Hard to believe this will all disappear." Brisa glanced around.

"True, but I believe God has a hand in it."

"What do you mean?"

Carlitos laughed again. "The delays. Doesn't it seem a little odd?"

"It's not God." Brisa stared up at the bell tower. "Sebastián Salguero is the one that's plaguing this place."

Carlitos didn't remove his eyes from the old convent. "I was hoping for a miracle from Mother Rosa. I was praying she could stop the demolition."

"If it's any consolation …" — Brisa laughed now — "… I presented the idea of renovating these buildings for weddings and other events. Maybe I can persuade Angela and the mayor."

Brisa headed for the office, and Carlitos walked beside her in silence. Rogelio stepped out as they approached. He looked sober today. Carlitos nodded at her and entered the house while she remained outside.

"Rogelio?" Brisa asked. "How are you?"

Rogelio nodded.

"The people who used to live here," Brisa said, "tell me about Juancho. About when you were kids. There was a girl named Sara?"

"All the answers are here, Miss Brisa," Rogelio whispered. "Or you can ask Sara yourself. She suffered so much as a child and young woman. I was the gardener's son. When my father worked the soil, I would run after Juancho and Sara. Lady Delfina despised our friendship because Sara and I were from poor families."

"What difference does money make?"

"Back in those days, wealth mattered." He shook his head. "We were teenagers when Juancho's father died. That's when Sara disappeared. Lady Delfina shipped my family to the lower fields and fired Sara's father. Gave the foreman job to an evil man who worked here until Lady Delfina's death. Then he died shortly after."

Rogelio's story was somewhat hard to follow. "Thanks, Mr. Rogelio."

The bell rang and Brisa glanced at the time — six in the afternoon. "Do you know why that bell rings twice a day?"

"The whispers ring that bell, Miss Brisa." He looked away. "The voices from the darkened halls that are far below us. Mother Rosa's whispers are the loudest. She wants her message to be heard. Sara is just begging for justice. The other ones ... well, they're the youngsters who suffered." Rogelio stared out at the horizon, and his gaze seemed somewhat watchful, as if he were replaying something terrible through his memory. "The convent and the school were closed when Lady Delfina died. Then the earthquake hit and finished the place off. The nuns left for various ends of our world. The Vatican refused to support them." He laughed and his chuckles sent chills all through her. "It's just voices crying out for justice, and the bell picks them up. Nothing more."

Brisa stood mesmerized. Her phone rang and she jumped. Angela's name filled the screen.

"Angela?"

Silence.

"Angela, something wrong? Is everything okay?"

"Brisa, the uncle is really missing."

"Uncle?"

"The paraplegic, Mr. Herradura."

Brisa could tell that Angela was holding back her anger. Her voice sounded tense and short.

"I'm on my way to your office now. Should be there within the hour."

Brisa thought about the log cabin on Sebastián's property. It was strange that he refused to talk about it. "There's a cabin on Sebastián Salguero's ranch. He may have his uncle there."

"Oh?"

"I was up there the weekend I visited the coast. Went to see the land for the road. When we walked near a cabin, I asked about it. He said it was an old hunting lodge, but he acted nervous." *I just betrayed Sebastián. Why is it bothering me? Do I feel something for him? Is it resentment or ... love?* "Angela? I suggest you look for the uncle at that ranch."

"I can't just barge in there," she said. "It's as if we're stuck inside a vicious cycle."

"If we start construction, Sebastián will probably show up and turn everything around. Go to the police!"

"Brisa, calm down." Angela laughed. "Going to the police is not a way to be successful. Only makes people more angry." She sighed. "I called so you could encourage me, and instead, you're feeling agitated."

After the call, Brisa needed a few minutes to calm down. She lit a cigarette and walked toward the school. She stepped into the old office and glanced out between the boards of a window. The sun was hovering just above the distant mountain ridge. As she walked through the empty halls, a small light from inside the darkness grabbed her attention. It was coming from the library. The door was slightly ajar, and Brisa glanced inside. It was a small desk lamp.

"The electricity is still on?"

She clicked on her flashlight and glanced around. Various papers and documents were still strewn about. Cobwebs covered the past due-dates on some of the notices. She walked back to the hallway and stood. Soft voices echoed from off the walls.

Marta?

Brisa listened. As she walked, the sounds of her footfalls bounced around her. Iron grids near the floor, placed every ten feet or so, grabbed her attention — probably for ventilation. *But ventilation for what?* Brisa knelt and tried to pry one open. The rusted screws fell away, and the grid clanked to the floor. Flashing the light into the rectangular hole gave away no clues. Nothing but another wall. Below, the area seemed to open up, and from what Brisa could tell, it was nothing small. She dropped one of the old screws into the rectangle hole and heard nothing. The same as what happened back at the mansion's fireplace with the glass bottle, the item simply disappeared without making a sound. *Are there secret rooms or passageways below this school? Rogelio had said that the sprits walked the halls below.*

A larger grid near a corner grabbed her attention. Just like the other one, the screws were rusted. Brisa unhooked her small mallet from her work belt and hit the grid. A different sound, perhaps not as deep, echoed through the hallway. Using her knees for balance, she noticed that something was wrong with the floor. The wood felt lumpy or uneven. The floorboards were loose. She grabbed her chisel and pried up one of the wooden slats. Shining her flashlight into the darkness, something flashed back. She gasped as she pried up several more floorboards. Brisa had found a secret treasure . . . a large metal box. The lid opened freely, and her heart pounded. Record books, photographs, and assorted papers filled the inside.

She glanced around and prayed that Marta was at home and not snooping around here somewhere. She browsed through the ancient material, and from what she could tell, she had found a stash of old student records — names of graduating girls, novices and their dates of investiture, and so much more. Most of the material was just accounting records and donation receipts, along with the school's debts. The last sheet was larger and was folded over several times. She carefully laid it out. As her eyes ran through the words, she slapped her hand over her mouth when she realized what she had found.

"Is this what Marta's looking for?"

A small scrapbook was wedged into the bottom of the metal box. She carefully pulled it out and gasped. Inside were old news clippings and stories about high-society happenings and . . . adoptions! Brisa read over an article from the sixties about a girl who had disappeared. The authorities investigated the school, but the girl was never found. The next few pages were photos of various novices. Brisa placed everything back inside the box and walked out of the school. As she sauntered up the hill toward home, her phone beeped.

```
Angela:     Where are you?

Brisa:      On the property.
```

Brisa glanced at the box and wondered. She walked over to her car and popped opened the trunk. After placing the box inside, she entered the mansion and smiled at a now-pacing Angela.

"You got here fast," Angela said. "Did you hire a plane or copter?"

"Neither. I was just outside."

"The whole thing's falling apart." Angela sat in Brisa's chair and rested her chin on her hands. "Partners are pressuring to demolish everything and now! I know that projects have their problems and it's normal, but I feel as if I'm walking with a pebble in my shoe." She stood and sighed. "Do you have any tea?"

Brisa shook her head. "Is there something new I should know about? Something else that's going on?"

"When you registered the plans, did you register them yourself?"

Brisa frowned. "I don't remember."

"Your ex is claiming that he's the *sole* owner of those plans."

"Because of the company we owned together?"

"He now owns that company alone." Angela folded her arms.

"What do you mean?"

"He has threatened a lawsuit if we don't remove *you* from the project." Angela pointed at her.

"I was with child and —"

"I pray things do not escalate." Angela glared at Brisa. "Are those plans registered here, in Antaño?"

Brisa nodded.

"Good, that helps." Angela walked across the room and whispered something to herself before adding, "Maybe Pablo can fix it. Thank God he's connected."

"I'm sorry, Angela." Brisa walked over to the fireplace and stared into the darkness. "This project is the largest I've ever done. I'll do whatever is necessary to ensure its success."

"Maybe I'm worrying over nothing." Angela glanced out the window. "Oh, good, Pablo's here."

The mayor walked in and smiled. "Hello, Brisa … Angela."

"Hello, Pablo." Angela walked over and accepted a brief hug.

"I'm tired of chasing after *your* Salguero Herradura." Pablo rolled his eyes at Brisa. "How are you holding up around here … alone? Locals don't like outside, professional women." He raised a brow. "Whenever you want a little company … just call."

The mayor walked over to the pot of day-old coffee and poured a cup.

Angela whispered to Brisa. "The mayor likes you."

Brisa ignored the comment and glanced into the silent and dark fireplace. The papers, binders, and photos that she had locked inside her trunk remained the center of her attention. She wanted to sit and take her time reading through the material.

After what seemed like an eternity, Angela finally spoke. "How about a ride to the lodge?"

Pablo nodded.

They bid their good nights and Brisa watched as Pablo drove down the hill. After a few minutes, she ran to her car and pulled out her newly found treasure. She sat on her bedroom floor and studied the photos while reading over the papers. A picture of a young nun grabbed her attention … a novice?

"Could this be Sara?" Sebastián had said that Sara was the love of his uncle's life.

Several photos of Lady Delfina handing out Christmas gifts looked interesting. *What a fake.* Brisa separated the photos and documents by person and date the best she could. When she finished browsing through the material, she knew she had to hide the heavy box and black binder inside the chimney. She wasn't sure why she felt the need to hide them in there, just that they needed protection. As Brisa stood and dusted herself off, Selena walked into the bedroom and gasped.

"Miss Brisa! What are you doing?" Selena pulled Brisa's hair from her eyes. "You frightened me."

"I'm sorry," Brisa replied. "Just looking a few things over."

Selena stared at the pile of papers and nodded. "Do you need me to toss anything out?"

"No … no, thank you. I was working on some things and was thinking about taking a closer look at the downstairs fireplace. Would be nice if it worked properly."

Selena nodded before leaving. Brisa sighed. The remainder of the night ended uneventfully, and the following morning, Sonia arrived in a mini taxi.

"There's an event going on in town!" she said with her voice high and excited. "Women will be wearing customary dresses from Antaño!" Her eyes widened. "Be good for marketing and public relations."

Brisa nodded and grabbed her bag. "We'll have coffee at the lodge and relax a little. I need to talk to someone."

The two jumped into the mini taxi.

"What's wrong?" Sonia asked.

"Mariano is threating a lawsuit. He claims the plans are his and not mine."

"What a jerk! The company's lawyers will put him in his place. Angela works with sharks all the time. Don't worry about it."

"I'm sure Pablo will take care of it," Brisa said, trying to push it out of her mind. "After all, the plans are registered in his jurisdiction."

"What else is worrying you?"

"Sebastián."

"What about Sebastián?"

Brisa did not reply. Instead, she looked down at her feet.

"You went out with Sebastián again?" Sonia asked.

Brisa nodded.

"He turned out to be your public enemy number one. Why would you?"

Brisa shook her head.

"If the company knew about you and Salguero!"

"Don't you dare say anything. He used me to find out what I know about the project. I can't stand him. He keeps trying to manipulate me."

Sonia sighed. "Men!"

"He's a lowlife. I won't fail the project or Angela." Brisa laughed. "Neither Salguero-Herradura, regardless of his lineage, nor Mariano will stop *my* project! They don't know the true Brisa. I won't stop until I put them in their places." Her hands shook and her heart pounded.

Sonia patted Brisa on the leg. "Enough … let's just rest. I'll not tell anyone. After all, the handsome peasant does have his charms."

Brisa looked around as the taxi stopped, and the two stepped out.

"That man is educated, and his name is gaining prominence toward winning the mayor slot in the next election," Sonia said. "I'm not saying this so you'll feel bad. It should make you happy."

"Why?"

"Half the females around here are chasing after him," Sonia said. "Know what he tells them that he loves the most?"

Brisa shook her head.

"Cows and cattle." Sonia laughed. "That's why he doesn't iron his shirts. You're too serious. Laugh a little."

The conversation didn't cheer her up. "I'll be back." Brisa hurried toward the bathroom. A panic attack was on its way.

Sonia followed.

Brisa sat on a bench that was just outside the lady's room.

"Are you okay?" Sonia asked.

"I just want to go home," she whispered. "Don't feel well." Brisa's chest ached and her breathing felt choppy.

Sonia held Brisa's hand as her tears fell.

"They all leave ... they either leave or betray me."

"That house is making you feel alone."

"No, Sonia. I *am* alone." Brisa wiped her eyes. "Every one of them left me for one reason or another. That house is the only place that wants me. I'm safe when I'm there. Don't ask me to explain."

"You're really not frightened by that place, are you? Noise echoes from upstairs ... doors open and close on their own ... a spirit walks down the stairs after everyone is gone. It's hard to believe it doesn't bother you. Remember the other day —"

"I'm afraid of the living, Sonia." Brisa stared at her. "Not the dead."

Brisa returned to the mansion with a new bottle of liquor. She stared at it. She had bought it as a security blanket, and just having it nearby was enough. She entered her bedroom and rested her head on her pillow. The carved, Spanish-style ceiling made her feel welcomed. After a while, she ran downstairs and pulled out the metal box. She sat on her bed and carefully studied the photos.

Glancing out the window at the boarding school, Brisa sighed. She compared several of the photos to the old buildings and yawned. A few of the pictures were of nuns who were busy in various church activities. Identification cards, with photos of the novices, gave her reason to pause. A group picture of uniformed students switched Brisa from a frown to a smile. The graduation ceremonies looked like happy events.

"Smiles can be misleading," she whispered.

The nomination dates for nuns were interesting. As she rummaged through the large pile, she held up a sealed envelope. Printed on the outside and in dark bold letters were two words — *Confidential Information*. Brisa slowly opened the envelope and looked over the content. It was a letter about the nuns in cloister but no photos. On the top of the page, CONFIDENTIAL was again printed in black lettering. Seemed as if the list was a dark secret or something. The square where a photo was supposed to have been placed was marked with an X. Under the X, the name *Sara Beatriz Urrutia* was printed in small lettering.

Brisa didn't understand. Where was Sara's photo? She set the papers aside and glanced out at the darkening outline of Antaño. She sighed. It was time to prioritize her thoughts and stop thinking of stupid things like the past. A strong longing for Sebastián filled her with a solemn loneliness and she frowned. Despite the circumstances, she felt strangely tied to the man. Why did he feel so familiar? It was as if she had known him for years. At times, her feelings felt reciprocated. Other times, she felt totally rejected. Brisa sighed. *So what?* She grabbed a few of the papers and tossed them into the trashcan. The metal box she slid under the bed.

"Pure bullshit!" She shook her head. "Get to work, Brisa … get down to it. Enough of old schoolgirl games!"

Her phone rang. It was Sonia.

"Turn on the news … hurry!" Sonia hung up.

Brisa turned on the TV and almost fell over. Sebastián had been arrested. She wanted to smile. Instead, her eyes filled with tears, and her legs grew weak, and her hands shook. She watched as he was handcuffed and escorted to a patrol car.

Pablo stood at a podium and raised his hands. "Good afternoon." He looked around and smiled. "Sebastián Salguero is charged with the kidnapping of his uncle, Mr. Juan Ignacio Herradura." He grinned as he announced that other charges would soon follow.

Sebastián sat on the back seat of the flashing squad car and stared forward. His face remained emotionless and void of expression. The camera zoomed in and Sebastián turned. It was as if he were looking directly at Brisa. Next to him sat a beautiful woman. The newscaster mentioned her name as Alina … something or other, his lawyer. Brisa smiled and then cried.

Her phone rang again. It was Angela. "Are you watching?"

"Yes," Brisa replied in a low whisper.

"The horizon is finally clearing." Angela hooted. "Get to work … full throttle. We need to celebrate! I don't know if there'll be a better time, but we need to make up the lost time that man has caused. Oh, and Pablo doesn't share in your suggestion of renovating the ruins or the mansion. Not that he doesn't like the idea, he just prefers to start fresh."

"Demolish everything?" Brisa asked.

"He *is* the main partner. Although, that's only known by us. He's solving our problems, Brisa. Get to work. It's time to build our new town."

Brisa now faced two rejections — Sebastián's detention and the denial of the renovations. Her feelings flew to Cami, since her father was now in jail. She turned off the TV and stared out the window. None of Sebastián's problems were any of her concern. He had brought them all upon himself. In a way, it felt good that he was arrested. *Vengeance? I'm wanting vengeance for him not loving me enough to agree to the project? How foolish!*

Brisa's mind whirled through her questions and thoughts, and her voice pounded from inside her mind. With all her doubts and conflictions rising, her emotions held no real meaning. She glanced at the papers in the trashcan and frowned.

Angela kept pushing for Brisa to join in the celebration of Sebastián's arrest but she couldn't. Her heart ached for young Cami. That poor girl … what had she done to deserve this dilemma? Why must she be punished? As ideas ran through her frazzled head, a small thought refused to stop nudging at her.

"Angela," Brisa said. "I've got a bad feeling about this. I'm not trying to ruin your excitement or anything, but the demolition will destroy any evidence of what happened at that convent."

"What?"

"What do you know about the school or Lady Delfina de Herradura?"

"What are you talking about?" Angela's voice was loud. "Why bring this crap up now?"

"Never mind," she whispered.

"Brisa, those are just silly ghost stories from the past. Nothing more."

"What's your impression of Marta?"

"Marta who?" Angela sighed. "You mean that lady with the gold tooth?"

"I don't trust her. She's up to something. I've heard her talking. And the other day —"

"She's just a government bureaucrat," Angela stated. "Harmless. You're paranoid." A long silence. "Have you been drinking again?"

"Not since I arrived here."

Angela sighed. "Marta's a small fry who's looking for notoriety. Ignore her."

"She's looking for something …" Brisa paused. "There *may* be something in that school worth keeping." She glanced over at the trash can.

"Brisa!" Angela yelled into the phone. "Enjoy Sebastián's arrest. Don't be a party pooper. We'll talk later. Ciao."

Brisa walked downstairs and stepped outside. She lit a cigarette and looked over at the convent and the school. The old man was ambling about.

"Morning, Brisa." Pablo entered the office and headed straight for the coffee. "We have the wind at our backs, so let's go." He turned and smiled. "Want to congratulate me for erasing one of our problems?"

"Congratulations, Pablo," Brisa said.

He stepped closer. "We help each other," he whispered. "Teamwork."

Brisa pretended to be looking for a drawing on the shelf when José walked in.

"Hello, Engineer," the mayor said to José. "Good news."

"Let's hurry on the demolition." José smiled and nodded.

Both men laughed and gave a thumbs up.

"You asked to see me?" Pablo turned back toward Brisa.

"Yes, I did." Brisa stared at him. "Angela said that you don't agree with preserving the ruins or the mansion."

"No, I do not."

"But why use explosives?" Brisa asked. "Mechanical is more than enough. I don't understand the need to blow everything apart."

"Your original plans are wonderful." Pablo took a sip of his coffee. "Let's not complicate things."

Brisa smiled but inside she was fuming.

When José walked into the kitchen, the mayor grabbed Brisa around the waist. He leaned in to kiss her, and she pushed him away.

"There are workers here! What's with you?" Should she flirt with the man? Pretend to be receptive of his sexual games? Could she like him if given a chance? Rumor was that he was newly divorced.

"You and I were made for this project," he whispered. "One for the other. I'm a free man." He walked over to Brisa's desk and pulled out a bottle of whiskey from his jacket. "Shall we toast to our success?"

"It's a little early." Are other alcoholics attracted to her for a reason? Maybe others knew of her relationship with the brew and had already spread the word.

Brisa shook her head and the ground vibrated. She watched as the heavy chandelier swayed. A tremor? They stepped into the lobby and employees were asking if they should leave the house. The chandelier continued to swing, and everyone stood frozen in place. When a stronger quake hit, they ran outside.

CHAPTER IX

A couple of days had passed, and according to the mayor, the sailed ship was traveling at full speed. At times, Brisa worked as part of the crew. Other times, she concentrated on Sebastián and Cami. She tried to convince herself that the reason for his detention was valid. However, she could not stop thinking that, just maybe, the mayor had him arrested without cause … just to get him out of the way. Cami was probably distraught and that bothered her. The whole situation broke her heart. Cami without her father? She now felt a strong urge to comfort and protect the child.

Today, however, was another matter. The time had arrived when she could no longer deny the mayor of his *personal* attention. Maybe Brisa could be truthful. *Sorry Pablo, you're just not Sebastián.* It would be a crazy thing to say, although, it would also be quite satisfying. Saturday morning arrived and Brisa met Pablo for breakfast.

"It's only eggs," Brisa whispered, entering the restaurant and accepting a quick peek at herself in the mirror. She nodded and then shrugged.

"Brisa!" the mayor stated, walking up. "You keep hiding from me. Always leaving me alone to talk to Angela. I never get to talk to you. Don't you like me even a little bit?"

Brisa smiled. "I'm sorry, Pablo. Just busy with the field work."

It was a new restaurant that was just outside of Antaño with a splendid view of the volcanoes and the fields of wild roses. The tables were full and everyone looked happy. With a clear and sunny day ahead, only Brisa's mind and heart were cloudy with a chance of heavy downpours. They sat inside since the terrace was full. Not to mention that Pablo required heavy security. As soon as they stepped up to the counter, the restaurant staff rushed the two into a secluded and dark corner.

"You are beautiful," Pablo said, reaching for her hand.

Brisa grabbed her water and took a long drink.

He laughed. "You look wonderful wearing casual clothes. You should put your boots and hardhat away more often." He winked.

The server arrived and the mayor ordered two glasses of champagne. Brisa did not object.

"Pablo," Brisa said, taking another sip of water. "I've been meaning to ask you about Marta."

"What about Marta?" He frowned.

"She works in the same building as you."

"We didn't come here to talk about work." He took a sip of his champagne and smiled. "How about a more intimate conversation. One about you and me?"

"She's up to something," Brisa said, ignoring his almost question.

He sat his glass down and clasped his hands together. "Marta's assigned to the Ministry of Culture. She's harmless."

"I don't agree," she said, pretending to take a sip of her champagne. "She wants something."

"What? An old brick?" He laughed. "Marta is just one link in a long chain of unending government bureaucracy. Let her fill out her forms and walk the empty halls. Very soon that school will no longer exist, and Marta will be out of our hair."

"Any news on Sebastián Salguero? Or his uncle? The arrest was what? Two weeks ago?"

"No news yet." He glanced around and sighed. "I guess —" His phone chirped and he frowned. "Mayor Mencos speaking …"

While he talked, Brisa looked around the room. Her heart stopped as Sebastián entered the restaurant. Now it was her semblance that changed. *Why is he here?* Brisa felt livid and unable to believe what she was seeing. She patted the table and glared at Pablo. Her hands shook and her heart pounded.

The mayor's face turned a bright red. He slammed his cell phone against the table and growled. "They let that damn Sebastián Salguero out!"

"When?" Brisa kept an eye on Sebastián who was walking in their direction.

"They had to let him go," he said between clenched teeth. "Lack of evidence. And … he made bail." The mayor hit the table again before gulping down the rest of his champagne. "What's this I hear about the plans and your ex? I understand he wants to challenge their authorship. Have you replaced on the project."

"I don't know exactly," Brisa replied. "This problem popped up from out of nowhere. I suggested that we show he doesn't have citizenship in this country. He is from Mexico."

"You are the clever one." He laughed. "That's why I like you so much."

Brisa continued to watch Sebastián. He was now standing at the bar and ordering a drink.

"If your ex keeps bothering you, I can ensure you peace of mind. Someone like him is easy to deal with. Easy enough to frighten away. I have my ways."

Brisa heard Pablo's words, but her mind and heart were focused on someone else. "And Sebastián?" she whispered.

"He's a little more difficult." Pablo talked as if oblivious to where her gaze was planted.

"I doubt they'd take the project from me," Brisa said.

"Would you like more champagne or a mimosa?" he asked as the waiter brought out their food.

"A mimosa, thank you."

Her first drink in months. Besides, she was just socializing. Brisa wanted to be friendly on account of the project. Then again, it may have been an excuse to enjoy a cocktail. Either way, Pablo's behavior had spiraled downward since taking the call. Every so often, he'd glanced nervously at his phone before playing with his fingers.

"Forgive me, Brisa. I must leave. Since they released that son-of-a-bitch ..."

Her heart soared.

Pablo grabbed her hand and kissed it. "We'll do this another time. Count on it, and I *will* protect you. We make a good team, you and me." Pablo stood and gulped down his mimosa. Before leaving, he signed for the breakfast. The mayor darted out of the restaurant not noticing who was sitting at the bar.

Sebastián stood and glanced around. Then his eyes landed on Brisa. He smiled and walked toward her. Brisa stared down at the floor, hoping he would not believe she was excited to see him. He would say something any minute ... but nothing.

Brisa looked up and Sebastián was gone. He had simply disappeared. She stepped out onto the terrace and looked around, however, he wasn't there. Why was she chasing after him in this manner? She thought about their intimate times together and smiled. But why had he left? And more importantly ... why did she want to see him so desperately? She drove home feeling elated, disappointed, and foolish all at the same time. As soon as she entered the house, Brisa turned on the news. There had to be something about Sebastián's release ... but nothing.

The morning freshness had ended, and the noonday sky had turned suddenly gray. The weather was quick to change in this area, and therefore, the wind was picking up. The house shook with each strong breeze. *A storm?* Brisa felt exhausted. The day already seemed to stretch on for hours, even though it was just approaching noon. The house even seemed more somber. Brisa shivered. It was freezing now between her ancient walls.

A strange sensation flew through her. Perhaps it was the cocktail from breakfast. Perhaps it was from … Brisa stood at the foot of the stairs and glanced up. Something was different and whatever it was felt sinister. She lit a cigarette and aimed for her office. Something was definitely off. She studied the papers that were shuffled across her desk. A few plans had fallen on the floor. A drawer was half opened. Someone had been in her office.

"Selena?" Brisa yelled out.

Selena had left earlier, for Saturdays were her days off. Brisa was supposedly alone, but when she stepped into the kitchen, the back door was standing wide open. She closed and locked it, and a whirlwind of light smoke floated through the kitchen. Noise echoed out from somewhere upstairs — loud banging, as if someone were busy slamming windows.

"Rogelio?" she yelled out.

No reply.

Brisa took in a deep breath and held it for a few seconds. She was now completely over this day. When the urge for a drink hit her, so did the guilt.

"Come on, Brisa … it was only a cocktail and diluted at that." She grabbed the bottle from the fridge, and the sound of footsteps echoed through the room … someone was on the second floor! Brisa turned and stared down the hallway. The small light that Carlitos had installed to brighten the stairs was flickering. Wind howled through the broken panes of the tall windows and sent chills all through her.

She sat the liquor back in the fridge before inching her way down the hallway. She glanced up the stairs. A strong breeze surrounded her and she shivered. A door slammed shut and the stairs darkened.

Maybe the wind knocked down a transformer or something?

Brisa turned on her phone light and slowly walked up the stairs. A loud banging again echoed down the hallway. She glanced into her room and all looked normal. The banging continued as she inched herself through the darkness. Glancing into an empty room, she sighed. A rod had loosened and was now entangled in the curtains. It was slamming against the open window with each strong breeze. Brisa struggled with the window that didn't want to close. Outside, the gray clouds completely hid the bright sun. Hard to believe that the day had turned so wicked so quickly. Another sound and this time it was coming from her bedroom.

"I just checked in there!"

The door was now half open, and she had opened it all the way just a few moments before. Brisa stood in the hallway and listened. Nothing, all quiet. She breathed in deeply and pushed the door open. The dark room didn't feel inviting. Carlitos had installed a foot lamp near the window, but it was off.

There was something odd going on, and she could feel it. Something or someone was in her room. Then, she saw him sitting in a chair in the corner. A silhouette of a man.

"Who are you?"

The dark silhouette was faint against the dim light. He was heavy built and wore a hat. She could feel his penetrating gaze despite the fact that he was enshrouded in darkness. His sparkling eyes were obvious, and she knew who it was …

"Sebastián?" she yelled out. "You scared the shit out of me!"

"Were you looking for this?" He clicked on the lamp.

"What are you doing here? How did you sneak past me?" Her heart pounded and she wanted to either hit or hug him.

"Secret passageways are everywhere." He laughed. "I grew up here, remember?" He looked tired. His hazel-coffee eyes had suddenly lost their glow. His beard was thick and untrimmed, and he looked a mess. "As a kid, I used to play hide-and-seek in this house." He nodded. "Besides, the door to the kitchen was open. A young girl told me I could wait for you up here."

"Selena let you in?" Brisa glanced into the hallway. "I'm sure she meant for you to wait in the living room … not my bedroom. I believe it's time for you to leave." Brisa turned and aimed for the hallway.

"Wait!" He followed her down the stairs. "Please, Brisa. Can I have just five minutes?"

"Five," she said as she walked into her office.

He began telling a story as if it were the answer to something that she was waiting to hear. "When I was awarded custody of Camelia, I promised myself that I would live only for her …"

"You owe me no explanations," she said, sitting down at her desk.

Sebastián didn't look well. He seemed uneasy, and at the same time, carried a certain amount of heaviness within him.

"How did you get out of jail?" Brisa asked. "And get to the point or leave."

"I'm not here for what you think."

"Oh?"

"I'm not here to start a romantic relationship. It's just that … she's asking for you."

"Who's asking for me?"

"Cami," Sebastian replied.

"Really?"

"Yes, children seem to like you."

"Unfortunately, I don't like children."

"I'm not interested in you or the project." His attitude darkened. "If you want to be involved with *those* people, then so be it."

"Well, thank you."

"I'm also not interested in the land."

"Then why did you take Uncle Juancho away? Don't tell me you're not interested in the inheritance."

"You seem to know a lot about me."

She shrugged. "Apparently not."

He shook his head. "You honestly believe that I would harm my uncle?"

"I would hope not."

"You know nothing about the history of the Herradura family. You show up with your building plans and postgraduate degrees ... then you flirt with the mayor —"

"Flirt, my ass!" she yelled. "I was *ordered* to go with him for the betterment of the project." Brisa could have sworn that his eyes had turned a soft shade of green. Was that even possible? Was he jealous?

"What are you doing? That man will only cause you trouble. I want to protect you, nothing more."

"Seems as if everyone wants to protect me these days," she replied.

"On this property, many terrible things happened. There's so much you just don't know ... I did play here as a kid. We were a happy family once. Before everything turned."

"What is it that you want, Sebastián?"

"I want to provide my daughter with a family she's never had. I want to recover my roots. Cami's mother's not interested in her and just left her on my doorstep."

"I'm sorry to hear that. But how does that concern me?"

"I want to bring to light the good of our family. My step-grandmother, Delfina, was pure evil. I don't want my daughter growing up in a city full of corruption. Cami will have to live and study here." He walked to the window and stared out. "Herradura was a good last name once. It was loved by everyone. With her false Catholicism and prudishness, that evil lady caused so much suffering. The school in Palmas Rojas only goes to the fourth grade. By then, I pray that Antaño will be different." He shook his head. Holding his hat, he ran his fingers through his oily hair. "It's difficult to explain."

"What does that have to do with me?"

He looked out toward the belfry. "You came along and complicated things."

"You said you never wanted to see me again."

He glanced at Brisa for only a moment before looking back out the window.

Brisa sighed. "Your sentimental statements do not impress me. Your reasons for caring for your uncle are purely financial. You're interested in the land just for the money. You're not fooling anyone, especially me. You want to claim custody of your uncle in order to stop my project."

Again, he looked at her before staring back out the window.

"You'll not stop it, Sebastián. Antaño Heights *will* happen."

He turned and took a step toward the door. "Over my dead body!" His eyes darkened and his frown grew. "You don't know me, Brisa." His tone changed and he looked … menacing … threatening.

"Who are you really?"

He took in a deeper breath and wiped his eyes. "A simple man with a complicated history. A man who's not allowing his passion for a woman to get in his way." He grabbed Brisa by the arm and pulled her in close. His eyes widened as his arms embraced her.

She felt herself falling into that hole again. The same dark hole she had fallen into before. Once again, she was caught in his web. Brisa was allowing herself to be manipulated. "Sebastián," she whispered. "Make love to me now with that rage that's boiling within you. Love me now!"

His eyes cut through her like sharp, little daggers. He pulled her in tighter, and she became nothing more than a rag doll. His rag doll. Frozen together in space and time, it was a battle between two beating hearts. Soon his lips would be on hers. His breath was familiar and sweet smelling, and she closed her eyes and waited as his breathing turned into gasps.

"You're ready to give yourself to me? Mind, body, and soul?" He gently pushed her away. "I think I'll save you the trouble. You'd only regret it later."

"Sebastián?"

He grabbed his jacket. "Goodbye, Brisa."

The disdain and hatred he held for her seeped eerily from his skin. Brisa could almost taste it. She stood speechless and her tears fell.

"What do you want from me?"

He had already left. How could she endure the same hurt over and over again? Her sobs blew through her as the waves of pain hit. She ran to her bedroom, which seemed hollow, and when her eyes fell upon the empty wastepaper basket, she gasped.

"Empty?"

The old photos and school papers were gone. Just like Sebastián, the papers had vanished. *Had he taken them?* What was Sebastián looking for? Was he searching for the same things as Marta? He said he knew about the passageways. Brisa looked under her bed and turned on her phone light. The metal box and documents were still there. He had not found them. She sat on her bed and cried. *A drink! Damn, I need a drink.*

"Son of a bitch!" she whispered, rubbing her hands together. "You damn son of a bitch!"

Brisa woke early. After her little encounter with Sebastián, her mind and heart simply refused to relax. She grabbed her work gear and tried to concentrate on the project. It was important to forget about her personal disappointments. As the coffee perked, she glanced outside. The sun was just cresting a distant mountain ridge. The bright orange and yellow clouds filled the sky, as if the sun were smiling at just her.

"I was looking for you last night," Angela said now standing by the coffee maker. "You had company?"

Brisa turned and frowned.

"I didn't want to interrupt." Angela's smile was more of a smirk.

Brisa could mentally see Sebastián sitting in her bedroom. Then, her thoughts flew to the mayor and how she had flirted … a little. *My God, when will this come to an end?*

"Talk," Angela said.

Brisa closed her eyes and clenched her fists. As the coffee machine sputtered, she yanked a cup from the shelf.

"You and Sebastián … is that the problem now? Here." Angela handed Brisa some papers.

"What's this?"

"Mariano has officially filed … for fraud." Angela frowned before taking a sip and adding, "And for theft of the building plans."

More complications with Mariano. Would that man ever leave her alone? Losing the baby was hard enough, but to be blamed for it and accepting his betrayal? And then, him leaving her alone like that?

"I'm not worried about the legal stuff," Angela said. "But I hadn't counted on you and Sebastián becoming a thing."

"A thing? Me and Sebastián? What a joke. It's not what you —"

"Yes, it is! This is serious. Sebastián was released from jail and you receive a lawsuit … all in the same day? Our number one enemy is free, and you stand by his side? I don't understand."

Brisa refused to reply. Anything she said now would simply be reversed and used against her. Instead, she stared out at the rising sun and prayed for … she didn't know what she was praying for exactly.

"Are you okay?" Angela lowered her voice.

Brisa's chest pounded and her throat felt dry and sore.

"Something wrong?"

"I just need a little air." Brisa almost ran for the door.

The fresh breeze felt cool and crisp. She walked up the small hill and stared out at the horizon. Everything looked peaceful and serene. It was obvious that Angela knew something about her and Sebastián. However, how could she ever explain what had happened between them and how she now felt? She was being used by a man who tried to control her through sex. Perhaps that was worse than the booze.

"Okay, Brisa," she whispered to herself. "Breathe in slowly."

Angela walked up the small hill, sipping on her coffee. Brisa grinned at her and nodded.

"Let's start over," Angela said more to herself than to Brisa. "I'm sure our legal team will find a way to block Mariano." Angela patted her on the shoulder. "I didn't mean to upset you." She glanced at her watch. "Though, I do need to talk to Pablo." The woman turned and then stopped. "I'm having lunch with him today. He's our best chance. Our only chance to stop your ex …" As she walked away, Angela glanced over her shoulder and smiled. "Don't you dare start drinking again."

Brisa sighed and yelled out, "I don't have any liquor!"

She had just betrayed her mentor. The woman who had helped her get back on her feet by offering her this project. What was wrong with her? Brisa watched as Angela walked down the path.

She ran directly to the refrigerator and pulled out the new bottle of liquor. She poured herself a tall glass and stared at the golden liquid, frowning as her mind and heart screamed out in all directions. Walking to her bedroom, she passed a mirror. Taking a step back, she stared at herself.

"You were at the point of losing everything," Brisa whispered. "Are you planning on failing those who trust you now?" She held up the golden brew. "I offer you a toast, my dear reflection. And … to Angela, and … to Pablo. Brisa will not disappoint you!"

She placed the glass to her lips and smelled the sweet aroma. Taking in a long, deep breath, she ran to the bathroom and poured the stuff down the drain. Running the water for what seemed like an eternity, it felt as if her life were nothing more than a few ounces of disappointment. She brushed her teeth.

The weekend passed slowly. On Monday, Brisa again woke early. Only this time, she remained in bed. The weekly meeting had been canceled. She allowed her mind to wander as the sun slowly rose into the morning sky. The office workers soon arrived, and Brisa tried to remain busy. As lunch approached, she thought about the binder that was stored inside the chimney. Was *that* what Sebastián was looking for? After all, he had taken what she had thrown away. Brisa shook the crazy thoughts and feelings from her mind. Best to just allow those old pages to turn to dust inside that forgotten crypt.

She sat outside on the bench and lit a cigarette. The enigmatic buildings of the old school and convent sent somewhat of a calming sensation all through her. The bell rang. No need to glance at her watch, for the thing only sounded at noon and six. What was it trying to tell her? And what was that irresistible magnetism that she held for this place? These buildings were nothing but ruins, and she felt privileged to just sleep inside the old and decaying house.

Marta probably wouldn't answer her phone. But she'd be the one to have the answers to Brisa's questions. It was time that the woman came clean about her antics anyway. Maybe Brisa could confront her about wanting her dead. As the phone rang, she studied the old buildings. They seemed to be reaching out to her. Begging her to uncover their secrets. Still no answer from Marta.

She darted into her office and grabbed her bag. After pouring herself a cup of coffee, she climbed into her car. The morning traffic was busy with people starting off their day. She parked and watched as the mayor climbed the steps and shivered at the thought of having to stand naked in front of the man.

The hallway was pristine and almost empty. As she walked, she thought about the crypt under the mansion. She stepped toward Marta's office, which was not far from the mayor's, and sighed. The sound of Pablo's voice made her shiver. Making a small fist, she knocked on Marta's door.

"Come in." The woman's voice sounded short.

She entered and closed the door behind her. The desk was covered with papers and binders. "I need to talk to you."

"I'm very busy." Marta looked up and frowned. "I don't have the time."

Brisa glanced around. The room was of medium size, with large windows that allowed in the morning light. Her beautiful mahogany desk was covered with a disheveled mess of a filing system. Several wooden cabinets occupied over half of the room. Three pictures of older men, with their eyes looking down, to Brisa, felt like another judgment. Two plush chairs faced the desk, and Brisa sat in one of them.

"I need information about the boarding school."

Marta smiled but kept her eyes on something she was reading. "Why? You're about to knock the place down."

"I know you're angry, and I'm not trying to block your work. I must follow orders from my company just as you follow orders from your agency."

"I do my job," Marta replied.

"What happened at that school?"

Marta huffed and flipped a few pages.

"The school's not colonial," Brisa said, leaning in a little closer. "It was built during the sixties, so what historical value could there be? I did find some obsolete information about the school's operating budget but nothing more."

Marta flipped another page.

"That ruin of an old convent ... you've been through it many times."

Marta glanced up before returning to her papers.

"I heard the whispers. Your little game was quite convincing. Why all the hush-hush now?"

Marta set her papers aside and placed her arms on her desk.

Brisa smiled. "You've taken inventory of the belongings of Mother Rosa. Please, what else are you looking for?"

Marta shrugged.

"Why mention the spooks and echoes that fill the empty halls? And that bell? It rings on time every day. What happened in 1961 that no one wants to remember or talk about?"

"I'm not trying to hide anything, and what happened is public information. I'll be removing Mother Rosa's portrait later today. A delegate from the ministry will be here. The Lord Bishop wishes to exhibit the portrait at the cathedral. Since you'll not allow us to enter the school, could someone from your staff remove it for us? Keep it in your office until I can arrange for shipping?"

This was her opportunity to gain Marta's trust. "Of course. Would be my pleasure. When you arrive, ask for Carlitos. He's my lead engineer. I'll inform him to place it in my office."

Marta nodded. "Thank you."

"Was Mother Rosa the founder of the boarding school?"

"No!" Marta yelled and her voice bounced around the small room. She stood and stared out the window. "It was in the fifteenth century when she founded that institution for down-and-out girls. It was never a place for rich women to hide away with their shame."

"Who changed everything?"

"Lady Delfina de Herradura."

"Why?"

"She felt that the girls from high society needed more of a *structured* education. That they needed *proper* discipline. Do you understand what I'm saying? *Proper discipline?*"

Brisa shook her head. "No, I'm sorry. I don't."

"Use your imagination!" Marta shuffled through her papers again. "I don't know much more."

"Was Lady Delfina Catholic? Definitely not a nun."

"That evil bitch was a Catholic zealot!" A tear rolled down Marta's cheek. "Her fanatic ideas almost destroyed this town and everyone in it."

Brisa was at loss for words. Even Sebastián had called that woman, his step-grandmother, a person of pure evil.

"She kept the school alive through generous donations. After a few years, she bought the property outright. That way, she could do whatever she wanted whenever she wanted."

Brisa nodded. "I see."

"I'm sorry ..." Marta stood. "But you've caught me at a bad time, and I honestly do not wish to discuss this matter any further. I'm expecting the delegate to arrive any minute now."

Brisa stood and turned to leave.

"What I *can* tell you is that Lady Delfina, or Mrs. de Herradura, undid all the good that Mother Rosa had done for Antaño. That convent was controlled by only a few nuns ... nuns that the Catholic church would no longer endorse."

"No longer endorse?" Brisa repeated, not turning around.

Marta laughed. "What does that tell you? The church closed that school after that witch's death. Now, the voices of those tortured young girls echo through those empty hallways. *Rich* girls ..." Marta sighed. "Imagine how much those spirits suffered up there between those brick walls."

Brisa opened the door and stepped out.

Pablo nodded at her from his office door. He walked over and took her hand. "What a nice surprise!" he said. "Three times in one week. Such a pleasure."

"Pablo," Brisa whispered. "Where can I find information about Mother Rosa?"

He laughed. "You're so much fun. So many obstacles ... Sebastián and your ex, and now, you're interested in Mother Rosa? Are you Catholic?"

"Just interested," Brisa replied, pulling away her hand.

"Nothing more than poorly contrived legends. Old tales to bring in the tourists. The miracles are to help sell the trinkets. Unless …" He laughed again. "Perhaps you can ask that old nun to create a miracle by removing our two idiots? Sebastián and your ex."

Brisa didn't appreciate him mocking her. "I'm not religious, Pablo, and I don't believe in miracles."

"Actually, that nun performed a miracle for me. You using my first name and then seeing you three times in one week." He stepped closer.

Brisa turned to leave and almost stepped right into Marta.

"Speak to Lorenzo Choc," the mayor said. "You'll find him in the tourism office. Just down this hall."

She turned back to the mayor and nodded. "Thank you."

"He knows the history of Antaño better than anyone. Have a little fun, you precious thing. A little distraction never hurts."

"Thank you." Brisa took a step, and the mayor grabbed her arm.

"Dinner? Wednesday?" He winked. "You need a drink?"

"Yes, a drink," she repeated. "Thanks for the information."

He pulled on her arm again. "You won't cancel?"

"I'll talk to you soon, Pablo."

She walked down the hall, avoiding Marta's glaring eyes. The tourist office was empty except for a receptionist. When she inquired about Lorenzo Choc, the lady said he was out giving tours. As she walked down the stairs, she called Sonia on her phone. It would be fun to have a partner for this little adventure. At first, Sonia said she was busy but when Brisa told her it was about tourism she agreed. They waved down a mini taxi and found Mr. Choc not far from town. They climbed aboard his tour bus and sat on an empty front seat. The two remained silent as Mr. Choc handed out small sheets of information.

"Why the sudden interest in the nun?" Sonia whispered. "It's all nonsense. Just old stories to frighten kids. I'm only interested because a mystic nun with red roses will sell, but why you?"

"I want to see what this famous nun had to do with what's stopping the project. Besides, I'm off the clock, so it's time for fun!"

"I think that you are your own worst enemy sometimes."

"If that nun performs miracles, I want one." Brisa smiled and nodded.

"Hope José falls for me." Sonia laughed. "Do me a miracle, and I'll become a believer. He's so cute! Poor guy's super frustrated…" Sonia continued to talk, and Brisa continued to tune her out.

They sat through the bus tour and listened to the old stories. Nothing of any real interest was covered. As the other passengers left, the two waited quietly on the front seat. When the bus was empty, Mr. Choc stopped and looked at them.

"May I help you?" he asked.

"I have some questions about Mother Rosa," Brisa said. "May we talk … privately?"

"I have an office," he replied. "Follow me."

It wasn't really an office but more of a small used bookstore. He was a tourist guide and a seller of old literature about Antaño. As she perused the aisles, Brisa stopped to examine the candles and various other religious objects that were for sale.

"What would you like to know about Mother Rosa?" he asked. "The young no longer care about such tales. It's a miracle that she was ever beatified by the church. They only recognized her because the Vatican corroborated her miracles."

"Oh?" Brisa picked up a small statue of the Blessed Mother holding a tiny baby. She smiled at it and nodded.

"Yes. Mother Rosa's teachings were revealed by the sacred heart of our Lord. Unfortunately, no one seems to want her teachings anymore." He handed her an old brochure. "Here are the basics."

Brisa glanced through the material. On the front, she read over the words that discussed Mr. Francisco de Herradura, the founder of the city, and how Mother Rosa had arrived from Spain about fifty-some years later. Mother Rosa had provided the original funding for the construction of the convent and named it *The Servants of the Crown of Thorns*.

"The original plans of the convent were lost," Mr. Choc said. "The Holy Mother died in the early 1600s, and in 1750, an earthquake buried most of the buildings."

"Mother Rosa was well loved?" Sonia asked, seeming somewhat interested.

Brisa looked at her and smiled.

"Marketing, marketing," Sonia whispered.

"Mother Rosa had a big heart," he said. "She always sheltered the needy. Mostly abandoned and abused single mothers. She'd educate them and place their unwanted newborns in loving homes. She was admired by many and performed daily miracles."

"Daily?" Brisa repeated.

"When an earthquake destroyed the convent, workers found the Mother's coffin. It was as if she were only sleeping. Her body was in perfect condition. When the workers returned the following morning, she was gone."

"Gone?" Brisa repeated. "You mean, the casket was empty?"

"No, everything was gone," he said. "No one ever found out what happened to her or her casket. Prophecy says that one day they'll find her again. When they do, they'll declare her Patroness of Antaño, and her body will be the same as when she first closed her eyes."

"Anything else?" Brisa asked. "Anything that's not written down?"

Mr. Choc walked over to a small table and picked up a miniature statue. He stared at it for a moment before adding, "Ask your friend to step outside."

Brisa looked over at Sonia and shrugged. Sonia walked out, stamping her feet. Mr. Choc pulled back a curtain that hid a small room filled with candles and many tiny statues of various saints.

"Only for you, ma'am." He nodded toward the front door. "She needs to remain outside." The man mumbled and closed his eyes. He swayed as he stood near the flaming candles. When he opened his eyes, his pupils had turned white.

His strange words sent chills all through Brisa. *Is he having a seizure?*

It was not something Brisa wanted to watch. She thought of calling Sonia when he grabbed her arm. Without looking directly at her, he continued his strange chanting. The words were a combination of Latin, Spanish, and an indigenous tongue she couldn't recognize. She was not able to make sense of anything he was saying but his grip tightened. When his pupils returned back to normal, he whispered, "The Venerable Mother gave me a vision. Within your aura, she saw it. You have *the mark* … the mark of the rose!" He pointed to Brisa's chest.

She looked toward the door with the thought of leaving. Another ridiculous prophecy. What was wrong with the people of this town? And … how could he possibly know about her mark? It was the first time she had ever seen this man, and her blouse hid her small birthmark.

"A Crown of Thorns appeared and then the roses," he said. "The omnipotent spoke — *I am the Heart of God represented by a single red rose. The thorns are the pain for the sins and sufferings of many. Help me save them!'* And that is how," — he released his grip and took a step back — "He converted Mother Rosa into a pilgrim for the cause." Mr. Choc took in several deep breaths.

"Please, just tell me about Mother Rosa," Brisa said, holding back a nervous giggle. "And stay to the point without the theatrics."

He placed a few roses on the little table between the two of them. He recited a short prayer before handing her the red flowers. "We need to find her hidden writings … her original teachings!" Mr. Choc stepped closer and whispered, "The Mother wishes to denounce what happened at the school after her death." He walked over to a heating pot and poured a hot liquid into a cup. He took a sip and glared at her. "Stop the demolition, lady architect. Stop the abomination of our Lord!"

"I … I can't —"

"You must cleanse yourself."

"Cleanse myself?" Brisa repeated.

"The liquor," he whispered.

Her heart pounded and her head spun. "Enough of this stupid talk. All stupid shit!"

Sonia ran into the small room and stood next to Brisa. "Are you okay?" She frowned at the man. "What did you say to her?"

"He's talking about stupid old stories," Brisa said. "Crazy things."

"He wants a big tip," Sonia said, placing her hands on her hips. "It's how people in Antaño give out information. It's just for show and money. They become angry if you don't pay. Forget it. Let's get out of here."

Sonia complained about being asked to leave as they sat in the mini taxi. "I can't believe that nut kicked me out!"

Brisa shrugged.

When they arrived at Brisa's office, they shared a pot of hot tea. After a while, Sonia stood and walked toward the front door.

"You're not sleeping at night, are you?" Sonia asked.

Brisa shrugged.

"I left a couple of sleeping pills on the desk. Take them!"

"See you later." Brisa glanced at her phone. "Thanks." It was six in the afternoon, and the bell had remained silent. She poured a small glass of wine and tossed the empty bottle into the trash. She paused but her mind refused to rest. Sebastián had taken the old papers from out of her trash. *Why?* Then that crazy Mr. Choc.

The portrait of Mother Rosa was leaning against her desk. She lifted if off the floor and placed it over the mantel. From within the dark shadows, the religious woman looked as if she were studying her … analyzing her. It felt like the woman knew Brisa … personally. She stepped closer and tried to make out the woman's fine features, but the oils had blended and faded with time. The lady's gaze made Brisa shiver. The old woman's eyes stared at her; almost judging her. Those eyes … dark and menacing that could penetrate deeply into a person's soul sent a hot ray of dread straight into Brisa.

"To your health!" Brisa said as she took a long, slow drink of the wine. Then she flipped the portrait around and cried.

CHAPTER X

The following morning, Brisa entered the boarding school before the office staff arrived. As she walked through the empty halls, a strange sensation settled over her. It was as if she had just traveled back in time. The tall arches and long hallways seemed to have been recently remodeled. Strangers now filled the rooms. Brisa aimed for the library and listened as the ringing of the bell echoed through the walls and into the floor.

"Hail, most pure Mary!" a voice yelled out from one of the rooms.

Many voices now reverberated in prayers. Where was the sound coming from? Perfectly clear, a choir sang out from somewhere nearby.

"Conceived without sin," another voice said.

Brisa walked into the library, and something was very wrong. Fresh books now lined the shelves. The floor was spotless. The ceiling lights were brighter now and completely lit the room. A nun walked in carrying an armful of books.

"You can't come in here without permission!" A nun tapped Brisa on her back.

Brisa turned and froze. It was Marta wearing a nun's black habit. Brisa took a step back and saw her reflection in the clean window. She was wearing a school uniform with blue stockings pulled up to her knees.

"What in the world?"

The bell sounded again and Brisa screamed. She ran down the hall and aimed for the front doors. The nun, Marta, ran after her. Just before she reached the outside, Marta's strong hands grabbed hold and Brisa screamed.

"What's wrong?" It was Selena. "Is something wrong, ma'am?"

Gasping for air and wiping the sweat from her eyes, Brisa stared at the girl.

"Just a nightmare," Selena said. "Can I make you some tea?"

Brisa glanced around her dark bedroom and sighed. "Only a dream?" she repeated.

"Yes, ma'am. You were screaming."

"I'm sorry. Some tea would be nice. Would you sit with me awhile?" Brisa needed someone who was alive and breathing, and Selena did feel a little like family.

"I'll bring the cups up." Selena smiled. "Yours and mine."

It was Monday and the week's meeting in the capital was marked as urgent. Brisa rose early so to not be rushed. She thought about driving by her old apartment and then thought better of it. To remind herself of her greatest loss would only be stupid and add additional stress to her already-hectic life. Her baby entered her thoughts and a tear fell. A little person that left this world before ever experiencing a breath. He had been no larger than her fist and never opened his eyes. She never heard him cry. And now … Mariano was trying to ruin her with a frivolous lawsuit. Hadn't he punished her enough with the annulment?

Brisa refused to tell him that she would never abort their child. A miscarriage, the doctors had said. Would it hurt Mariano more if he knew the truth? How many nights had he tortured her with his infidelity? No, she would never forgive him. It was inside their apartment in Mexico where she first gave in to her drinking. For six months, she remained hidden in seclusion and almost lost her life.

Today, however, their annulment no longer haunted her. Now that she thought back on it, she didn't believe they ever really loved each other. They had rushed into marriage because of the pregnancy. In their minds, they honestly believed that they could live together, work together, and have a child together. Then again, their marriage and a child would have pushed his residency as a citizen.

After she rescinded her Mexican nationality, she wondered what her adoptive parents would think. It was the nationality they had offered as a gift of their love when they adopted her. She didn't want to feel ungrateful, but her decision to return to her birthplace and start a new life was all that she had left. And now it seemed as if Mariano was haunting her.

As she drove through the countryside, Brisa knew she had to change her mental outlook on things. Otherwise, she'd walk into the meeting too depressed to think. Forcing herself to enjoy what the beautiful vista had to offer, she started to relax and feel a little more like herself. When the city traffic became heavy, it was then that her job concerns reappeared. *What could the urgency be about? Had she somehow provoked this unexpected urgency?*

A bad feeling almost overwhelmed her as she walked in. Several lawyers, standing next to Angela and the mayor, frowned. Brisa smiled and took a seat at the large table.

"We're all together … finally," one of the lawyers said. "Brisa? I now have the pleasure of meeting you in person."

Angela nodded. "Let's get to the point," Angela said. "It seems that your ex is winning the battle. You know how much we appreciate you, and I hope you won't take this personally, but unless you're legally free to manage the Antaño Heights project, we'll have to turn it over to Mariano Fuentes. This is where we are. I'm sorry."

Brisa glanced between the lawyers and Pablo. Angela's tone had just pushed her off a fragile cliff and directly toward the brink of hell. She studied the faces studying her and an unusual surge of strength suddenly consumed her. From somewhere inside the darkened corners of her mind, a figure of a nun stepped forward and held out a rosary. The woman remained silent, but the energy was still there. Brisa took in a deep breath and released all her built-up emotions, and the sensation was tremendously liberating.

"The stipulations state that the professionals involved must be citizens of this country." Brisa's voice was loud and stern. "The construction company must also be from here. I was born in Antaño, and Mariano was born in Mexico. The company we founded together was also incorporated there."

"He became a citizen when he married you, and you switched your citizenship," Angela added impatiently.

"Yes and no." Brisa kept her eyes on Angela. "He annulled our marriage just after we arrived here. I already explained that to you, Angela, and I won't stand for Mariano stealing this project from me."

Pablo smiled and rocked back on his heels. The lawyers talked amongst themselves, and after a few moments, they asked for a short recess.

Brisa stepped into the lobby and pulled out a cigarette. Her hands trembled but she knew she had to act confident. As she watched the outside traffic, a young lady walked up and said that it was time for Brisa to return to the conference room.

"Architect Murillo is correct in her position," one of the attorneys said. "If the marriage was in fact annulled, then his citizenship was also. Mariano Fuentes does not have a legal leg to stand on."

Everyone smiled and left. Brisa remained behind to review some data on her laptop. A little alone time would do her some good.

Pablo walked into the room, smiling. He looked … satisfied. "Wednesday night?" Pablo placed his hand on Brisa's shoulder. "A drink … just you and me?"

The following afternoon, Brisa pulled out the project plans and tried to imagine how the new buildings would look. The thought of many homes facing the volcanoes with their wide streets running down the hill made her smile. Then she thought about the land without the mansion or the ruins. Could she redesign the access without a majestic driveway? The old school plans that Carlitos had dropped off grabbed her attention.

"Goodbye, school," Brisa said as she tossed the old plans into the trash. "To hell with your documents and stupid, hidden treasures!"

She walked outside and lit a cigarette. Marta was aiming straight for the boarding school. Brisa shrugged for she didn't care anymore.

"Last visit, Brisa!" Marta yelled out. "We're abandoning the project. You should be happy."

"I hope you found what you were looking for," Brisa hollered back. "You must hurry. Soon, this will be nothing but an empty field!" Brisa's attitude was childish and she knew it. At least she was able to accept her acquired indifferences about saving the buildings. From today onward, her mind would be focused exclusively on pushing the project forward. "Take that stupid bell with you!"

"You'll soon see it at the Museum of the Captaincy General," Marta yelled back.

Just as she entered the mansion, Pablo arrived to pick her up for their early and intimate dinner. As he drove to the restaurant, she studied him a little closer. He was attractive and carried himself with a surety that she admired. Now, Brisa wondered if his tacky smile was a personal and self-indulged boast or was he covering up for something? After he ordered a bottle of the most expensive red wine, he looked at her and winked.

"What if Angela sees us together?" Brisa asked.

"Angela only cares about the project."

"The success of the project does matter to her."

"Doesn't mean we can't have a good time," he said. "You and me. We make a good team."

"Perhaps."

Pablo thanked the waiter and poured two glasses of wine. Brisa took a sip and smiled — dry and tart.

"The lawyers had an interesting conversation with your former husband." He laughed. "I believe that Angela is actually feeling sorry for the guy."

"Oh?" Brisa took another sip.

"Since he annulled the marriage, he's now an illegal in this country. Shot himself in his own damn foot. Since he's not a citizen, he has no right to sue. He'll be lucky if they grant him a work visa."

The mayor seemed to be in a celebratory mood. Could she ever be interested in him — handsome, tall, dark, and wealthy — why not? *What can I lose?* After all, Angela had acted indifferent about their romantic plays. Her thoughts flew to Sebastián and Mariano. She felt nothing for either of them. Shouldn't she be happy? After all, vengeance was hers. Why was she not savoring the victories?

They finished dinner and not without several more drinks. Brisa had lost count after the fourth or fifth one.

"We need to know each other better ..." — Pablo took her hand — "... more intimately. Soon, we'll be involved in many projects together. We should fill our future with passion." He raised his drink in a toast.

She raised her glass and smiled. They hugged on the way to the car. Across the street, Sonia stood silent and watched. Brisa acted as if she hadn't seen her, but her friend's gaze was a combination of surprise and remorse.

Brisa remained quiet as Pablo drove to his small townhouse that was closed to City Hall. He parked out front, and they climbed the few steps to the front door. He hugged her again as he used his keys and led her inside.

"My studio," he said.

"Studio?"

"Music studio," he added. "And it's close to my work."

She glanced inside. The room was filled with electronic equipment and large speakers.

"I play the guitar," he said. "Mexican music with my friends. We have a band and we practice here. A hobby of course. We all work for the government, but we enjoy making noise together."

"I see."

"I had the room soundproofed. Touch here." He ran her hand down the wall. "You can make as much noise as you want and no one will hear a thing."

The mayor poured them each another glass of wine. He hugged and kissed her neck. As she took a sip, the room spun.

"I don't feel so good."

"You've not had *that* much to drink," he said.

"I took something for my nerves," Brisa whispered. "Please, forgive me. I need to lie down." Her stomach churned and she felt as if she were about to be sick.

"Coffee?"

She shook her head. "I'm not well. I want to go home. I'm sorry."

He frowned but nodded. "I'll drive. We have *all* the *time* we need. All during construction, and who knows, maybe even longer. Depends on you. Many things do, and we should begin by knocking down that damn school."

Pablo drove Brisa back to the mansion. She struggled with the urge to be sick in his car. After giving her a quick kiss on the cheek, he left her on the doorstep. Her only thought was running to the bathroom. Now, she was angry with herself. Maybe a good night's sleep would fix everything.

Brisa woke feeling terrible. The effects of the previous night's drinking were obvious. Her eyes were bloodshot, and she couldn't stop shaking. She walked outside with her coffee and sat on the bench.

Rogelio glanced over and his smile displayed a certain type of understanding that bothered her. It was as if he knew what had happened. "Good morning, ma'am."

"Hello, Rogelio."

"You sometimes remind me of Miss Sara," he said as he followed her through the old ruins. "They left her here to die."

"To die?" Brisa repeated.

"Hasn't Miss Sara tried to talk to you?"

"Talk to me? I thought you said she was dead."

He didn't respond.

"Mr. Rogelio?"

"You were sent here to die, too, but on the inside." He tapped on his chest.

"Oh, Rogelio!" Brisa took a sip of her coffee.

Rogelio turned and stared over at the small chapel. "Mother Rosa performed a miracle for Sara, and now she gave one to me."

"What are you talking about?"

"You should ask for your miracle, ma'am. The omnipotent asked the Holy Mother to protect women. She taught them how to protect themselves from the abuse of men."

"I am not abused by a man." Brisa laughed.

"Perhaps you are abusing yourself. We can sometimes be our own worst enemy."

She turned and frowned. "You're nothing but an old fool. Never speak to me again!" That man had just poured salt into her seeping wound — her pride. "Don't you *dare* come near me. I'm in charge here. You're just an old field hand."

Rogelio's eyes softened. He didn't smile, but he also didn't frown.

"Don't you dare act like you're better than me. Stay away from *me* and *my* office!" As she yelled out her words, the release of her built-up anger felt almost wonderful.

"With all due respect, ma'am, you don't need a man to abuse you. You hurt yourself enough. That's precisely what Mother Rosa taught the women she rescued. Sara learned, although … it cost her a life."

Brisa stood and entered house. Her body ached and she wanted nothing more than to lie down and sleep out the day. If the old man ever approached her again, she would have him removed permanently from the work site.

The day passed and everything seemed normal except for her pounding headache. Fighting with her thoughts about her ex and Sebastián somewhat helped her to ignore her inner pain … not to mention a little assistance from several cups of coffee, a pair of Alka-Seltzer tablets, and an anti-anxiety pill. Brisa sat and updated several drawings before signing a few others. When the afternoon finally arrived, she stood at her bedroom door and sighed as her fears seeped, deeper and deeper, into her inner core. Then … she spotted it! A freshly cut, long-stemmed, red rose rested somberly on her pillow.

"Sebastián?"

Brisa searched the mansion. The place was empty except for Selena who was in the kitchen preparing dinner.

"Someone left this on my bed," Brisa said, setting the rose on the counter. "Did you see anyone come in?"

"No, ma'am. I saw no one. I cleaned your room just a while ago and there was no rose on your bed."

It couldn't have been Sebastián. What a stupid thing to believe. She was simply tired. If nightfall would only come, she could close her eyes and not have to think. She ate dinner in the kitchen with Selena sitting across from her, and after helping with the dishes, Brisa excused herself for the night. Before heading upstairs, she stepped outside to smoke a cigarette. The more she thought about curling up in her bed, the closer she stepped toward the old school.

"The building's about to come down!" a female voice yelled out. "Everyone out now!"

Brisa ran toward the exit as the nuns, wearing long, black gowns, closed in around her. She needed to hide, but a picket fence blocked her way.

"Nuns?" Brisa whispered.

She turned to run and something soft brushed against her knees. She glanced down. Dark-blue, knee-high socks, again, covered her legs. She screamed and an explosion shook the ground as dirt splattered across her face. She stared at her hands, and they were nothing more than dried bones. She screamed again.

Brisa grabbed her blankets and jumped from the bed. She gasped for air and her heart pounded. A bright light and then a loud boom announced a pending storm. As she relieved herself in the bathroom, the rain splattered against the windows. She flicked on the lights but all remained dark. No power.

It was time for some tea. Holding a lit candle, she carefully descended the stairs. It was dark and her heart was still pounding. With her bare feet slapping against the cold living room floor, lightning lit the sky and another loud boom rattled through the large, old house. She entered the kitchen and a strong wind blew open the outside door. The breeze soared through the house and straight to the fireplace. The portrait of Mother Rosa crashed to the floor. Brisa ran and picked it up when another flash illuminated the old woman's face. Brisa could not move. It was as if the woman were looking directly at her! Another flash and her candle fell from her hand. Now standing solemnly in the dark, an odd sensation, as if she were the invading storm, washed over her. She leaned the portrait against the fireplace and searched for her candle but couldn't find it.

Another strong breeze and a rumble rolled across the floor. Brisa ran to Selena's room and stumbled into a table. A trashcan tumbled over.

"Seleeeena!" Brisa screamed.

Selena lit a candle. "What's going on, miss?"

Brisa hugged Selena and cried.

"You're trembling!"

"Hug me, Selena," Brisa cried out. "Hug me, please! Would you sleep with me tonight?"

The day began with Brisa signing checks. She had hardly slept and couldn't stop yawning. Selena had remained by her side until the first morning light. But now, her hands shook and her stomach ached. An important meeting was scheduled for later that afternoon, and it was important that she kept a clear head. Needing a break, Brisa walked down to the lodge and ordered coffee on the veranda. Feeling a little better, she paid her bill and left. Cami ran out of an ice cream shop, and Brisa opened her arms. They hugged.

"Hello, Brisa!" Cami yelled.

A woman's hand reached out and pulled Cami away.

Brisa stared at the stranger who now frowned at the child.

"Come, Cami!" She pulled Cami to the car while giving Brisa an evil glare. "I told you not to run away from me when we're outside the ranch!" The woman scowled over at Brisa. "You must be careful in this city. There are really bad people here." She scolded Cami without removing her eyes from Brisa.

Sebastián stepped out of the store and frowned. "Let's go, Alina!" he stated firmly.

"She's not a stranger, Papa!" Cami whined. "It's Brisa!"

Brisa watched as they drove away. It was as if she were stranded on an iceberg and the darn thing was sinking. Taking in a deep breath, she inched her way toward the mansion. It felt as if her feet weighed a ton. A blurry haze and an empty heart plagued her as she moved. If it were not for the fact that her body knew the way home, she would have ended up a hundred miles away.

The house looked larger and emptier than before. Not because the workers had left, but because everything felt different. Everyone's life she touched turned desolate, sad, or disquieting, and it was all because of her. Brisa walked through the rooms without a direction in mind. She meandered through the offices, not looking at anything in particular. When she walked up the stairs and stared down the empty hallway that led to more empty rooms, she stopped at her bedroom door. The pristinely made bed was the only part of the house that didn't feel hostile. She stretched out on the blankets and wiped her eyes. Her phone rang.

"Sonia!" She almost yelled out the words. "Good to hear from you!"

"Is everything okay?"

"Yes," Brisa replied. "Just needed to talk to somebody."

"Same here." Sonia laughed. "I'm almost in Antaño. Why don't we have lunch at the new restaurant just outside of town?"

Brisa danced as she changed her clothes. It was still early, but a drive would be wonderful right now. A torrent of thoughts and images flew through her mind as she walked downstairs. Her romantic moments with Sebastián gave her reason to pause until Carlitos' warnings hit. "He has a lot of enemies. They say to stay away from him!"

After typing the restaurant's address into her GPS, Brisa glanced into her rear-view mirror. She sighed for her blonde roots were showing again. She reached into her bag and felt for the little bottle of liquor. It was still there.

"Tonight," she told the small bottle, as if they were old traveling mates. She glared up at the bell tower and frowned. "You don't ring anymore. Why not?" She despised that old tower with the large bell that used to ring twice a day. In many ways, it sent waves of revulsion all through her. Now it felt as if that old bell had somehow abandoned her, just like the ones she had loved. She pointed at it. "I have the power to bring you down!"

Brisa drove down the hill and through the city streets. The noonday was alive with friends gathering and young children playing. She exited onto the highway and glanced over at the mountains. As she reached to turn up the radio, a white car slammed into her from behind.

That's it ... need this like a hole in the head!

Brisa pulled over to the side of the road and turned off her car. She stepped out and stared at the new dent. "It's just a fender." She shrugged. "Happens to everyone."

The car that hit her sat idling. A black vehicle with dark windows pulled in front of Brisa and stopped. A man stepped out. He stood quietly and just stared at her. Another man walked over from the car in back, and an odd feeling crept up her spine. She grabbed her cell phone and ... no signal!

"Shit!" she whispered.

"What happened, ma'am?" the man from the white car asked. "Why did you stop so suddenly?"

"You hit me," she said, still tapping on her phone.

Her cell phone rang. It was Sonia. As she tapped on the name to answer, the man grabbed her phone and threw it into the field. When the phone bounced twice, two men wearing brown robes, walked out from between the tall grass.

"What do you want?" Brisa asked, taking several steps back. "I have no money."

The man from the front car grabbed her by the arms. He pulled her to his door and pushed her onto his backseat. Someone was already sitting in the dark and shoved a gun up to her head.

"Kill her if she resists," the man ordered.

The men wearing brown robes squeezed themselves inside. The man holding the gun placed a damp handkerchief over her face. The strange odor of something pungent made her stomach twist as the darkness ...

CHAPTER XI

The room was lit with only black candles. Her eyes burned and her chest ached. Brisa glanced around and only a light haze filled the room. She took in a deep breath and gagged. The air was stiff and stale. She tried to wipe her eyes, but her hands were tied behind her back. Taking in another deep breath made her chest rattle. As she coughed, her damp clothes clung to her body. She was covered in mud.

"You had a long trip," a deep voice said. "They will not find you here."

"Where am I?"

"You are here," the voice replied.

With a pounding head and fuzzy vision, Brisa tried to sit up but couldn't — not without her arms or hands for support. She struggled and her skin rubbed raw against the ropes.

"I can't breathe." Brisa coughed.

"Stand up," a man said, pulling on her arm.

The pain shot across her back and she screamed. He yanked again, and as her feet hit the cold floor, the room swayed and her head pounded harder.

"I will take you to the hallway for fresh air," he said, pulling on her again.

The damp floor sent chills all through her. She glanced down and sighed. No shoes. He pulled her to an old, wooden door and paused. After picking up a black sack, he shoved it over her head. Brisa tried to walk, but it was difficult with her eyes covered.

"Where am I?"

"Keep walking," he ordered, yanking on her arm.

Brisa felt a slight breeze and took in a deep breath — fresh air? "May I stay out here?"

"No," he said.

They soon returned to the stuffy, candle-lit room, and he gently pushed her onto the cot. Her shoulders ached and her chest pounded as he yanked off the musky sack.

"Blow out the candles," Brisa ordered. "They're using up the oxygen."

"In an hour. After they pay for you, and the rite of passage has been fulfilled."

"They?"

"Shut up or I'll have to kill you!"

A rite? Am I a sacrifice?

Brisa had heard of religious groups being in the area but never gave them much thought. Then again, she had also read about several recent and unsolved murders. Now, this man was talking about a rite of passage and a payment?

"Who are you?"

"Silence!" he shouted. The man stood and walked over to her. "Follow my instructions and you'll be fine."

He looked to be in his late fifties or early sixties. Short, graying hair hung just below his ears. He wore a brown robe and no shoes. When he sat in the chair near the door, he leaned over as if his back was hurting.

Brisa stared at the hundred or so black candles that surrounded her. She watched the flames flicker, and when static voices echoed through the room, she gasped. *A radio?* She glanced around for her phone and remembered that one of men had thrown it into a field.

"What rites do you do here?" she asked.

"Rites of adoration," he replied. "Rites of passage. Take your pick."

"Witchcraft?"

No reply.

"Are you the caretaker?"

"Hmm." He grunted.

"What do you want from me?"

Again, no reply.

Voices of men talking over a radio echoed through the room. "Eagle calling Hawk … over …" "It's best to remain armed … over …" The man clicked off the radio.

Marta had been armed. Could Marta have taken her? Brisa thought about Sebastián and when he used a radio that day he rescued her at the emergency ramp. She didn't know anyone else who used a radio. At the project site, they used their cellphones.

"Sebastián!" Brisa yelled to the man who didn't move. "This is Sebastián's doing, isn't it?"

The man ignored her.

"Sebastián Salguero?"

The man stood and walked over. He knelt and stared into her eyes. "Welcome to your final home." He went back to his chair and sat.

"Who are you?" Brisa screamed out the words. "Where am I?"

The man laughed.

"I need to use the bathroom."

The man laughed again. He grabbed a plastic bucket and threw it at her.

She shook her head as the bucket bounced to a stop near her feet. "Untie my hands?"

"No."

She stared at the tiny bucket. How could she pull down her pants without using her hands? "What do you want from me?" Brisa couldn't remove her eyes from the bucket, and the room remained silent. Her heart pounded and she felt dizzy and sick. A panic attack was aiming for her. "Water?"

The man picked up a bottle of water. He stood in front of Brisa, and she gulped until the bottle was empty. He laughed again before sitting back down on his chair.

Again, the room remained quiet. With nothing else to do, Brisa counted the flames. When she passed a hundred, someone knocked on the door. The old man opened it partway and peeked out.

"All good?" a deep voice asked.

The old man nodded.

"If she gives you any problems, shoot her."

"Can I negotiate with you?" Brisa screamed out. "What do you want? Money? Call Angela Gaitán or Pablo. I'm a close friend of Lord Mayor of Antaño! Please!"

The man in the hallway laughed, and the door slammed shut. Brisa coughed again. She rested on the bed and closed her eyes. Her body ached and she felt beyond exhausted. What were Marta's last words? "*We're abandoning the project!*" Images of Marta filled her vision, and the woman's golden tooth shone brightly inside that dark room. Was Marta abandoning her inside this cave from hell? She thought about when Marta was watching the interaction with her and the mayor at City Hall that day. That alone was a nightmarish situation that still haunted her. Were her evil glares a warning? Brisa cried silently as her sleep engulfed her.

She woke praying everything had been nothing more than a bad dream. Unfortunately, she was still lying on the cot with her hands tied behind her back. She glanced over at the man, and he held up a slice of bread.

"Breakfast?" he asked.

"No." Brisa's stomach churned and she felt nauseated. Her tears fell. As her thoughts ran to her ex-husband, she sighed. Could Mariano be behind any of this? Maybe he felt it was the only way to remove her from the project. Could he be capable of such a thing?

"Mariano? Is Mariano Fuentes your boss?"

No reply.

"I want to talk to your boss!" Brisa screamed out between sobs.

The man picked up the black sack. He grabbed her arms and yanked her to her feet. After shoving the sack over her head, he pushed her back onto the bed. The sound of the door opening grabbed her attention.

"Hello?" Brisa said from under the canvas sack. "I can tell someone is here."

The room remained silent.

"Tell Angela to talk to Mariano. I'll sign whatever you want." Her sobs racked through her. "They understand each other. Please …"

A man laughed. She could detect … *what* in his voice? Disdain … disgust?

"I'm a partner in the project." Brisa held back her sobs. "I can pay if you let me go."

A shadow of a man walked toward her. He shoved her against a wall and stated sternly, "Shut up!" His footfalls faded as he walked toward the door. "Make her drink water. She needs to stay alive."

The door shut and after a few moments the old man jerked off the black hood. He helped her to sit up. "You, an engineer or architect?" he asked.

"Architect."

"Have you been in a crypt before?" he asked.

Was he bored from guarding her? "Why?"

"Just asking."

"I need fresh air. Can we go outside again?"

The man stood and helped her to her feet. They walked out and she took in several deep breaths.

"Five minutes," he whispered.

The hood was not properly placed over her head this time, and Brisa could see a little through the bottom. If she tilted her head, she could just make out … vents! The vents were just like the ones at the boarding school and catacombs, and the floor looked like polished rock or concrete — the same! She took in a deeper breath and enjoyed the air before he shoved her back onto the cot.

The old man locked the door. "Combination lock."

"So?"

"I will untie your hands. Use the bucket and eat." He used a knife to slice through the ropes.

Brisa rubbed her wrists that were raw and bleeding.

"Eat." He pointed to a small table. "Bread … cheese and cola."

The man turned his back and waited. Brisa grabbed the bucket and balanced herself the best she could. It took a while before she could relieve herself. She sat on the cot and stared at the food.

"I'm not hungry."

He stood, picked up the bucket, and placed it by a far wall. "You need to eat and drink something."

She shook her head, and an old movie ran through her mind. Images of what could happen filled her with a strong sense of dread. Again, her thoughts fell on Sebastián's recent erratic behavior. They had made love twice, and she knew he felt something for her. How could he be so cruel to do something like this? She thought about the woman who pulled Cami away, and the way Sebastián had glared at her. There was so much hate and anger flowing from his eyes. And what about the documents and photos he had stolen from the trash? He had sat there bragging about how he knew all the secret passageways that were inside that mansion. Selena would never have given him permission to enter her bedroom. If he were responsible for this, then why did Brisa love him so much? That was it, wasn't it? She *loved* him. Her mind whirled and then it hit her. She was attracted to men who were mean to her.

Brisa must have slept too soundly, for she woke up agitated. The caretaker was leaning against the door, snoring. Brisa shook him. He opened his eyes and frowned.

"What do you want?"

"Any news?"

"Tonight, they will come."

"Do you know Sebastián Salguero?" she asked.

"Many people know of him."

"Is he a bad man?" she asked, sitting back down on the cot.

"Not someone you'd want to mess with. I'm paid to guard you. Not to answer questions."

"Is Sebastián your boss?"

No reply.

"Can you tell your boss that Mr. Salguero knows me personally? I can negotiate directly with him. Please ... I need to talk to him." Her heart pounded and she gasped as her tears fell. "I beg you ... please let me talk to him!"

"Lady, shut up!" He stared at her and frowned. "Do you believe in God?"

"Me?"

"Yes, you." He pointed at her. "I've got a feeling that God loves you."

"What?"

He shook his head. "Do you believe in Mother Rosa and her miracles?"

"I don't know."

"She performs miracles for women." He nodded and smiled.

"I need a phone."

He rummaged through a large bag and tossed Brisa her cracked phone. She grabbed it and pushed the buttons. The battery was charged, but no signal.

"No chip," he said.

She sighed.

"You need to drink water. They want you alive, not dead."

The hours passed and Brisa slept before waking and then sleeping again. After what had to be days, someone finally knocked on the door ... just more cheese and crackers.

"It's late," the old man said. "Get some sleep. Negotiations with your friends are falling apart."

"What do you mean?"

"Maybe they don't love you very much. Talks are breaking down."

"Talks, who are they talking to?"

"Your ex-husband, your boss, your friends." He laughed. "Strange how we interpret our relationships. They're never quite as we imagine, are they?"

"I can talk to them and they'll pay. Prove to them I'm really here. Take a photo with my phone and send it to them. Please!"

"We sent them proof. Everything you were wearing."

Brisa glanced down at herself and the muddy sweats.

"Tomorrow we will send more proof. Something that belongs to only you."

She glared at him. "I have nothing else."

"You still have fingers." He chuckled.

Her tears fell and then the sobs. Brisa couldn't stop crying. Her hands shook and her heart pounded.

The man held out a bottle of liquor. "Want some?"

"No!"

He opened the bottle and gulped down the golden brew. "It's late, go to sleep."

She closed her eyes. She was shaking uncontrollably. A loud screeching echoed through the room, as if a freight train were running over her at a high speed. Brisa listened and the sound vibrated from somewhere deeper inside the earth. *An earthquake?* Was she going to die underground ... alone? A private grave made just for her? A strong jolt bolted through the room, and Brisa flew off the cot. The floor rolled under her. The vibrations inched up through her arms and into her darkened soul. When she glanced over at the old man, her eyes froze. The door was standing open, and the chair was empty.

Where did he go?

Silence. The ground stopped rumbling, and the flames of the candles had somehow frozen in place. It looked like someone had just taken a photo. Brisa pushed herself off the floor and stared at the black candles. She glanced up and the dust was no longer dancing inside the dim light. Even the little particles now remained frozen in the air that once flowed freely. Brisa closed her eyes and counted to five. Opening them slowly changed nothing.

A woman's voice whispered gently into her ear.

"Angela?" Brisa yelled. "Is that you?"

"Shhhh," the woman's voice said.

Someone gently held her arm and helped her to her feet. She could almost sense, more than see, the woman. But whoever it was stood about her height and was about her weight. She wore a long, flowing gown, and her head was covered by a long, thick cloth. The ground now felt firm and unmoving under her feet, but the air was still motionless. Time had stopped, for not even gravity had any pull on her.

"Am I dead?" Brisa asked. *Is this what happens when a person dies?*

"Come with me," the woman whispered. "We have little time."

Brisa could see nothing. Although the candles were lit, the room was darker than dark.

"Hold on to me. Quickly now."

The two hurried through the emptiness. Brisa couldn't see a thing but the woman seemed to know where she was going. What was it that Sonia had said she saw on the stairs that day? A white shadow? Or had it been just the light from the morning sun?

The woman's grip was strong but gentle, and Brisa felt a warmness emanating from her that was almost angelic. As they ran huddled together, the sound of a heavy cloak dragging across the floor echoed through Brisa's ears. How the woman could see anything was beyond comprehension. A shadowy halo somewhat shaded the woman's face. It was almost painful to try and look directly into her eyes.

Suddenly, Brisa was running down the hallway to her bedroom in the old mansion. Then she was walking down the path toward the school. Now, she was ambling up to the old tree where Rogelio was waiting for her. Although barefoot, her feet felt neither cold nor warmth. With everything so hectic, Brisa simply obeyed the woman's commands, as if her words were somehow connected to her soul.

Her chest no longer ached, and the air tasted neither fresh nor stale. However, with each step, her breathing improved. They ran and the sounds of running water filled her with dread. As they ran deeper into the darkness, the woman's cloak changed from an aged brown to a bright white. An iridescent glow now painted a shining oval around the woman's silhouette.

"Mother Rosa?" Brisa whispered.

If there were an explanation for all of this, then Mother Rosa would be the best guess. It had felt as if she were being carried away on a warm current of air. The security that now surrounded her was comparable to a mother cradling their young child. Brisa didn't want the sensation to ever end. They stopped running and Brisa tried to look around. She clung tightly to her phone, for it was the only scrap of reality that tethered her to life — the phone without a chip. As the woman pushed her deeper into the folds of Mother Earth, the hands that had cradled and protected her from the evil forces faded into the dimming light.

"In here, quickly," the woman whispered. "Deeper, go much deeper!" The woman gently pushed Brisa into what or where, she had no idea.

Was she dreaming? Was the woman an apparition or someone real? Maybe Brisa was dead … or maybe just suffering from hallucinations?

"You're safe now," the woman whispered, and the angelic voice slowly blended into the darkness. "You're safe now, my beautiful girl." The woman had disappeared into the shadows as quickly and as silently as she had arrived from beyond the light.

Brisa relaxed a little, hiding inside that dark cavity. She closed her eyes and rested her head against the cool bricks. The air, now free from the aroma of stale candles, seemed invigorating and rejuvenating. She must have dozed off, for a dim light woke her and clouded her vision. As her heart pounded, she shielded her eyes from the brightness. Her eyes slowly adjusted, and a metal grate, only a few feet in front of her, grabbed her attention. Black boots darted back and force from the other side. They were frantically searching for something … someone … perhaps her?

"You let her go?" an angry voice yelled out. "You stupid fool!"

The voices accused each other of her escape.

"It was the quake!" the old man said.

Brisa recognized the voice as that of the keeper.

"There was no quake, you stupid idiot!" A loud bang blasted through the grate, and the old man dropped to the floor.

Brisa held back a scream as the dead man's eyes stared blankly at her. The other men continued to dash about, screaming and demanding answers. Brisa snuggled deeper into the folds of the living earth and tried to breathe in a more calming and soothing rhythm. *How can I escape?* She turned on her phone light and studied what was behind her. A pile of loose bricks and dirt blocked her path. The ground shook again, and a few bricks rolled gently to the floor. The men were still arguing, and several times, she heard gunshots. After struggling to turn around, Brisa pulled on a couple of bricks. When she did, several fell away along with a bucket's worth of dirt. Stale air caressed her face. Brisa dug and dug until a space large enough for her hand to reach through opened up.

Her hiding space was just tall enough for her to rest on her knees. As her head brushed along the ceiling, tiny rocks and dirt dug into her skin. She pushed on the bricks, and the ground, again, rolled beneath her. Only this time, larger chucks of the earth fell away. Brisa poked her head through the small opening and looked around. It was too dark to see anything. She struggled and placed her feet toward the bricks and dirt that were blocking her. Now sitting on her butt, she pushed. With each tremor, she shoved her feet against the earth that surrounded her. The barrier finally gave way, and a wave of stale air greeted her.

She inched her way through the opening, and as the world fell away, she screamed. She landed hard on a solid rock floor. Brisa gasped as the wonderful, life-giving air slowly filled her lungs. Rubbing her hands together, her heart pounded. She sighed when she spotted her phone laying only inches away. With the help of a nearby wall, she stood. Grabbing her phone, she frantically searched the area with her light. The passageway was more of a corridor than an actual room, but a corridor to where? Soft voices echoed through her ears and she panicked. After flipping off the phone, she leaned against the wall and panted. All remained quiet. She was alone. As she walked, the place began to look somewhat familiar.

Could it be? Oh, yes it could!

Brisa was standing in the old coal room that was next to the entrance of the ancient church. *"It was a long trip,"* the caretaker had said. Brisa laughed. She was in Antaño the whole time. She stepped up to the vent that faced the outside and breathed in the fresh air. With each fresh and wonderful breath, her mind cleared a little more.

Brisa entered the church and sighed. The room was empty. She glanced up at the huge cross and nodded. She ran and her bare feet slapped against the cold rock floor. Several times, a small pebble would dig into her skin, but she kept running. She hit the wooden front door at full speed, and water splattered against her face. A bright light and a loud bang vibrated all through her. It was raining and raining hard. Her eyes landed on the mansion. She ran through the heavy downpour, and the muddy earth sucked at her feet. The night sky never looked so good. Brisa slipped several times as she struggled up the small hill. She half-crawled, half-ran to the mansion's front door. She hit the sidewalk, and as her feet flew out from under her, she fell hard against the ground. She gasped for air and crawled to the stoop. After inching herself up, she pushed opened the front door and landed inside.

A woman screamed.

Brisa neither smiled nor frowned. Angela ran up and wrapped her arms around her, and the woman's cries echoed around the large room. Brisa could feel her friend shaking. She leaned into the warm embrace, and after several deep breaths, the aroma from Angela's hair sent waves of emotion all through her. A police officer stepped over and helped Brisa into the living room. She glanced around and sighed. The room was filled with police and strangers wearing dark suits.

"Is this Brisa?" one of the men asked.

"Yes," Angela said between sobs. "My God, Brisa, what happened? Where were you?" Angela pulled her in close for another hug.

Brisa was crying so hard she could barely see. She was soaking wet from the rain and still caked with mud.

"We need to get you cleaned up." Angela laughed and cried at the same time. "Brisa escaped, everyone … Brisa escaped!"

Pablo stepped up and wrapped his arms around her. "Thank God you are safe."

Brisa thought it strange that the man didn't seem to care about the mud. She glanced around and locked eyes with Selena.

Sonia ran over and gently touched her cheek. Her eyes were red and swollen. "You can't stay here anymore. Not safe."

Brisa nodded.

"You'll stay at Los Arcos with me," Angela said, pulling Brisa toward the stairs. "We need to get you washed up first. You can talk to the detectives later."

Brisa nodded again.

After a long, hot shower, she sat on the couch as Selena spoon-fed her hot vegetable soup.

"Brisa," a man wearing a dark suit said softly. "I'm Detective Perez. I need to ask you a few questions."

Brisa wasn't sure how much she told him or how much he asked. She was still in shock. A doctor arrived and checked her vitals. He tended to her wrists and feet and bandaged them. He handed Angela a few sleeping pills and said she needed water and rest. Brisa was now surviving inside of a nightmare, for she watched as their lips moved with no sound. She remembered the soup but not what happened to the bowl or who took it.

"We've been searching for you," Angela said finally, directly to Brisa. "I was so worried! How did you escape?"

"The earthquake," Brisa replied.

"What quake?" Angela asked.

Brisa stared at her and shrugged.

"That's okay," Angela said. "We need to leave this place so you can relax. You need to feel safe. Tonight, we'll sleep at the lodge. Sonia has agreed to sleep with you. You'll have twenty-four-seven security."

Brisa glanced around at the worried faces and smiled. Her head pounded and she still felt a little dizzy, but at least she was safe.

It was Sonia who welcomed her at the lodge. Everything felt strange and not all there. Sonia acted a little distant and that felt unnerving as Brisa needed the old Sonia in her life right now. Her best friend who never gave her a chance to say anything — the nosy Sonia, and the Sonia who always asked for details.

"What's wrong?" Brisa asked when they were finally alone.

"I'm scared." Sonia cried into her hands. "I feel paralyzed because of what happened. Maybe I just need some sleep."

Brisa slept soundly that night at the lodge, and in the morning, she felt wonderful. The nightmare had finally ended. She didn't want to blink, or else she might end up back in that crypt. Her mind was no longer foggy, and what she could see clearly was that a presence had helped her escape. She had never felt such tenderness or love before.

Should she tell the detectives, *"Oh, it was Mother Rosa who showed me the way out."* Yeah right, that would get her placed in a mental hospital for a very long time. The detectives asked questions that were never-ending, and Brisa tried to explain but so much was still just a fuzzy cloud. Could she confess that an illuminated spirit, a white shadow of a woman, helped her escape? She could hardly believe it herself. Maybe she imagined it all. Maybe she was losing her mind.

Brisa sat with Sonia on the veranda, and they ate their breakfast in silence. Every so often, Sonia would glance at her only to quickly look away.

"I need to go to the bank," Sonia said as they entered their room. "The ATM here is not working. Don't go anywhere. I hate to leave you, but I need cash. Angela wants to take you to the capital, but the police still have questions. Please, don't leave this room or answer the door while I'm gone."

"Don't worry," Brisa said. "I'm okay."

A phone dinged ... it was Sonia's. Brisa grabbed it and ran to the door. Her friend had already left. She frowned when she saw the name. The text was from Angela.

```
Angela:      Continue to keep me posted. Keep tabs on her. Alert
             me to anything no matter how small.
```

Brisa found the wording a little off. Why would Sonia be keeping tabs on her? As her curiosity grew, she flipped through the older messages. Hundreds of calls and texts existed that were between just them. Why would they chat so much? Sonia had definitely been acting a little distant since Brisa's return, but still ... a knock on the door pulled her from her thoughts. She sat the phone on the desk, took in a deep breath, and waited for a second knock before saying anything.

"Who is it?"

"It's me, Pablo. Can I come in?" Brisa opened the door, and the mayor stepped inside. "We've had quite the scare." He hugged her. "Are you okay?

We'll punish those who did this, you can be sure. The police have your car. It was found on the outskirts of town. They looked for fingerprints but nothing. Wiped clean."

"I'm not surprised. They seemed to know what they were doing. Was it Mariano? Sebastián? Who were they negotiating with?"

"We don't know," he said, kissing her cheek. "We were in talks, but they never revealed anything. We were close to finding out what they wanted when they suddenly refused to say anything else. After scheduling a meeting, everything just stopped. I thought the worst, and Angela was sick with worry."

"Thanks," Brisa said, sitting down on the bed.

"There's something else." He lowered his eyes. "Please don't think that because of this terrible ordeal that I've forgotten. I still owe you a night out … at least an afternoon."

She shrugged.

"However —"

"How could this happen?" Brisa glared at him. How would this affect her work? When would these obstacles come to an end? She wanted to get back to the project to show her value to the company. There just wasn't any time to waste, and this was not a good time for her to go to the city. Would Angela understand? Maybe she could convince her that all she needed was some alone time to heal. "Pablo …" — Brisa stood — "… tell me what the kidnappers wanted. Was it money?"

"We can't talk here," he said, glancing around. "I'll explain it all later, but you'll need legal advice first." Pablo glanced out at the veranda. "You're safe and that's all that matters. I must get back to work. Take care, Brisa. The security guards will protect you." Pablo darted out the door without saying goodbye.

Brisa needed to return to the mansion. After all, it was still her home. She wanted *her* bedroom and *her* stuff. It was the only place where she could clear her mind. She could no longer be closed up in a tiny room with Sonia avoiding her.

She grabbed her bag and snuck down the stairs. Two guards sat in the lobby talking. She nonchalantly wandered out a side door and ran to the street. A mini taxi was parked on the corner, and she paid the fare. When she arrived at the mansion, she crept through the rooms to ensure she was alone. Not even Selena was there.

Brisa took the opened bottle of wine from the fridge and poured herself a tall glass. The belfry remained eerily quiet. She walked outside and stared down at the old boarding school. She wanted answers, but again, none came. After gulping down the wine, she poured herself another glass, and then another, until the bottle was empty. Finishing off the last few drops, the catacombs and black, flickering candles filled her vision.

"How could anyone hate me so much?"

When she walked back into her office, the anxiety pills called out to her. She took one. The pill bottle sat idle and reminded her of being alone. One at a time, Brisa counted out the little, white pills and with each count, she swallowed. Tossing the empty bottle into the trash felt like an honest release, but a release from what, she wasn't sure. She walked aimlessly through the mansion and allowed her inner pain to radiate and grow. A bottle of vodka sat idle inside a small fridge in the corner of one of the offices.

"Why can't I find someone to love me for me!" She screamed out the words, and a sudden rush of anger soared through her.

The house remained quiet.

"Am I an expert at making people *hate* me enough to *torture* me?"

Brisa stepped outside and threw the empty liquor bottle against the house. The loud clanging of shattering glass echoed through the yard. She ran down to the ruins and stared at the large rose bushes. Red and white flowers swayed in the wind and sent a wave of resentment and disappointment deep into her core. She grabbed a flower and tore off the petals. She grabbed another and another.

"Mother Rosa!" Brisa screamed out. "If you're so damn powerful, why do you keep me locked inside this dungeon? Why take me out of captivity only to put me in another? What do you want from me?"

Brisa grabbed more roses and threw the petals high into the sky. They rained down around her. And they rained. And they rained. Staring at the falling petals, she screamed.

"Tell me!" Brisa fell to the ground and cried. "Where are you? Stop playing hide and seek, or am I too much for you? Someone even the great Mother Rosa can't save!"

She stood and ran to another rose bush. She yanked off the petals and screamed. As they fell around her, she pulled off more — yanking and tearing and yanking and tearing until her hands were red and full of blood.

"It's okay," Brisa whispered. "Can we call it a truce? If you will just stop me from feeling this way, I promise I'll never bother you again." She threw another handful into the air. "Are you nothing more than a cheap parlor trick?"

The petals fell and continued to fall. Brisa looked up as a scarlet hue surrounded her. The torn flowers continued to rain down and fill her with a sense of doom.

"I want to sleep, Mother Rosa," Brisa cried out. "Please, just let me sleep ..."

She fell to the ground and rested her head against the thick blanket of petals. A fragrance of death, mixed with the sweet scent of life, surrounded her. She closed her eyes and allowed her heart to fall numb. For the first time in months, Brisa's pain was gone.

Footsteps echoed across the yard. She glanced up through the fuzzy haze and smiled at the familiar face.

"Ma'am?" Rogelio whispered and shook her arm.

"Mr. Rogelio." Brisa closed her eyes and sighed. "I saw Mother Rosa." Silence caressed her, and as she floated away on a soft cloud of tranquility, a slice of God's presence comforted her. Non-life was ever so wonderful.

CHAPTER XII

The following morning, Brisa thought for several moments that her head had actually exploded. The room spun and her stomach churned.

"How do you feel?" a woman's voice barely registered in Brisa's mind. "You've had a stomach wash and we're hydrating you."

"Where am I?" Brisa reached up and grabbed her throat.

"Antaño Hospital," the woman's voice replied.

"Who are you?"

"A nurse." The woman adjusted the sheet.

"How did I get here?" Brisa's voice cracked. "I want to go home."

"In a few days. The doctor must discuss a therapy regimen before you're released."

"Doctor? What doctor?"

"The psychiatrist. He'll be by soon. Would you like some breakfast?"

Brisa tried to look around, but the light burned her eyes. She couldn't make any sense as to what had happened. *What did I do to myself now?* "Who brought me in?" Brisa asked.

"I don't know. I wasn't on duty when you were admitted." The woman walked around the bed and held out her hand. "An older gentleman stopped by to bring you this envelope and those roses." The nurse pointed to the other side of the room.

Brisa glanced over at the window and frowned. A large vase was filled with a dozen, red roses.

"He sat next to you while you slept. Maybe he was the one who brought you in?"

Brisa opened the brownish envelope and pulled out a scribbled note. The paper looked water-stained and crinkled.

It was the old drunk, Rogelio, who had called an ambulance. Brisa thought about him and understood. They were now partners inside this strange game of trying to stay alive. She waited until the nurse left before sitting up. She stood and had to grab onto the bed for support. Her clothes were stuffed inside a brown paper bag that sat on a small table. Slowly and methodically, Brisa pulled out her IV. She dressed, and after glancing into a mirror, she frowned. In many ways, she already resembled the dead.

I must return home before Angela finds out. What was I thinking?

She peeked out the door and glanced down the hallway — empty. An outside door was only a few steps away. Shielding her eyes with her hand, she stepped into the afternoon sunlight. It had to be just a little after lunchtime. After waving down a mini taxi, she sat and sighed. Watching others walking through the streets gave her a reason to pause.

"Can you drop me off on the corner?"

He nodded.

The driver knew her, and she simply told him that she owed him one. Brisa ran up the hill and entered the mansion through Selena's bedroom. The workers didn't see her, as they were busy talking. Marta was down by the school, and someone was standing next to her.

Hypocrite! Brisa would denounce Marta to the authorities. She picked up the phone to make the call when she stopped. *Authorities?*

Brisa slammed the phone down and sighed. Before she could call anyone, she had to think things through. Why was Marta still here? She locked the kitchen door and aimed for the living room. Stepping in front of the old fireplace, the portrait of Mother Rosa grabbed her attention. Marta never came to pick it up. Why not?

Why had she always felt that something was off when it came to Marta? The woman acted as if she were always up to something. Could it be that the documents Brisa had found protected a dangerous secret? What if Marta knew about them? Were *they* the treasure everyone was searching for?

"The documents!"

Would they still be there, or had someone found them? Not that they were relevant to Brisa, but her instincts were telling her they were important. She crawled into the fireplace and maneuvered her way into the underground tunnel that led to the boarding school.

I wonder how many times someone traveled this way to spy on someone or to secretly communicate?

Ambling through the empty underground hallways, the air felt cool and damp. She thought about the room with the black candles. Glancing over her shoulder, she could almost imagine someone hiding in the shadows, ready to pounce. She spotted the metal box and smiled. Light from the upper grates cast weird lines across the floor and sent chills down her spine. *I must be walking under the school now.* Peeking through a grate, she could see Marta's feet. Using the unusually placed bricks, Brisa slowly climbed up the wall for a better view.

What did Marta do while alone in this building? Did she talk to the ghosts? Marta was now carrying a flashlight and ... a gun! It was tucked under her jacket, and when she turned around, the sun from one of the library windows reflected briefly off the handle. Brisa wasn't surprised.

Her foot slipped and a rock bounced across the floor. Marta froze and slowly turned around. She pulled out her gun and flashed it across the room. She stood still, probably trying to hear more. After a few moments, she shoved her gun into her waistband and walked out of the library.

With her hands shaking, Brisa darted for the mansion. She crawled out of the fireplace and called the mayor.

"Hello, gorgeous!" Pablo's voice was chipper as usual. "Where have you been? We're looking for you."

"It's Marta!" Brisa whispered. "She's a gang member! You need to arrest her."

"You're talking about an employee of the ministry." Pablo sighed. "Now honestly, where have you been? Sonia and I have been looking everywhere for you. I'll stop by in a bit and we can talk. Are you at the lodge?"

"Yes," Brisa lied.

"If it makes you feel better, I'll have Marta followed for a few days. Now, take it easy and get some rest."

"Thank you, Pablo." Brisa nodded and a tear ran down her cheek.

She didn't want to call Sonia. Not yet. Sonia had been acting strange since her escape, and she didn't feel comfortable around her. Suddenly, she realized that she didn't feel comfortable anywhere. Now, more than ever, she depended on just Angela and Pablo.

Brisa glanced out the window, and José was talking to someone near the school. The stranger wore a dark suit, and she couldn't tell who it was. The two were looking over what looked like plans. As they pointed at the construction site, Brisa stepped out from behind the door.

Yellow caution tape and danger signs were now wrapped around the mansion. She darted back into the living room and glanced into the offices.

The rooms were empty. She ran to a window and looked out. The demolition crew was standing in a circle near the old tree.

"Oh my God!" Brisa screamed out. "They're going to blow this place apart!"

That stranger José was talking to was probably the explosive engineer. The fog that had clogged her thinking lifted, and everything became crystal clear. The micro charges were in place, and they were going to detonate without telling her. Brisa ran to the phone, and it seemed eerie that it still worked.

"Brisa?" José said. "So good to hear from you."

"What are you doing? Where's the heavy-duty bulldozers?"

"We won't need them," he said. "Charges are ready and we just need to place the dynamite. Angela said you both were in agreement."

"Wait, José!" Brisa screamed. "Why explosives? Why now? There are catacombs under these buildings. We never agreed on anything. You need to explain the plans in detail to me."

"It's too late for that," he said and he sounded a little confused. "I'm sorry. You'll need to talk with Angela. I'm just following orders." José hung up and had acted as if he were in a hurry.

But why?

Brisa ran into the front yard and spotted a worker. "Where's the rest of my staff?"

"Over there, Architect," he said, pointing to an old galley that they were now using as an office. "They are housed there while the demolition takes place. Trailers will be set where the mansion is once the ground's leveled."

Where was that old man, Rogelio? Why wasn't he walking around the place as usual? Brisa needed to talk to him.

She didn't want to barge into the temporary office and face her staff while feeling disoriented. Besides, her staff was probably just as confused as she was. Not only from the change in venue but with the abrupt change of direct orders. So much had happened within just a few, short days. She needed her car. *Where had she parked it?* Then she remembered, it was still with the police. Brisa walked to the parking lot and glanced around.

"Brisa!" Carlitos ran up and wrapped his arms around her shoulders. "How nice to see you. Do you need something?"

"Your car," Brisa replied. "Lend me your car for a couple hours."

"Of course," he said, handing her the keys. "Are you okay?"

Brisa nodded.

Avoiding the main road that led to the lodge, she drove around the park. Who could she call? Sonia? No, she didn't want to talk to her. Angela? No, Angela wanted to move her to the city. Then again, Angela owed her an explanation for the decision to blow the place up.

She could talk to Rogelio, but the old man had disappeared. Marta? Brisa laughed. Marta was her main suspect in her kidnapping. Sebastián? *Oh, hell no.* Not realizing it, Brisa was approaching the road that led to the older catacombs. The ones Sebastián had taken her to on horseback. She took in a deep breath and thought about Mother Rosa. Maybe her arriving here wasn't a coincidence. The catacombs that those creeps had locked her in definitely resembled the ones she had made love to Sebastián in.

She took in a deeper breath, and again, Mother Rosa came to mind. Brisa thought about the impeccable image of the benevolent figure that had led her to safety. What a marvelous experience or was it divine? She still needed to digest everything that had happened. A loud knock on the car window yanked her from her thoughts. Believing that it was an officer who would be telling her she was improperly parked, she rolled down the window. Brisa turned and stared directly into a holster with a gun.

"Get out, Brisa!" Sebastián ordered.

Her heart pounded and her head whirled. It was the same panic she endured as a hostage. Brisa obeyed Sebastián's orders. He was armed and she was not. He never raised his gun, but she still felt threatened. He grabbed her by the arm and pulled her into the catacombs.

"Brisa ..." he started. They stepped deeper into the tunnel and stopped. "I have to get this off my chest." He glared at her. "I know this isn't the right time, but I have to say something." Another pause and he glanced around as if feeling guilty about something. "Are you with ... him?"

"Him?" Brisa's mind fell blank. What kidnapper asks about a *him*? "Him who?"

"That man doesn't appreciate you!" Sebastián lowered his eyes. "He just wants to use you."

"What are you talking about? I'm not with him!"

His shoulders relaxed as he grabbed her arms. "Where are the documents you found in the school?"

"I don't have any documents. You took them, remember?"

He took a step back. "Someday you'll understand. I'm not what you think!" He ran his fingers through his hair and scratched his nose. "I need the rest of those documents. I know you found them. Please, it's a matter of life and death. Cami has disappeared. She's nowhere to be found."

"What? Cami? When?"

"For a few days now." Tears filled his eyes. "Help me, please!"

Would Sebastián invent such a story for a bunch of old papers? Then again, they were probably standing in the same catacombs from where she had just escaped.

Brisa glanced over at the opening and shook her head. "Don't lie to me about Cami! Don't use your daughter as a ploy. Is that what you wanted all along? The damn documents? Was that why you made love to me?" Brisa aimed for the outside light. Her heart wanted to burst, and she wasn't sure if it was from love or hate.

"Cami's gone," Sebastián yelled out. "And she ..."

Brisa stopped but didn't turn. She just listened.

"Please!" His voice cracked. "You don't believe me, but ..."

"There you go again!" Brisa yelled, holding back a sob. "Stop using your daughter against me!"

She started the car and aimed for the mansion. It was important to grab a few things that she had left behind. But Sebastián had never looked so desperate. She almost wished that she possessed the courage to stay and listen to him ... to believe in him. However, her newly acquired distrust for the man was just too overpowering.

She turned on the radio and thought about how she needed to fix her phone. Any lost contacts she could pull from her computer, so that shouldn't be an issue. As she drove through the town, she spotted an electronic store. *Phone!* It felt as if she were escaping all over again. Then again, escaping from whom?

It took a while at the store, but eventually she walked out with a new sim card. Her phone was cracked but still worked. Brisa sat in the car and stared out at the people who were busy living their lives, and here she was acting as if she didn't have one. She shook her head and turned on the radio. A newscaster was talking. Reaching out to change the channel, she paused when the name Camelia smacked her across the back of the head.

"A few days ago, we reported on the disappearance of young Camelia Salguero. As of today, there's still no trace of the girl. No individual or group has come forward to take credit for the disappearance. Mr. Sebastián Salguero, father of the child, has denied all involvement and refuses to give a statement ..."

Brisa stared at the radio as the words echoed through her mind. It was all true, and Cami was actually missing. The poor child. Poor Sebastián! She should have stayed and listened to him.

She pulled out of the parking lot and aimed for the mansion. The buildings and fields flew by, as if they never existed. The place looked empty. Brisa ran inside and grabbed Mother Rosa's portrait from the mantel before crawling into the fireplace. She struggled since the frame barely fit through the secret tunnel. She grabbed the metal box with the photos and papers and walked deeper into the crypt. As she struggled with the large frame and heavy box, she allowed her mind to wander. Underground, everything should be safe. Brisa still felt confused and paralyzed by the recent events, because everything had happened so quickly and strangely. When she found a nice, little nook, she stored her treasures.

Climbing back out through the fireplace, she darted into the yard and searched for Rogelio. Again, the yard was empty. No Rogelio. Now, she was worried. Brisa had not seen him since she had passed out at the ruins. She sat on the bench and allowed the wind to caress her face as her mind drew blank.

She had left this place without any thoughts, theories, or resolutions. It was as if she were a robot and her software had just crashed. Between her heart and soul, nothing remained except an empty vessel. Brisa stood and walked over to Carlitos' car. She sat in it like a prisoner that was giving up. After a few minutes of driving, she stepped out and walked to the lodge. Nothing felt important anymore. Why should she care what happened next? And besides, what could she do to change anything? Whatever she decided to do would only turn to chaos and negatively affect her and those she cared about. No, she would simply allow Angela to place her wherever she wanted.

Just like a criminal tired of escaping, Brisa was tired of running. She entered the room at the lodge, and Angela was standing near a window. When Brisa walked in, the woman turned and looked … what? Agitated? Sonia glared at her, and the look of her eyes just about summed everything up.

"Why did you disappear?" Angela asked, flailing her arms through the air. "We want to help you, but you have to stop this craziness. You probably need more help than I can provide. Still, you're coming back to the city with me … today!"

"We've looked for you everywhere," Sonia said.

Angela's phone rang. "Angela here … yes, the demolition is imminent."

Brisa felt like a beaten-down dog. With her tail between her legs, she whispered, "Angela, with respect to the demolition … why did you make that decision and not include me?"

"Brisa!" Angela yelled out. "You're not up for this!" She turned back to her phone conversation. "I'll call you back." Angela glared at her. Her eyes were saying more than Brisa cared to know. "You're off the job. You need rest. You're putting yourself in danger, and I'm the one having to protect you. This protection is a distraction, and not just for me but for everyone."

Brisa sat on the bed and wiped away a tear.

"You'll be back soon enough. But since you can't stay at the mansion, you'll remain in my apartment until you're better. The ruins will fall any minute now."

"Why? Why the hurry?"

"Forget it!" Angela screamed and then shrugged. She smiled and walked over to Brisa. With her voice softened, she added, "Don't think about work. Relax. Now is when you need my help the most. Not work help but personal help. Mental help."

"Angela?" Brisa frowned. "There's more going on …"

"No!" Angela stepped back and laughed. "You just need to get your strength back. You've experienced something horrible. Sonia?"

Sonia startled and took a step forward. Obviously, she wasn't paying close attention to their conversation.

"Stay with Brisa. When she's ready, help her put her things in my car … please. I'll be right back."

Brisa had, once again, lost everything that was important to her. Picking up the remote, she turned on the TV and closed her eyes. Perhaps something would be on that could entertain her or clear her mind. At least the TV made some noise. Noise that would block out her thinking.

A young female reporter looking distraught stared into the camera.

BREAKING NEWS

"The kidnapped daughter of Sebastián Salguero is still missing. The police have not been able ..."

Cami? The poor girl was still in danger. Sebastián had to be completely out of his mind by now. Was it a ruse? Would Sebastián hide her at the ranch for such attention? A strategy to divert everything to the girl to gain time for his legal battles? No, Sebastián would never play with his child that way. His daughter *was* his whole life. Cami was such a happy-go-lucky and loving child. Brisa watched and tried to figure out how she could help. How could she do something for Cami? She was not in the best of spots to help, but then again ... Glancing over at Sonia, she frowned.

It would probably be best to just stop resisting and do what Angela told her to do. Rest and get better. She turned off the TV and her tears fell. Instead of wallowing in her self-pity, she stepped out on the veranda. A loud voice grabbed her attention. Angela was downstairs and yelling into her phone. As she stepped closer to the railing, she peered over and listened.

"Pay no attention to Cami!" Angela shouted. "That girl has a huge imagination. Pablo ... you're allowing her to manipulate you!"

Brisa stared out at the horizon and frowned. *Pablo has Cami? Pablo, the mayor, and Angela kidnapped Cami? Why?*

"Remember," Angela said. "She knows the man, but I know him better. Believe me when I say that Sebastián will agree to everything that we're demanding, all because of the child ... our child! He's convinced I don't have her and that I'm just as worried as he is." Angela glanced around.

Brisa took several steps away from the railing.

"Remember ... I was the one talking to him when you performed the drama about Brisa's kidnapping. Everything's fine. I have everything under control."

Brisa's mind flew through all the possibilities. Her reality had just faded from a bad dream and reappeared as a complicated nightmare.

"Sonia is keeping tabs on Brisa," Angela said. "Her help has been vital. I'll give her a bonus for her troubles."

Brisa's heart was beating so loud that she feared Angela would hear it. Angela had known all along where Cami was and who had her. What else was Angela hiding? Suddenly, she understood. Angela had hand-picked Brisa to run the project because she believed she was a pushover. Because of her drinking problem, she was seen as easy to manipulate and not capable.

Brisa sat on an outside chair and rubbed her stomach. The knot she was feeling was growing. What could she do? Thank God she had never disclosed her intimate relationship with Sebastián to Angela.

Breathe, Brisa, breathe.

Brisa had to tell Sebastián. When Cami's words echoed through her mind, *"They say my mom doesn't love me ..."* she accepted the fact that it was time to do something. Perhaps something brave and foolish ... *but what?* Come on, Brisa, you can do this.

A warm light descended through the clouds and gently caressed her face. It was the same warmth she had felt when that ghostly woman carried her to safety.

She entered the room and sat on the bed. She allowed her mind to flow through everything that had recently happened. Just before two plus two equaled four, Angela entered.

"Brisa, I've arranged everything."

"I haven't taken her stuff down yet," Sonia interjected.

Angela shook her head. "Sonia will follow us with your things. Let's go to my car."

Brisa studied Angela as they walked. The woman was very good at lying. What was she up to now, and how deep was Sonia a part of it? Sonia walked silently behind Angela, but it was obvious that her mind was someplace else.

Many livid scenes reminded Brisa as to when a person experienced a life-or-death situation. Perhaps these emotions explained why Sonia was acting so strangely toward her lately. Then the hundreds of texts between Angela and Sonia flashed before her eyes and she understood.

Angela really despised Sebastián. In a way, it was almost an obsession. And ... she *was* fighting a custody battle. Angela never said who her child was or who was the father. But now, Brisa solved the mysterious equation. Angela was, indeed, Cami's mother.

When Brisa glanced over at Angela, she saw a whole new woman. But why didn't Angela tell Brisa who was who? And ... how could a mother kidnap her own daughter? Was all of this ... *everything* ... just for that damn project, or was something more dark and more deadly happening around her? Angela had already hidden Cami, so why was she now including Brisa in her little game of hide-and-seek?

Once dedicating herself completely to the project, Brisa had fallen into a void that blinded her to what was really going on. If she had not been so focused on Sebastián, would she have figured it all out earlier?

And then there was Sonia. Why hadn't Sonia told Brisa about the relationship between Angela and Sebastián? Sonia *was* the one who had told her he was handsome and wonderful and ... why hide stuff? Brisa slapped her forehead — *I'm so damn stupid!*

They stepped up to Angela's car. It had seemed to take only a second but was enough time for Brisa to run the recent events through her mind.

"I need to pick up some things at the mansion," Brisa said. "They're personal and I can't leave them. I'll be quick. Pick me up in an hour?"

Angela nodded and grabbed her phone.

CHAPTER XIII

As Angela walked back inside the lodge, Brisa ran as fast as she could to the mansion. She wanted to get away from Angela and Sonia and call Sebastián. Each time the phone rang only his voice mail answered. Brisa tried several more times before finally giving up.

"Sebastián!" Brisa yelled out to no one. She ran up the hill, and when she stopped to catch her breath, José walked over.

"I'm sorry, Brisa." José blocked her. "Even if Angela did give you permission, I have strict orders from the engineer not to allow anyone in."

"I don't need any damn authorization from any engineer!" Brisa pushed past José and shoved open the door.

"These are orders!" José shrugged and waved his arms through the air.

Brisa entered and nodded. The incriminating documents were well-hidden and safe. Apparently, everyone was looking for them, and Sebastián was still not answering. Those documents were meant for Sebastián and Cami, no one else.

"Damn, Sebastián, where are you?"

Angela's car flew up the road and skidded to a stop only a few feet from Carlitos. After a few, brief seconds, the woman aimed for the mansion. She was coming after Brisa.

Brisa crawled into the fireplace and climbed up the bricks as Angela's footsteps echoed through the now-empty mansion.

"Brisa!" Angela yelled out. "I'm here to pick you up!"

Her footsteps pounded through the different rooms. When all quieted, Brisa figured that the woman must be on the second floor. After a few more minutes, Angela yelled out again.

"Damn it, Brisa!"

The front door slammed and everything silenced. Brisa remained hidden inside the fireplace. She shifted through the small tunnel and climbed down the brick stairs. She made herself as comfortable as she could inside the crypt. The next time she checked, two hours had passed. She climbed back up and entered the fireplace. When she crawled out, she sighed. The house was now dark. Again, Brisa tried Sebastián's number. Still no answer.

She had to find him, but how could she leave the mansion without being seen? Brisa darted up the stairs and glanced out the bedroom windows. She almost yelled when she spotted her car. Someone had returned it and parked it by the mansion. But why was it parked so close? It would have been destroyed during the demolition.

She ran down the stairs and exited through the servant's quarters. Standing outside in the dark, her skin crawled. Inching her way along the house, she sighed when she reached the far end. Her car was unlocked, and the keys were in the ignition. Glancing over at the old nun's quarters, she smiled. "Thank you, Mother Rosa," she whispered.

The car started and she drove out through the back entrance since not many used this route. After a few miles, she took in a deep breath. It was time to think. Where could Angela have taken Cami? She tried to remember everything she had experienced over the last several months — emails, voicemail, and sticky notes or writings on whiteboards. Angela was hiding Cami so Sebastián would believe she'd been kidnapped. Unbelievable.

The main road was deserted, and she drove with no destination in mind. She passed the lodge, and a woman ran into the street. It was Sonia. At a red light, Sonia jumped in front of the car, blocking her way.

"Brisa," Sonia yelled. "Stop! We need to talk." She stepped up to the driver's window with tear-stained cheeks. "I need to explain. Will you listen for just a moment?"

Brisa looked straight ahead. "Another day, perhaps."

"Please, Brisa —"

"You betrayed me!"

Sonia pounded on the car. "Brisa! You were ill. You were acting weird. Please … let me in, and I'll tell you everything!"

Brisa glanced away and sighed.

"Please?"

"Fine!" Brisa pushed on the door locks.

Sonia ran around the car and hopped inside. With wide eyes and a large frown, she whispered, "She said she was doing everything to help you …"

The light turned green, and Brisa pushed on the gas pedal. "Help me?" Brisa repeated. "Now who's the crazy one?"

"You were acting out of it." Sonia wiped her eyes with her shirt. "Angela asked me to watch you and report everything you did back to her … and only her. She said she was worried and wanted to help. Then, I noticed something."

"Something with me?"

"No, with Angela. Her attitude seemed off. Did you know that Angela is Cami's mother?"

"I figured that one out already. Why didn't you tell me?"

Sonia stared into her hands and another tear fell. "I only found out a few days ago myself. I had no idea. When Cami suddenly went missing … well, that was when I put two and two together. And …"

"And what?"

"There's something else."

Brisa frowned and stared out the front window. "I'm listening."

"I believe that because of me, you were kidnapped."

"What?" The road crested a small hill, and the vast ocean filled their view. Brisa followed the car in front and soon entered a small parking lot. She turned off the engine and looked at Sonia. "Let's walk."

They stepped out and Brisa locked the car. An empty boardwalk and pier seemed like the perfect place to talk … privately. The sand sucked at their feet with each step, and the cool breeze felt somewhat calming.

"I handed you over to Angela that day. I betrayed our friendship."

"What do you mean?" Brisa asked.

"You said you were desperate and I told Angela. She took the opportunity and ran with it."

Brisa stopped and glanced down. A small critter ran across her foot before digging itself deeply into the sand. She sighed.

"Remember when I invited you to dinner?"

Brisa nodded.

"She was the one who told the kidnappers to wait for you on that road."

"What? What do you mean?"

"Are you even listening to me? Angela and Pablo were the ones who ordered and paid for your kidnapping!"

"Why? What for?"

"To blackmail Sebastián."

Brisa shook her head. "Blackmail Sebastián? That's just crazy." She stepped onto the boardwalk, and the aging planks creaked with each step. The old railing, faded from time, felt rough and cold. The ocean breeze again caressed her face, and she wiped her eyes. Together, they walked to the end of the pier. All remained quiet except for a few gulls that were arguing over a newly caught fish.

"They were negotiating with Sebastián for the land."

"I know that." Brisa sighed again.

"Sebastián was close to giving up. Was ready to walk away from the project and sell you the land for the back road to the beach."

"Really?"

"Yes, really. Sebastián was doing it all for you! He was the one who was negotiating the trade for your life. Wanted to give the kidnappers what they wanted, just for your release. That's why I left you alone at the lodge that day."

"I don't understand."

"I lied to you, Brisa! I didn't need to go to the bank."

"Then what were you doing?"

"Checking in with Angela. She made me so mad that I returned to tell you the truth, but you'd already left." Sonia's eyes filled with tears, and she used her hand to wipe them away. "Sebastián was upset that he couldn't track you with your phone."

"The night I returned, the mansion was filled with police and investigators. Was that a farse, too?"

"No." Sonia shook her head. "That was real. The police *were* searching for you. However, Angela and Pablo provided the detectives false clues. The police would never have found you if you hadn't escaped. Sebastián agreed to all their demands, just for your life. He's in love with you, Brisa."

Brisa's heart and soul cracked as the wind stroked her face. The thought of Cami flew through her mind and her stomach tightened.

"Angela and Pablo are holding Cami," Brisa said. "I overhead Angela talking on her phone to Pablo. We *have* to rescue her. I have to find her for Sebastián."

"We have quite a mess to clean up." Sonia sighed and shrugged.

"It's Pablo who's hiding Cami. He's from around here and knows the people he can buy."

Sonia rubbed her eyes. She stared out at the water and frowned. "Cami is probably at his studio. It's soundproofed."

"He took me there after dinner." Brisa shrugged. "Damn, I'm so stupid. He told *me* it was soundproof. Oh my God!"

"You're not the only fool who's ever slept with a lowlife, yah know."

Brisa laughed and shook her head.

"Pablo's as evil as Angela," Sonia said.

"Not really." Brisa shrugged. "Just an opportunist."

"There may be a lot of bad blood in that man, but Angela ... now she's a practicing witch."

"There was witchcraft stuff in the catacomb. I saw it."

"This is not good."

"What about Cami?" Brisa wiped her eyes. "Can we save her?"

"I can get us inside Pablo's studio," Sonia replied. "We just need a different car. Yours is too obvious."

"We'll take both cars," Brisa replied. "I'll park down the street. Cami doesn't know you. But she'll come to me."

"Okay, then what do I do?"

"You distract whoever is holding her," Brisa said. "That way, I can take her to my car."

"I know the housekeeper. She sells cosmetics through a catalog. I've bought from her before. I'll knock and when she comes out, I'll place an order and act confused. I can even fumble finding my money."

"Sounds like a plan." Brisa sighed and glanced up at the heavens.

Sonia rang the bell, and the lady answered through the intercom. Sonia backed down several stairs and waited. When the lady stepped out, she left the front door half opened. Sonia pointed at the catalogue, and the lady stepped out a little farther. The stairs didn't have a railing, which gave Brisa an idea. She crept along the building, and when the lady looked completely absorbed in her conversation with Sonia, she snuck inside. Cami was playing with a couple of dolls on the living room floor. Brisa walked up to the child with her finger over her lips.

Cami eyes brightened and she nodded.

"Are you okay?" Brisa whispered.

"Just bored," Cami whispered back. "Mom's punishing me."

"I can take you to your dad. Would you like that?"

Cami nodded.

"You'll have to come with me and do exactly as I say. Can you do that?"

Cami nodded again.

"You know I'm not a stranger? And that I'd never hurt you."

Again, Cami nodded.

"Would you like to bring your dolls?"

"Yes."

Cami didn't seem afraid. It was as if she were used to such things happening. Brisa texted Sonia and told her to, somehow, get the lady to go to her car. Sonia replied with, "*K*."

Cami followed Brisa to the front door. Brisa peeked out and the lady was looking at something on Sonia's backseat. Sonia was yelling at her.

"It's no good!" Sonia said. "I tried it and it didn't work. I want my money back!"

"You're not using the product correctly," the woman said, placing her hands on her hips.

Brisa guided Cami by the hand, and they inched along the house behind the bushes. When they reached the car, Brisa sat her on the backseat and fastened her seatbelt.

"Can you lie down?"

"Why?" Cami asked.

"It's a game I'm playing with Sonia, my friend."

Cami rested her head on the seat and laughed. "Like this?"

"Exactly, now don't move." Brisa started the car and pulled away from the curb. When she stopped for the light, she honked once and waved. Sonia glanced up before going back to arguing with the woman.

Brisa drove straight to the mansion. Cami looked confused when she parked between the tall bushes.

"I need you to trust me."

Cami nodded.

"Just do as I say, okay?"

She nodded again.

The place was empty. No workers and no furniture. Brisa glanced at her watch, and within a few minutes, Sonia drove up.

"Phew, that was close," Sonia said, giving Brisa a quick hug.

"Too close." Brisa nodded. "We need to hide Cami until I can find her father."

"In here?" Sonia asked.

"No, follow me."

They crawled into the fireplace and Sonia giggled.

"Cami," Brisa said, "we're going into a secret passageway. I'll carry you. But you need to hold onto me like you're a baby monkey. Can you do that?"

"Is this a magic chimney?" Cami asked.

Brisa nodded. "Yes, a magic chimney."

They climbed up the small ledge and scooted into the square passageway. After maneuvering down the narrow stairs, they entered the crypts. Brisa carried Cami and she clung on as instructed. Sonia didn't say a word. They sat down inside the darkness near the portrait of Mother Rosa. Brisa's heart pounded and her mind whirled.

"You *do* keep secrets," Sonia said, giggling a nervous laugh.

Brisa just looked at her. "You're safe here. Cami, do you know the person in this portrait?"

Cami nodded. "It's Mother Rosa."

"Yes. The Mother will protect you until I return with your father. I need you to stay right here with Sonia. Okay?"

Sonia hugged Cami. Brisa stared at the old painting and took in several deep breaths as Sonia's phone dinged.

"Angela?" Brisa whispered.

Sonia nodded. "There are twelve missed calls from her."

"Turn it off to conserve the battery and to shut off the location tracker."

"It's stuffy in here." Sonia looked around. "Is it safe?"

"There's fresh air coming in from those vents. Take Cami over to one every now and then. But don't talk. Your voices will carry. I don't want you exposing yourselves. It's safer if you just stay put. There's enough oxygen, it's just stuffy. And no matter what you hear, don't talk to anyone!"

"What's painted up there?" Cami asked, pointing up to the domed ceiling.

"An old fresco," Brisa replied, glancing up. A little light from one of the vents allowed for a hint of the beauty that was displayed above them.

"They're roses," Cami whispered. "Red roses … the Mother's favorite."

Brisa flashed her light up at the ceiling. Cami was right. The ceiling was covered in faded roses.

"Wow," Brisa said. "But stay here. I'll bring water back. Tell Sonia about your stamps and the other objects of Mother Rosa's that you've collected."

Cami laughed.

"But whisper." Brisa nodded and so did Cami.

"Where are you going?" Sonia asked.

"To the school," Brisa replied. "I must stop the demolition. And no matter what you hear or see, do not move from his spot!"

Brisa walked up to the grid of the old school. It was dark but she didn't want to use her phone light. The library light was on, and harsh voices echoed out. People were arguing and it sounded like a rather heated debate. One person was definitely Pablo. Brisa couldn't make out what he was saying. The other voices she couldn't recognize. She shrugged and aimed for the fireplace. Once outside, she ran to the boarding school. She slowly opened the school's door, and the explosive engineer stopped her.

"I'm Brisa Murillo, lead architect for this project." She flashed him her ID and kept walking.

"I'm sorry, Architect. I do not know you. You cannot enter. We're waiting on orders from Angela Gaitán to detonate."

"Angela is not in charge, I am. I hired your firm, not her. You work for me. And I give the orders. Right now, I order you to stand down until further notice."

"But Angela ..."

Brisa held up her hand. "I will handle Angela. And I order you ... do not detonate!"

The man nodded and pulled out his phone.

"And don't talk to Angela! I will."

As Brisa walked toward the library, Pablo's deep voice echoed out through the halls. Several people were standing around arguing. Angela's voice rang out the loudest. It was hard to understand exactly what they were saying.

Brisa tiptoed closer and slid along the wall. She glanced into each room to ensure she was alone. Stepping into the library, her heart pounded. A large column hid her from Pablo and Angela. It looked like they were yelling at someone who was sitting on a bench. She could just barely make out the top of a head with dark, curly hair.

Angela was more than angry. Brisa knelt and inched her way closer. Now, she could see what they were doing by looking at the reflections in the windows. Angela and Pablo were pointing at Sebastián, whose hands were tied behind his back. Pablo held a gun to Sebastián's head, and Angela flashed around a pistol. Sebastián's eyes were wide, and Brisa could almost taste his fear.

"Sign, Sebastián!" Angela yelled. "Sign if you want to see your little girl again!"

Sebastián's sighed. "I can't sign. My hands are tied."

Angela screamed. "Mr. Salguero's acting like the perfect nephew. Taking care of his paraplegic uncle. I don't know what's more pathetic. You and your puppy love for Brisa or your fake dedication for your uncle." She laughed an evil laugh.

Sebastián glanced over at the window and frowned.

"Your little love interest is nothing more than a drunk, and she's being just a little too nosey these days. Snooping around and asking questions that are none of her business!" Angela laughed again. "And you! Stupid guy falling for her like that. Incredible! I didn't see that one coming." Angela's eyes reddened as her scowl grew. She paced across the floor and continued to flash the pistol through the air. "You always rejected me. You could have had it all. A home and the lands that your uncle had fought so hard for. I wasn't asking for that much from you. I gave you our daughter!"

Sebastián shook his head. "Your father did every evil things that my step-grandmother desired. Then, he wanted the land that was just not his to own. This place is *my* family's legacy."

"Lady Delfina inherited it all when your grandfather died. And *she* promised the land to *my* father!" She yelled out the words. "Besides, your uncle can't enjoy any of it. He's nothing but a damn cripple. You never cared for him before. Why the sudden change of heart?"

"It was you and your father who gave my uncle those drugs. It was probably Lady Delfina's idea, so she could sign everything over to your father as his guardian. Only problem? My uncle outlived your dad. And now, me and my daughter are the only living blood relatives."

Angela released the safety of the gun.

Sebastián shook his head. "Keep it all. Enjoy it! I hope that someday you'll think about Cami. At least once before you die. I don't want any of the money or properties. I just want full custody of our daughter and legal guardianship of my uncle."

"Sign … now!" Angela pointed the gun between Sebastián's eyes. "Sign over the land and *without* conditions!"

"Calm down, Angela." Pablo stated. "Let's do this … calmly. We'll have our life together, just like we always wanted. But let's use reason here and not be impulsive."

"What?" Angela turned on Pablo. "You said these stupid peasants want Sebastián as their mayor. You want *him* in power? He'd turn everyone against us. We must disqualify him, once and for all!" Angela pushed Pablo away and turned back to Sebastián. She took a step forward and hit the gun across Sebastián face. Blood ran down his chin. "Falling in love with a stupid bitch who can't even take care of herself. She did design the plans, I'll confess that much. And her work is good, but she's no good for anything else!" Angela laughed. "Know why I hired her? Because … she's a puppet. Someone I can use for *my* purpose. And now it's all over." Angela screamed and pushed the gun against Sebastián's forehead. "What was her goal, huh? I'll tell you. You were her goal … Sebastián Salguero! I underestimated that bitch. Even Pablo here was flirting with her." Angela now pointed the gun at Pablo who took several steps backward. "Our relationship is one of convenience, isn't it, Pablo? No love. Just convenience." She sighed. "I'm still surprised by your nerve, though."

"I never loved you, Angela," Sebastián said. "I've always been sincere about that. Not to mention, you're no good for Cami."

"You've always loved me, even if you won't admit it!" She screamed out the words and pushed the gun harder into his forehead. After hopping a little on her toes, she stepped back. "Sign and you can keep that brat all to yourself. Renounce everything and never come back here. Take your lovely Brisa with you. But you'll need an insane asylum. Great taste, Sebastián. And … I want the documents you stole from this school. Everything having to do with Lady Delfina and my father. I don't need any nasty rumors floating around."

"What documents?" Sebastián asked.

"If we had married, all of this would have been ours. Instead, you ruined everything and now you'll die by your own gun. Do you want your daughter or not? Give me those damn documents that incriminate my father … and sign this now!"

"I don't have them."

Angela pushed the pistol into Sebastián's neck.

"I don't have them, Angela. I'll help you find them but give me back our daughter first!"

"Let's not complicate matters, Angela." Pablo said as he wiped his forehead with his handkerchief. "He'll sign away the mansion and the ruins, and we'll give him his uncle and the girl. No one will investigate your father. I'm in power and I'll take care of things."

She ignored Pablo and raised the gun back up to Sebastián's forehead. "The documents … now!"

"I have them," Brisa said, taking a step out from behind the pillar. "Angela … leave Sebastián alone."

Angela swerved on her heels and pointed the gun at Brisa. Pablo, looking confused and afraid, flashed his gun between Brisa and Sebastián.

"Shouldn't you be in a drunken stupor by now?" Angela waved the gun toward the bench, indicating that Brisa should sit down next to Sebastián.

Brisa didn't move.

"You had no business in any of this." Angela sighed. "You're just a damn fool. A huge fool. Were you not tortured enough after being kidnapped that you had to show up here, now?" Angela laughed. "We bartered you like a cheap piece of furniture. In the end, you became valuable as this idiot's treasure." She pointed the gun back at Sebastián. "A ranch that runs from the highest peak of all the land down to the endless sea. That's the price we placed on your pretty, little head. And this cretin here fell for it all. Was willing to give it all up and just for you!"

Angela crossed her arms and glared at Brisa. It was obvious that the woman was losing her mind. Angela paced across the room several more times before saying, "The only thing you had to do was stay drunk, Brisa! Not hard for you, is it?" Angela glared at her. "Now, I have Cami and she's worth much more than this land or the ranch. She's now worth the documents and your uncle." Angela glared at Sebastián. "Am I clear? Or must I repeat my words!"

"I don't have any documents," he replied.

"Do you realize how pathetic you look? Forsaking it all for the love of a drunk? Willing to leave it all behind for this … this … slut? You're an idiot." Angela walked around the room and every so often glanced over at Brisa, as if calculating her next move.

"Again," Brisa said, "I have the secret papers. Found them under the floor in this school."

"So, *you* have the papers?" Angela pointed the gun at Brisa. "Interesting. You have the papers … Pablo has Sebastián … and I have Cami." Her voice crackled as if an aged witch were talking. "What would be the best trade?" She glanced between everyone as if mentally filing through her options.

Brisa chuckled.

"What's so funny?" Angela asked. "I find nothing funny about any of this!"

"I also have Cami."

Sebastián's face instantly relaxed. He smiled and shook his head.

"You're bluffing!" Angela yelled. "There's no way." She glared over at Pablo before adding, "You'll never see her alive again, Sebastián! I will kill you both and be done with it."

"Angela!" Pablo shouted. "Calm down!"

"Better yet …" Angela stepped up to a boarded-up window and tried to look out. "You will remain in here and die in the explosion. More romantic that way. Don't you think? The workers are awaiting my orders. Buried under the rubble. Just like Mother Rosa or that famous bitch, Sara."

"Angela, take it easy." Pablo's eyes were begging her. He wiped his forehead again, only this time, his hand shook. "We don't have to kill them. Let him sign and they'll leave."

Angela pushed Brisa toward Sebastián. "Here is your breeze of alcohol!" A noise from the hallway grabbed Angela's attention. She paused as she tried to see what it was.

"The engineer will not obey your instructions anymore," Brisa said.

"José will," Angela replied as another noise echoed in from the corridor.

"Who's there?" Pablo asked as the gun shook in his grip.

Brisa sat next to Sebastián and smiled. "Cami's okay," she whispered. "She's in a safe place."

His eyes softened and he nodded.

Angela and Pablo ran to the door and glanced into the hallway. Sebastián played with the ropes, and when they fell to the floor, Brisa giggled. He kept his hands behind his back and smiled.

"Sign and let's get this over with," Pablo said but his voice sounded softer.

Angela pushed the gun into Brisa's head now and laughed. "You will both die soon. Give her a farewell kiss, Sebastián." More noise and footsteps echoed in from down the hall, and Angela flashed the gun around the room. Her eyes now burned red with anger.

Pablo shoved his pistol into his back pocket and stepped into the hallway.

"Want a drink, Brisa?" Angela laughed. "You'll never marry Sebastián. I'll never allow you to get an inch closer to *my* daughter. You've been in my way for too long already." Angela pointed her gun at Brisa's head. "I'm done with you!"

After rushing back into the room, Pablo reached out for Angela's arm, and a loud boom blasted through the air. Angela's gun slid across the floor as she pulled her hand to her chest. Blood stained her blouse, and she screamed out.

Sebastián jumped up and rammed into Pablo who fell backward. Now *his* gun slid across the floor toward Sebastián who kicked it into the hallway.

Another loud boom and Brisa glanced around, trying to figure out what was happening. Who had the guns, and who was shooting who?

Sebastián jumped on top of Pablo and pinned him to the ground. Angela ran over and picked up her gun with her good hand. She pointed it at Brisa, and as her fingers tightened around the trigger, a soft click sounded and another loud bang scorched the air. Angela collapsed to the ground and gasped. Blood pooled around her and her eyes widened.

"Hands up!" Marta's voice echoed out from the hallway.

Sebastián froze on top of Pablo, trying to raise his hands.

Marta stepped in flashing a detective badge. "Judicial Police!" Marta stated. "Pablo Mencos and Angela Gaitán, you are both under arrest!"

Angela held her stomach, as tears filled her eyes. Sebastián crawled over to her, and she whispered something that Brisa couldn't hear. Angela then spat at Sebastián and screamed out, "I hate you!"

Several uniformed officers darted in from behind Marta and pulled out their handcuffs.

Angela held up her phone and screamed out, "Blow it, now!" Fear filled her eyes as she yelled out, "José … blow the place up … please!"

"No! You'll kill us all!" Pablo shouted the words as his hands were pulled behind his back.

Brisa ran to the window and waved at José. "Ignore Angela's orders," she yelled.

José nodded before turning his attention back to several police officers.

Sebastián walked over and hugged Brisa. "You, okay?"

Brisa smiled.

"Marta," Sebastián said. "Brisa has my daughter. She's safe."

Marta holstered her gun and walked toward them with a smile. "Brisa, I don't know whether to congratulate you or admonish you. You've complicated things quite a bit. I believe you know that now." Marta shook her head.

Paramedics arrived and placed Angela on a stretcher.

"She's still breathing, Marta," a detective said. "Your aim was not off, after all."

Marta shrugged.

CHAPTER XIV

Brisa awoke feeling tired. She crept down the stairs of the lodge and glanced around. A couple of officers were talking and enjoying a cup of coffee as Marta and Sonia entered the lobby, both wearing large grins.

"What a day!" Sonia said, accepting a cup of steaming brew from an attendant.

"Yes." Marta glanced over at Brisa. "I knew you were a good person. Just didn't know how good. So, tell, me … what will you do when you return to the city?"

"Not sure yet."

Marta accepted coffee from the attendant and smiled. "There will be an official investigation of PROE S.A. Those responsible will be charged for their illegal dealings." She blew on her coffee before taking a sip. "We know you have nothing to do with the inner workings of the company, however, you'll still need to be prepared to answer questions and make a statement."

"And Pablo?" Brisa asked.

"Held on charges of kidnapping, obstruction of justice, corruption, fraud, abuse of power … just add to the list. Sebastián will follow up on the legal process as a Herradura. The lands are a family affair. Thank God you were able to put a stop to their plans. Without you, the ruins and buildings would have been destroyed, and any legal rights forever lost. But there's still a lot of work to be done."

"How's Angela?" Brisa asked.

"Out of surgery," Marta replied. "Lost a lot of blood. Doesn't look good. She hasn't awakened yet. Could be some brain damage. Hit her head pretty hard when she fell."

"Sorry to hear that," Brisa replied.

"Such a shame that it had to get to this point." She took another sip of coffee. "I wanted to avoid another shot, but she was ready to shoot you. How's Cami? Does she know?"

"Sebastián took her home. Poor, little thing." Brisa draped her arm over Marta's shoulder. "Thank you. You probably saved my life."

"I've got to go," Marta said. "Still need to find the documents to see what really happened in that boarding school."

Brisa's tears welled and she couldn't hold back her sobs.

"Why are you crying?"

"Thinking of Cami," Brisa whispered. "She's only a little girl. I never really knew my mother. Sebastián was both mother and father to her. She needs his attention now more than ever. Do you know what she knows about her mother?"

"Cami never knew she was kidnapped," Marta said. "She just thought she was being punished for something."

Sebastián walked in and sat on the couch. He pulled off his hat and leaned back.

"Any news?" Marta asked.

"The mayor's assistant was just arrested," he replied.

Brisa wiped her eyes. "How's Cami?"

"Fine. I told her that her mom was sick." He grinned.

"Not a complete lie," Brisa said.

"She's at the ranch. She'll be safe with my people."

"Sebastián, I found the documents that were hidden at the school." Brisa glanced at Marta. "I hid them until I could figure out what was going on."

He smiled. "I thought you were a step or two ahead of me."

"I hid them from you both. I thought Marta was up to something sinister, and I just didn't trust you. Then, when Cami was taken, I tried to call you but you never answered … I didn't know you were busy with Angela and Pablo."

"I need to get something from my car," Sebastián said, standing.

Marta and Brisa sat on the couch and waited. Sebastián returned with the photos and loose papers he had taken from Brisa's trashcan. He held up a photo of one of the novices.

"This was Sara," he said.

Brisa studied the photo. A beautiful blonde, very young looking, stood next to another young girl that was shorter and a bit stockier. Both wore the habit of a novice. Brisa turned the photo over and read the words, "Sara and Conchita, Novitiate Servants of the Crown of Thorns, 1961."

"Sara was Uncle Juancho's one true love. I wish to tell him the truth of what happened to her before he dies. He's lived all these years, longing and suffering for her. He never heard from her once she went missing. I want to bring him the truth, so he can die with peace in his heart."

"The documents may be relevant for the investigation," Marta said.

Brisa darted up the stairs and gathered the material she had kept a secret. When she returned, Marta smiled. Brisa handed her the binder and the green, metal box.

"I believe this is what you've been looking for. The treasure."

Marta laughed and her golden tooth twinkled in the sunlight that had entered through the large front windows.

"This is valuable, Brisa!" Marta glanced through the material, looking rather excited. "I'll reopen the investigation into what really happened at that school and convent. This is exactly what we were looking for. The legal, accounting, and private records of the girls."

Sebastián nodded at Brisa and smiled.

"Look at this!" Marta said. "Dates of the entrances and exits of each girl from the school, the convent, and the monastery. Dates of the babies' births.

A veritable treasure trove!" Marta gathered up the material and nodded before walking out the door.

Brisa sat next to Sebastián and rested her head on his shoulder. She glanced up at him. "You never told me about Angela. That she's Cami's mother ..."

"I wanted to tell you. But you didn't want to hear me out. You ran away ... remember?"

"I'm sorry about that," Brisa whispered.

"I felt it important that you discover Cami for yourself and not through the lens of her mother." He sighed. "I didn't put any of this together right away. I honestly didn't know that you two were working so closely. Then when we ... well, let's just say that I didn't want to bring any toxic feelings I had for Angela into *our* relationship." He sighed deeply. "Bringing Angela into our relationship would have only darkened the scant moments we shared ... you and me."

"They were scant," Brisa replied.

Sebastián sat up straight. He placed his fingers gently on her chin and turned her head toward him. Their eyes met and he smiled. "The last time I saw you, my intentions were to tell you everything. I wanted to bring you up to speed about Angela and what she was capable of. You were upset and I understood, but I was too." He shook his head. "I've been a brute toward you."

Brisa looked at him tenderly. His eyes were trying to explain what his words couldn't. Brisa hugged him. "I fear that Angela will never leave us alone. If she dies, and if what Marta says is true, even from the grave she'll haunt us. I hope she recovers. I'd rather fight her in the courts than in the catacombs."

"She'll never hurt you ... hurt us," he corrected. "I promise."

They walked outside and aimed for the mansion. The air felt warm, and the aroma of fresh roses seemed to touch the air. It was good to walk in the morning sunlight with Sebastián. Marta was still hanging around the convent, which made Brisa chuckle.

"That woman's tireless!" Brisa's phone dinged. "It's Marta. She wants us to make a statement at the police station tomorrow."

"Don't see why not," Sebastián said, taking Brisa's hand in his.

They sat on the bench just outside the big house. After a while, Marta walked up and sat next to them. They stared out into the distance without talking. There was so much to say, however, no one said a word. Marta held the knowledge, Sebastián held the hope, and Brisa held the fear — and no one took the initiative.

After a few more moments of awkward silence, Brisa spoke. "Marta, if Mother Rosa founded this convent, and now she's a saint, how could such terrible things have happened in the sixties? Wouldn't she have stopped it somehow?" Brisa glanced up at the bell tower and frowned.

"Mother Rosa died many years before that. A couple of centuries, in fact. When Lady Delfina married Sebastián's grandfather, it was his second marriage. That woman wasn't all there," Marta pointed to her head and frowned. "She was obsessed with purging all non-religious activities from society."

"Why?"

Marta shrugged. "She started off by buying the trust of the convent with generous donations. Then, she found a few nuns who had strayed from the true path of God. Women available for a price, let's say. Lady Delfina was a part of high society at that time, and she opened a boarding school for rich girls. She promised the parents that she would reform their daughters ... let's just say that she moved right in."

"How could anyone fall for such a thing?"

"If your children are involved in premarital relations of the scandalous type ... not hard. The goal was to reform the girls and return them to society properly re-educated ... or ... educated to Lady Delfina's standards." Marta laughed. "Unfortunately, things turned wicked and no girl ever returned home."

"Wow!" Brisa whispered.

"Disastrous abuse of young, pregnant women. Women who were stolen from society and their families."

Sebastián sighed. "There was talk of human trafficking of the girls' babies. A full investigation should be done. Angela's father was a key player. Too bad he died. But we still should know what really happened to those newborns. I hope you get to the bottom of it all. Maybe we'll find out who Sara was and where she ended up."

"We'll do what we can," Marta replied. "The case was opened in the sixties, and given Lady Delfina's over-reaching power, the investigation went nowhere. That woman bribed anyone who'd reach out their hand."

"I want to see any evidence you find," Sebastián said.

"Of course." Marta nodded. "What Brisa found in that school should help. Mother Rosa is a saint, and when the Vatican finally canonizes her, this town will fall back to her teachings. If only we could find her original writings. I've searched everywhere." Marta frowned as she gazed deeply into Brisa's eyes. "If we're able to excavate underground ..." — Marta sighed — "we'd probably find the vestiges of the original convent. The one that was Mother Rosa's —"

"Where *are* her writings?" Brisa asked.

"They were lost in a major earthquake. When the original convent was buried," Marta replied. "Now, they're passed down by word of mouth. I can only share what I've gathered so far and it isn't much. Remember the picture of Mother Rosa with her notebook and rosary that has a rose engraved in the beads?"

"Yes."

"Well ..." Marta glanced across the yard. "By the way, where is the painting of the Mother?"

"Hidden and safe."

Marta sighed. "Thanks for keeping it safe. I'll make arrangements to ship it to the cathedral. I was worried about the demolition." Marta smiled. "Brisa, you have the rose tattoo. Maybe you'll be the one to solve the mystery."

Sebastián nodded. "We need you, Brisa …" He smiled now. "I know many of the underground passages, however, there are many that are still hidden. You have an architectural background. We'll probably need geo-radar equipment."

Brisa didn't reply for she didn't know anything about her life at that particular moment. Her world was nothing more than a whirlwind of happenings. She stared at the photo of Sara and Conchita. "Conchita!" Brisa whispered. A memory flashed briefly through her mind. Selena's aunt, the witch who said she was once a nun … was there a relationship there? Her heart pounded. Brisa stared at Sebastián and frowned. "Come with me."

"Where?" he asked.

Marta stood and nodded. "I'll catch up later."

Sebastián opened the neck of Brisa's blouse and ran his finger over her birth mark. "I always thought it looked like a rose." Sebastián smiled.

It felt to Brisa as if he wanted to kiss her but was holding back. "Please, come with me. No time to waste." Brisa placed the photo of the novices into her bag. "We're going after answers." She pulled out her phone and clicked on Selena's name.

"Yes, miss?"

"I need to see your Aunt Conchita," Brisa said.

Sebastián pulled on her arm. "Brisa, leave it for later. We have too much to talk about. The ranch and Cami …"

"No!" Brisa shook her head. "You must come with me now."

"My aunt is sick and not giving appointments," Selena replied. "My mom says she is dying."

"I would not ask if it were not very … very important."

Selena sighed.

"Please, ask your mother."

Time was not moving as the two sat in Sebastián's car. He talked on his phone, and Brisa watched the birds. Her phone rang and she jumped. It was Selena, and she was waiting for them. Sebastián looked serious, although he had no idea where they were going.

"This way," Brisa said, walking into the humble and aging building.

Sebastián glanced around and frowned. They climbed the stairs and entered the small apartment.

"What are we doing here?" Sebastián whispered. "You should rest. You've been through so much. I'll take you to the ranch for a few days … clear your head."

Brisa smiled and ignored his comment. She walked solemnly behind Selena as they entered Conchita's room.

"She's awake, although a bit feverish," Selena said.

The room was plastered with candles, photos, and various statues of saints. Selena pulled two chairs next to Conchita's bed.

The old woman's voice was weak, and she spoke with a whisper. "My daughter. I've been waiting for you."

"Hello, Conchita." Brisa glanced at Sebastián to make sure he was still paying attention. He was frowning but listening.

Conchita extended her shriveled and wrinkled hand and Brisa grabbed it. "The horseshoe and the rose." Conchita laughed. "You're here, together at last!"

Was she referring to Sebastián? Herradura did mean horseshoe.

"Juancho?" Conchita whispered.

"No, Conchita," Brisa said. "It is not Juancho. It's Sebastián Salguero."

"Is Juancho alive?"

"Yes," Brisa replied.

"How do you know of my uncle?" Sebastián asked then whispered to Brisa, "Who is this woman?"

"You are a Herradura," the old woman said, staring at him. "You are Lucía's son. Juancho was her brother."

Sebastián nodded.

"Juancho and I could never die without finding you, Brisa." Conchita's voice cracked. "I swore to deliver you to him. He's been waiting for so long. Another of Mother Rosa's greatest miracles is finally fulfilled."

Sebastián sat back and grunted. "I don't know what we're doing here. This poor woman is senile."

"This is Sara's diary." Conchita waved at her niece who handed Brisa a small and aged notebook. "She always kept one. Take it with you, my daughter."

"Thank you," Brisa said, glancing through it.

"She wrote in it since we were novices at the convent. I kept it safe for you, Brisa." Conchita took in a few deep, raspy breaths. Selena helped her to take a sip of water.

"Don't talk anymore, my aunt," an older woman said, stepping into the room.

Brisa stood to leave, and Conchita grabbed tightly onto her hand. "I do not have much time." Conchita's eyes widened.

"I'm here," Brisa whispered.

"Lady Delfina discovered that Sara was pregnant with Juancho's child. She did everything she could to stop the birth."

Sebastián sat up straighter.

"Sara was forced to become a nun and to remain hidden inside that convent. That girl was a prisoner. Never allowed to venture outside. Juancho was told that Sara decided on her own to take the vows."

"I'm listening," Brisa whispered.

"I met Sara at the convent. We became friends. We were both assigned a new destiny. Isolated and alone, we were living in a prison disguised as a school. A place for girls who dishonored their families." Conchita coughed. "So many pregnant girls died in front of me. Many never laid eyes on their babies or ever looked into a clear, blue sky again. The parents were told that their daughters took the vows or had left town."

"What happened to the babies?" Brisa asked.

"Smuggled into Mexico."

Brisa looked over at Sebastián and he nodded.

"True," he whispered. "Rumors of illegal adoptions ran wild through my family."

"Were you pregnant, too?" Brisa asked Conchita.

"No, my sins were much greater. I preferred women to boys. A mortal sin back then. My punishments were tougher and more painful. I fell in love with another woman. Society expelled me. My time there was tougher than Sara's. It was only much later that I learned how the other girls had suffered a pain worse than death."

Conchita's breathing became labored.

"Conchita," Brisa whispered, "we can return another day. You should rest."

Conchita shook Brisa's arm. "We made plans to escape when the opportunity presented itself. At noon and six, they would ring that bell for prayer. Two times a day, we stood inside that chapel. We hated that bell!"

It still rings at six and twelve.

"Our rooms were underground. Sara and I communicated through the walls. We planned our escape that day, and exactly at six, the bell rang and the ground shook. When the nuns ran, Sara screamed out with the first contraction. She was ready to give birth. She was too large and could not fit through our escape hole in the wall. I tried to pull her through. I tried so hard!"

"How sad," Brisa said.

"The shaking stopped and someone grabbed Sara. No one ever saw me. Then another tremor hit. The nuns took Sara away. I waited and listened. The lights went out, and terrified voices echoed throughout the night. I felt horrible for leaving Sara behind.

"I heard the cries. Cries from Sara's room. She screamed and screamed. She was delivering her child. The nuns ran around as if a wildfire had spread. Someone yelled that the baby was a girl. *'Cell number twenty! Call the midwife!'* I knew the baby would soon disappear and I felt powerless. I fell to my knees and prayed to Mother Rosa for help. But the moans and cries just kept coming! Then, a long silence. I thought they both had died. But then I heard someone say that the baby was alive ... an angelic voice I had never heard before."

Conchita's breathing looked painful.

"Someone asked if the infant was dead. They ordered more candles, hot water, and clean cloth. I snuck into Sara's room when the nuns left. Sara lay on the floor ... bleeding ... oh, there was so much blood. Sara grabbed my arm and begged me to take the baby away. She wanted me to give the child to Juancho."

"My God," Brisa whispered.

"I wrapped that little package inside a pillowcase. Sara pointed to her diary, and without saying another word, I ran with that baby and book. The ground shook again, only stronger. I kept falling as the dirt and rocks surrounded me. I ran to our escape hole and the baby cried. Those tremors never stopped that night. As the building collapsed around me, I snuggled the baby inside my arms and tried to protect her. Then, I gave myself up to Mother Rosa. Someone touched my arm and helped me up."

"Who?" Brisa asked.

"It was a mist. A white shadow that felt benevolent ... peaceful. It led us through the falling rubble. Reminded me of when the Red Sea opened up for

Moses. I followed that mist with Sara's baby in my arms. To this day, I swear that my feet never touched the ground."

Selena placed a wet cloth on Conchita's forehead. The other woman signaled for them to leave. They stood but Conchita sat up and yelled.

"Wait!"

Brisa turned.

"Rogelio lived nearby and helped me. He hid us in his house. His mother took care of us. The baby was a girl … a girl with a special, little birthmark on her chest. It was in the shape of a rose." Conchita coughed and fell back on her pillow. "The rose birthmark matched the one on Sara's neck. Brisa, you are Sara's and Juancho's daughter. Mother Rosa saved you for a purpose. Once I laid my eyes upon Mother Rosa, I could no longer see. I had become blind. Find Mother Rosa and Sara. They are calling for you!"

Brisa took several steps toward the door and paused. Her mind twirled and her heart pounded.

"The Horseshoe and the Rose!" Conchita yelled out. "The Horseshoe and the Rose … the Horseshoe and the Rose …" Conchita's voice softened and she closed her eyes.

Selena's mother walked up to Brisa and whispered, "Best to leave her to sleep."

"I'll stay with you, mother," Selena said.

Brisa stared at Sebastián and he frowned. They walked down the stairs without talking.

He opened the car door and she slid in. When he started the car, he glanced over at her.

"Can we trust what this woman is saying?"

"It was a long story, how else would she know all of it unless it was true. If I'm Sara's and your uncle's daughter, then I'm your … cousin?"

"You've met the dark side of Antaño … the criminal side. All types of evil. Who knows what her intentions are."

"Conchita is dying. No need to lie."

"You? Sara's daughter? You're not even from here. You're Mexican."

Brisa sighed and shook her head. "Sebastián … I was born in Antaño."

"Are you serious? How?"

Brisa glared at him.

"I don't mean that."

"I know Rogelio," Brisa said. "He works on the project."

"This is such foolishness. Are you going to believe what that old woman was saying? I don't want to be disrespectful with people's beliefs, but we must apply common sense here. How would it be possible that you know someone named Rogelio?"

"It sounds ridiculous, and yes, it's almost impossible, but …" Brisa stared out the window. "I do have the birthmark on my chest."

"We need a break. Let's eat and talk. We need to absorb this."

Brisa thought about her experience with Mother Rosa and how she helped her to escape. Sebastián, of course, would never believe her story. When they parked at the mansion, Sebastián received a call. Brisa left him alone to heat up the left-over dinner.

As they ate, Brisa couldn't stop thinking. Although it seemed crazy, too many strange things had happened recently to not make her believe. Events she couldn't ignore. Sebastián, however, was more skeptical. Would Conchita use such a story for money? Mother Rosa had helped Conchita to escape just as she had freed Brisa from the kidnappers. But how could she be Sara's daughter? Was it even possible for Sara to be her biological mother?

They finished their meal and Sebastián stepped outside. Brisa joined him and they walked toward the school and convent.

"You don't believe her, do you?" Brisa asked.

He shook his head. "You do? That would make Uncle Juancho your father. For God's sake, Brisa! That's ridiculous. I respect the stories about Mother Rosa, but this is just too much." They stopped at the school doors, and Sebastián placed a hand on her shoulder. "I'll investigate this once you're settled at the ranch. When you're safe. Marta will want to know about these stories."

"This will make us ... cousins!"

"I don't believe it. I'm a practical man." He stared out at the horizon and the setting sun.

"You may be right," Brisa whispered, "but I need a glass of wine."

Brisa woke late. Pushing herself out of bed, she noticed that Sebastián's hat was on the chair next to her bed. The memory of sleeping together and making love until the wee hours of the morning gave her a moment of reflection — their love making had become more of an instinctual reaction than a real love. Perhaps he was guarding her as she slept. A noise grabbed her attention. She walked down the old mansion's stairs as voices echoed up from the living room. Sebastián and Marta were near the fireplace.

"Brisa?" Marta asked. "Feeling better?"

Selena handed Brisa a cup of coffee. Brisa nodded to Marta.

Sebastián's eyes looked full of questions. Had he told Marta about what happened at the old lady's house?

"I'm sorry I took you to see Conchita yesterday," Brisa said.

"You don't believe in God or Mother Rosa?" Marta asked. "You have said that many times, but the story that Sebastián just shared merits an investigation. He mentioned that Conchita gave you Sara's diary?"

Brisa nodded. "Supposedly, Sara was my mother." The two stared at Brisa and shook their heads. "I do have the rose-shaped birthmark." Brisa touched her chest. "Perhaps these are stupid thoughts after all."

"Marta!" Sebastián's eyes widened. "As a homicide detective, you don't believe these old stories, do you?"

"Everything's important in an investigation, Sebastián." Marta shook her head again. "Everything."

Sebastián's grunted and stepped away.

"There are many things that we'll look into. The diary for one. Brisa, will you permit me to make copies of it?"

"Of course," Brisa replied.

"If any of this were to be true, and if it is found that you are in fact Juancho's daughter, you might want to consider ... he is still alive." Marta turned to Sebastián and nodded. "There's always the paternity test."

Brisa walked to the stairs and stopped.

"Where are you going?" Sebastián asked. "If it's true, then you'll be the true heir of Uncle Juancho's estate. Why don't we find out for sure."

Brisa's eyes filled with tears. Tears of frustration. New parents, new lands, new inheritances, and a life that pointed in the direction of a great loss. The hope she held that they would be together tomorrow had simply vanished.

"I'm going to pack," she yelled down. "Do what you feel is best. I'm leaving. I don't want to mess up any more lives ..."

She thought about Rogelio. He could help clear things up. Brisa turned and walked back into the living room.

"I want you to meet someone ... Rogelio."

"Where?" Sebastián asked.

Brisa ran out the front door and up toward the old tree. Marta and Sebastián followed. Rogelio could explain about Sara and the truth behind her birth. Sebastián would see that she was not demented and imagining things. Then, she would be able to talk about her experience with Mother Rosa. After that, she would enter herself into a treatment center. Brisa reached the old tree and there was no Rogelio.

"Rogelio!" she screamed out. "Rogelio!"

The old man was nowhere to be seen.

Carlitos stepped out of his car and ran up to her. "Architect!" Carlitos yelled out. "Thank God you are okay. I can't believe everything that has happened."

Brisa smiled and nodded. "Thank you, Carlitos. Have you seen Rogelio?"

"Who?" he asked.

"You know … the old man that's always walking around. Do you know where he is? The old guy?"

"Old guy?" Carlitos repeated.

"Yes, the old guy. He sometimes shows up here drunk," she said, frowning.

"Rogelio who?" he asked.

She glared at him. "Marta, surely you've seen him. He walks around here every single day."

Marta looked at Brisa and frowned.

"Carlitos?" Brisa stared at him. "Rogelio! He's here every day."

"Brisa, we do not have a Rogelio on the payroll."

Brisa was at a loss for words. She looked deeply into Carlitos' eyes and frowned. "No Rogelio?"

Carlitos shook his head.

"Go to the ranch and rest," Marta said, now shaking her head.

Carlitos sighed and turned. He walked away nodding.

"I want to go to rehab," Brisa said.

Sebastián sighed. "You just need rest."

"I'll leave you two alone." Marta gave Brisa a hug and shook Sebastián's hand. "I'll be in touch."

Sebastián glanced into the sky and sighed again. He grunted a few times before saying, "I'll take you wherever you want to go." His eyes lowered and he smiled. "Please, may I ask for just one favor?"

Brisa nodded.

"Spend a few days at the ranch. Cami wants to see you, and you can get to know Uncle Juancho."

"I would like to see Cami," she replied. "But then, I enter rehab."

They stood together in silence. The church bell rang. It was noon. The message of the bell was loud and clear. Brisa looked over at the ruins and thought of Mother Rosa. *I know what you need of me.*

"I'm being pressured to run for mayor," Sebastián said as he maneuvered the car down the road. His voice sounded flat.

Brisa waited for him to say more … to tell her more, but his workers were talking to him over the radio. She stared out at the horizon and thought about the last time she drove down this road alone. Angela had sent her to look at the land, and she had made love to Sebastián at Camela Ranch.

Over the last few weeks, so much had happened. Brisa saw an apparition of Mother Rosa, and she had overdosed on alcohol and pills, she endured the horrors of being kidnapped, was thrown about in an earthquake, and talked to an old man that no one else could see. She needed help, and a rehab center was the best place for her.

During her last trip to Palmas Rojas, she had been trying very hard to please Angela and reach an agreement with Alberto for the benefit of PROE S.A. It was strange how life had turned everything around in only a short couple of weeks. Angela was now lying in a hospital bed and could possibly die, and Brisa was seeking out a rehab center. Despite everything bad that had happened, she had unmasked Angela and that felt incredible. Although she had feared the woman as a boss, she now feared her as an enemy. Even when the woman was unconscious, Angela frightened her, for the woman was capable of anything. How could Angela hate her enough to actually kill her?

Then Pablo flew into her mind. What a dangerous ride on a carousel he was. Those two flourished inside a very strange and twisted relationship.

The landscape was changing, and the beautiful flora had turned somewhat tropical. Brisa thought of Cami and how much she wanted to hold her. For some odd reason, they held something special between them. Brisa wasn't sure how or why since she was never any good around children.

Sebastián's phone rang. "Yes?" His face paled. "When?" He stared straight ahead as he listened. "I'll be back tomorrow." A long silence. "Thank you." He looked over at Brisa and frowned.

"What is it?" Brisa asked not sure if she wanted to know.

"Angela … just died."

Brisa's mind drew a blank. She stared out at the flowers and frowned. "I'm sorry."

He squeezed her hand.

"Cami?" she whispered.

They didn't talk for the rest of the ride to the ranch. There was nothing else to say. Before stepping out of the car, Sebastián slid closer and planted a kiss on her cheek.

"I'll not telling Cami about her mother until after you leave. I don't want to ruin anything." His eyes looked sad and somewhat darker.

Cami ran to them, and they said their hellos.

"Time to meet Uncle Juancho," Sebastián said.

They walked together up to the small country house — a gorgeous log cabin.

"We fixed it up for him," Cami said. "This is where he likes to be."

"An old hunting cabin?" Brisa mused.

Sebastián smiled.

"Uncle Juancho loves to hear my stories," Cami said, "especially the ones about Mother Rosa."

"She spends time up here," Sebastián added. "Drawing and reading to him."

Cami ran into the cabin.

"Both are alone most of the time," Sebastián said, glancing at Brisa. "My girl and my uncle. I see so little of them."

They stepped onto the porch and stared at each other.

"The man could very well be your father, Brisa." He smiled. "I no longer know what makes sense and what doesn't."

Brisa shrugged and Sebastián stepped inside. He stopped and stared into her eyes. "It's just a DNA test," he said. "What have you got to lose?"

"You're not serious?" she asked. "You've worked so hard to convince me to be doubtful."

"I understand," he replied. "But after these last few months, I'm convinced that there's something else beyond this world. Something that is more than what we can see or hear."

Now, she wondered how much she could share with him. *I'm probably crazy anyway ... so why not?* "I saw Mother Rosa, Sebastián." She paused and waited for his reaction. When none came, she continued, "She was the one who helped me out of the catacombs. I won't pretend to try and convince you." She looked away. "I need help to stop drinking. You have no idea what I would give for one right now."

Sebastián nodded.

"Introduce me to your uncle?"

"I need you, Brisa," he whispered. "You're important to me. But ... I never thought you'd be the missing link that completes the puzzle. Please don't leave me ... us."

Her eyes filled with tears.

"You and I ..."

"Papa! Uncle Juancho is awake." Cami yelled out. "He's sitting up on his bed!"

"Sitting? On the bed?" Sebastián ran inside.

"Yes, Papa." Cami smiled. "Nanita and I made him walk a little."

Brisa looked at the man who had already relented his world to time. He was not as handsome as the man in the old photos, for life had definitely taken its toll. Now, only a small mixture of country elegance and class flared from inside his tired eyes.

Cami pulled on Brisa's arm. "A woman comes to see him," she whispered. "But don't tell anyone. It's our secret. Yours and mine and Uncle Juancho's. Okay?" Cami placed a finger over her mouth.

The girl's sudden statement came as an unpleasant surprise. Once again, Brisa was placed in a situation where she had to keep a secret. "Do you know who it is?" Brisa asked.

Cami shook her head. "She doesn't allow anyone to see her face."

"Tell me more about her later." Brisa smiled. "It's our secret for now."

Uncle Juancho sat on his bed, and his gaze focused on a scene only he could see.

Brisa knelt before him and smiled. "Hello ... Uncle Juancho?"

"This is Brisa," Cami said. "She came to meet you."

Sebastián took his uncle's hand. Brisa took the other, and a strange sensation flew up her arm and into her chest. She felt hot and her cheeks flushed, but she remained silent. Sebastián let go of his uncle's hand and moved to the chair next to the bed. Brisa did the same, except she sat on the bed.

Cami knelt in front of her great-uncle. "He's looking at me. He's really looking at me!" Cami gasped when Uncle Juancho squeezed her hand.

Sebastián's eyes widened. "Involuntary movements," Sebastián whispered. "That's what the doctors say."

Uncle Juancho closed his eyes and then opened them. It felt as if he had been praying, but the enchantment suddenly shattered. From a dark place deep inside, the urge to run overwhelmed Brisa and she stood.

"We can come back later," Sebastián said.

Uncle Juancho continued to gaze into nothing, as if unaware of life and all that surrounded him.

That night, the three dined at the ranch. No liquor was placed on the table, and Brisa didn't ask for any. They retired early. As Brisa headed for the guest room, Sebastián yelled out from his bedroom. "Brisa? Quick … come see."

Brisa entered his room and stared at the glaring TV …

"… the unexplained disappearance of girls from the Servers of the Crown of Thorns that shut down in 1962. Angela Gaitán passed away today. She was implicated as an accomplice to her father, Alvaro Gaitán, the atrocities committed at that school. The first investigation of Lady Delfina de Herradura was closed in the late sixties and …

Sebastián turned off the TV. "Enough of that," he whispered.

Brisa stepped closer with the intention of kissing him good night. He stepped forward and hugged her. Then, he kissed her on the forehead.

"Good night, Sebastián," Brisa whispered.

CHAPTER XV

Six months later

She finished drying her hair and stared at the reflection. Brisa was again a blonde. She smiled since she could now look at herself without judging, without doubting, without hating. Her face radiated with a freshness that felt empowering. She glanced at the paternity papers again.

```
DNA PROOF OF LEGAL PATERNITY
Laboratory results:
Child:          Brisa Murillo
Paternal:       Juan Ignacio Herradura
                Possibility of paternity: 99.9999%
Maternal:       Unknown
                Possibility of maternity: N/A
```

Within her eyes she could now see her father's. Since rehab seemed to be working, she believed it would be a good thing to spend a little time with her aging father before he reunited with her mother. The clock ticked and she sighed. Sonia would arrive any minute to pick her up, although, it did feel strange to have Sonia in her life again. She glanced around.

"This room will be missed."

She stood in the doorway and looked at the lobby. It felt like a graduation of some type and maybe it was. For the last six months, Brisa had crawled inch-by-inch out of a deep and darkened pit that had held her captive for so long. She read the sign that hung over the office door for the last time. At least, she hoped it would be the last time.

Lost Angels Center for Alcohol and Drug Rehabilitation

She was only a short five-hour drive from the ranch, but it still felt as if she were in a world far away from everyone. The rehab center was called *Lost Angels*, which matched her inner struggles — a city of solitude. Perhaps a few stray or stranded angels had helped the mortals to help her? And perhaps her mother was one of those angels — her real mother — Sara. After she read her mother's diary, Brisa understood how difficult her mother's life had been. And from the tarnished pages, she was able to absorb her strength. Her mother's words both comforted and saddened her soul before sending her the resilience she needed. And of course, Mother Rosa was probably the other angel.

Her phone buzzed. Sonia had arrived. Sebastián, Marta, and Sonia offered to pick her up. However, Brisa felt it'd be easier if only Sonia came. After all, Sebastián was busy working in his new position as mayor. Marta, of course, was busy playing detective. Not to mention, that having Sonia here made it easier to prove that she had forgiven her for her betrayal.

Brisa glanced at the graduation card from Sebastián and smiled — Mayor of Antaño. She still couldn't believe it. He wrote weekly and each time apologized for everything. During her six months of solitude, she used the time to reflect. There was just so much to figure out, discard, or accept. The drawings that Cami had sent that decorated her room had helped the most. Those drawings were the last things she packed. Brisa walked back into her room and sat on the bed. She glanced at her phone, and a light rap on the door grabbed her attention.

She stood and Sonia ran to her. They hugged without talking. Sonia picked up the teddy bear that had fallen to the floor and smiled. "Cami's?"

Brisa nodded before stuffing it back into her bag.

"You've gained a little weight," Sonia said. "You look … healthy."

"Thank you," Brisa replied.

"You're cured and now you can come home."

"Cured?" Brisa shook her head. "That term doesn't exist in the world of addiction. I will struggle every day for the rest of my life."

"You have so much to tell me." Sonia grabbed one of the suitcases.

"You, too." Brisa nodded. "I know nothing of what's happened back home. Aside from the letters, I'm in the dark."

"You start," Sonia said as they walked down the hall. "What do you want to know first?"

Brisa stopped by the office and said her goodbyes. A few tears fell, although it was wonderful to leave. Stepping outside felt odd and refreshing. The sun hitting her face warmed her heart but still chilled her soul. *Will I survive?*

"What happened with PROE S.A.? Any legal issues?" Brisa asked.

Sonia shook her head. "None. They questioned us several times. The whole mess centered around Angela and Pablo. Everything came out during his trial. So many times, we had to state that we were just doing our jobs … me, José, and Carlitos. The investors scattered and disappeared."

"Sounds typical."

"Angela was listed as majority partner for the land that she was trying to dispose, which would have happened if the courts had given her power of attorney." Sonia sighed as she placed Brisa's stuff in the trunk. "What irony."

"What's an irony?"

"The true investor was actually you all along. Funny how things turn around, huh? Who'd have thought?"

"I still ask myself how we never knew the kind of people they were," Brisa said. "I always felt that Pablo's involvement was not ethical but the rest? I guess Angela ran everything directly. She hid so much from us all."

"Yes, she did," Sonia replied, pulling away from the building.

Brisa glanced out the window and sighed. She felt free but also restricted. Now, it was up to her to make the decisions about what to eat ... what to wear ... what to drink ... "Angela's rush to demolish everything really bothered me." Brisa turned her attention back to their conversation. "Somehow, I knew something was wrong about the whole project. At first, I believed it was Marta." Brisa laughed.

"Why no visitors while in the clinic?" Sonia asked. "So many wanted to come and support you. Cami is very happy that you're coming home."

"I was not alone." Brisa stared out the window and watched as the buildings and people and trees passed. "I had roommates and mentors who were just like me. They understood what I was going through. And ... my mother was there."

"Oh?"

"I talked to her at night when the lights were out. And ... I had a great mentor."

"Oh? Who?"

"Mother Rosa."

"Mother Rosa? The nun?" Sonia looked over at Brisa and frowned. "Remember the apparition I saw in that old house? That beam of light really scared the crap out of me."

Brisa laughed.

"You knew that light was her. Didn't you?"

Brisa patted her on the shoulder. "Not really."

"Maybe it was." Sonia shrugged. "Perhaps lucky for us." She nodded. "Definitely lucky for you!"

"I've dedicated myself to writing about her teachings. I want to put them into practice. The program at the clinic relied heavily on spiritualism. Made me realize that I want to follow in Mother Rosa's footsteps."

"You want to become a nun?"

Brisa laughed and shook her head.

"You scare me sometimes. You know that don't you?"

"I want to *follow* in her steps. Not walk in them."

"Your handsome rancher wanted to rescue you on horseback."

Brisa laughed and nodded. "Are you still looking for a job?"

"After PROE S.A., I was so traumatized I could barely think." Sonia sighed. "I'm living in Antaño now. Fell in love with that cobblestone town. And … José."

"José?" Brisa shifted in her seat and raised a brow. "Tell me."

"He's in Mexico right now but should return soon. The whole project was canceled. Unemployment has its ups and downs." Sonia glanced at Brisa and frowned. "Do we still want to demolish something?" Sonia laughed. "I could order the explosives. We could continue with Antaño Heights."

Brisa took in a deep breath and shifted again. She glanced out the window and sighed.

"The plans and the land are yours …"

Brisa shook her head and smiled. "Have you been back to the boarding school?"

"Yes, and the town restored it. It's beautiful. What's left of the convent is still there. Carlitos is the architect for the municipality now."

Brisa smiled.

"You're needed there. So much to be uncovered."

"I'm sure there are many hidden secrets inside those crypts. I need to talk to José."

"Why?" Sonia frowned.

"Tell him hello … don't want to destroy or knock anything down. Well, nothing besides my pride," Brisa said. "I want to build. Mother Rosa dedicated her life to helping women. Her mission was … *is* … women suffering from domestic violence." Brisa glanced away. "I don't want the Herradura inheritance."

"You are a Herradura!"

"I only want the school."

"Why?"

"To rebuild Mother Rosa's dream. I want to establish a center for all women … based on Mother Rosa's teachings. It will be a religious retreat. I contacted the congregation of the Servers of the Crown of Thorns in Mexico. I've invited them to tour the ruins. If I can return it to what it should have been … in honor of the Mother, of course."

"I'd love to work with you on that. What a delight. I'm interested."

"Look, Sonia, the ocean!" It was a wonderful and awakening sight. Not seeing or smelling the ocean breeze for six months was torture.

They drove in silence down the coast. During the quiet times, Brisa reflected upon her relationship with Sebastián. He insisted that she spend a little time with him at the ranch. In his letters, he constantly reminded her that they were family. The dissonance of that word, *family*, threw her for a loop, and at the same time comforted her. Besides, she had nowhere else to go. Sebastián and Cami were, in fact, her only family now. Over the last six months, they only discussed the DNA results once. The other letters were about him accepting the mayorship of Antaño, or Cami and her obsession with Mother Rosa.

"I've gotten to know Alina better," Sonia said, pulling Brisa from her thoughts. "She's crazy over Sebastián."

Her comment slapped Brisa across the face so hard that she had to touch her cheek. Was she gossiping or trying to make her lose interest in her religious aspirations? Brisa swallowed but didn't reply.

"If you go all nun-ish on us, you'll be delivering Sebastián to her on a silver platter." Sonia sighed.

Listening to her talk made Brisa's head spin. She leaned back and closed her eyes. Sonia's words ran into one ear and never out the other. Instead, they bounced around inside, attacking her nerves. Her mentor at the clinic said to take it easy with life and relationships … baby steps. To jump back into her old ways could push her into a relapse. They also suggested to stay away from any romantic entanglement. For a few years, at least. According to the clinic, she was vulnerable in her heart, mind, and soul.

Sonia hit the brakes and pulled over to the side of the road. Dust surrounded them as the car skidded to a stop.

"What's wrong?"

Sonia stared at Brisa and her face paled. "I just saw Mother Rosa sitting at that bus stop!"

Brisa sighed.

"A strange light was shining on just her! I swear it." Sonia's phone rang and she jerked back. Shaking her head, she said, "It's Sebastián. Must be for you."

Sonia handed Brisa the phone. It was a video call.

Brisa tapped the talk button and said, "Hello." She watched as Sonia's hands shook. "Want me to drive for a while?"

"Brisa?" Sebastián handsome face filled the screen. "Everything okay?"

"Yes, Sebastián, thank you. On our way. Not far. Can't wait to see you and Cami."

"You changed your hair. Blonde? You look …" — He glanced down and grinned — "… pretty."

"No hair dye at the clinic." Brisa shrugged.

Sebastián's beautiful coffee-colored eyes lit up. "Crazy down here with the elections in Antaño and the inauguration scheduled at City Hall. Really crazy."

"I'm happy for you, and the city needs you … Mayor of Antaño …" Brisa laughed. "Are you happy?"

Brisa turned to Sonia who was staring out the window and taking in several deep breaths.

"Don't like the politics or bureaucracy, to be honest … just don't like people." He grinned. "My parents built us that ranch in Palmas Rojas. Always loved the coast."

Brisa smiled. Sebastián seemed interested in talking to her. "I miss Cami. And … an opportunity to return to where I was born. You'll make your daughter proud of her last name."

"Brisa," he said. "Everything'll be fine. We have a lot to discuss. I'll try to return home soon."

"Cami and I will be okay. Take your time with that City Hall stuff."

Her chest tightened. For the first time in her life, it felt as if she really belonged to a family. Then at the same time, it was a great loss, giving up Sebastián's romantic love. A love similar to the one Sara and Juancho had shared. Maybe Mother Rosa would help her begin a new life without his love and devotion.

She handed Sonia her phone. "I saw that nun, too." Brisa smiled. "It was just a religious woman. Probably a novice waiting for the bus. We could have offered her a ride. But between slamming on the brakes and the phone …"

For the rest of the ride, they talked about ghosts and where their lives would lead them. Time passed and they soon arrived at the ranch. Brisa stared out at the setting sun and sighed. Cami ran up and anxiously handed out hugs. She had grown so much during the last six months. It saddened Brisa a little for things had changed.

They watched the recordings about the inauguration of the new mayor, and Cami praised her father. Brisa enjoyed just seeing his handsome face again.

"We'll begin conservation of Antaño," Sebastián said to the reporters, "… and my priority during my term is to rediscover our traditions … our heritage. I want to make our home a special town. We'll preserve our history and culture and bring in the tourists. Antaño will be restored by principles on which it was founded and as Mr. Francisco de Herradura would have wanted. We will do honor to our future title as World Legacy of Humanity."

A beautiful woman stood next to Sebastián. As the woman beamed with pride, Brisa's heart broke.

"Look," Cami said, pointing to the screen. "That's Alina … my dad's liar."

"Lawyer," Brisa said, correcting her.

The program was short. When a local documentary about Mother Rosa flashed across the screen, Brisa couldn't move. The program discussed recent miracles after her beatification twenty years ago. The announcer discussed the possibility that the canonization could take place during the visit by the Holy Father in a few years.

"Cami," Nanita said, tugging on Cami's arm, "time to sleep."

Cami and Brisa spent many hours visiting with Uncle Juancho. Brisa tried calling him Papa, Father, or Dad, but it was difficult. She read him Sara's diary and emphasized the passages that explored their love, omitting the painful parts about her birth. A few times, she thought she saw a small smile when she showed him photos of Sara, her mother. When she showed him her rose birthmark, his eyes would widened and he'd nod.

Brisa gave Cami most of her time. They talked or rode horses, and Cami would tell her stories about her mother. Cami would sometimes draw while Brisa's father stared into the distance. Their favorite place was on the log cabin's porch. From on top of that the hill, it seemed like the ocean continued on forever. Brisa felt at peace sitting only a few feet from her father.

A week into her stay, Cami ran into the cabin. "My Papa is home! My Papa is home!"

Brisa held the girl's hand as they walked together toward the ranch house. Several cars parked out front gave Brisa her first clue that more than just Sebastián had arrived.

"Go to your father, Cami. I'll be in shortly."

Brisa was in no hurry to see Sebastián. She was still feeling vulnerable and unsure of her reaction. Too many months in rehabilitation were spent on introspection, and this was just the beginnings of a new path. A path for her to control, not someone else. She remained out front and stared at the beautiful ranch. A home that Sebastián's father had made for his wife and two sons. A place where she could escape and be far away from her evil stepmother.

Brisa slowly climbed the steps and stood at the opened front door.

"Brisa!" Sebastián walked up and planted a kiss on her cheek.

It felt wonderful to see him, although the meeting also felt tense.

"Come in," Sebastián said. "I'll introduce you."

Sebastián walked Brisa around to various strangers who were members of his team or local politicians from neighboring towns.

"Marta's busy and unable to come," Sebastián said, "but she sends you a hug." Sebastián held on tightly and kissed her forehead.

A stunning redhead, who she had seen many times with Sebastián and Cami, stepped forward.

"Alina," Sebastián said, "this is Brisa."

"Pleasure meeting you, Brisa," Alina said. "I've heard so much about you."

Alina stared at Brisa as if she would challenge her or something. Instead, Brisa ignored her and followed Sebastián around the room. She nodded to those he introduced her to. Everyone seemed to be enjoying themselves, however, Brisa felt uncomfortable.

Wanting to be alone, she let the cook know she would eat in her room with Cami. As she headed for the stairs, Sebastián stopped her.

"Brisa," he said, "I need you."

"What?"

"I have plans for the old convent, the one founded by Mother Rosa. I need someone to work the excavation. So much is underground that must be uncovered. Your professional knowledge will help. We have expert archaeologists, but it's not the same. These are delicate structures. I need someone to inject passion and a dedication only you can provide."

Brisa stared at him and couldn't answer. Her stomach cringed and her chest pounded.

"I don't have time to go into everything right now," he said. "So much to clean up at City Hall first. You have no idea. The Ministry of Culture needs a capable person like you. Marta was just a plant. Part of the judicial police."

Brisa frowned. Her mind refused to grasp what he was saying.

"I need *you* in charge of the project," he said. "You're perfect. Imagine digging out the secrets buried under the ground. All to be presented before Mother Rosa's canonization. What do you say? We would be working together." He shook her shoulders and smiled. His eyes widened.

"Sebastián," Brisa whispered. "That work is for the archaeologists." Brisa looked away. "There is no us. We never should have … besides, I need about six months to finish *my* project."

"What project?" he asked. "Are you building something?"

"No, I'm compiling Mother Rosa's teachings. I desire to publish a book about her and rescue her doctrines. Record her miracles and honor her life. I've felt her calling to me. Sara had heard her calling, too. Sara, my mother. I believe she stayed at the convent under her own will. I don't want to yield to the temptations that led me to confusion and chaos as before."

"Desire?" he asked.

"There are many abused or abandoned women who need a better life." Brisa sighed. "I want to put into practice Mother Rosa's teachings. I want to dedicate my life to her to help girls as Sara once did. Maybe become a novice and allow myself to be guided by my mother and Mother Rosa. I've already spoken to the Mother Superior of Mother Rosa's congregation in Mexico."

"Novice? You've got to be kidding."

"I'm not kidding, Sebastián. I wish to experience the time of novitiate to determine if I want to move forward and dedicate myself to our Lord."

"You mean … to wear a habit? A nun's habit!"

Brisa nodded. "To take the perpetual vows." She was surprised that she had said anything. Brisa wasn't sure herself if she were at that point in the considerations. Sebastián stared at her and frowned.

"Come, Sebastián!" Alina stepped up and handed Sebastián a drink.

He stared at Brisa and frowned again. "I'll leave you in peace. Do whatever makes you happy."

Brisa sat on her bed and stared out the window. It was late and she couldn't sleep. After the noise died down, she snuck downstairs and walked onto the porch. She needed some fresh air. Sebastián was sitting in a rocking chair and looking up at the dark cabin.

"Where's Alina?" Brisa asked, sitting next to him.

"Everyone went to bed."

Brisa looked up at the log cabin and smiled. "Deep down, I somehow sensed that my father was up there."

Sebastián smiled. "Somehow, I knew that you knew."

"I'm so sorry for all the trouble I put you through."

"Me, too. We both hurt each other. What if we start over?"

"You seemed a little overwhelmed in there," Brisa said, trying to change the subject.

Sebastián continued to stare at the cabin.

"Was she a witch?" Brisa asked.

"Who?"

"Angela?"

"I don't know. She was interested in the occult." He laughed and shifted in the chair. "She threatened me several times with a curse. Does that count?" He laughed again. "I was beginning to believe that maybe she was." He looked at Brisa and frowned. "Those last words that Angela whispered to me after being shot …"

"When you bent over her?"

He nodded. "Said that Cami wasn't my daughter."

Brisa gasped. She had heard something that day but couldn't quite make out the exact words.

"Paternity test?"

"Hell no!" His voice was stern. "Cami *is* my daughter!"

Brisa sighed.

He looked at her and scratched his head. "I have a lot on my mind. You're needed around here. There are family matters to attend to, and you're involved whether you like it or not. Many new projects now in the National Council for the Protection of Antaño. CONADA needs a person they can trust. I trust you. You can coordinate the activities with the archaeologist and excavations. I really need you here and not running off to some damn nunnery." He stared up at the cabin again and sighed. "Pablo confessed to some terrible things. Although, he was not here when Angela's father was working for my step-grandmother." He rubbed his head.

Brisa nodded.

"Angela would have been a little girl at the time. Pablo made her his accomplice when she turned eighteen, or maybe it was the other way around. But Angela's father was the right-hand man for Delfina in trafficking the newborns ... among other outrageous things."

"Yes, it's something all right. What was the goal of your step-grandmother?"

Sebastián laughed. "She was your step-grandmother too."

Brisa rolled her eyes. "Damn, hadn't thought about that."

"Just another religious fanatic. With her money and power, she could judge like a god. Wanted to reform society to her wishes. A true character from the old inquisitions. In reality ... she was a sadist. Incredible how she molded Angela's father to commit her crimes."

"Murders ...?"

He nodded. "Among other things, and how he brainwashed Angela to keep everything for herself and make Juancho an invalid."

"Sebastián … I need to talk to Pablo. In fact, I need to see him. Can you make it happen?"

He looked at her, and once again, his eyes turned a darker shade of gray. "I suppose … is it absolutely necessary?"

Brisa nodded now. "I have questions about the Herraduras, and he's the only person who'll know."

"I'll set up an interview." His voice had flattened.

Brisa felt the need to lighten things up a little. "Come with me to the cabin? I want to show you something."

"Uncle Juancho will be asleep."

"I don't believe so."

The small cabin was lit with a soft light. The boy who stayed with Juancho whispered, "He just finished his tea."

Brisa nodded and entered the room. Her father was staring out the window. He turned toward her and grinned. Brisa waved for Sebastián to watch.

"Who am I?" she asked Juancho. Brisa reached down and took his hand in hers.

Juancho's eyes watered and he smiled. "Sara," he said in a soft voice.

Sebastián raised his brows. "I've never heard him speak before," he whispered. "Uncle, this is Brisa … your daughter."

"Sara," Juancho repeated, pointing at the rose birthmark on Brisa's chest.

"Good night, Papa." She kissed him on the forehead.

Sebastián placed another blanket on the bed. They sat next to him, and the three being together as a family felt good … as it should. That night Brisa slept with a peaceful heart.

The following morning, Brisa was enjoying a soda on the porch when Sebastián and Alina returned from horseback riding. They were smiling and laughing.

"Good morning," Alina said, sliding from the horse and hurrying toward Brisa.

Sebastián held onto the horses until a worker came to fetch them.

"Brisa …" Alina said, using her sweet and syrupy voice. She pulled Brisa aside and grinned. "Brisa —"

Sebastián's hand grabbed Brisa's arm and pulled her away. Brisa nodded to Alina as they entered the house. A heated debate was being argued between the politicians.

"Brisa!" the governor said, waving at Sebastián. "Come in … let's talk. It's been confirmed about Mother Rosa's canonization."

"Yes," Brisa replied, stepping away from Sebastián. "We're planning on building her a place she deserves."

Cami ran over to Brisa and grabbed her hand. "And they'll find her whole and incor … incor —"

"Incorrupt," Brisa said, smiling. "That's the legend."

"How can people die and not turn to dust, Brisa?" Cami asked. "Is it a miracle?"

"I don't know." Brisa smiled at her. "Probably depends on how each person perceives it."

The minister of culture stepped forward and nodded. "It's incredible that a human body can remain intact for centuries. It would indeed be a gift from God if the body is still whole."

"Frauds!" Alina stated, stepping forward. "The work of charlatans and not possible. I don't want to be disrespectful, but —"

"And what do you say, Brisa?" The minister turned to Brisa and smiled. "You've walked those crypts."

"I'm not a scientist." Brisa glanced around the room. "However, perhaps if the nun's diet and fasting was just right, or the construction of the crypt and dryness of the climate? No insects or fat. Maybe there will be a scientific explanation … that is, if the body had not yet decayed."

A man she had not met stepped forward. "Good stuff to sell to tourists!"

"We can either hold the view that everything is a miracle," Brisa said, smiling, "or that nothing is a miracle."

Alina took a long drink of her beer and added, "I don't know. Sounds sinister and macabre to me. Reminds me of zombies or ghosts." Her air of smugness was starting to rub raw on Brisa's nerves. "Besides, no one has found anything … not Mother Rosa or a crypt. Just a glorified fairytale."

"But they will find her!" Cami stated firmly.

Sebastián stepped forward. "It's a shame that your trip must be cut short." His voice was so loud that Brisa almost laughed. "I'm happy that you were able to see my ranch."

"In an hour," Alina told Sebastián, gently touching his arm.

Brisa had had enough and walked outside. She shook her head as she headed to her father's cabin. She sat next to him and stared out the window.

After a few minutes, Sebastián entered and nodded. "Came to say goodbye."

Juancho looked at peace sitting by the fireplace in his wheelchair.

"Sebastián …" Brisa stood. "I believe I know where Mother Rosa's crypt is. I've been researching and —"

"You mean her coffin?"

She nodded. "I saw her. She spoke to me."

Sebastián took a step back and smiled.

"Don't look at me like that. I'm not crazy and I'm not trying to impress you."

He shook his head.

Brisa thought about Rogelio and how no one believed her when she went searching for him. Why was she the only one to have seen him? She had been drinking, however, he was so real. "Remember when I looked for Rogelio?"

"The man that hid you as a baby or the drunk by the tree?" Sebastián laughed.

"Very funny. So, I have an imaginary friend. Who cares?"

"You're a little old for an imaginary friend."

"Don't mock me. I'm not crazy. Behind the old fireplace in the mansion, I found a hidden catacomb. I'm fairly sure her mausoleum might be there. They haven't demolished the house yet, have they?"

"The mansion?" Sebastián smiled. "That house is yours, Brisa."

"Great, it'll become the center I want to open someday. A place for abused women."

Sebastián sighed. "I'm leaving and must pack. Alina's waiting for me."

She turned and walked toward him. "There's more."

"More?" he asked, not turning around.

"I've signed up for a contemplation. It's official."

He didn't respond.

"I'm now a candidate to become a nun."

He shook his head and sighed. "You'll never marry ... never have children ... no love ... no carnal relations. I admire your faith. Your family left Antaño and the church because of Delfina's fanatical beliefs. She used religion as a front for her outrageous actions. My dad raised me here at Camelia Ranch away from all that. I'm sorry if I cannot identify with your sudden change of heart."

"I must make amends for our relationship." Brisa stared at him.

He turned around and frowned. "Our relationship? You act as if it were a sin!"

"Sebastián! It's almost incest!"

"Alina must be wondering where I am," he said. "I'm leaving now. Let me know when you're off for your … contemplation. It'll hurt Cami." Sebastián turned and nodded to his uncle. "Goodbye, Uncle." He frowned. "Talk some sense into your daughter." He glanced at Brisa, and she could feel his anger. His eyes were now black and his lips tight and pale. "Write down where that crypt you're talking about is located. I'll have an archaeologist dig it up." He sighed again. "I've had it with this shit about nuns and holiness." He shuffled down the stairs and aimed for the house.

Brisa felt lost. She had tried to do what was right, but everything felt so wrong. Her crazy life was again pushing against the urgencies that her addiction carried. She ran to her room and cried. Looking out the window, she watched as the sun blared down and heated the earth. Brisa didn't feel warm, in fact she felt cold.

She sat in front of her laptop and flipped through the photos she had taken of the crypt where she had hidden the portrait of Mother Rosa. She glanced through a few articles about the Mother that she had found on the internet. Her heart yearned to walk again under that mansion, but her mind told her that she was being crazy. Her soul wanted to explore every nook and cranny of that vault while her mind desired to have nothing to do with it. The last time she was there, Cami had noticed that the water stains on the ceiling looked like roses.

She searched the internet and flipped through pictures of baroque structures found in the Americas — convents, monasteries, missions. Specifically, she searched for similar mausoleums and urns with similar reliefs. There was something very similar in Peru. It was a rectangular crypt with an engraved cross above a heavy granite tile. However, the image gave her no answers. She glanced out the window, and the sun was about to set. It was almost time for dinner, and she wanted to see Cami.

Brisa began her day with coffee in the kitchen with Nanita. Cami was still asleep. It was a time she enjoyed before the workers arrived, and the kitchen always seemed the most comfortable place to be.

"Is this my father's breakfast?" Brisa asked, examining the tray of food.

"Yes," Nanita replied.

"I'll take it." Brisa nodded. "I want to surprise him."

As she walked up the hill to the cabin, she spotted an outline of a woman wearing a long, black cape. Her pace was slow, but then again, she was moving fast. The woman's features were vague and dark.

Brisa's hands shook and her heart pounded. She stopped and blinked several times. The woman's outline was so clear. She was slightly hunched over, as if old or in pain. Along the hem of her cape was a rim of brown — *a scapulary?*

Whoever it was that was sneaking into her father's cabin, she had to confront them. Her legs felt heavy when she stepped onto the porch. She glanced inside. Her father was alone and still resting in bed. Brisa sat his breakfast on the table.

She could feel the woman's presence. Whoever she was, Brisa could almost see her from the corner of her eyes. The woman was sitting in her father's rocking chair. Brisa couldn't turn, not even her head. The woman walked … no, she floated toward her. As she moved closer — their gazes briefly met. The woman's cool breath brushed against Brisa's skin. *Will she float through me?* The woman was not a vision, or an ethereal apparition, or a white shadow. She was as human and as solid as Cami had said. Brisa turned at the last moment as the woman floated past and stopped near the end of the bed.

As the woman moved, Brisa could hear her tunic drag across the rough, wooden floor. The air felt suddenly cooler, and the woman seemed to shimmer in the morning light. What was holding Brisa in place … fear? She allowed her eyes to follow the woman. The nun grinned and Brisa's fear exploded from somewhere within. Her heart vibrated and she could feel it radiating throughout her body. Was this the same apparition that had saved her while inside the crypt? She was not a flash of light or a wisp of smoke. Whatever it was, it was definitely a woman made of flesh and blood …

The woman's nose was long and sharp and resembled the figure in the painting but with a slight and subtle difference — she was younger, much younger. Her habit dragged along the floor, carrying a dusting of dried grass with an aroma of stale musk. A white scapulary flashed out from under the brownish material. Her bare and soiled feet reminded Brisa of someone who had suffered a long pilgrimage from some faraway place. Around her waist hung a common frayed ribbon that was ripped and stained. Her cape puffed out as she moved. If courage had found her, Brisa would have run away or maybe have confronted the intruder. She wasn't sure which.

The woman floated toward the fireplace and stopped next to the old rocker. She turned toward Brisa, and her cold, dark gaze penetrated deeply into Brisa's soul. She wanted to face the woman, but an invisible force held her firmly in place. The woman's lips moved as if speaking, but Brisa could not hear a word. *What is she saying?* The woman lowered her head and frowned. Taking another step toward the fireplace, the woman reached out her hand before vanishing. No mist, no smoke … she was just gone.

Brisa took in a deep breath, and her body suddenly released. She fell hard against the floor and held back a scream as the old chair rocked back and forth.

Cami had seen her, too, she reminded herself.

Who was the nun, and what was she trying to say? Could that nun have been her mother? Were the people who once walked this earth sending her a message? Mother Rosa, her mother, and Rogelio were all talking to her, and she couldn't understand a word. Instead of running or turning away, Brisa needed to find her inner strength to guide her. Logical decisions never did her any favors before. Therefore, Brisa had to decipher the message within her spirit. They were clearly asking for something. But what?

CHAPTER XVI

Sonia drove Brisa to the old mansion in Antaño. It felt as if it had been waiting for her to return. The school looked recently painted, and many of the windows had been replaced.

Carlitos stepped out of his car and waved. "Brisa!"

Brisa hugged him. "Carlitos, I've missed you!"

"Your house has been waiting for you. It was just cleaned, and here are your keys. Selena's inside."

Brisa walked through the front door, and the chandelier swayed as if welcoming her home. The first floor still held its antique furniture but no more office desks. The view from the great windows felt warm and inviting.

"You're working with Sebastián now?" Brisa asked. "In City Hall?"

"Different projects around the town," Carlitos replied. "Wherever he needs me. Right now, I'm measuring the land and marking out the catacombs."

"The catacombs near here?"

He shook his head. "No, the ones on his land. They've been declared an archaeological site, and Sebastián is giving that property to the city for preservation. He's there now with the topographers."

"You know what? I'll go say hi to him," Brisa said, walking out the front door. "Stay in touch, Carlitos, and thanks."

He started to walk to his car but stopped. "Brisa?"

She stopped and turned toward him.

"Ring if you need anything."

She nodded and walked down the long path to the lower lot with the older catacombs. Brisa counted about thirty workers on the site. Sebastián was talking to who she assumed were topographers. As she approached, he looked over at her. She could tell he was a bit surprised. Sebastián pushed his hat up higher on his head and nodded. He stared at her with wide eyes and a stern expression. It almost felt as if they were enemies once again. It was the Sebastián from about a year ago. The one who didn't trust her. The one who feared being involved emotionally with her.

"Hi." Brisa glanced over at the entrance that was now cleared and mowed. "I'd like to walk the tunnels, if you don't mind."

"After you," Sebastián said as if she were a client. "We've reopened some of the passageways that were sealed."

Brisa stepped inside and her heart and soul flooded with memories both good and bad. "Hello!" Brisa yelled out, starting an echo.

Sebastián's eyes seemed indifferent. "This is where the ghost of Mother Rosa took you?"

"You don't have to be mean, Sebastián." She snapped at him since his attitude of coldness was starting to show. "You believed me when I first told you. But now you don't. Just because we are cousins doesn't mean we can't be friends. Or would you prefer not?" Brisa stepped closer and breathed in deeply. She wanted to kiss him but held back the urge. "Please don't hate me, Sebastián."

"Friends, Brisa?" He bit his lip. "Never!"

He pulled her into his arms. "Let's go to hell … you and me. To hell with everything and everyone. Let's see what *your* nun and *your* saints have to say about this!"

Sebastián kissed her, and she melted into his warm embrace. She had lost the battle from the moment they stepped into that cold crypt. His moist lips and sweet aroma filled her with a yearning she couldn't resist. Slowly, he undressed her. First her shirt, then her shoes, and then her pants. They made love on that cold rock floor with passion that was filled with fury and rage. The emotions were so strong it was almost painful. Brisa had to submit to the heavenly design that was now outside her control.

"Could this be hell?" he asked, challenging her beliefs.

The time flew through the echoes of their heated breaths. Their voices sliced across the air before bouncing off the walls. The dark void of the hallways became a sanctuary for their passion. They breathed in, deeply gasping for the air that seeped through the vents. Between the silence, it was only him and her that existed on the vibrating waves of lust. Sebastián stared at her with an unknown rage that flew from his eyes, as if he had suddenly released a million tiny daggers.

"This is what you wanted?" He panted and gasped. "When you begged me to make love to you in the mansion. Well … at that time, I was too decent." Sebastián grunted and panted and sighed. He rested on her and snuggled deeply into her neck. He took in several breaths before rising up on his arms. "I've tried to understand you, I really have. To accept everything that's happened and act with decency … to *hell* with your decency! I'm in love with you, and you just …"

They dressed without words, without looking at each other. Her cheeks warmed and she felt … annoyed with herself … with him. Brisa had once again lowered her guard and allowed him to insult her with his love.

"Goodbye, Brisa," he said, looking her directly in the eyes. "Alina is waiting for me to have lunch with her."

He walked toward the gate as she stood there alone in the darkness. Her thoughts, doubts, and insecurities were only inches away, ready to attack. As her tears fell, she refused to wipe them away.

She ran back to the mansion feeling confused and humiliated. Selena had prepared her room, and her clothes were back in the closet and drawers. She stared at the bell tower and screamed. Then, total silence.

"Miss Brisa?" Selena yelled up. "I stopped coming here after Aunt Conchita died. Are you okay?"

Brisa walked to the top of the stairs and nodded. "Did your aunt suffer?" She wiped her eyes. "I'm sorry, Selena."

"No, she didn't suffer. Just fell asleep. I brought you this." Selena climbed the stairs and handed Brisa a rosary. "She said it once belonged to Sara … your mother. That it was always meant for you."

"Thank you, Selena." Brisa stared at the religious relic. It was the one from the diary. The one her mother had given to Conchita at the novitiate. Then again, it was different. No. This one once belonged to Mother Rosa. It was the one from the portrait with an engraved rose that marked the First Mystery. Brisa hung it around her neck.

Thanks, Mama.

Brisa touched the beads that had once touched the fingers of her mother and Mother Rosa.

"I'll start dinner," Selena said.

"Thank you."

Brisa walked into the living room and glanced at the fireplace. The portrait of Mother Rosa was gone. Could it still be in the crypt? She crawled into the passageway and climbed through the small tunnel. The narrow stairs felt familiar and welcoming. Using her phone, she lit the passageway. After a while, Mother Rosa stared back at her from inside the frame.

"You tell me," Brisa screamed out at her. "You show *me* the way!"

The following morning, Sebastián arrived early and Brisa treated him with a strong dose of indifference. It was the only way she could continue on with what he wanted her to do in Antaño. She was in the living room enjoying her morning coffee when he walked past the front door.

"Do you want a cup?" Brisa offered.

He shook his head. "Good morning."

"Sleep well?"

He didn't answer.

"Coffee's good." Brisa took another sip.

"Sorry about yesterday," he said, taking a step closer. "Where did you say you saw that crypt? Finding her coffin before the sanctification ceremony would be great for morale."

"And for the popularity of your mayorship?" Brisa added sarcastically.

He responded without taking his eyes off her. "My only interest is Mother Rosa. I want her citizens to enjoy her rites and beliefs."

As he rambled on, Brisa gave him the once-over look.

"Of course, once the authenticity of the body …"

She allowed her eyes to follow the curve of his head, shoulders, and chest.

"… it would be the Department of Archaeology, in addition to the professionals they are already working with." It was as if he were talking to a stranger.

"Excellent," Brisa said, using her professional voice. It was the Brisa from a time long past. Pride was now guiding her. "I'll show you the crypt. And I demand a team of professionals that can adapt to *my* schedule, and I'll need a legal witness. Will also require a geographer …" Brisa grabbed her tool belt and strapped it around her waist. After she tied up her work boots, she glared at him. "Hardhat, Sebastián!" Bossing him around as if he were her underling felt rewarding. "This way." She pointed at the hearth.

"The fireplace?" He laughed and took a step back.

She nodded and crawled into the hearth.

"Are you crazy? I'm not going to fit!"

Brisa turned around while on her knees and glanced up at him. "Knock down that wall for all I care. It's not colonial." She turned and kept crawling.

Sebastián walked out and returned with a pickaxe and hammer.

Brisa laughed. "By yourself?"

Using his tools, Sebastián pounded until a larger opening appeared.

"Our step-grandmother or Angela's father moved through here to enter the school clandestinely." She laughed again. "And you can't fit? Ha!"

It was hard for her to say that. It felt odd and frightening. He pounded until enough bricks fell and he could fit through. Brisa looked at the mess and sighed.

"If it don't fit, men make it fit."

Sebastián panted as they crawled up and over the bricks. They inched their way to the passageway and stepped into the part that divided the two corridors. Sebastián had to scoot through on his belly.

"I can't make it through here," he whispered.

Brisa kept crawling and ignoring his words. She refused to look back. As she listened to him grunt and struggle, she held back a giggle. After a few moments, he was well inside the space and they, together, stared down into the shadows. After descending the makeshift stairs, they walked and searched, and when Brisa pointed her flashlight through an iron grid, he laughed.

"The boarding school and the office where Angela and Pablo had detained you."

He didn't say anything.

"On the other side is the hallway of another crypt. It's the one I want to search."

They walked a little farther in silence, as the strange echoes of their footsteps resonated off the walls.

"See these bricks?" Brisa hit various spots with a small mallet. "There's a void here and in other places. An archaic system of insulation. You hear the emptiness." She hit the wall again. "There is no layer of earth behind it. That means that there are more rooms ... hidden rooms."

"I can hear the echo," he said.

"That's why there's no humidity. These walls are insulated."

They reached the crypt, and the deafening silence was overwhelming. Sebastián seemed delighted and changed his tone from aggressive to one of curiosity and wonderment. As if a child on Christmas morning, Sebastián ran from wall to wall and nook to nook, pounding on the rocks.

"We need professional excavation equipment," Brisa said, putting away her mallet. "We must document this before we touch anything."

"Give me the orders and I'll obey," he replied.

"You're the mayor, not me." She placed her hands against her hips. "This place belongs to the city now. After you've rented the equipment and obtain the permits, and if you still need me, I'll help." She sighed. "If I'm still here."

Deep down, she was hoping that her final words would hurt him. Instead, Sebastián fell back into a more professional mode.

"I'll let you know." His tone was quick and stern. "Thanks for showing me this. The city will be thankful."

His eyes fixated upon her in the same manner he looked at others who he worked with. Brisa felt suddenly intimidated.

"I'll have the house sealed off … except for you, of course, and post security since this is a new discovery."

They crawled out of the fireplace together. He pulled out his phone and called someone. Sebastián nodded as he walked out the front door.

Sebastián rented the excavation equipment through CONADA. With all the commotion and people running around, Brisa returned to the ranch to live. Spending time with Cami gave her a sense of peace and purpose. She also found the time to study to become a novice. Her crazy, hectic days were all behind her now.

The early morning light felt inviting. After saddling a horse, she rode toward the river. When the horse stopped to drink, she glanced around and admired the beautiful countryside. A small person was running toward her. Cami was in school, so who was it? As the individual approached, they smiled. Something twinkled in the sunlight … a golden tooth? Was it Marta? What would she be doing out here? Whoever it was wore jeans and a gray sweatshirt.

"Marta?" Brisa shouted.

"Hi, Brisa!" Marta's voice echoed through the trees.

Brisa slid off the horse and ran to her. They hugged.

"I wanted to come earlier, but it's been a hectic year. For you too, I believe."

Brisa nodded. It felt odd because the woman was acting as if they were long, lost friends.

"It's incredible," Marta said. "So much has happened since the investigation, and all under our new mayor. Antaño is slowly changing for the better." They walked and stopped by the river. Marta sat on a rock and took in a deep breath. "Thanks for your help in the investigation," Marta said, covering her eyes from the bright sun. "Your statements and Sonia's have been very instrumental. PROE S.A. is about to close their doors for good. Antaño will have its historic legacies, and the Herraduras will have their true family history finally revealed. Mr. Francisco de Herradura would be proud." Marta glanced out at the water and sighed.

Brisa look over to make sure that her horse hadn't moved.

"We'll soon be a world heritage site," Marta said.

Brisa nodded.

"Almost the same time that Mother Rosa is branded a saint."

"Incredible." Brisa smiled.

They sat on that rock and watched as the sparkling water flowed. So much had happened, and they had not seen or talked to each other since before Brisa left for the Lost Angels clinic.

"Marta?" Brisa pulled her hair from her eyes. "Remember when you said that neither of us should say that we know Sebastián?"

Marta nodded. "We were in the whispering room."

"I didn't understand it then but I do now. I never would have believed that you were investigating Pablo and Angela. Incredible job."

Marta nodded again and smiled. "Do you still have the Mother's portrait?"

"I do." Brisa nodded now. "It's in the mansion."

"It's yours. I never reported it. You decide on what to do with it."

"I'll talk to the bishop. Know what else I want to deliver to the church?"

Marta looked at her before tilting her head.

"My life."

"Your life?" Marta repeated.

"I want to enter the novitiate. To dedicate myself to Mother Rosa's teachings. To honor her. It's the home I've longed for. My life is in the heart of the church."

Marta squinted and frowned. "Weren't you married once? The church doesn't allow for divorced women."

"The marriage was annulled."

"If you say so, and if you're sure that's what you want. Just be very certain because you'll never be allowed to marry."

"I'll marry our Lord and wear a bride's dress."

Marta nodded. "And Sara? Your mother? What legacy did she leave you?"

"She remained in the convent and delivered her life to God."

Marta sighed. "You're not seeing the whole picture, Brisa."

"What do you mean?"

"Sara didn't know that you were alive. Remember? I read her diary too, and it's given me great information for the investigation."

"What difference does it make if she thought I was alive or dead?"

"Makes a big difference. Pablo told us about the love between Sara and Juancho. At least, what he knew from Angela. However, Sara never knew her little girl was taken away alive. She thought her baby had died. That is what she was told. Sara lived a cloistered life because she believed that she killed her daughter. She did not remain a nun of her own free will. She remained by deception. It became her humble evidence of her acceptance of God's design. However, only from her perspective. Sara delivered her pain to God as a sacrifice. A final punishment for killing you!"

Marta's comments sounded logical. Looking at it from that angle, who knows what Sara's destiny could have been? If she had not believed that her baby and Juancho were dead, perhaps her decisions and choices would have been different. If her mother remained a nun as a self-punishment, then what was Brisa doing? Who was she punishing?

Brisa looked deeply into Marta's eyes and said, "I saw Mother Rosa. You probably won't believe me and think it was from my drinking. That I was just hallucinating. However, I know that I'm obeying a calling."

"I believe you." Marta stood and stretched. "Remember the old man? The drunkard?"

"Yes," Brisa said, looking away. "How crazy was that? I don't speak to him anymore, but our conversations felt so real. I feel ashamed about it now."

"Brisa …" Marta shook her head. "What if he's your guardian angel? Ever thought about that? I would love to have a guardian angel who took care of me." Marta grabbed Brisa by the shoulders. "Someone called for help that day you overdosed."

"So?"

"Who made that call?" Marta asked. "If it wasn't Rogelio, then who was it? He appeared as a paternal figure … a guardian … *your* guardian. And you don't even realize it. You're not crazy. Never were."

"But —"

Marta raised her hand. "Why did he appear to you so many times? Brisa, listen to me … you need to interpret his message. And for that matter, how are you so sure about what Mother Rosa wants from you? Did she say you should become a nun? Did you hear those exact words?"

Brisa shook her head. "Of course not —"

Again, Marta raised her hand. "Is *that* what Sara would have asked of her daughter? What your own mother would have wished? And what's even more important … what do *you* desire?" Marta touched Brisa's chest where her heart was pounding. "What is *your* heart conveying to you?"

Brisa nodded. "I understand what you're saying. Perhaps you're right, perhaps not. I just don't know."

"When was the last time you were truly sober?" Marta asked.

"Not in a long time."

"Exactly." Marta smiled. "Now that you *are* sober, you'll see and hear things a little differently."

"I believe you're telling me to think things over. To reflect on what my guardians are trying to tell me and not jump to conclusions."

"Becoming a nun is easy," Marta said with a laugh. "Living as a human is not."

Now Brisa laughed. "Okay, Marta. I'll take the time for retrospection and to rediscover who I am —"

"Before you take any vows," Marta said with a smile.

"I will." Brisa hugged her.

"Here …" Marta handed Brisa a sheet of paper with the Antaño seal on the top. "The interview with Pablo that you requested. It will not be a long one. The date, time, and address is on there. Will you go?"

Brisa read over the paper and nodded. "Thank you."

Marta sighed. "We still need to find the time for a little wine and cheese. We should celebrate the rose … your birthmark." She hesitated and looked away. "I'm sorry, I should not have mentioned the wine."

"It's okay." Brisa hugged her again. "I can have a soda, and you can have wine."

Together, they walked back to the stables with Brisa pulling the horse. They spent the rest of the morning talking about this or that and other unimportant matters. For the first time, Marta and Brisa were acting as comrades and not opponents. It felt good to share their time together as friends.

As she walked to her car, Marta waved. When she opened her door, she yelled out, "Brisa! The bell still chimes at the convent twice a day!"

The city jail was one that Pablo had finished building when he was elected mayor. He was sleeping in a special wing nowhere near the other prisoners. Brisa was led to a small room, which looked more like an office with the exception of two guards. Pablo walked in through a side door wearing street clothing and no handcuffs.

"What did you expect?" he asked. "Black and white pajamas?" He smiled and winked.

"We don't have much time," she replied.

They sat with a table between them.

"I'm here relaxing," he said. "Although, I will be out soon. They don't have much against me." He kept his eyes on Brisa and laughed. "Is it true? Now that you're a blonde, you have a boyfriend … your cousin!" He shook his head and lowered his eyes. "Tsk, tsk, tsk. Such a sin." As he smiled, he leaned back. "You still owe me a drink, remember?"

"Why are you in this jail?" she asked. "Thought you were on house arrest."

"The trial was prolonged. They really have nothing on me. I may get a couple of years but that's about it."

"Despite everything you did?"

"Me?" Pablo laughed. "I accepted a few payments under the table. Big deal. They were gifts, nothing more. Your boyfriend is the one calling it corruption." He laughed again. "What do they have? That the legal representative of PROE S.A. was my accountant. Now that poor man is facing serious charges." He sighed.

Brisa placed her hands on the table and frowned again.

"Don't get me wound up, Brisa. The fraud belonged to Angela and Angela alone. I only went along for the ride."

Brisa stared at the man. Pablo was evil, a charlatan, and not to mention abusive and corrupt. She closed her eyes and counted to five before looking at him again.

"The biggest crime against me is illegal urban land development and fraudulent authorization of municipal permits. That's it!" He threw his hands into the air. "I've fully collaborated with the authorities. Now, the evidence of what Angela's father did was far worse. However, there's no one left to slap into jail for that ... is there?"

"And what if Angela had lived?"

"She'd be facing fraud charges about now. I knew that her father was keeping that man, Juancho, sick ... your father, by the way." Pablo pointed at her and laughed. "I knew all about those secrets and said nothing. But as for the stew, cooked up by Angela's father as legal guardian of the uncle, well ... " Pablo stared up at the ceiling, as if watching something only he could see. "They could also proceed against her for the irregular handling of the company's funds." He nodded. "That's where the deceased really had a field day. Yep!" Pablo sat back and sighed. "Too late now!"

Brisa raised a brow and smiled. "I'm glad you feel so optimistic. Did Angela ever say what her father and Lady Delfina were doing in that boarding school?"

He laughed and wiped his forehead. "Angela knew everything. Her father kept nothing from her," he said. "Want it in chronological order or alphabetical?"

She took in a deep breath and let it out slowly.

"Lady Delfina, your grandmother, wanted to clean up Antaño. Get rid of the undesirables. What she called the *wicked city people*. She didn't like fast and loose girls, despite once being one herself. Had a desire to teach them all a lesson. Maybe to ensure that she entered heaven or something." He shrugged. "The convent was practically hers. The religious would do whatever she demanded." He sighed and stared up at the ceiling. "That woman hated Sara." He laughed. "All your mother ever wanted was to be with Juancho. But to get rid of her, Lady Delfina locked her up inside that convent. Told Sara that Juancho had killed himself. When the old lady discovered that Sara was pregnant ..." He shook his head. "Let's just say that Sara was never allowed to leave those walls again. Turned that poor girl into a cloistered nun, they did."

"Can you tell me more, but spare the mockery?"

Pablo frowned. "I'm locked in here while your sinful boyfriend runs around on his white horse and rids the city of evils of corruption." He took in a deep breath and shifted in his chair. "Angela's father made a fortune selling contraband across the border ... babies, babies, and more babies. Lady Delfina enjoyed punishing the women ... the mommies. The man made a ton, and the woman had her fun. Your grandfather was long dead and forgotten by then. Therefore, Angela's father was the perfect man for the perfect woman, and that created ... the *perfect* team for the *perfect* crime."

"And what do you know about Sara's mother and father?"

"Not much. But your father didn't know that you survived until after you were adopted. And ... I do *not* know who told him. I do know that when Juan Ignacio was told that Sara was about to deliver *his* baby inside that filthy convent, well, he made a big scene. All in front of Lady Delfina. Not wise on his part. Her hired men and Angela's father ambushed the poor guy. And ... well ... the rest you pretty much know about. A girl, whose name Angela couldn't recall, and a young man named Rogelio took the baby away. I remember his name because Angela had met him as a child. When that old witch found you with Rogelio, let's just say that you were sold to the highest bidder and he was …"

"Time's up!" a guard said, holding the door open.

She turned to Pablo and asked, "Why did Angela hate me? And … why did she hire me?"

"She didn't hate you, Brisa." He shook his head. "She just thought of you as a manipulative, double-faced woman. It took her a while to find out about you and Sebastián. I really underestimated you. But to be sure, your kidnapping *was* a punishment. Don't ask me if I had anything to do with it." Pablo pointed at her and frowned. "I will not talk about that." Pablo stood and walked toward the guard. Then, he turned and said, "Holding a grudge against me, Brisa?" He shrugged. "No, I don't believe so."

"Goodbye, Pablo," Brisa said, turning to leave. "I'm glad they're treating you so well."

Several weeks passed and life with Cami seemed to be falling into place. Every morning, Brisa took her coffee on the porch, which allowed her to see the ocean that touched the horizon. As she took a sip, her phone beeped.

"Sebastián …?"

"Brisa! I need you at the ruins. A group of archaeologists and the official team from the National Council for the Protection of Antaño are working the convent and excavations are scheduled to start in about two weeks. They'll make an initial assessment of the crypt that you showed me. I don't know if you're interested, given your religious commitments and all, but since you told me …"

"Sebastián, can it please wait?" Brisa sat her coffee down. "I'm leaving the country for a few days but not going to the convent. It's a personal trip. Please do not proceed with the assessment without me. They may be archaeologists, but they don't know about the weak foundations or the structural integrity of the buildings. Please … don't start anything without me."

"Where are you going?"

"Mexico."

"Oh, okay, I won't ask anything more. I have everything scheduled to start in two weeks. Will you be back by then?"

Her phone dinged for Sebastián had texted her the dates and times. "Yes, of course."

"Good. I'll have to get with you later since it's Alina's birthday that week. I'll be late to arrive."

With a feeling of cold water splashing her between the eyes, Brisa stood and gazed out at the horizon. Had she just lost Sebastián forever? She looked at the now-silent phone. Sebastián had not even said goodbye.

The flight to Mexico City felt a lot shorter than she'd imagined. Although she didn't know a lot of things, she did understand that this trip could not be postponed. Brisa was allowing herself to be guided by instinct and not by her mind. Her logic had never taken her to anything good before, for her logic was derived from the voice of an addict. Could it be that her heart was directing her now?

The taxi drove her directly from the airport to the private cemetery located in the center of the federal district. For the first time in many years, Brisa felt the need to reconnect with her adoptive parents. And for the first time, she was showing them the love and thankfulness they so deserved. They had chosen her as their daughter and raised her the best they knew how, constantly offering her their love. Brisa had left her resentment behind and wanted to talk to them with gratitude. Even if they could not answer back in words.

She placed the red roses near their headstone. Kneeling over, she kissed the earth, giving them the kisses she had failed to give before their deaths. That couple gave her a safe and secure home with the best of intentions.

"Mom … Dad … I'm sorry. I should not have left so angry." She wiped away a tear. "I love and miss you and need your support more than ever." Brisa stared at the headstone and allowed her fingers to trace over their names. "Please understand. I had a wonderful childhood because of you. Know that I'm here and that I miss you both."

Brisa remained for a few moments before standing and smiling. She walked away feeling the most peace and calm that she had felt in a very long time. She climbed into the taxi and headed to the small apartment she had not visited in several years. She rang the bell. The street noise was loud, and it was hard to answer the intercom.

"It's me … Brisa!"

A loud buzz sounded and the door opened. Brisa climbed the stairs and rang the bell for apartment eleven. Mariano stood in the doorway and frowned. He didn't look surprised or angry, just evasive.

"What brings you here?" Mariano asked.

"Only one thing and I'll be brief. Can I come in?"

Mariano stood aside and Brisa walked into the living room. Nothing had really changed. The couch and chair were in the same location against the one wall. The TV looked newer, and the curtains had been changed. Other than that, everything was as she remembered.

"I'm returning to Antaño later today," she said, sitting on the arm of a chair.

Mariano sat on the couch.

"I didn't do well by you," she said. "I've been in rehab recovering from my addiction. It's time I make amends to the people I've offended. I should not have taken the project you wanted. I accepted it more out of revenge. It was my way of showing you my pain. I want to apologize."

"It was yours anyway," he said, looking away.

"Doesn't matter. I did things to hurt you. Like our child, for one."

"Am I to forgive you?" he asked.

"It wasn't an abortion," she whispered. "I miscarried. I lied to hurt you. Your affair had changed me somehow. And then when you pushed for the annulment ..." She sighed. "I won't be long. I just want to ask for forgiveness and to wish you the best."

"The company we had ..."

"It's yours," she said. "I'll sign whatever you need."

"I shut it down. There are no loose ends."

She nodded. "Okay, thank you, Mariano." Brisa stood and walked to the door.

Mariano stood and grabbed her arm. "Brisa, I also didn't behave well with you."

Brisa smiled. "It's all good," she said, patting him on the shoulder. "Goodbye, Mariano."

"Goodbye, Brisa."

CHAPTER XVII

Once again, Brisa was back in Antaño. The volcanoes, rose bushes, and cobbled streets filled her with a sense of belonging. She stared at the familiar Herradura mansion and felt instantly at home. Although the place always looked sinister and spooky, she felt as if she belonged. Now, she understood why her connections were so strong. Brisa could actually feel and see Sara, Juancho, and Rogelio running through the fields as kids. Her bedroom, the one where Lady Delfina once slept, also belonged to her grandparents. Brisa could visualize Sebastián playing in the halls when he visited.

She sat on the old bench that remained just outside the front door and sipped on a hot cup of coffee. The old bell tower that blocked the noonday sun drew out so many memories. She watched as a couple of young men walked through the field with an excavation team — probably the archaeologists hired by Sebastián. Carlitos had just arrived and ran to greet them. Brisa took another sip as they headed her way.

Sebastián had said he would arrive later in the day. since it had been Alina's birthday the night before. He had made sure to emphasize his hot date. Brisa stood and walked toward the ruins to smoke a cigarette before joining the team. She laughed as she remembered that she'd already quit the nasty habit.

Near the ruins, the roses were in full bloom, and the petals reminded her of a red carpet. A bald spot on the grass grabbed her attention. It was where she had passed out the night she drank and took the pills. Someone was sitting near one of the old buildings. The worn-out, old hat gave him away as did the shadow that formed in his old shirt. It was Rogelio. Brisa ran toward him, and he laughed as she smiled. His twisted and yellow teeth, that she knew so well, made her giggle. They looked at each other and did not speak. Brisa wrapped her arms around him and squeezed. They looked at each other again and smiled.

"You are cured, Miss Brisa?" he asked with a wink.

"Cured?" She laughed. "Are you cured?"

They laughed and hugged again.

"It's an everyday job, right, miss?" He patted her shoulder.

"Yep. If you can, then I can."

"You must hurry," he said, giving her a little nudge. "They're waiting for you." He pointed out at the field.

"How do you know they're waiting for me?" She turned and stared out at the small group.

Rogelio laughed. "Mother Rosa … the Most Holy of Mothers is also waiting for you." He stood and nodded.

Brisa took a step back and walked over to the rose bushes.

"Brisa …"

As she stared at the man, he faded into the ruins and vanished. If he were an angel, he had no wings. Although, she knew that he was watching over her. Then again, it no longer mattered if he was just a figment of her imagination.

She walked back to the mansion and several of the archaeologists nodded. They were young, maybe late teens, early twenties? Carlitos and Sebastián walked up and smiled. Brisa glared at Sebastián and frowned.

"Thought you'd be a little late," Brisa stated.

Sebastián shrugged. "Shall we enter the catacombs?" Sebastián's breath held a strong odor of alcohol. His eyes were red and puffy.

"Too much celebrating?" she asked, shaking her head.

Sebastián smiled and shrugged again.

She grabbed her tool belt before handing out hardhats.

Sebastián nodded and grabbed a pickaxe.

They crawled into the fireplace and Sebastián laughed. "Sorry," he said to the others. "This is the only way in. I've looked for other points of entry but they're sealed with debris … probably earthquakes."

The archaeologists didn't respond. Instead, a couple snapped photos as they crawled.

"This is a place of great historical value, Mr. Mayor and Miss Architect," one of the youths said. "There's a whole city down here."

"There are many hidden places like this throughout the town," Sebastián said, acting official. "Antaño will thank you for your discoveries."

The young archaeologists stayed behind to document the strange entrance through the fireplace as Sebastián and Brisa continued to explore. They reached the grid that led to the floor of the school and stopped.

"We're checking all the vents," Sebastián said.

Brisa nodded. "The school must have had direct access to this chamber and others at one time."

They searched every wall and brick, and no words were spoken. The silence felt deafening.

"Are you still interested in the novitiate?" Sebastián asked in almost a whisper. "In taking your first vows?"

Brisa didn't reply. Sebastián was either concerned or angry. She couldn't tell which. However, he had Alina so why would he care where she ended up?

"The city needs someone like you." Sebastián glanced at her and frowned.

"This is not the time or place to discuss such matters." Brisa used her small mallet on the walls. "There are chambers here." She marked a brick with chalk. "We need equipment." She pointed toward the hallway of the crypt where she believed Mother Rosa was resting.

The young architects strolled nonchalantly toward them.

Brisa sighed and shook her head. Pointing back the way they came, she yelled, "You need hardhats!" Brisa almost screamed out the words. "Even though no excavation is taking place, you must wear them. You should know better."

The men shook their heads and sighed. They glared at Sebastián who shrugged. He shook his head and pointed back down the hall. The young men turned and ambled away. The halls, again, fell silent.

Sebastián pulled out his phone. "I'm requesting a geographer." He nodded as he typed.

They continued their walk and after turning a few corners, they arrived at a crypt.

"There's a cross on the floor." Sebastián stood back and his eyes widened. "Why is it here? Crosses are normally on the walls or ceilings." He knelt and ran his fingers along the tile. "What could this mean?"

"I had asked myself that question many times," Brisa replied as she knelt next to him. She studied the contours of his face before continuing. "I couldn't make out the design at first. Didn't have a good enough light at the time. Cami was the one who gave me a clue."

"Cami?" he said, looking at her now with concern. "My Cami?"

Brisa nodded. "She saw the roses." Brisa pointed her light up to the ceiling.

Sebastián glanced up and gasped.

"I always wondered how roses could remain forever on top of the Mother's coffin and never wilt. Flowers will not mummify. They eventually turn to dust and float away. The roses from the legend are actually referring to those stains." Again, she pointed up. "The ceiling ... what Cami saw before anyone else did. The stains look like roses!"

Sebastián slowly stood and looked up at the beautiful red roses that covered the ceiling.

"I believe her coffin is here ... underneath this cross." She hit the cross with her mallet and a fine layer of dust floated up toward the ceiling. "But then again, it could be nothing but a relief ... a sculpted border." She hit the cross again, softly. "What if it's a lid?" She struck with more force, and the sound echoed around them. "Sounds hollow underneath."

Sebastián knelt and rubbed his hand along the floor. "Another chamber?"

Brisa stood and stepped back. "You have the axe," she said, pointing to the metal item in his hand.

Sebastián raised the axe over his head and swung toward the cross. The sound of metal hitting metal echoed through the halls, and a spark lit the room for only a second. For some odd reason, it felt as if they were destroying something that should be left alone.

Brisa touched his shoulder and knelt. "It's not a crack." She flashed her light along the dark line and sighed again. Standing, she took a step back and whispered, "It's an opening." Brisa pulled out a brush and swept the floor. A plate slowly came into view. She stood back and unhooked a small crowbar from her belt. Handing it to Sebastián, she pointed.

He sighed and rubbed the back of his head. After glancing around, as if he half-expected to see Mother Rosa or something, he slowly pushed the metal slab enough to where a small opening gave just a slight hint of another room or corridor. "Fascinating!" Sebastián said as he pulled out his phone.

"What are you doing?" Brisa asked. "You're an archaeologist … act like one!"

He clicked off his phone.

"This is probably why I should have studied archaeology in school," she said with a laugh.

They tried to pull the lid aside and their hearts pounded.

"Stop," Brisa said, trying to catch her breath. "It's too heavy."

"We'd better find the others." Sebastián took off his gloves and shoved them into his pocket. "They should have been here by now."

The ground vibrated and they stared at each other.

"A tremor?" he asked.

Another wave, and this time they were lifted off the floor. Brisa grabbed his arm and pulled him toward the only entrance she knew — the stairs and fireplace.

"Hurry!" Sebastián yelled now pulling her toward the entrance.

Again, a large shock hit, and the room suddenly moved vertical and horizontal at the same time. Brisa stumbled and Sebastián grabbed her around the waist.

"It's a big one," he yelled.

Sebastián pushed her toward the stairs. She leaned against the wall and climbed. She refused to look down. Instead, she concentrated on the opening above her head. The bricks felt loose as she scrambled over and fell into the fireplace. After scurrying into the living room, she stood and ran out the front door. The young archaeologists were standing under the tree shaking.

"Sebastián!" Brisa said, turning around. "That was too …."

Sebastián was not behind her. The ground shook again, and it was hard to stand. She glanced at the young men for only a second before darting back into the mansion. The chandelier rocked and hit the ceiling. Large chucks of plaster fell to the floor. The windows rattled and the walls cracked. Brisa crawled into the fireplace and dodged several falling bricks. She scurried through the small tunnel and onto the stairs.

"Sebastián!" she yelled out.

"Brisa!" He had fallen off the stairs and was lying on the floor. "Get out of here!"

"You're hurt," Brisa said, examining his swollen ankle.

"Get out, the place is going to collapse." Sebastián pushed her away.

Brisa stood and felt something, then she heard it. The floor continued to roll and rumble. It was as if Mother Rosa had awakened from her sleep and was angry for being disturbed.

Something urged Brisa to go back to the crypt. First, she walked and then she ran. Dirt, rocks, and dust surrounded her but she kept running. The ground shook harder and stronger. She stopped at the lid with the cross. Mother Rosa's crypt was now half opened. Debris fell from the ceiling, but the stairs leading down still beckoned her. It was a calling she couldn't resist. The ground shook stronger, and the lid slid across the floor. Brisa took the stairs two at a time, dodging rocks and falling debris. Stepping onto a solid, shiny floor, Brisa froze and stared at the mysterious but beautiful coffin. The shaking suddenly stopped.

The sarcophagus had been placed in the middle of the chamber — a chamber about the size of a child's bedroom. A fine dust covered the surface. Brisa reached out and touched the fragile silk cape that covered it. She pulled it off and slowly, as if magically, the material hovered for only a few moments before floating softly to the floor. A thick glass window was near the head. Brisa pulled out her brush and cleaned away the remaining dirt. She leaned over and rested her hands on the coffin. Her eyes looked upon a woman ... a beautiful woman ... a nun.

"Mother Rosa," Brisa whispered.

The woman's face seemed calm and at peace. Her hands rested one over the other. The woman's veins were visible just under her sheer, white skin. It were as if she was only sleeping. Between her delicate fingers clung a small notebook. The same little book that was in her portrait. On her wrist was the mark of a rose.

Brisa's hands shook and the ground rumbled. She held onto the coffin and screamed. The walls shook with such force that they screeched out in agony. A strong wave rolled through the room, and the coffin rose several feet. Brisa rested her head over Mother Rosa's and closed her eyes. The earth would soon open and swallow them both. She crouched upon that coffin and cried. Keeping her eyes closed, she allowed herself to be carried away. Several bricks hit her on the back. One smashed against her hip, and she yelled out in pain. The room darkened and a black void opened as the ground shook harder and stronger. The room was falling, and the earth was closing in around them. Debris fell over the coffin … then silence.

No movements, no sounds, no bricks.

Brisa glanced up and stared into a shower of red rose petals. Mother Rosa's room was filling up with soft, red petals and a bright, white light. Instead of fear, Brisa felt only a peaceful tranquility that was going to consume her. Time no longer held any meaning. Every day, every year, every second no longer seemed to exist.

A far away sound echoed through the room. Was she alive or dead?

"Brisa!" a soft voice rang out.

It seemed to be the voice of Sebastián, or was it just an echo from the catacombs? She could not tell nor did she care.

"Brisa!" She heard the voice again before the world darkened around her.

Brisa opened her eyes and glanced around. Her arms reached out for Mother Rosa. Instead, she touched the blankets of her bed. Her body ached as if she had just woken from an eternal sleep. She was alive.

"Brisa! Wake up!"

She was in her bedroom, and Sebastián was sitting next to her.

"We could barely get you out. The fireplace is gone, and the entrance is now blocked." He leaned in closer. "An ambulance is on its way."

"The tremor," she whispered. "Was it a big one?"

"No," he said. "Just a little one. Because I opened the chimney, I weakened it. It fell and covered the entrance."

"And the crypt? Did the mausoleum get destroyed?"

"It's fine," he said. "We had to unblock the area around the fireplace to get you out."

"I was with Mother Rosa, Sebastián. I saw her. The lid to the mausoleum was opened by the quake. She's intact. Just as the legend says. I was there and she was just sleeping. We have to …"

He stared at her and frowned. "We must make sure you're okay."

Brisa shook her head.

"The area is closed. I'll go with you to the hospital and —"

"No!" She gripped his arm. "I'm fine." An uncontrollable urge to sleep ran through her. She lay back and sighed. "Please, I don't want a doctor. We have to call an anthropologist. My colleague in Mexico who I told you about!"

"We'll contact him," Sebastián said. "I already called our bishop and explained that we're close to finding Mother Rosa's mausoleum. He'll send a delegation as soon as he can. Brisa, you might have a concussion."

She stared at him.

"You're correct about the Mother's sarcophagus. I believe it's there. But your health is more —"

"I'm fine. Listen …" Brisa told Sebastián everything that had happened to her. "… after the roses fell, I fell asleep."

He sat back and his eyes widened.

"It's her and she is beautiful and at peace. The serenity is unreal. She was indeed a pilgrim. I can tell she once suffered, but she looks … happy now."

"The bishop will work with Rome. The postulator of Mother Rosa will be corroborated as soon as we can confirm it." He wiped his forehead and pushed his hair from his eyes. "If it's really her, her sanctification is imminent. But you need rest —"

"She has the mark of the rose on her wrist!"

Sebastián leaned over and hugged her. "I'll cancel the ambulance if you'll allow a doctor to come see you."

Brisa shook her head.

"But Brisa," he whispered, "we found you lying on top of the lid. Not inside the crypt. The crypt is still intact."

The doctor left saying that she was healthy and fit, and not a thing was wrong with her. Just a few scratches. Brisa walked through the living room and stopped when her eyes landed on the destroyed fireplace. Glancing up at the chandelier, she frowned. The ceiling was fine, no gashes from where the chandelier had hit. *Why not?* Workers had placed a tarp over the fireplace to keep out the rainwater. That night, Brisa slept deeply as Sebastián remained by her side throughout the hours.

The following morning, Sebastián cooked breakfast with the help of Selena.

Brisa entered the kitchen and yawned. "Smells wonderful."

Sebastián placed a plate of food in front of her. "Eat."

Brisa nodded.

"How are you feeling?" Selena asked.

"Fine, thanks."

Sebastián left and she ate with Selena by her side. As Selena cleaned, Brisa walked outside. Workers were everywhere, both civilian and municipal.

Carlitos walked over and gave her a hug. "Ironic."

"What is?"

"We're now protecting what we were about to knock down."

"I was just thinking the same thing."

They laughed and continued to talk as Sebastián rode up on a horse. He nodded.

"Coming?"

Brisa reached out her hand, and he pulled her up. They rode around the site without exchanging words. Several times, they galloped across the rolling hills. Everything belonged to them now. They stopped on a hill and watched the people below.

"It was never my intention to demand these lands be returned to me," he said, glancing across the vast property. "However, we do have a few decisions to make … you and me. We're now co-owners of this. Relatives and partners."

Brisa ran everything through her mind and smiled. It was a new concept for her. "I'll stay for a while."

"Do whatever makes you happy, Brisa," he said. "At some point, you'll have to work the legal matters as a Herradura. How do you plan to live? Do you have a place in the city you can rent?"

Brisa shook her head. "I have some savings."

They rode back toward the mansion, and Brisa looked down at her hands. She sighed.

"I have many things to tend to," Sebastián said. "If you can take care of Cami, I'd appreciate it. I'll drop some funds into your bank account … expenses for my daughter. The moment you decide to work, a thousand opportunities will pop up. I do have one question."

She nodded.

"Just out of curiosity, can you aspire to be a novitiate after marriage?"

Brisa nodded. "It was annulled."

He stopped the horse and they slid off. They stared out at the horizon and breathed in the fresh aroma of the roses.

"Ironic," he said. "You were married to another, and now you'll marry the church. You'll soon be a nun. I, however, will remain stuck in the middle with nothing. I simply do not appear anywhere along the horizon of your life." He stared directly out at the ocean. "Must be a reason."

Brisa shrugged.

"Managing this town is not easy, and soon a big event will come … canonizations," Sebastián said. "Antaño will be declared a world heritage —"

"Will you do it for Cami?"

"It's the Antaño I promised her. There's something else I'll do for her … and for me."

"Oh?"

"I'm asking Alina to marry me," he said and his words were cold and blunt. "I'd like you at the wedding. You're the only family I have aside from Cami and my uncle."

Brisa's stomach turned and she felt the world sway. She stared at him and frowned. "You love her?"

"Yes, or whatever love is."

Her heart broke and she stared at the ground. "I'm glad for you. But not just for Cami, right? I mean, Cami *does* have me."

"Living inside a convent?" he said, pulling the horse by the reins. "You are in contemplation. The spiritual stuff. After the discovery of the body of Mother Rosa, you'll have an even stronger pull for your spiritual mission. City Hall and the church will take over when you move to Mexico."

"Sebastián …" — Brisa stopped walking and grabbed his arm — "… when I was alone with the Mother, I had a revelation."

"Brisa, I respect your devotion." He pulled his arm away. "I'm just made from a different material."

"Wait, Sebastián …" Brisa ran in front of him and placed her hands on his chest. "I have to tell you this."

"Tell me what?"

"I saw her … for a moment. When I closed my eyes, everything fell in around me. I'm not going to tell you everything, because I don't expect you to believe me. But when I woke up, I knew what I had to do."

"And I respect that —"

"Would you just listen!" Brisa wiped away a tear and he frowned. "For years, perhaps for my whole life, I've been waiting to hear … to understand the messages of the universe. I wanted to find the divine meaning of things.

Then a voice guided me. And this time I listened, really listened … and I understood. The words were clear."

"Mother Rosa talked to you when you were with her?" He rolled his eyes and stared into the sky. "I see."

"It was not a voice exactly … but it was her voice. Mother Rosa didn't talk to me directly. The voice came from inside me. I finally heard her message!"

"Okay, so you talked to yourself."

"Sebastián, the inner voice of Brisa finally spoke up. I know what I want to be." She yelled out the words.

"I'm listening."

"I want to be a mother." She wiped away another tear.

"I know!" He yelled back. "You've said that several times. How many times must I hear it?"

"I want to be *Cami's* mother." She grabbed his arm and shook it. Her tears fell. "That is my true destiny. Not a religious mother. Mother Rosa is not asking me to become a nun but to honor women. And I have to start with me. I want to be the woman who raises Cami. My mother *had* to be a nun. But she actually wanted to be my mother."

Sebastián stared at her.

"That was Sara's message, too. I love Cami. I want to be her mother. Or at least the closest thing to it. I want to ask your forgiveness for everything. I don't want you to separate me from us. Cami is the abandoned girl that was found in the teachings. Inside Mother Rosa's doctrines. I'm the one who's called on to protect, recognize, rejoice, and love. Cami needs a mother to guide and protect her."

"I don't know what to say." His eyes were wide and a tear formed.

"You've done an excellent job. Now, I ask that you allow me to be a part of her life. The mother she never had. It's girls like Cami, with an absent mom, those are the ones that Mother Rosa wants to reach. That was the basis of her catechism." Brisa panted to catch her breath.

Sebastián stared down at her and shook his head. His eyes flashed through different hues of gray.

"I will not go to the convent." Brisa sighed. "It is not my calling. When I discovered the coffin of Mother Rosa, I heard a voice. The voice and light was so intense that they overpowered everything. I lost consciousness and didn't know who had given me that message. After a while, I figured it out. The voice was mine."

Sebastián wiped his eyes.

"Do you believe me?"

"I do. I truly do. If you want to be with Cami, stay here with us. I respect that you cannot get over the fact that we're cousins. Do you think this is another curse?"

"Neither a curse nor a blessing," she replied, looking away. "I cannot have children. I lost the one I was carrying when I was married. Mariano believed I aborted it and never forgave me. But I lost it. I cannot have others."

He cleared his throat and coughed. He walked around the horse and petted it several times.

"Alina wants children," he said, not looking at her.

"And you?"

"Yes, and I plan on spending my life with her. I deserve it."

"It is your life, Sebastián," Brisa whispered. "I just ask that you don't forget your time with Cami."

He nodded. "Of course not. No wedding until I hand over the mayorship. I want to take Cami on a trip first. It's just that ... Alina's in such a hurry for everything to happen." He petted the horse and stared out at the horizon. "You and me ... *we* have Cami. Right now and in the present. It doesn't matter if you can't have kids. We already have one together. There's no impediment for you and me to still —"

"Stop!" Brisa held up her hand.

He walked around the horse. "Since you do not want me to wait for you, then I'll just marry Alina." He picked up his hat up and nodded. He jumped onto his horse and held out his hand. "Coming?"

"I prefer to walk."

Brisa returned from dropping Cami off at her summer day camp. She wanted to spend as much time as possible with her. The months were flying by, and her efforts in re-establishing the school and adding dormitories to the convent kept her busy. Not to mention, it was now her responsibility to supervise the archaeologists at the excavation site.

A light knock on her bedroom door and Selena stepped in.

"Miss Alina is looking for you."

"Alina?" Brisa repeated. "What could she possibly want?"

Brisa turned and Alina was standing at her bedroom door … looking as beautiful as ever. She stood strong and firm and reminded Brisa of a powerful lawyer. She felt as if she were her client and had been late to an appointment or something.

"What a surprise," Brisa said. "Please, come in."

"You live in such a beautiful mansion." Alina walked in and glanced around.

Brisa picked up Cami's pajamas and folded them as the woman talked.

"We live in such a small apartment. That's why we can't have Cami with us."

Her comment was absurd. They lived in a beautiful apartment that overlooked the central park and was only a block from City Hall. Brisa ignored her statement and smiled. Alina and Sebastián could have Cami all the time if they really wanted her. However, Alina did not seem interested in the girl, only in controlling Sebastián.

"I'm listening," Brisa said, without looking at her.

"I'll get to the point," Alina said, taking a step closer. "You and Sebastián have this love game going on … kissing cousins?"

Brisa turned and glared at her. Instead of seeing a beautiful woman, she noticed a dark and evil soul.

"He's told me and I'm no fool. I can see how you look at him. I think that with what I'm about to tell you, you'll leave him alone. He deserves to be happy and without distractions." She sighed. "I believe that over time, he'll come to love me as he loves you."

Brisa shook her head.

"There's something you need to know. Angela's still carrying on with her legal case from wherever her soul is now living."

"Oh?"

"When Angela was alive, and during the legal battle regarding Camelia's custody, Sebastián signed off on Uncle Juancho's inheritance. Therefore, upon the uncle's death, the inheritor would be Cami. That was the agreement the two had reached. Until you appeared." Alina walked over to the window and glanced out. She turned to Brisa and frowned. "To make matters worse, you're the legitimate daughter of Juancho … goodbye Cami as the heiress." She waved her arms through the air.

"Go on."

"Brisa … you're an alcoholic. You've tried to pass yourself off as a nun, and in addition … you're cousins in the fourth degree of consanguinity. The law prohibits a marriage."

"Not with special permission," Brisa stated. "I'm not a lawyer, but I'm also not a fool." This woman was threatening her with taking Cami away, and she was not about to let that happen. She had a great inner urgency to fight for Sebastián too, and not be rolled over by this evil woman. For some odd reason, Brisa seemed to attract corrupt people into her life whether she wanted them around or not.

"Not a good example for Camelia." Alina sighed and laughed. "I've watched you leave the AA meetings in Antaño. Can you imagine the embarrassment if she finds out that you're really just an old drunk? You've been playing with both of their feelings by bouncing back and forth about becoming a nun." She sighed. "You should reconsider delivering yourself to the church. Become a nun. It would be a road of redemption for you. And … everyone else can finally live in peace."

Brisa placed Cami's pajamas on the bed and walked over to Alina. After surviving everything over the last few months, having to endure manipulation was the last thing Brisa needed. Obviously, Alina feared her. Feared the love Sebastián still held for her.

Brisa sighed. "I'm allowing you to speak because I understand you are afraid and need to get this off your chest." She took in a deeper breath and let it out slowly. "At the same time, my patience is running thin."

Alina glared at Brisa and squinted. Her mouth tightened and her eyes widened. "Leave Sebastián alone! You can keep Cami until we marry, but then she comes with us. Sebastián has a brilliant political career in front of him … although he does not appreciate it. Since you've returned, he's reverted to his old, country ways. He wants his cows, not politics."

"What do I have to do with his wants and desires?"

"Since the canonization of the nun, he's dedicated himself to it with a fervor that's not worthy of him. He's acting like a common villager! It's embarrassing. He's ignoring his official obligations. I think he's starting to believe in this dead nun of yours. He's regressing and acting like an ignorant field hand. All this noise for a dead body in the name of a phony religion!" She yelled out the words as she stared out the window.

Brisa walked across the room and stood by the door.

"You've made progress in the renovation of the convent." Alina allowed the curtains to fall. "I invite you to reconsider your true destiny. To wear the habit, Brisa. If you don't, you'll start drinking again. You know you will. At least in a convent you'd be safe."

Brisa took in another deep breath and counted to ten.

"When Sebastián and I marry, I'll take him away from this backward town. My sons will be raised in the city. Never as farmhands!"

Brisa let her breath out slowly.

"I warn you …" Alina said, "if you tell him about our conversation today, I'll deny it and destroy you!"

"The door?" Brisa said in a low voice, pointing. "Alina?"

"I'm leaving. Promise that you'll not go looking for him."

"I'm staying here." Brisa smiled. "Not because of my love for Sebastián, but because this is my true vocation. Sebastián is a big boy. Why don't you talk to him about staying away from me? Just remember, we are cousins by blood, and therefore I have a right to be with him. With respect to Cami, she will always be in my life while she needs me. Please leave, Alina. You are no longer welcome in my house!"

The days had turned into weeks and the weeks into months. When the months turned into years, Brisa realized that her life was full even without Sebastián in it. Between her professional duties at the mansion and caring for her father and Cami, not much time was left for anything else. Cami and Juancho remained her first priority. Time passed and never once did she crave a drink. As her father's health improved, she and Cami immersed themselves in his ability to walk through life. Juancho could not pronounce their names properly but was fully aware that Brisa was his daughter and Cami was his niece.

Brisa moved her father from the cabin to the mansion. He still could not speak clearly, however, she could perceive a certain unease when he was in the big house. There were a few rooms he simply refused to enter. Brisa created a picturesque apartment for him in the service wing one room away from Selena. He loved it there because he could see the garden from the window. And … he was near Brisa. He never mentioned Lady Delfina or his father. Framed photos of Sara were placed where he could easily see them. He seemed happy.

Cami slept in the room across the hall from Brisa. Many a night, Brisa would wake and find her asleep in her bed. Life was wonderful and she was happy.

During the last six months of her father's life, she would visit him just before bed to kiss his forehead. Every night he would whisper, "Daughter," and a big smile would decorate his face along with his twinkling eyes.

Sebastián would stop by and say hello when he'd come to pick up or drop off Cami. They never talked unless they needed to share information about the child. A couple of times they discussed starting back on the Antaño Heights project, but it would have to wait until his term as mayor had ended. Still no official marriage date for Alina and Sebastián, and Brisa never asked. Maybe Alina had resigned to waiting until Sebastián handed over the mayor's position. Cami and Brisa avoided the subject, for Cami's private life with her father was not a part of hers. Sebastián no longer searched for Brisa, and she no longer searched for him. They now existed within their own separate worlds.

The project, Antaño Heights, began to show a few signs of reawakening. Brisa could accomplish it using her own designs, but she would need a new focus. The original supporters were not only willing but eager to replay their parts. However, no demolition. José would switch his priorities from civil to restoration. Sonia talked and talked about it, but instead it reminded Brisa that she had a more pressing project — a center for young women abused by violence and neglect. Sebastián, as mayor and part owner, would be part of it too, of course.

Still, they needed to finalize the legal Herradura issues and reassign the deeds. And everything had to wait until Sebastián was out of City Hall. The idea to resuscitate the project had to come from him. Therefore, they decided to wait.

Marta showed up one morning to give Brisa her weekly update on the investigation of the PROE S.A. — a talk Brisa always enjoyed.

"Pablo is about to be sentenced," Marta said, smiling. "He's such a good negotiator. His time was reduced ... since he gave up so much information and helped to incriminate the key players and all. He's implicated so many who operated from inside the city. Mostly for misappropriation of funds."

"How many charges were place against Pablo?"

"In addition to abuse of power, he was accused of accepting bribes and bribing others. His biggest crime would be the project. However, with the project scrapped, we couldn't make anything stick."

"That's too bad."

"He's a clever one. I underestimated him. Since I never suspected his undercover activities, I believed he would be an easy catch." Marta smiled. "He took advantage of his position to pull false permits. He's a phony and a swindler. He'll probably get ten years. Although with his luck, I'd bet on five."

"Any time is better than none," Brisa replied.

"Now the atrocities committed by Lady Delfina and Angela's father ... just about all of those secrets are out in the open now. Of course, everyone involved is dead, so no charges for the crimes. Thus, the secrets will remain the history of Antaño to bear. The best news ... the church had nothing to do with it. The nuns who were managing the boarding school never knew what was happening at the convent ... in the cloister wing. The church jumped in when rumors spread about the young women who became novices against their will, and they eventually removed their financial backing. And so …" Marta sighed.

"What about the smuggling of babies?"

"It was Angela's father who headed that up." Marta laughed. "He was the one who paid to sneak the babies across the border. He charged a lot for each newborn. A Mexican adoption agency was involved too. The investigation there is quite complicated, and it's outside our jurisdiction."

Brisa's mind fell blank. There was nothing else to say. She took a sip of her coffee and smiled. "The new convent will be finished soon. It'll begin small with religious sisters from the congregation who'll establish a foundation. This religious institution will coordinate a center for abused women, married or single. Sonia will manage the place along with the nuns." She shrugged. "Later, I may revive the Antaño Heights project. So much to do."

"Sebastián told me something about that." Marta nodded. "I'm happy for you, Brisa. Antaño is recovering its reputation and ethical principles. It's turning into a place for old culture and renewed values."

It was hard to believe that Marta and Brisa held the same objectives. Could that be another treasure or a miracle?

Marta walked to the door and stopped. "Been holding on to this …" She held out a folded piece of paper.

"What is this?"

"Received it yesterday from the Mexican adoption agency."

"Oh?"

Marta handed the paper to Brisa.

Brisa's eyes teared as she read over the names — Mother - Sara Beatriz Urrutia — Father - Juan Ignacio Herradura … Brisa wiped her eyes. "Thank you."

CHAPTER XVIII

Brisa's father passed in his sleep. She found him on a bright and sunny morning. When she entered his room, he looked like he was sleeping. Brisa knew, however, that he would not be waking up. Her feelings of sadness turned to peace when she imagined him with her mother, Sara. She glanced at her birth certificate that she had framed and which now sat on his nightstand. *Can you both see me?* She could perceive their presence in his room and felt blessed.

She organized her father's funeral in the simplest of ways. Cami and Brisa were the first to arrive at the cemetery. They watched as Sebastián's black car slowly rolled to a stop. He and Alina stepped out, and the woman instantly grabbed his arm.

They approached wearing dark sunglasses. It was one of the few times Brisa saw him without a cowboy hat. He looked odd and uncomfortable wearing a black suit.

"I'm sorry for your loss, Brisa." Sebastián reached out to hug her, but Alina stepped between them.

"Me, too," Alina said a little too civilized and cordial.

"It's your loss too," Brisa whispered to Sebastián.

They buried Juancho next to Sara, and for eternity, they would be together. A forever love. Alina and Sebastián placed a flower on the graves. Cami and Brisa had brought a wagon full of red roses. Sebastián chuckled as he watched them lay each one separately. Brisa placed a kiss in her hands and rubbed it onto their tombstones.

Sara Beatriz Urrutia and Juan Ignacio Herradura

"Cami and I are leaving," Brisa said coldly to Sebastián. "We brought flowers for Rogelio. His tombstone is just over there."

"We'll go with you," Sebastián said and Alina forced a smile. "I'd like for Cami to spend the weekend with us. She's sad and it would be a good distraction."

"Of course," Brisa replied. "I would just ask that you discuss it with her first."

"Are you okay?" he asked as they walked down the path.

"Long time no see, Brisa," Alina said, clinging to Sebastián's arm as if her life depended on it.

"Yes, I'm good."

"I want to thank you for caring for Cami," he said. "Our apartment downtown is just too small."

"After the wedding," Alina said, "we'll have room for all. We'll take her then. She'll have siblings soon." Alina smiled. "You and Sebastián are such a united family. You haven't seen each other recently, have you? How has life been for you and Cami at the mansion?"

"Cami is happy," Brisa replied. "You and Sebastián can decide with respect to Cami, and if she agrees, it's fine with me. I'll always be here for her."

"I'll always share the girl with you," Sebastián said.

"Of course!" Alina said, smiling a fake smile. "You're the only family Sebastián has now. You will be the aunt to our children."

"What have you heard about the convent?" Sebastián asked.

"It's official. Now that Cami and I live in the house, I can supervise the restoration. We started on the new building for the rooms, and the convent will be in the same vein as the home for displaced girls. Managed by Sonia, of course."

"Is it ready?" Alina asked. It was as if she didn't want Sebastián and Brisa talking alone. "Is it not dangerous for Cami to live so close to girls that have gone astray?"

"There will be a convent next to them, Alina," Sebastián said calmly. "It's a safe place."

Alina smiled and nodded. "It was good to see you again, Brisa."

"Let me know when you'll be returning Cami," Brisa replied. "She has practice with her basketball team."

Brisa had not seen Sebastián for many months. He had aged quite a bit, or maybe he was just tired. However, through her eyes, he looked more handsome than ever.

Just seven days were left before two great and simultaneous happenings — the sanctification of Mother Rosa by the church and the declaration by UNESCO granting Antaño the title of World Heritage of Humanity.

Sebastián was sprayed all over the local TV and radio. He was interviewed almost daily about the discovery of the remains of Mother Rosa and the corroboration by anthropologists and religious authorities. Next to him, as always, stood Alina.

The sacred remains of the Most Holy Mother Rosa were to be viewed at Antaño's cathedral under the supervision of the archbishop. The church scheduled the dates that the Holy Mother would be available for veneration.

She turned off the news and sat back. It was time to sleep and rest. Tomorrow would be busy with a weekend full of activities. Her new position required her to prepare speeches and coordinate the festivities. She now presided over CONADA, the National Council for the Protection of Antaño, for the inauguration of the new archaeological sites. Brisa and Cami attended a private ceremony to honor Mother Rosa in person before they opened the casket. As soon as they returned home, Brisa tossed off her shoes and fell onto the couch.

"Mother Rosa has a tattoo just like yours." Cami sat next to Brisa and rested her head on her shoulder.

"Were you nervous today?" Brisa asked. "You held my hand throughout the whole ceremony."

"It was okay," she said. "I think your rose looks like hers."

"It's a birthmark, Cami."

"Can I get a tattoo when I'm older?"

Brisa nodded. "Go change. Get comfortable."

Marta, Sonia, and Carlitos walked in.

Sonia sat next to Brisa and wrapped her arms around her shoulders. "How nice to celebrate as a family and not with so many people around."

"You gave a great speech, Brisa," Marta said.

"And you, Marta?" Brisa laughed. "Being handed the *key* to the city?"

"And handed to me by Sebastián himself!" Marta smiled and her golden tooth shined. "I hate talking in public."

"It didn't show," Sonia said

Marta looked proud.

"Who will come later today?" Sonia asked.

"Us and some members of CONADA."

"To Antaño's progress!" Marta said, holding up a large bottle. "Non-alcoholic champagne. All the beverages are non-alcoholic." She smiled.

"Thanks, Marta." Brisa stood.

Marta popped the top and handed out glasses. "To Antaño!"

They all yelled out a toast.

"Cheers!" Brisa said.

"Look, Brisa," Marta said, pointing out the window. "The minister of culture is driving up. I'd recognize that car anywhere. Those closest to him call him Willy."

"Did you see how he looked at you when you were at the podium?" Sonia asked.

"Sonia!" Brisa laughed. "I thought you gave up being a *nosy busybody?*"

"You like?" Sonia asked.

"Perhaps," Brisa replied. "I'm just getting to know him."

"I love what you've done with Dracula's mansion," Sonia said, walking across the living room. "It's precious. Poor little ghosts, there's no place for them anymore."

"It's the most welcoming place in the whole city," Carlitos said. "Has Sebastián seen the house remodeled yet?"

"Not yet," Brisa replied.

Willy stood out front and rapped on the door.

"Come in, Willy," Sonia said, running to greet him.

"Congratulations, Brisa! President of the Council for the Protection of Antaño. I didn't know you spoke so well in public."

"Thanks, Willy, for coming." Brisa stretched out her hand.

"Me, neither." An unexpected voice followed Willy through the door. It was Sebastián.

Willy turned to him, but Sebastián ignored him and pushed his way through.

"Good job in your administration," Willy said to Sebastián, extending his hand, but Sebastián ignored him again.

Sebastián didn't look so good. He was unkempt, wearing jeans and an old t-shirt. He turned to the minister and frowned. "And you? Are you moving to Antaño? If not, when are you leaving? You don't have anything else to do, do you?"

The minister squinted and frowned. He glanced over at Brisa and Sonia and shrugged.

Brisa grabbed Sebastián by the arm and pulled him outside. "What's wrong with you?" She took in a deep breath and gagged. "My god, you've been drinking!"

"Not really." He shook his head while trying to talk, but his words slurred together. "I think … I think I'm tired of people filling my head with bull … shit!"

"And Alina?" It was the only name that came to her mind.

"At the apartment," he said, almost tripping over his feet.

"You should leave … please?" Brisa said as she pushed him toward the waiting driver.

"You invited me."

The minister kept looking over at them. Brisa pushed Sebastián again toward the idling car and whispered, "Goodbye, Sebastián!"

"Cami," Brisa yelled out. "Hurry! Your dad's handing over the mayorship."

A year had passed, and now Sebastián was free to marry Alina. They could finally revive the Heights project. Working next to Sebastián would be pure hell, albeit rewarding. The newscast was almost over, and they sat together to watch the end of the interview with Sebastián.

Cami frowned. "When will I get to see him? I've not seen my dad in months. When he marries Alina, he'll be too busy for me."

"I'm sure he's going to give you a lot of time."

"You two hardly ever see each other anymore."

Brisa shrugged.

"Do you think Alina will have a baby? She said it would be my little brother. How would she know if it'd be a girl or a boy?"

"Why do you ask?"

"Whenever we go to the stores, she always has to stop by the baby section. If she's going to have a baby, can I just live with you?" Cami frowned.

"Everything will be fine. Your father will always love you. I will always love you. You know what, it's time to go to bed, okay?"

"Can I sleep with you tonight?"

Brisa nodded.

A few weeks later, Brisa sat out front drinking her morning coffee. She admired the new convent, the renovated school, and the restored entryway to the catacombs. Everything had changed so much. A man on horseback entering the property grabbed her attention.

Sebastián?

He had not ridden a horse on this property in years. The few times he dropped off Cami, he had sent his driver or Nanita. Brisa sat her cup on the bench and stood. She walked out and greeted him. Sebastián was sitting on a new horse. He wore his usual hat and wrinkled denim shirt. He suddenly looked very happy.

"It's the new mare for Cami," he said, sliding down. "Is she up yet?"

Brisa nodded. "She's a bit tall." She caressed the beautiful white and tan horse.

The sounds of Cami running down the stairs filled Brisa's heart with warmth. The girl threw herself on Sebastián before reaching out to caress the mare.

"Can I ride her?" Cami asked. "Is she mine?"

Sebastián nodded.

Cami took the reins and led the horse to the small stable they had built near the back of the house. Sebastián took off his hat.

"Can I come in?" he asked.

Brisa nodded. "I didn't expect to see you. With all the commotion that you've had with the farewell from the city and all."

"Brisa ..." he said, holding her shoulders. "I'm no longer mayor."

Brisa nodded.

"No more armored cars ... or politicians ... or people all decked out. Cami can walk around without a security detail." He let go and looked away.

"She detested all of that," Brisa said, walking into the house. "And I don't blame her."

He looked around. "Looks great. How long did it take to restore the place?" He sighed and frowned. "I must apologize for the last time I was here."

"A little over two years." Brisa shrugged. "Look at the chandelier ... completely restored."

They walked into the kitchen.

"Coffee?" she asked.

He shook his head and opened the refrigerator. "May I?" he asked, grabbing a can of soda.

Brisa nodded.

"Can we walk outside and talk about the Antaño Heights project?"

"No hurry, you must have so much to do."

"The land is in your name. You can dispose of it or negotiate with the banks. Did the lawyer give you the papers?"

Brisa nodded.

"I want to look at your new plans. First, I want to show you where we plan on living."

"The ranch?" Brisa asked.

"No, I want something bigger."

They walked to her car. Sebastián looked way too happy. His gaze flashed that golden sparkle that always tinted his eyes. He drove them down the hill and into the mountainous terrain. In some places, the car struggled to make it up the steep incline.

"Why way up here?" Brisa asked.

Rather than answering, he kept driving. The car was soaring down the road when he suddenly stopped. They stepped out and she took in a deep breath.

"A house up here?" Brisa asked. "Here is where you want to live?"

"Look at that view!"

Brisa nodded as she walked around.

"That mountain is called Mount of the Virgin!" he said. "And look what's coming up from below. That's the Coastal Mountain Range. And those plains. Can you see them?"

She glanced over at him and sighed. "Looks like it's in another county."

"Palmas Rojas," he said. "What you see over there is Alberto's farm. And right here is where I want our house."

"Are you crazy.? It would cost a fortune. Did you talk to Alina about this?"

Sebastián took in a deep breath and pounded on his chest.

"Wait … your ranch begins here? You want to build a house on your ranch? Why? I thought Alina wanted to live in the city."

"I want to live on my ranch. It's a surprise for Cami. When I was at City Hall, I worked on a new project. Not the corrupt one started by Angela. It would mean easy access to the coast and be close to Antaño. I could sell part of Camelia Ranch, and if you agreed, you could do the same. That would add value to everything and generate a bunch of new jobs for the people of Palmas Rojas and Antaño. I mentioned it to José. He's an expert on roads and has confirmed it's doable. The three of us would live at the ranch until the Heights development was finished."

"The three." Brisa counted on her fingers. "You, Cami, and Alina?"

He shook his head. "No, silly. You, me, and Cami." Sebastián walked around the car and stood next to Brisa.

She took a step back and stared out at the horizon. The view was beautiful. "You're nuts. Did you talk to Alina about this?"

He nodded and smiled.

"And?"

"Oh, she's already moved back to the city," he said, without taking his eyes off the horizon. "Many months ago."

"I don't understand."

"What is there to understand?" he said. "You, me, and Cami."

"Are you … proposing?"

Sebastián laughed. He extended his hand and held out a ring that looked old … very old. "It was our grandmother's. Our grandfather had given it to my mother."

Brisa didn't know what to say. She walked around the car and switched from looking at the ground to up at the horizon. Her mind flew in all directions. She stepped over and stared at the ring. Tears filled her eyes.

"Brisa," he said, taking her in his arms. "Marry me? Please?"

Questions flew through her mind. What about Angela's and Pablo's charges? What about them being cousins? Instead, she looked into his beautiful face and smiled. "Yes," she whispered.

Her answer was as abrupt and as decisive as his proposal. They kissed and hugged. It felt wonderful and she never wanted to let go.

"You're going to marry me?" He looked at her with those grayish eyes and her heart melted. They stood there just looking at each other for a very long time. Their souls and bodies knew that they belonged together. Again, their lips met and they kissed.

After a while, Sebastián placed the ring on her finger and it fit perfectly.

"We are getting married?" Her heart pounded as she stared at the ring on her finger.

"It's not from our step-grandmother," he mused. "It's from our biological grandmother."

Brisa laughed.

"Pulling the marriage permit will be easy," he said. "The church and the bishop approved it already, can you believe it?"

There was nothing to say. They kissed again and this time more passionately. Each of their intense kisses felt like a short stroll through heaven.

"What about Alina?" she asked.

"Alina never loved me, and I never loved her. She only wanted the fame that politics could bring."

"We are still cousins, Sebastián."

"Did Mother Rosa say anything about that? Did she say it was a sin? I don't think so."

"No." Brisa hesitated. "What if we don't go to heaven?"

"Keep on kissing me, and I'll show you how we'll get there."

They lost themselves inside their love. A love they had wanted for so long.

"What about Cami? We should give her the good news."

Sebastián smiled and took her hand. "First, we drive back to the house, and if the car doesn't quit on us, we will give her the news."

It took almost an hour to return to the highland at the ranch. Cami was in her saddle enjoying the new mare. Very calmly, and with the natural demeanor of a young teen, she asked with a smile, "Did you say yes?"

EPILOGUE

The three old-timers looked cautiously through the window. They were tired. It had not been easy to summarize Brisa's life. For Sara, especially, it was hard to remember the moments that were compiled within her diary. Sara closed the book, and the three sat solemnly together.

"We have not finished yet," Rogelio said, still staring out the window. "Weren't you going to show us the photo album?"

Sara stood and Juancho grabbed her by the arm. "Take a break, dear. Finish your tea first." He looked at his shaking hands. "Haven't you noticed? We've aged since we started telling this tale." He pointed at his fingers that were even thinner than before. "The mansion, on the other hand, has rejuvenated itself. It's no longer a place for a family to sleep, but it's still beautiful."

They sat together and admired the mansion and old school for a while longer. Some of the original furniture was still there and gave them comfort. The baroque chandelier still swung from the ceiling, and the painting of Mother Rosa sat proudly above the rebuilt fireplace.

Rogelio stood. He pulled the photo album from off the bookshelf and sat next to his friends. He wiped away a tear. He took in a deep breath and slowly browsed through the photos.

"Brisa was not with them when many of these were taken," Juancho said, running his fingers over the glossy pictures. "Most were taken when she was in rehab. However, she would probably say that with the sanctification of

Mother Rosa, they finally started living a full life. Not without some obstacles, mind you. Right, Rogelio? Such as her relapse?"

"It was just a short fall," Rogelio said. "Brisa had to put in practice all her knowledge about the addiction. You saw me relapse several times, remember, Juancho? Like when Lady Delfina fired my father and kicked us out of the farm? Rather than helping my family, I turned to drinking. There are always catalysts. Brisa was able to get herself back to her AA group. The same group she took me to." Rogelio chuckled.

"And what about the others?" Sara asked.

"Sonia married José!" Rogelio said. "Wasn't that a big surprise? They even have children now. Look at the photos from the start of the project. Here's Brisa with their adopted baby boy." He sat back and sighed. "And here are the rest of the photos. The cornerstone of Antaño Heights. Here is everyone. Marta appears in many, and always with her golden tooth. Maybe one day she can join us to tell us the rest of the story."

They stared at the last few pictures. José and Carlitos were part of the original team, and Brisa was always smiling and wearing her hardhat. Sebastián continued to wear his cowboy hat. They closed the album and looked at the mansion again from the inside. It was now the clubhouse for Antaño Heights. The last phase of the project had been concluded.

Rogelio spoke again. "Oh, the celebration has begun. All those people are gathered in the atrium that they built from the ruins. How they have decorated it!"

"Yes," Sara said. "It is a magnificent rose garden."

"Looks like they're waiting for the mayor," Juancho said. "He doesn't seem to be here yet."

They finished their tea and smiled.

"We have only a little longer to be together." Sara sighed. "It's not easy being a guardian."

"You're telling me?" Rogelio said. "This girl gave me gray hair."

"And Conchita? When will she join us?" Juancho asked.

Sara shrugged.

"Her time has not yet come for this mission," Rogelio replied. "She'll be here at the proper time."

Sara grabbed a hand from both men. "You look tired."

"You, too." Rogelio rested his head upon Sara's shoulder.

"I miss the kids," Juancho said, gazing at Sebastián's photo that sat on a nearby shelf.

"Don't tell me you're thinking of applying for guardianship of the boy?" Rogelio asked.

"Boy? He's no boy, he's a man!" Sara laughed. "Sebastián's almost an old man now."

The main door of the mansion flew open, and a small child ran inside with his nursemaid, Selena, close behind.

"Wait up, little Ignacio!" Selena shouted. "We should not go in yet!"

The little boy stopped and looked up at Sara and smiled before walking back to the frantic, young woman.

Sara turned to Juancho. "The boy saw me?" she asked.

Juancho nodded. "Do not all children see us?"

"They named him Ignacio in your honor," Sara said to Juancho. "You definitely left your mark on them. Brisa initially didn't like children, but they ended up with two."

Brisa and Sebastián walked in with a beautiful, young woman, Miss Cami, following.

"Couldn't you have worn the shirt I set out for you. The new one?" Brisa asked, laughing. "This one is so ... wrinkled."

"There was no time," he replied. "This one's fine." Sebastián's phone beeped. "The mayor has arrived. Forget about the shirt. It's your project, Brisa. Your long-awaited project is now a reality."

They left the house in a hurry and aimed for the renovated ruins. Cami glanced back one last time and winked before following Selena who was dragging little Ignacio by the hand.

Sara stood and wrapped her shawl across her shoulders. "I think we can go now," Sara said. "I need to rest for a while."

They took one last look through the window at the celebration. Holding hands, they walked out the front door. Behind them, the volcanoes majestically rose to the heavens as witnesses to their story.

The afternoon was waning, and the sun's rays were painting the sky with splashes of orange and magenta. The illuminated mansion that once held everyone's past now glowed against the oncoming evening sky.

Brisa looked over at the mansion and smiled. She loved that old house. As she turned to listen to the mayor, something grabbed her attention. Three elderly individuals ambled up the hill toward the old tree and into the growing shadows. As she watched, a feeling of warmth filled her with love and devotion. Brisa nodded and smiled.

"Love you, Mom … Dad … and Rogelio!"

PATRICIA SORG

Born in Guatemala City in 1956, Patricia Sorg is an international artist who tells stories through her writings and paintings and has earned several awards in both Latin America and the United States.

Her first work of fiction: *Mountains That Touch The Sky* [*Montañas Que Tocan El Cielo*], published in Spanish and English, was inspired by her native land. Now, Patricia launches her second work of literature, *Habits That Haunt Me* [*Tan Cerca Que No Se Mira*], and as always, she remains close to her ancestral traditions by evoking the magic of local legends that give life to the supernatural nuances that takes the reader from the colonial era to present day by means of its colorful and enigmatic characters.

Now a United States citizen, Patricia lives in Sarasota, Florida where she works as an artist and Fine Art instructor.

https://www.patriciasorg.com/

308

Floricanto Press (August 6, 2019)

ISBN 0915745054

Sofi is a rural teacher who arrives at Casa Montesanto to be the assistant of the Vega sisters. Unsuspectingly, she finds herself at the service of a dark and greedy family, obsessed with power and wealth, that hides a sinister past.

"The author inter-weaves three different timelines and three different voices, not allowing the reader to put down the book from beginning to end. A true masterpiece!"

—VIDA AMOR DE PAZ
Columnist, Writer, TV Personality and Environmentalist

"A journey into a volcano. Magic and verb are the key ingredients of this great story, which challenges the reader from the first to the last paragraph."

—ANDRES CORREA GUATARASMA
North American Academy of the Spanish Language

311

PATRICIA SORG'S

PAINTINGS

Krishantia

Sarasota Sunset

Misty Forest

Cecilia

Portrait of Christa, my daughter

HABITS THAT HAUNT ME

Enchanted